Mashiro got to his feet and gestured toward the bowl of cherries. Nagai grabbed a handful of cherries in disgust and threw them at him.

Mashiro drew both swords. Flashing steel surrounded him like an evil mist. He was a goddamn human food processor, sending specks of neon red flying in every direction. His final slash was with the short sword. A cherry half flew straight up into the air. When it came down, he caught it on the flat of his blade. "There will be no trouble with D'Urso and no trouble with Hamabuchi. You will be happy. I am dedicating myself to it. Please do not worry." He flipped the sword up and tossed the cherry into his mouth. He bowed, grinned, and chewed.

Also by Anthony Bruno

BAD GUYS
BAD LUCK
BAD BUSINESS

BAD BLOOD

ANTHONY BRUNO

A DELL BOOK

For Mia, the little sweetie

Published by
Dell Publishing
a division of
Bantam Doubleday Dell Publishing Group, Inc.
666 Fifth Avenue
New York, New York 10103

ISBN: 0-440-20705-3

Reprinted by arrangement with G. P. Putnam's Sons

Printed in the United States of America

Published simultaneously in Canada

July 1990

10 9 8 7 6 5 4 3 2

RAD

1

The orange Volkswagen Beetle emerged from the dawn mist and thumped over the old, uneven planks of the weathered pier followed closely by a black 1960 Cadillac De Ville, which in turn was followed by an executive-gray Mercedes SEL limousine—little fish, big fish, bigger fish. The Beetle stopped a few feet from the end of the pier, the Cadillac about twenty feet behind the Beetle, the limo nosing up under the Caddy's lethal-looking tailfins. They stood there in check, the Volkswagen's air-cooled motor wheezing and twittering, the Cadillac rumbling low, the Mercedes issuing a barely audible but insistent hiss.

The man behind the wheel of the Caddy, Katsumi Nagai, turned off the engine, wearily ran a hand through his hair, and draped his arms over the steering wheel. It was too fucking early for this shit. He looked across the cracked, black leather seats at Mashiro's broad back as he bent over to take off his shoes and socks. Mashiro folded his socks neatly and placed them inside the black lace-up shoes which he then tucked under the seat. Nagai stared at him. After all these years, Mashiro still made him stop and wonder. The squat, expressionless man then reached for the sheathed sword lying on the backseat and placed it in his lap. He looked at Nagai, waiting for the go-ahead from his boss. Nagai stared at the long, curved *katana*, the samurai's primary weapon, then looked Mashiro in the eye and nodded wearily. The man bowed his head curtly but respectfully, then got out of the car. As Mashiro walked around the front of the car, Nagai wondered what he was thinking, or if he thought at all.

Nagai watched him unsheathe the sword and set the black leather scabbard on the hood. Mashiro then marched over to the Volkswagen, back straight, sword at his side, and ordered the two inside to shut off the engine and get out.

The couple didn't move. Nagai reached over to the glove compartment and took out the small automatic he kept there. He pressed the button to open the power window on his side, then stuck his arm out and fired a shot left-handed over the VW. The sound of the shot rolled over the river, a sharp crack on the dull cold air. The girl started sobbing again. He could see her head bobbing up and down. He rested his elbow on the door, the gun leveled on them out the window so they could see it.

"Hurry," Mashiro shouted in his harsh Osaka-accented Japanese. The young Japanese couple started to come out, reluctantly, like small animals forced to abandon a temporary shelter. They stood before Mashiro who eyed them with neither hate nor compassion. The girl held her hand over her mouth. Mashiro abruptly raised his sword like a spear and thrust its point into the rotting head of the nearest timber. It stood there glinting in the gloom of the gray dawn, swaying slightly, as staunch and deadly as its owner.

My faithful monster, Nagai thought.

Nagai glanced into the rearview mirror, feeling slow and heavy, then got out of his car and walked over to the back door of the limo. He stared at himself in the dark-tinted window, waiting for it to open. His face looked too sad and drawn, he thought, and his hair was streaked with gray now. He wished he looked more like his man Mashiro, robust and stone-faced, dangerous. And Mashiro was even two years older than him. When the rear power window started to glide down, he changed his expression and attempted to look properly grim for his boss.

"Good morning, Nagai," the old man in the backseat said, not looking up. He was carefully prying the lid off a paper coffee cup, holding it away from his dark, Hong Kong-made silk suit.

"Good morning, Mr. Hamabuchi," Nagai said with a respectful bow of the head. Nagai was suddenly hit with a memory of serving breakfast tea to Hamabuchi when he lived at the boss's Tokyo house as part of the apprenticeship that was supposed to teach him how to obey his boss like a father. That was a long time ago. A dull ache started to throb at the back of his head as he thought about the course his life had taken and the fact that if he hadn't been so bull-headed back in Japan, he probably would've been sitting pretty now, running his own night club in the Ginza. But that's not how it worked out. You have to pay for your mistakes.

The old man blew over the surface of the steaming coffee as he squinted through the tinted windshield at the trembling couple standing before Mashiro. His brow was furrowed, his expression quizzical. He seemed to be studying them. Nagai recognized this look. It was the prelude to a Hamabuchi homily. The old man took a slow, careful sip.

Sometime today please, Nagai thought.

Hamabuchi suddenly looked Nagai in the eye.

Here it comes.

"Does the girl weep for their lost honor, Nagai, or for their unfortunate fate?" Hamabuchi asked with that inscrutable grin of his. It was a well-practiced gesture, one he cultivated years ago. Americans expect this kind of Oriental bullshit, he once confided.

Nagai glanced back at the couple, the girl sobbing softly into her boyfriend's shoulder as the boy tried unsuccessfully to look Mashiro in the face. He had no sympathy for them. They signed a contract and they broke it. You have to pay for your mistakes.

"She weeps for their lost honor, I would think." Nagai knew all the expected responses.

Hamabuchi lowered the cup to his lap, shaking his head almost imperceptively. "No. I don't think so. Only old people concern themselves with honor these days. Old ones like me and Mr. Antonelli."

Here we go again with the old stories about the Occupation and the black market in Kobe and the clever American corporal who knew how to play ball. The great Antonelli.

"I'm concerned about my honor," Nagai said pointedly, hoping to cut him off. "I want it restored."

"I know, I know you do." Hamabuchi took another sip.

"My promise still holds. If you succeed here in America, everything will be all right."

Nagai nodded tactfully, trying to hold onto the fading mental picture of the faces of his three children back in Japan. Sweet Hatsu is eleven now; next year she'll like boys. Kenji is eight; he must be a real hellion. And the baby will be going to school this year. Incredible.

"Tell me, Nagai, how are you getting along with D'Urso?"

"What?"

"D'Urso. How are you getting along with him? I ask because he impresses me as a man of convenient loyalties, a man who thinks his own thoughts, if you know what I mean. I didn't think our Mafia friends tolerated such individuality within their ranks."

Nagai wondered whether this was some kind of backhanded reference to himself. Probably. "D'Urso's an arrogant prick, but he's holding up his end. So far we've had no trouble with the law here, and his demand happily exceeds our supply."

The old man looked up at him from under his brows. "And you are keeping up your end?"

He nodded. "Every delivery has been on time and to their satisfaction. The number of uncooperatives and runaways is minimal now, thanks to Mashiro and the extra men you've sent us. Only four in the last month, including these two." He smiled at his man who was standing motionless before the scared couple at the end of the dock. "They fear him worse than death."

"Ah, yes . . . the samurai. Gozo Mashiro, isn't it?" Hamabuchi muttered, scratching his eyebrow. "A very loyal man, I'm told."

"None better."

"May he never disappoint you." Hamabuchi stared up at him.

Nagai put the hand with the gun on the roof of the limo and stared at the stump where the last joint of his pinky had been. Yes, yes, tell me again.

Hamabuchi blew his nose into a paper napkin, balled it up, and put it in the bag. "Well, let's get this over with," he said. "You seem to be handling things adequately here. Very good, Nagai."

"Thank you, Mr. Hamabuchi." But when the fuck can I go back to Japan, old man?

Nagai watched the old man's face disappear as the dark window closed and the limo started to move backward, gliding back toward the fog on shore. Hamabuchi, man of the black mists. He comes and goes without warning, never letting anyone know what continent he'll be on next. Nagai had learned long ago that it was useless to try to keep tabs on his boss's movements. "I want you to always act as though I am three steps behind you," the old man often told his people, "for you never know. I just may be there."

Nagai stepped away from the limo and saw in the Mercedes's dark windshield the reflection of the rising sun peeking through the skyscrapers of Wall Street on the other side of the river. He turned away from the glare and looked at Mashiro who was looking at him. Nagai gave him the nod and waved with the gun as he went back to his own car. He felt very tired. It *was* time to get this over with.

Mashiro bowed to his boss, then faced the couple again and separated them. They both stared at the glinting sword out of the corners of their eyes as Mashiro took a step back and positioned himself in front of the young man. Nagai could hear the departing limousine whining backward in reverse.

The sudden force of the blow—Mashiro pivoting on one foot, swinging his other leg up high, his heel crashing into the side of the boy's neck—made no sound of its own as far as Nagai could tell. The involuntary grunt emitted through flaccid lips and the thud of the already lifeless body hitting the wooden planks came a half-second later. Only the victim can hear the quick crunch of shattering vertebrae, Mashiro once told him. Almost totally painless. Nagai shook his head. What did that matter? When you're gonna die, you're gonna die.

Nagai watched the girl absorbing the hard truth of the moment as she hovered over her lover's body, leaning toward him but not touching him, petrified on her feet, terror painted on her face, fingers spread, mouth open but voiceless. She looked like someone poised to catch a cannonball. Nagai thought of his daughter and sighed. He shielded his eyes from the sun and took in the magnificent Manhattan skyline. Contracts must be honored, my dear.

The girl's body falling to the pier made a hollow thud.

Mashiro immediately rolled the boy's body over onto the girl's, stacking them face to face. His head was buried in her neck; she was looking up at the sky, her mouth open. She looked like she was about to have an orgasm. Mashiro reached for the gleaming *katana* then. Nagai looked away. He didn't think he could stomach this.

He stared instead at the silvery swells of the Hudson and let his mind drift. He heard the sudden swoosh of the blade then, felt the referred impact on the boards under his feet, but he didn't look. He concentrated on the gentle, lulling lapping of the river against the timbers below and longed for home again.

A moment later, he started to hear the blood. A steady dripping that quickly turned into a heavy, uneven splatter, blood hitting water. He looked down. A dark tide gradually seeped out from under the shadow of the dock, a drifting stain on the quiet brown-green waters. He looked up at Mashiro who was carefully wiping his blade. The samurai bowed to him. Nagai thought he saw the hint of a grin. Maybe . . . maybe not.

He couldn't help looking now. Dark pink guts spilled out of their sides. The girl's face was speckled with blood. Nagai turned away and reached for the car door. "Get rid of them, Mashiro. Hurry up."

"*Hai.*"

2

The cop in the wet suit tugged hard on the cable a couple of times, then swam over to the police boat. He hung onto the gunwale with one hand as he gave the crane operator the high sign with the other. The crane drums started to turn slowly, tightening up the slack cable. Then the engine growled and a second later a chrome bumper emerged from the oily water. Even though they pulled it out slowly, the water rushing out of the little car created enough of a wake to rock the police boat. The crane operator—a red-faced, gray-haired guy wearing a kelly green cap with a shamrock on the peak—left the orange Volkswagen hanging a few feet over the water, still dripping. The Transit guys milled around, looking antsy. Ferries had been stacked up in the harbor all afternoon, forced to operate short one berth space, and now the Staten Island natives were getting restless.

Gibbons looked over at the mob of people hanging over the rail of the ferry in the next berth, all rubbernecking to get a look at the VW, all of them mad because they'd been delayed. Gibbons tipped his hat back and squinted up at them, showing his teeth. He took his hat off and smoothed down what hair he had left. What the hell did they expect for a quarter ride, for chrissake?

Gibbons stood off to the side and squinted at the sun glinting off what was left of the Beetle's windshield. He put his sunglasses back on. Indian summer had come back with a vengeance, but Gibbons didn't pay much attention to the heat. He always kept his jacket on, his collar buttoned, his tie up. That was an old FBI rule from J. Edgar's day, and Gibbons had followed it for so long it just became a habit with him. The Bureau dress code had been relaxed a little since then, and there was nothing that said a special agent couldn't unbutton his collar if he was uncomfortable; it was just something that never occurred to Gibbons.

"Lieutenant Elam? Lieutenant?" The ranking member of the antsy Transit officials was trying to get the officer-in-charge's attention from behind the yellow tape police barrier, and Elam was doing the sensible thing under the circumstances. Ignoring the asshole.

"Lieutenant! The mayor's office assured me that we would regain use of this slip as soon as possible." The guy was getting testy with Elam, which was pretty ballsy for a guy who looked like a maitre d'. Tyrone Elam was six-eight and once played basketball for Michigan. Or Michigan State, Gibbons wasn't sure. Might've played pro for a season, too. He always reminded Gibbons of Willis Reed, the guy who played center for the Knicks back when New York knew how to win. No one could slam the boards as hard as Reed. No one has since. Two hundred and forty pounds of unadulterated intimidation. Elam had that same look. Not the kind of guy most white people want to argue with.

Elam had his foot up on the bumper of a patrol car, tapping a pen on the messy-looking clipboard on his knee as he talked to a uniformed sergeant. It looked like he was doing police business, but what he was really doing was wishing the little Transit frog would get lost before he picked him up and heaved him into the water.

The maitre d' wouldn't give up, though. He unbuttoned his suit jacket, stepped under the yellow tape, and crossed the police line. This guy did have balls.

"Lieutenant, I'm getting a little tired of your rude—"

Elam turned his head and shot the guy a look that shut him up *toute de suite*. It was one of those slow, sharp-eyed looks that komodo dragons have when they smell meat. Gibbons remembered it from a documentary he saw on Channel 13 about the giant carnivorous lizards of Malaysia. That's exactly what Elam looked like right now. Gibbons smiled like a crocodile.

Elam stood up and looked straight down at the hair-transplant scars in the maitre d's very thin scalp. "Mr. Shapiro," he said with dangerous tranquility, "it has been explained to you that this is out of the police's jurisdiction and that we cannot do a thing until federal authorities arrive."

"But—"

"No buts, Mr. Shapiro. A federal crime has been committed here, and my duty is to keep the crime scene sealed until the FBI gets here. That's the way it is. *Capisce*, Mr. Shapiro?"

Gibbons figured this was his cue to get involved. "Gibbons, FBI," he said, walking up to them and flashing his ID. "Who's in charge here?"

"Me," Elam said.

"And who're you?" Gibbons said, thrusting his mean Aztec deity face into Shapiro's.

"Addison Shapiro, deputy transit commissioner in charge of Waterway—"

"You authorize him to be here?" Gibbons said to Elam.

"No."

"Crossing police lines and violating a federal crime scene is a federal offense. Please leave." Gibbons jerked his thumb at the yellow tape.

Shapiro scuttled back under it immediately. He tried to plead his case to Gibbons from over there, but Gibbons turned his back and ignored him.

"That true about violating a federal crime scene being a federal crime?" Elam said as he propped his big foot back up on the fender.

"Probably," Gibbons said, then turned his attention to the dripping VW. "So what's this? The catch of the day?"

Elam smiled and showed the gap between his front teeth. "Whatever it is, Gib, it's yours."

Gibbons crossed his arms and shook his head. "You guys don't handle homicides anymore? What was it they used to say back in the bad ole days about 'lazy and shiftless'?"

"You don't have to prove to me what a racist bastard you are, Gib. I already know."

Gibbons flashed a saccharine grin. "I like you too, Elam. So now tell me why I'm here."

Elam flipped a few sheets on his clipboard. "About two this afternoon, 911 started getting calls about something floating in the harbor. Only the roof and part of the windshield were visible in the water. One woman reported it as a dead whale."

"An *orange* whale?"

"She was a dumb blonde," Elam said with a shrug.

"Now who's the racist?"

Elam rolled his eyes at Gibbons, then flipped another sheet and continued. "Harbor Unit responded, and they sent a diver in to investigate. The diver reported that the doors were locked, two bodies in the front seat."

Elam looked at Gibbons again, waiting for a reaction. Gibbons stared back at him stone-faced. He wanted the details first.

Elam went on with the report. "Apparently the killer didn't know that VW Bugs are airtight. I don't suppose he wanted this thing to float on him. Anyway, the Harbor guys towed it into this slip. They said it'd be easier to pull it out from here. I dunno. Said they'd have it out before rush hour, no problem. But as soon as they started to lift it out of the water, the front axle snapped. Pulled it up too fast. That's what the crane guy told me. The windshield smashed somehow when it hit the water and the car started to sink then. They told me it might take all night to pull the damn thing out now, so I told them to go ahead and take the bodies out."

"What the hell did you do that for?"

"Didn't want the fish to start eating them."

Gibbons shook his head and snorted a laugh. "Sharks?"

"Anything's possible in New York, man."

"Go on. I like this. First you dump this ass-pain on the FBI, now you're telling me you fucked up whatever evidence we might've had. The lab boys in Washington are gonna send you flowers for this one, Elam."

"Division okayed taking the bodies out. You take it up with them."

"That's right, pass the buck. You guys are good at that." Gibbons pushed his sunglasses up his nose. "I still don't get why you called us. This isn't a federal crime."

"Keep your pants on. I'm getting to that." Lieutenant Elam flipped another page. "If you look closely, Gib, you'll see that the car has Jersey plates. It floated here to Manhattan from Jersey, which is where the murders must've occurred, which makes this an interstate crime, which, as you know, makes this all yours, Gib." Elam put his thumb and forefinger over his eyes and laughed with his shoulders.

"You check the water inside the engine? Can you prove it's Jersey water?"

The lieutenant just shrugged. Not my job, man.

"All right, I'm here now," Gibbons said. "I may as well solve this one for you. Where are the bodies now?"

Elam's grin suddenly disappeared at the mention of the bodies. "The ME did the preliminaries and took them to the morgue a little while ago."

"And?"

"Not pretty." Elam exhaled deeply and looked down at his notes for a moment before he went on. "The victims were a male and a female. Both Asian. Exact cause of death is unknown at this time." Elam looked up from the clipboard. "But if you saw them, it wouldn't be too hard to guess."

Gibbons squinted at Elam. "What do you mean?"

Elam scratched his ear. "They were practically cut in half. Right through the middle. They weren't hacked, though. You know, the way a guy does it when he wants to stuff his wife in garbage bags and put her out with the trash. These cuts were different. They were . . . well, neater than that."

Gibbons tried to imagine what he was talking about and all he could think of was the big roasts in the meat case at ShopRite. "What do you mean, 'neater'?"

"From what I saw, it looked like the killer actually tried to cut the victims in half. The gash on the male was on the left side. It cut right through the spine. The female's was on the right. Not quite as deep, but almost. The guys from the morgue had a hell of a time keeping them together when they moved them out of the car. The ME told me he wouldn't be surprised if there were a few organs missing. Lost in the water. That's how big these cuts were. But like I said, the weird thing is that they're very neat, precise cuts, Gib. No indication of sawing or chopping that I could see. Slices, I'd call them. I've never seen wounds like these on a body before. Clean, deep slices."

Gibbons took off his glasses and waited for his stomach to settle down. He could taste his lunch—brisket. "Slices, huh? You telling me I should go check out every cold-cut slicer in Jersey?"

Elam shook his head slowly. "You are one hard ass, aren't you? This kind of shit doesn't affect you anymore. You seen it all before, right?"

"What do you want me to do? Pull out my handkerchief and cry a little? Sympathy for the victim wasn't part of the job description when I joined the Bureau. I feel sorry on my own time. My job is to find the bastards who do this kind of shit so they can't do it again. Okay?" A rock-hard band of pain circled his gut. Bastard.

Elam stood up, stuck his hand in his pocket, and just looked at the veteran special agent. "They don't make 'em like you anymore . . . thank God."

Gibbons scowled. "Don't try to butter me up, Elam. You already dumped this case on us. It's not your headache anymore. Be happy."

"I'd love to see your annual job evaluation. What does your boss put under 'Attitude?' Peachy?"

Gibbons didn't bother answering. He stared at the orange Volkswagen hanging from that cable like the big one that didn't get away, trying to imagine what kind of weapon or device could make those "slices," wondering what kind of sick mind could do something like this, wondering why the hell a killer would bother doing something difficult when all he wanted to do was just kill his victims. Assuming, of course, that was his only purpose.

"Were there any other marks on the bodies?"

Elam shook his head. "Not that we could see."

"Any idea who they were?"

Elam shook his head again. "No identification on the bodies. No wallets, no money, no keys, just odds and ends."

"Anybody checking with Missing Persons?"

"Nope. Not our job, man. This is your baby now."

Gibbons shook his head and looked at the ground. "It gladdens my heart to see that the NYPD's attitude toward the Bureau has improved so dramatically." Couldn't expect a cop to go out of his way to help a fed. Unwritten police rule in every precinct from sea to shining sea: Screw the feds whenever you can.

The crane's engine started revving up then as it slowly started to pull the VW up away from the water. When they finally set the Bug down on its tires, Gibbons took out his notepad and went over to take a look. The first thing he did was jot down the license plate number. He looked through the side window on the driver's side, scanning the frontseats, then the backseats.

He could see Elam's reflection in the glass, looming behind him. "So what do you see, Gib?"

"A wet car, lieutenant."

Elam pursed his lips and nodded. "That's the kind of trenchant comment you come to expect from a seasoned investigative talent. I can see why the FBI pulled you out of retirement."

"Who says they pulled me out of retirement?" He walked around to the passenger side and peered in.

Elam stuck his hands in his pockets and cocked his head back. "Oh, you know how it is, Gib. Word gets around."

Gibbons ripped off a blank sheet of paper from his pad and used it to open the car door so as not to add his fingerprints to the handle. "So what's the word?" he asked. "Clue me in."

"That the Bureau had to call you out of retirement to chase down one of your guys in the Manhattan field office who went renegade."

Gibbons stuck his head inside the car and took a look under the dash, then jiggled the stick shift. It was in neutral just as he knew it would be. Bodies don't drive themselves into the river. They were pushed.

"The way I heard it, Gib, this dude started shooting up all these bad guys who walked in court, you know, cases he'd put together before he went nuts. A one-man judge, jury, and executioner."

"You see this one on TV, Elam?" Gibbons scowled under the dash. How the fuck did he know about Tozzi?

"Yeah, well, the way I heard it, you knew something about this guy, how he ticked and all that. They figured you were the only one who could bring him in before he did any more damage. Is that how it went down, Gib?"

There were a couple of people at the field office who could've pieced it all together and figured out that Tozzi had gone renegade, even though Ivers insisted that he was certain he'd kept the lid on it. Maybe it was Ivers himself, though. Maybe our dear Special Agent in Charge bragged to a few of his law-enforcement colleagues, modifying the story to make it look like a real management coup on his part. That wouldn't be out of character for the asshole.

"Come on, Gib, you can tell me. You are the Great White Renegade Hunter, aren't you?"

Gibbons stood up and looked at Elam over the roof of the Volkswagen. "I don't know what the fuck you're talking about. It's a good story, though. You ought to write it up in a book."

Elam just smiled, flashing a lot of big white teeth. "Yeah, I'll do that, Gib."

"Hey, Elam, can I ask you something?"

"What's that?"

"You used to play for Michigan, right?"

"Michigan State. I played forward and backup center. We tied with Indiana for Big Ten champs, my junior year." The lieutenant seemed very proud of his record.

"Didn't you play some pro ball, too?"

"Yeah, a little. I was drafted by the Bullets, but I only played a couple of games with them."

"What happened?"

"I wanted to stick it out, man, but I had bad knees."

"Bad knees, huh?" He studied Elam's size, noticing how his waist was almost even with the roof of the Bug. Willis Reed had bad knees. Didn't stop him.

Gibbons stared at the passenger seat of the VW. There were no blood stains; the river had washed the vinyl upholstery clean. He shut the door and pressed his hand against his sore gut, wondering if the killer was a short little shit.

3

John D'Urso watched his boss, Carmine Antonelli, slowly pouring out two cups of espresso and wondered just how he should bring it up, hoping that maybe today he could convince him. It was a great idea, a potential fucking gold mine. He knew from the first night last summer when Nagai took him to the yak whorehouse on Sixty-sixth Street, the one Hamabuchi set up to cater exclusively to Jap businessmen. Ever since that night, he couldn't stop thinking about the possibilities, the opportunities, those incredible girls.

The girl he had that night was unbelievable. To tell the God's honest truth, he wasn't even up for it that night, but she changed that quick enough. It was like she had a little hand up there. He never imagined one of these shy, quiet little things could be so sexy, so accommodating, so incredibly good. And as far as he could tell, they were all like that, walking fantasies, all of them. There was no question about it, he had to have Jap girls working a house for him. All he had to do was get Mr. Antonelli's okay. That's all he wanted. Antonelli was a stubborn old bastard, but he wasn't unreasonable all the time. If the old goat had enough left in him to make it with one of these Jap pros, he'd go for it like that. True, Antonelli already said no, but he could change the old man's mind if he played his cards right. Play it right and he just may go for it this time. Sure, why not?

"Nice suit, John," Antonelli said without looking up. "Shiny." He pushed a cup and saucer in front of D'Urso.

D'Urso knew what the old man really meant. He didn't like flash, never had. Gotta keep a "low-profile," he always says, a "low-profile." Always the goddamn "low-profile." A three grand, tailor-made, polished Italian silk suit and he calls it "shiny." Christ.

Antonelli carefully rubbed the slender piece of lemon rind around the rim of his espresso cup. His bony, wrinkled hands reminded D'Urso of the wicked queen's hands in *Snow White and the Seven Dwarfs* after she turns herself into a witch. They had the video at home, and his daughter watched it all the time. The old man's hands looked just like the wicked witch's when she held out the poison apple for Snow White.

D'Urso waited for the old *capo di capi* to speak next. It was considered very disrespectful to rush the boss, even if the senile old bastard did take a week to stir a little spoonful of sugar into his goddamn espresso. D'Urso glanced over at Vincent sitting at the bar, quietly sipping his own espresso. Vincent stared back at him dead-eyed, like a gorilla with an attitude. Vincent, of course, wouldn't agree that the old man was getting too old to run the family. Why should he? The old man wants to make him underboss. Vincent the bodyguard, the old man's goddamn driver, for chrissake! Vincent who ran the shittiest crew in Brooklyn. Now the old man wants to make him underboss. Unbelievable.

Antonelli reached for a pignoli cookie from the plate in front of him and broke it in half. He took a bite and chewed slowly and deliberately, then sipped from the small gold-rimmed cup. D'Urso felt like he was trapped in a fucking old age home. He looked out the window at the traffic inching down Mulberry Street, then focused on the backwards letters on the plate-glass window, the cracked gold-leaf lettering that spelled out CAMPANIA SPORTS SOCIETY. MEMBERS ONLY. He hated coming here, bowing and scraping to the old man, making a big production number out of giving him his cut when the goddamn guy didn't do shit for it really. Christ, the last time Antonelli was even in Jersey Nixon was president. Why the hell should he have to drive in here and give Antonelli fifty fucking percent, leaving him with a lousy ten percent after expenses? Good question. D'Urso held his tongue and sipped his espresso which was like poison in his throat. He hated espresso and only drank it when he was here, out of respect.

"So," Antonelli said, brushing cookie crumbs from the ridiculously wide lapels of his dark suit, "how are we making out with our Japanese friends?" He looked up for the first time, and D'Urso was startled by the clear blue of his eyes. The old man's hard, suspicious eyes always caught him by surprise. They just didn't go with the rest of him.

"Very good, Mr. Antonelli. Very good." He heard himself sucking up to Antonelli, and he hated the way he sounded. A bad taste lingered at the back of his throat as he reached for the attaché case on the floor by his leg and presented it to the old man. Four hundred and sixty-eight thousand dollars, freshly laundered from Atlantic City at his own expense. For what?

Antonelli took the leather attaché case and passed it to Vincent who opened it on the bar and started counting the packets of bills.

"I saw Hamabuchi last week," Antonelli said. "He's much happier now that the profits have started to come in. He never liked the idea of having to wait till we showed a profit before he got paid for his merchandise."

Merchandise, my ass. They're slaves, for chrissake. Why not just call them slaves?

"Hamabuchi has his doubts. He says he still can't see people in America using enforced labor." Antonelli stared him in the eye without blinking.

"Well . . . our customers don't know that these people are slaves." The old man knew all this. He just likes to make you lay out the whole operation for him to make sure you know what the fuck you're doing. Just to bust balls. "We lease the slaves to different employers, mostly factories but some domestic help too—maids, cooks, nannies—"

"What?"

"Nannies, live-in baby-sitters. You know. They're very popular these days. My wife handles them . . ."

Antonelli closed his eyes and nodded for D'Urso to go on, which made D'Urso's stomach tighten up. He treated him like a goddamn kid.

"Anyway, we've got two dummy employment agencies set up, besides my wife's nanny thing. As I said, our customers don't know they've got slaves working for them. They don't even question it because they're getting help at cut-rate prices. I imagine some of them suspect that everything's not totally kosher, but they don't want to know any of the details because they're getting such a great deal. All they ever say is that we've got some hell of an outfit. Our buses deliver the slaves first thing in the morning, pick 'em up at closing time, and the bosses don't want to know a thing beyond that."

The old man smiled benevolently and nodded. "That's just what I told Hamabuchi, John."

D'Urso grit his teeth. He could've punched him in his fucking face, the patronizing old bastard. Then he caught Vincent glaring over his tinted glasses at him. Vincent who carried two guns at all times.

Antonelli took the other half of the pignoli cookie, stuck it in his mouth, and sucked on it for a minute. "You know, John, I asked Hamabuchi why these Japanese kids agree to this crazy deal in the first place. Eighteen, nineteen years old, selling themselves, three years of hard work in exchange for a trip to America. Maybe I could understand it if their country was one of those poor and dirty places, but Japan isn't a poor country. You Japs got everything now, I told Hamabuchi. So why do they do it? I asked him."

D'Urso knew why, but he knew he was going to have to hear why again. Out of respect. "What did he say, Mr. Antonelli?"

"They make their kids crazy over there in Japan. Did you know they have to take tests to get into *kindergarten* over there? Can you imagine?"

He thought about pointing out to the old man that rich kids right here in New York have to take tests to get into ritzy preschools, but he decided not to bother. Antonelli was hip; he just liked to pretend he was an ignorant old fool from the old country.

"In Japan these kids take tests all the time, and if they don't pass, they're finished. It makes these kids cuckoo. Hamabuchi told me that a lot of these kids go to school ten hours a day, six, seven days a week. But why? I asked him. He said because they all want good jobs with Panasonic and Sony and Toyota, all those big companies they got over there, and the only way to get an executive job is to go to one of the top colleges, but if they don't get fantastic grades on these stupid tests, they end up going to a number-two school, which only gets them a so-

so job with a so-so salary in a country where a lousy cup of coffee in a diner costs you five bucks. That's why these kids agree to sell themselves to Hamabuchi's gang."

D'Urso nodded. "The Fugukai." He wanted to let the old man know he was still paying attention.

"Right, the Fugukai. These're kids who didn't pass their college entrance exams. They feel hopeless, John. They don't know where to turn. That's when Hamabuchi's people step in and sweet-talk them, show them that there's still a chance for them, a chance to restore their *honor*, which is a big thing with these people. The Fugukai promise them a trip to America, the land of opportunity. If they agree to commit themselves to three years of on-the-job training—that's just what they call it, too—then they can have room, board, and passage to America. These kids are so depressed, they agree to it like that." The old man snapped his fingers, but D'Urso didn't hear anything.

D'Urso figured it was his turn to look smart. "And the beauty of it all is that we don't have to honor their original deal with the Fugukai. They're ours for as long as we want them. We can work these people for twenty, thirty, forty years. We pay off Hamabuchi in three, then after that we pocket roughly eighteen to twenty grand annually on each one. We've got twelve hundred in the country now, eighteen more on order . . ." D'Urso pulled out a pen and did some figuring on his napkin. "Three thousand slaves times eighteen grand a year is . . . fifty-four million a year for forty years. Not too bad." So why don't you let me have a better cut, you fucking old bastard you.

Antonelli pressed his finger on top of a pignoli nut that had fallen off one of the cookies and put it in his mouth. D'Urso watched him chewing thoughtfully, staring out the window. It was just starting to rain. The old man was getting as inscrutable as the goddamn Japs.

"They can't all be cooperating. These kids aren't dummies. You must be having problems with some of them. It can't be running that smooth."

D'Urso's stomach tightened again. He suddenly remembered that priest who always interrogated him in the Confession box when he was a kid, the one who wouldn't take his word for anything, who always assumed he was hiding some big mortal sin.

"Hamabuchi's hitters take care of that end," he said.

"Are there enough yakuzas here to really control all these kids?" Antonelli seemed skeptical.

"We've counted at least a hundred of them, but it's hard to tell with these yakuza guys. Most of them don't talk, and they just seem to show up whenever they're needed. They're weird that way." He stopped and considered what he was going to say next. "I had hidden video cameras put in down at the docks and at a few of the factories just so we can keep tabs on the yaks."

Antonelli frowned. "I don't like that, John. That's not showing trust. Hamabuchi is an old friend of mine. We helped each other a lot after the war. He wouldn't have his people spying on us."

The hell he wouldn't.

"No more spying on them. Get rid of the video crap."

D'Urso lowered his eyes and nodded. "Okay." Yeah, just watch me.

"Now back to my original question. Are Hamabuchi's people keeping the kids in line?"

"Definitely. It's really only the ones doing the hard work in the factories that give us any trouble, and the yaks come down hard on them right away. No warnings. First time a kid starts complaining or drags his ass, they beat him silly. And then there's Nagai's right-hand man, Mashiro. I don't know what it is with him, but all he has to do is show up and *bing!* the slaves snap to it. I've seen it. They're terrified of him. Supposedly his specialty is tracking down runaways, and so far we've only had a few." He decided not to tell the old man about the two Mashiro tracked down just yesterday. He wondered if Antonelli knew what his old pal Hamabuchi's mandatory punishment for runaways was. An awful waste of good merchandise to his way of thinking.

"Well, I'm happy to see that things are going well. Very good, John." Antonelli had that tone of voice that implied the meeting was over and he should go.

"One more thing, Mr. Antonelli." He took a deep breath, hoping. "Have you reconsidered my idea for a high-class bordello in Atlantic City? I've got a line on a good place, close

to the casinos. I was thinking about doing it up like a geisha
house, you know? The girls could all wear kimonos. You
know, a lot of these kids are very very nice looking, and we
really shouldn't be wasting them on baby-sitting and that
kind of stuff. These girls really know what they're doing,
from what I hear. Most guys have never done it with an Oriental broad, and a lot of them are curious. I think we could
clean up—"

"No."

"But—"

"I said no, and that's it." The old man slapped the tabletop
and Vincent shifted in his seat, getting his feet on the floor in
case he'd have to do something. "I told you before that it's too
risky, too high-profile. Besides, Hamabuchi keeps the pretty
girls for his own house here in town."

"But, Mr. Antonelli, we could clean up with—"

"You're not stupid, John. Think. Cops go to whorehouses,
too. What if one of the girls started talking to the wrong guy.
What then?"

"We'd control that—"

"How? You gonna get in bed with them? Make sure they
don't talk?" The old man's eyes were wild now.

D'Urso's hands were shaking under the table, he was so
mad. He was biting the insides of his cheeks. Fuck you, old
man. Fuck you. I've already got my whorehouse going. A
month and a half we've been in business, you old fucking fart.

"Do we understand each other now, John?" Antonelli
leaned across the table and tilted his head like the kindly old
grandfather. Who the hell did he think he was? Papa Gep-
petto?

He glanced at Vincent. "Yes, Mr. Antonelli. I understand."

Vincent seemed to relax then.

"Okay. Good. Keep up the good work." Antonelli was dis-
missing him now.

D'Urso stood up. The old man wasn't looking at him. Vincent was.

"Take it easy, John," Vincent said. In other words, get going.

D'Urso buttoned his double-breasted jacket and headed for
the door, measuring his pace so it wouldn't seem like he was
rushing out. If he had a piece on him, he swore to God he'd

do it right now. Luccarelli had done it, he kept thinking. He did it and he got away with it. That was twenty years ago, but still, he did it.

The sky was gray and a cold rain was falling. He stepped briskly, sizing up his odds as he walked toward the car. How many *capi* were really that loyal to Antonelli? Besides Vincent, how many would really put up a fight? A lot, that's how many. But still, Luccarelli did it to Joe Coconuts, and there weren't that many guys who loved Luccarelli back then. They respected him *after* he did it. Kill the boss and you earn the position. *That's* how you do it.

He got into the black Mercedes 420 SEL and looked at his brother-in-law, Bobby Francione, sitting behind the wheel, feeding bullets into the clip of that little automatic he just gave him. "Whatta you, stupid? You playing with your dick or what? Put that fucking thing away before a cop comes by."

Bobby snapped his head up to get that strand of carefully crimped and moussed hair out of his eyes, the same stupid-looking strand he painstakingly worked on every morning to hang there like that. "Bad meeting, huh?"

He couldn't hold it in any longer. He threw a punch into the seatback so hard it made the whole car rock. Rain beaded on the windshield, throwing the world out of focus. "I run two car dealerships, a construction company, three night-clubs down the shore, and seven after-hours joints, and he treats me like a fucking nobody. I swear to Christ, Bobby, he's forcing my hand. I'm gonna have to do it. It's not right the way he treats me. He's holding me back, Bobby. There's no other way. He's got to go."

Bobby stuck the gun in his pocket, checked his hair in the rearview mirror, and grinned that shitty little grin he picked up in prison. "I keep telling you you should do it, John." He turned the key in the ignition and pulled the big car out into traffic.

He stared at Bobby's profile, his hands shaking, his heart pounding.

Yeah . . . I *should* do it.

4

Tozzi stared out the back window of the empty apartment at the pile of construction rubble in the backyard. A mangy-looking dog with a long, matted coat was pissing on a broken piece of wall board. Scraps of aluminum ductwork sparkled in the bright October sun. Yellow leaves from the junk tree that was uprooting the rickety back fence were beginning to fall on the pile. Several backyards on both sides had similar junk piles, the remains of recent renovations. Refocusing, he saw his own reflection in the glass—dark, deep-set eyes in a square, sad-looking face. He wondered if they'd ever get around to cleaning up the junk.

"What did you say the rent here was?" he asked, still staring out the window.

"Eight-fifty. That doesn't include heat or hot water," Mrs. Carlson, the real estate agent, said. She had a big ass, Coke-bottle glasses, wore ruby-red lipstick, and had a bad habit of standing over his shoulder and wringing her hands. She looked like Charley Chan in drag.

"Pretty steep," he said. "Adams Street isn't exactly the chicest part of Hoboken."

She smiled pleasantly around her buck teeth, ignoring his assessment. "Did I mention that Frank Sinatra once lived in this building? Actually it might've been this apartment. I'll have to check."

Tozzi had seen seven apartments in Hoboken this week,

and he'd been told that Sinatra lived in five of them. Old Blue Eyes really got around.

"Hoboken is a very desirable community," Mrs. Carlson started, launching into the same pitch Tozzi had already heard from every other real estate agent he'd talked to. "Everybody wants to live here. It's a very easy commute to Manhattan, but there's a very special feeling here. It's almost like a European village, don't you think? Nice little shops, bakeries, green grocers . . ."

Tozzi wondered how many villages in Europe had mesquite grills, quarter-million-dollar studio condos, a rock club where Bruce Springsteen films his videos, and an arson rate several times the national average. Ah, Hoboken, all that and more.

He walked back to the front of the apartment where sunlight was shining off the recently buffed wood floor. The place didn't have the old-world feeling that some of the others he'd seen had. But marble mantels and coffin corners cost you, and he didn't want to be rent poor, especially because he was still on probation. Ivers wouldn't need a great big reason to shitcan him this time, not after his little renegade adventure. Of course, he couldn't get into much trouble where he was now, relegated to a desk in the File Room, working for that dim bulb Hayes the librarian of all people, who was too shy or stupid or whatever to just come right out and say what he wanted done, which tended to make his days very long, boring guessing games.

Take your time and get yourself settled, Ivers had told him. Get your head back on straight, he'd said with that bullshit fatherly smile of his. That could almost be funny if it weren't so pathetic. It wasn't that long ago that everything he owned in the world fit into one suitcase: a suit, a few shirts, jeans, a few pairs of underwear, some socks, a pair of loafers, a pair of high-tops, a 9mm automatic, a .38 Special, a .44, and three boxes of cartridges. That was it. A couple of Mafia torpedoes had taken care of the rest of his worldly belongings when they ransacked his dead aunt's apartment, where he'd been hiding out. It depressed him whenever he thought about it. All in all, though, it was a lot better being back in the fold than out in the cold.

Tozzi looked the place over. It was clean, new fixtures,

white walls. He could fill it up, make it a home. Still, it was hard adjusting to the fact that just about everything he owned was brand new. Maybe that's why he'd decided on Hoboken. It sort of reminded him of the neighborhood he grew up in, the Vailsburg section of Newark.

"Our office has put together a little brochure that lists local shops, restaurants, services, schools, cultural events . . ." Mrs. Carlson opened her briefcase on the counter that separated the kitchen from the living room and rummaged through her papers. Tozzi ignored her. He was looking out the front window now at a tough-looking Hispanic teenager in a fringed, black leather jacket, sitting on the tenement stoop across the street, playing with a baby. He assumed she was the mother. The kid was just learning to walk, taking shaky steps on the cracked pavement, moving like Franken-stein in those gooney, white lace-up shoes, the kind people used to have bronzed when he was a kid. The baby was laughing, a big, drooly, toothless smile on his face. The girl was laughing, too. She snatched up the kid in her arms and gave it a big hug. Her face was pure joy. Tozzi smiled.

"Here it is," Mrs. Carlson said, pounding across the bare floors in her clunky heels to give Tozzi the brochure. "You may find this very helpful when—"

Just then Tozzi's beeper went off, which surprised the hell out of him. He was required to carry it, but he never expected anyone from the office to be calling him. Maybe it was a real crisis. Maybe Hayes ran out of the big paperclips.

"Excuse me," he said. "Is that phone hooked up?"

"Well . . . I don't know if the former tenant—but I don't think—"

"Don't worry. I'll reverse the charges." Tozzi unhooked the receiver from the white wall phone in the kitchen. There was a dial tone.

"By the way, Mr. Tozzi, I forgot to ask—what do you do for a living?"

Tozzi looked at a blank wall for a second and considered a lie. "I'm with the FBI," he said quickly, hoping she didn't catch his hesitation. "Informational Services," he added. "I'm in charge of data systems for the Manhattan field office."

"Oh . . . I see."

Instinctively he worried that she might have noticed the

bulge under his left armpit. But there was no bulge. He wasn't carrying a weapon these days. Ivers's orders.

He dialed the call-in number at the field office, reversing the charges, and identified himself to the operator who switched him to another line.

"Tozzi." The voice was vaguely sarcastic. It usually was.

He was surprised to hear Gibbons on the other end of the line. He hadn't seen much of his old partner in the past two months. It was no secret that Ivers was keeping them apart. "How's it going, Gib? Sorry you came out of retirement yet?"

"Sorry *you* came back?"

"No."

"You're gonna be. I've got some bad news for you."

Tozzi could hear the crocodile smile in his voice. He grinned in anticipation. "What?"

"You're going back into the field. With me."

"What're you talking about?"

"I had a talk with Ivers this morning. I fixed it all up. You're off probation."

"Cut the sh—" Tozzi suddenly remembered that Mrs. Carlson was right behind him. "Explain yourself."

"There's nothing to explain. We're short on manpower right now, NYPD unexpectedly shuffled this homicide case over to us, and nobody around here wants to work with me."

Tozzi coughed up a laugh into the phone. "Now we get to the real reason."

"Hey, I told Ivers straight out. If you can't get me a halfway decent partner, I'm going back into retirement. Give me Tozzi or else I'm gone, I said to him. Just like that. He caved right in. The asshole's got no backbone."

In his thirty years with the Bureau, Gibbons had rarely had a partner who lasted more than three days with him, except for Tozzi who'd been his partner for six years, right up until Gibbons retired. Tozzi sighed. It was nice to be wanted.

Tozzi glanced at Mrs. Carlson who was by the front windows, making believe she wasn't listening. "I thought Ivers was dead set against putting me back in the field. What really changed his mind?"

"Who knows? He's a shitty judge of character, though, if you ask me. One, for listening to me, and two, for letting a wacko like you back on the streets. Just get your ass back down here by five. Ivers wants to have a little talk with you before he sends you back out."

"Oh, yeah? Is he packing my lunchbox, too?"

"Yeah, with Twinkies. He may even give you a big kiss to send you on your way," Gibbons said with a snarl. "In his office at five—*comprende, goombah?*"

"I hear you."

"I'll fill you in on the case when you get here. A real Sherlock Holmes deal. Just your kind of thing."

"Why don't you give me a preview right now? I can't stand the suspense."

"You've got no patience, Tozzi. That's your whole problem. I bet you're even a premature ejaculator."

"Nope. No problems in that department." All I need is someone to do it with.

"Yeah, sure."

"Well, are you gonna tell me about it or what?"

Gibbons broadcast his annoyance with a long sigh into the phone. He seemed to be working harder these days at maintaining his image as a mean son of a bitch. God forbid anyone should think he was finally getting cooperative as he approached his golden years. Wouldn't want it to get around that he was getting soft.

"Okay, listen up, Tozzi. A VW Bug floated in with the tide and wound up in a Staten Island ferry berth in lower Manhattan yesterday, two stiffs inside. The bodies were nearly cut in half."

Tozzi's first thought was a magician sawing a woman in half. Then he thought of the mess of blood and guts, and he stopped breathing for a moment.

"The car had Jersey plates," Gibbons continued, "which is how the police managed to unload this thing on us. I ran down the plates with Motor Vehicle, and just as I figured, the car was stolen. The owner reported it last Saturday night to the Kearny police, ten hours before the estimated time of death."

"Is the owner a suspect?"

"No, his alibi checks out. He was at a chess club meeting in the Village that night. Witnesses confirm that he was there till at least ten-thirty. He got a ride home with a buddy of his from the club. His car, the VW, wasn't in the driveway when he got there."

"Why didn't he use his own car?"

"He says he only takes it to the grocery store. The guy's a retired math teacher, an old fart. He's not our man. I know it."

"A retired old fart, huh?" Tozzi laughed through his nose.

"Shut up and listen, will ya, Tozzi? The killer was definitely no rocket scientist. He closed all the windows in the car before he dumped it into the river. Beetles are airtight. They float. I thought everybody knew that. Christ, I think they even used to advertise them that way."

"Maybe he's not everybody."

"Obviously not. Not everybody has the crust to slice up two bodies like Thanksgiving turkey, then stick them in a car and dump them in the river."

"You put it so eloquently, Gib."

"Thank you. I just got a copy of the medical examiner's report. It's right here in front of me. One of the victims was cut on the right, the other one on the left. Initially we thought it was two cuts, but the ME says it was the same cut and that it was done *after* death. He thinks they were laid out on top of each other, or maybe even stood up face to face when it was done. Chew on that for a while."

"Sounds ritualistic to me." He lowered his voice, looking around for Mrs. Carlson. "You checking out the devil-worship angle?"

There was silence on the line.

"Gib? You still there?"

"Devil worshipers, huh? Why did I know you were gonna say that? Maybe it was Druids who did it. How about that?"

"Come on, give me a break."

"Five minutes on the case and you've already come up with one of your *Twilight Zone* theories. I knew you'd love this one, Sherlock."

"I have no theories or opinions until I see for myself what the labs come back with."

"And *then* you can start busting my balls with the cult shit."

Tozzi stretched the cord and looked down the hallway

Mrs. Carlson was poking through the linen closet now. "I'll see you later, Gib. I'm holding up a busy lady here."

"Oh, yeah? That sounds interesting."

"A real estate agent."

"She good-looking?"

"A very nice personality."

"Too bad. So how's that going? You find a place yet? And does the real estate lady come with it?"

"I hope the hell not," he mumbled. "This apartment search is a real pain. I just want to get it over with."

"So take a place, for chrissake, any place. All you need is three rooms and a bed. If it's clean, just take it. You're not Prince Charming, you don't need Buckingham Palace."

"Thanks for the advice. I'll see you at five. And by the way, thanks."

"For what?"

"Getting me back out on the street."

"Oh . . . you're welcome then. I'll see you later." Gibbons hung up.

Tozzi was grinning as he put the phone on the hook, then walked over to the front windows. The teenage mommy was still having a ball with her kid.

He could hear Charlene Chan's heavy footsteps coming down the hall behind him. The mommy flicked her cigarette butt into the street and hugged the baby tight, rocking him inside the open flaps of her leather jacket.

"Everything all right, Mr. Tozzi?" Mrs. Carlson asked.

"Oh, fine, fine." Then he remembered his lie to her. "Just a minor software problem." Dead flesh is soft . . . at least until rigor mortis sets in.

"So, what do you think?"

"How much did you say the rent was again?" The baby was arching his back, sticking his face into the folds of his mother's sweatshirt, laughing his head off.

"Eight-fifty. Not including heat and hot water."

He knew he wasn't going to find anything cheaper, not this clean. Anyway, he was sick of looking. He just wanted to get back to work now, real work. "I think I'll take it," he finally said, pressing his lips together and nodding.

"Good for you," she crooned with a well-practiced gush of enthusiasm. "I'm glad you like it, Mr. Tozzi. There is just one final thing we must do before I can draw up a lease. The landlord likes to know who his tenants are, and he does prefer married tenants. Since he does live in the building himself, and there are fewer than five units in the building, he is legally entitled to screen tenants and accept or reject them as he sees fit. But I'm sure there won't be a problem. There is a Mrs. Tozzi, I take it?"

"Oh . . . yes. Of course." His ringless hands froze in his pockets. "She couldn't make it today. Business."

"Oh, I understand. You must be DINKS." She smiled with all her teeth.

"Excuse me?"

"Dual Income, No Kids: DINKS. You've never heard that before?"

Tozzi shook his head and forced a smile. Bitch.

"Please forgive me. It's just an expression. No offense was intended."

"None taken." Offensive bitch.

"Your wife isn't a lawyer, is she? Mr. Halbasian doesn't rent to lawyers."

"No. She's not a lawyer." Fucking offensive bitch.

"Good. I'll get in touch with him today and we'll arrange for you all to meet. All right?"

"Sure, fine." Shit.

He glanced back out the window at the teenage mother and considered the possibility, then instantly rejected the idea. She'd never pass for a DINK.

Shit.

5

Nagai didn't like the way D'Urso was acting. He couldn't put his finger on it, but something wasn't right. He was too friendly, too smooth, not so arrogant. And too much smiling, considering why they were all here. He was up to something. Nagai looked to Mashiro for an opinion, but the samurai was preoccupied now, staring at his own hand. It was understandable. He's never done this before. Americans can just say "I'm sorry." Not so easy for us.

"Here, use this." Bobby Francione threw down a copy of *The New York Post* on the counter by the dirty sink. "And don't get blood all over the place."

Nagai picked up the newspaper and glanced at the headline: DEATH BUG FOUND IN HARBOR. A picture of the Volkswagen hanging over the water from a cable was under the headline. Very subtle, Bobby.

Mashiro stood off to the side as Nagai opened the newspaper over the old linoleum counter for him. The samurai put the small silver knife on the counter on top of the paper, then resumed his position, cradling one hand in the other like a small pet. Nagai looked at the man's thick, fleshy fingers. They reminded him of starfish arms. The one grimy window and the dim lightbulb hanging from the ceiling in that dingy backroom recreated the ominous gray light that precedes a storm. It seemed too appropriate.

"I'm all confused," Francione said, pointing to the small knife with the three-inch blade. "Is all this necessary?"

"It's a yakuza tradition," D'Urso said calmly. "Isn't that right, Nagai?"

Nagai nodded. "It's called *yubitsume*. When a man has made a serious mistake, traditionally this is how he must atone for it." He raised his right hand and showed his own mutilated pinkie and ring finger.

"It's like when we break legs," D'Urso said to his brother-in-law.

Francione suddenly snapped the newspaper closed and pointed to the headline. "For a major-league screwup like this, the fuck-up would be lucky if he was still breathing when we got through with him. If he was one of our guys, he'd be dead by now."

Why the hell did D'Urso have to drag that little asshole along wherever he went? Nagai wondered to himself. "How was Mashiro supposed to know that the car those kids stole would float? Floating cars. Who ever heard of such a stupid thing?"

"That's no excuse. You shoulda known. Now the cops must be all crazy about this. And why the hell did you have to cut 'em up like that? We don't need this kind of aggravation now. You people are walking liabilities as far as I'm concerned."

Nagai stared at Mashiro's hand. "And how is that?"

"Just look at yourselves for chrissake. I mean put yourself in our position. We're supposed to keep the law off your backs —right?—but you guys may as well wear signs around your necks, you're so damn obvious. Most of you yak guys dress like my Uncle Nunzio with those loud sports jackets and the gooney hats. Then there's the freakin' body tattoos all you guys have, even on your dicks . . . and this finger thing." He gestured at Mashiro's hand. "If any of you guys ever gets caught, they'll deport you in no time. You're all dead give-aways."

"Enough, Bobby," D'Urso said.

Nagai shrugged, unconcerned. He tugged on the cuffs of his royal blue shirt so they showed outside the sleeves of his sharkskin jacket. "You have your traditions, we have ours."

"Tooling around in an old black Caddy with fins? Is that tradition, too? That car looks like the fucking Batmobile. Is that supposed to be your idea of keeping a low-profile?"

Nagai glared at the punk, wondering why he was even having this conversation with this idiot. "That car belonged to Hamabuchi. He gave it to me. It would be dishonorable for me to give it up."

Francione threw up his hands. "Oh, for chrissake, that's all we ever hear from you people. Can't do shit because it would be dishonorable. Fuck. I think it's just a convenient excuse for not doing what you don't want to do."

Mashiro loudly sucked in a deep breath and picked up the knife. Francione's eyes bugged out at the sight of the knife in Mashiro's hand. Nagai forced a carefree chuckle. "It must be hard for you, Bobby, having to depend on slanty-eyed creeps like us to keep the slave trade going."

Francione's finger sprang out in front of Nagai's face like a switchblade. "Don't get wise, Nagie. You need us to buy the slaves just as much as we need you to get them over here, so just keep quiet."

"Tell me then. Where else can you get slaves in this kind of bulk? Slaves that *my* people keep in line for you."

"Don't try to throw your weight around with me, my friend. You've got people, my ass. I happen to know you've got nothing over here, Nagai. Zilch."

"I've got plenty of men here. More than you know."

Francione laughed in his face. "*You* don't have men. *Hamabuchi* has men. They answer to him, not you. Only Mishmosh here answers to you."

Nagai's heart started thumping. His throat felt dry. "You don't know what you're talking about."

"Oh, yes I do. We know all about you, Nagai. We know that you don't have any friends back home in Japan either because you fucked up royally over there. You're on the outs with the Fugukai because you tried to off Hamabuchi so that you could take over the family. But you blew it, right? But instead of having you whacked the way he shoulda, Hamabuchi keeps you around like a little dog on a leash. Am I right or am I right, Nagai? Coming here was your punishment, right?"

Nagai stared into Francione's eyes, wanting to take the knife from Mashiro and slit the little bastard's throat. Hamabuchi's words came ringing back out of the past: "*Now that you've gotten the treachery out of your system, you can be trusted not to try it again. Having realized your inadequacies, I believe that your loyalty to me will be that much stronger now. Atone for your error in America, Nagai. Work for me there, and I promise you, your honor will be restored."*

But when, goddamn it? When?

Francione looked at D'Urso and laughed. "He's got nothing to say. He knows I'm right."

"Shut up, Bobby, and go stand over there." D'Urso stepped between them. He put his hand on Nagai's shoulder and took him aside. Nagai was wary of his touch. "Don't mind Bobby. He's a hothead. He doesn't know what he's talking about."

"He knows quite a bit for someone who doesn't know what he's talking about."

D'Urso nodded apologetically. "Yeah, I know, well, that's my fault. Antonelli told me. I shouldn't have said anything to Bobby."

Nagai felt hot. They knew too much. He'd said too much himself.

"Listen," D'Urso said under his breath, "I want to talk to you about something. I can use more slaves, a lot more, as many as you can get, especially women. Can you arrange it?"

"The next shipment is due a week from Thursday—"

"No, no, no, those are already accounted for. I want to up the order. Get 'em over here as fast as you can. If you're willing to renegotiate the unit price, I'll put in a bulk order right now. Two thousand slaves, half women. But delivery can't be any longer than eight weeks. Can you do it?"

Nagai stared at him. "Hamabuchi and Antonelli make the deals, D'Urso. Not us."

D'Urso wrinkled his face and smiled. "Forget about them. I'm talking about something just between you and me. I've got some plans, which I can't really talk about just yet, but I definitely want to include you, Nagai. You're a very capable guy. I recognized that about you from the start. But it seems to me that Hamabuchi is keeping you down, and that's not right the way I see it."

"Just how do you see it?"

"Well, the way I see it, this whole slave thing is working out because of you and me. We work pretty good together, and I think we could work better if we were independent, if you know what I mean."

Nagai laughed. "You must be kidding."

"No, I'm not kidding. Who the hell needs these fucking

bosses? We do all the work and they take all the profits. We don't get anything back from them. You know the figures, I don't have to tell you. If we go out on our own, in three years we'll have more money than the two of them put together."

Nagai shook his head. "We'd never be able to get a shipment out of Japan by ourselves. Hamabuchi would block it."

"So who says we have to have Japanese kids? You told me once that you had connections in the Philippines. You used to buy girls over there to work as hookers in Hamabuchi's Tokyo nightclubs. Isn't that what you told me? We could start bringing Filipino kids over here. You could arrange it, couldn't you?"

Nagai stuck out his bottom lip and shrugged as he thought about it. "In theory we could . . . but in reality we'd be dead in a week if we tried to cross them."

D'Urso grinned and shook his head. "Not if you stick with me. I've got muscle behind me. Antonelli doesn't like to fight anymore, he's too old. He'll make noise, but he doesn't really have the numbers to go up against me now. And as long as you're here with me, we'll protect you from Hamabuchi's guys. I guarantee it. Hey, besides, you got Mashiro here to protect you. He won't abandon you for Hamabuchi, will he?"

"No, but—"

"*Hai.*" Mashiro suddenly came out of his trance, interrupting them. Nagai turned toward his man. This was important; he had to witness this. Mashiro had draped a towel over his front, and now he was bellying up to the counter and opening the newspaper again. He held the knife against the pinkie of the pet hand as if he were going to slice a carrot. He looked to Nagai for the go-ahead.

"Think about it, Nagai," D'Urso whispered in his ear. "Just think about it."

Nagai sighed inwardly and tried to concentrate on Mashiro. He kept thinking about what D'Urso had just said, though. It was crazy. He didn't want to live here permanently, even if he could have Hamabuchi's share of the profits. Still, with that much money, he could arrange to have his kids move here, kidnap them if he had to. And he wouldn't have to deal with their goddamn mother over here. You could do a lot with that much money—

A low, growly moan came out of Mashiro, and Nagai

snapped out of it, feeling guilty for not paying attention at such a crucial moment in the samurai's life. *"Hai,"* he said, trying to duplicate Mashiro's intimidating grunt. The samurai looked over his shoulder at him. A good man, Mashiro. It wasn't his fault, but still he is responsible. He met Mashiro's unwavering gaze and nodded curtly.

Without hesitation, Mashiro hunched over his hand. His shoulders heaved twice. Getting through the joint wasn't easy. Nagai knew. Blood quickly covered the newspaper and poured down the crease into the sink. Mashiro squeezed the base of the bleeding pinkie to staunch the flow. Nagai, in the meantime, took the knife and wiped it on the towel. He then pulled a Bic lighter out of his pocket and held the blade over a tall orange flame.

"Holy shit," Francione hissed. It was nice to see the punk looking so pale. "What're you gonna do with that?" Francione nodded at the severed chunk of finger on the blood-soaked newspaper. He was barking. Like a dog on a leash.

Nagai grinned as he watched the lapping flame. "Mashiro offers it to you. A token of his regret for his mistake."

Francione made a face. "Get that the fuck away from me."

"You could have an earring made out of it." Nagai laughed.

The punk touched the gold stud in his ear. "You're real funny, Nagai. Flush it down the toilet. And make sure it goes down."

"Perhaps I'll keep it." Nagai passed the knife to Mashiro who immediately pressed the flat of the blade to his wound, cauterizing it on the hot metal. Nagai took a gray plastic film container out of his pocket and dropped the bloody piece of finger into it. The stench of burning flesh filled the small room as Mashiro asked his boss in Japanese for the flame again so he could touch up the cauterization. Nagai noticed that Francione looked like he was going to be sick. Nagai held the flame and shook the film container to make the punk a little sicker. But the hollow rattling sound that the finger made suddenly made him sad. It reminded him of the sound that fuzzy, white mechanical bear made on his little toy drum, a gift he'd given Hatsu, his oldest daughter, so long ago.

After Mashiro had finished working on his finger, he

rubbed the ceremonial knife carefully with the towel and gave it back to Nagai.

Francione was shaking his head in astonishment. "You are one tough motherfucker, Mishmosh. Now I see why those slaves are so afraid of you." He had his hand on his earring again. "How'd this guy get so mean, Nagai? He go to sumo wrestler school or what?"

Nagai ignored the question, but Mashiro asked him in Japanese if he could answer the punk. Nagai shrugged and nodded. But why bother? He's an idiot American, he wouldn't understand.

"Once upon time," Mashiro began in his faulty English, "I was executive—not big boss, not small boss, middle boss. But my life make me sick. Nothing in my soul when I was executive. In company everybody worry about making better junk. I know one man he kill self because company no want his idea for clock in car. This no good. This is not Mashiro. Man must serve his spirit, not company. I am samurai. This my spirit. I must serve one lord, one lord who cares about more than clock in car. Mashiro can be no *ronin.*"

"What's that?" Francione asked.

Nagai paused, considering whether it was worth the effort to explain it to the punk. "A *ronin* is a wandering warrior, a samurai who has lost his lord."

Mashiro nodded vehemently. "Nagai-*san* is my lord. He tell me do this, I obey. He know best."

Nagai suddenly remembered the first time he ever saw Mashiro. It was a rainy morning, three, four years ago. He was coming out of his house and he nearly tripped over this strange man kneeling on his doorstep with his head bowed down on the concrete. With great reverence and formality, the stranger introduced himself as a descendent of the samurai Yamashita who served the great warlord Nagai of Kinki in the early days of the Tokugawa Shogunate. He thought the man was out of his mind. Mashiro kept calling him "lord," though, insisting that this old warlord Nagai was his ancestor, and that he'd come to carry on the tradition of their forefathers. Nagai laughed at him and pointed out that Nagai was a common name, but Mashiro said he was certain of the lineage, though he never said how he knew that. Mashiro explained that he'd gone to great lengths to seek him out so that he could offer his services. Nagai just stared at him, and suddenly it occurred to him that this stranger might be part of his shifting fate. This had happened less than a week after he tried to kill Hamabuchi, the period when he was preparing to face death for his blunder. He was all alone. No one in the Fugukai would talk to him, and his wife had fled to her mother's house with the children in fear. Normally he would have told the stranger he was crazy and kicked him off his property, but he needed a friend then. Someone to keep him company while he waited for Hamabuchi's punishment. He invited Mashiro inside and made him tea. That's how it started.

"Wait a minute, wait a minute," Francione said, pulling him out of his memories. "Mishmosh had a straight job and he gave it up to join the yaks?"

"There's much more to it than that. You wouldn't understand." Just go away.

"It has to do with honor, Bobby," D'Urso said softly, looking at Nagai.

"Honor, yes," Mashiro piped up. "More honor to be yakuza today. No honor in business. Nagai-*san* stand for something greater than junk. Nagai-*san* is *daimio*, warlord from long ago. System today is bad. Big factories make lots of junk. Old way is better. We succeed, we mock system. This is good."

Francione turned to D'Urso. "I'm not following any of this."

"What he means, Bobby, is that it's better to be a good yakuza than to be an ass-licker for some company. Mashiro knows bullshit when he sees it. All these big companies are all bullshit. They're just into waste and senseless consumerism. Mashiro holds higher values than that. Isn't that how it goes, Nagai?"

Nagai just stared at D'Urso. Amazing. In his own way D'Urso did understand. Amazing.

Mashiro was nodding again, smiling at D'Urso. "Yes, yes. Better to be samurai for Nagai than insect for Toyota, yes."

Francione shrugged. "If you say so. Hey, tell me something, Mishmosh. How will your finger there affect your karate chop?"

Mashiro looked puzzled, and Nagai translated. The samurai looked at Francione and grinned cryptically. Nagai laughed at the confused look on the punk's face. Let him wonder.

"Where is my cousin?"

Nagai stopped laughing. Heads turned toward the voice coming from the doorway, the insistent question in Japanese hanging in the air.

It was one of D'Urso's slaves, a kid in an oversized, stained, white lab coat, one of those ridiculous paper caps on his head. He stood there in the doorway, glaring at them, then abruptly he bowed to all four of them and spoke to Nagai and Mashiro in Japanese. "My name is Takayuki. My cousin left to find his girlfriend days ago. He has not returned. The rumor is that you killed them. I want to know if this is so." He stood firm, waiting for an answer.

"What the hell does he want?" D'Urso's face was a scowl.

"I want to know what has become of my cousin, Mr. D'Urso." The kid spoke perfect English. "He's been gone since last Saturday. This isn't right, how you treat us. This is not what we expected when we signed up for this program back home."

Takayuki . . . yes. Nagai knew who this kid was. The lovesick puppy who used to help Reiko with her English lessons after school. He remembered her saying that he spoke English just like an American. Nagai often thought he ought to be grateful to the little shit for training such an effective spy. Reiko . . . If D'Urso ever found out about her . . .

Nagai caught Mashiro's eye then and nodded abruptly. The eager samurai nodded back and turned toward the kid. Mashiro's broad back blocked his view of the slave's face. "Make sure all the others see," Nagai ordered. "Scare some sense into them."

Mashiro moved quickly, swinging his wide hips in long, round strides. He stood toe-to-toe with Takayuki, motionless, waiting. The boy glowered at him, then started to make his demand again in Japanese, but he was cut off sharply when Mashiro smashed him in the forehead with his own head. Mashiro pushed him out of the doorway and quickly followed after him. Nagai smiled. He knew Mashiro was going to do that.

From the hallway, Nagai could hear the kid trying to protest, but all his pleas were cut short. Then he heard a violent banging, the kid being thrown down the short flight of steps that led to this back wing. There was a moment of silence then. Nagai imagined the whole plant freezing at the sudden arrival of Mashiro with the kid. Whenever he appeared, they froze. He put dread in their hearts like a long, bitter winter. The sounds traveled up to that back room, scuffling feet on the tile floor and young Takayuki's body slamming against the metal vats as Mashiro's blows did their work. Then silence again followed by a weak, mounting wail of pain. Nagai looked at D'Urso and smiled. "He'll be a good boy now."

D'Urso smiled. "I'm sure he will be. Listen, I got some business to attend to over at my Honda dealership right now, but promise me you'll consider what I said."

Nagai nodded. "I'll let you know."

Francione looked confused again as he followed his brother-in-law out of the room. When he was alone, Nagai stared up at the gray light coming through the dirty window, trying not to be tempted by the possibilities. But in America anything was possible.

Mashiro reappeared then, his wide silhouette covering the doorway. He was holding onto his blood-smeared hand. The blackened stump was oozing. "The knife and the fire, please."

Nagai nodded and reached into his pocket. Yes . . . anything was possible.

6

Gibbons sucked on a butterscotch Life Saver and studied Tozzi sitting in the chair next to him. Tozzi's knee was bouncing as he scanned the top of Ivers's desk, trying to read the papers laid out there upside-down. He looked jumpy. He usually did these days.

Special Agent in Charge Brant Ivers sat behind his oversized mahogany desk, half-glasses perched on his pointy nose as he read the report in his hand. It might've been his imagination, but Gibbons could've sworn Ivers was beginning to let the gray show in his temples. The touch of gray combined with the plain navy suit and the white button-down shirt gave him an almost fatherly appearance. Sort of a Teddy Kennedy/Ozzie Nelson crossbreed. As a matter of fact, Ivers's demeanor had become quite fatherly since Tozzi had come back. Gibbons glanced at the photo of Ivers's three sons on the desk. Kids do make you old, Brant. Gibbons grinned meanly.

Ivers peered over his glasses, glanced at Gibbons, then let his skeptical gaze settle on Tozzi. It was another one of his practiced gestures that was supposed to mean something. Shit. If you don't trust Tozzi, why the hell did you agree to let him take part in this investigation in the first place, asshole? Come on, get on with it.

Ivers let out a long, resigned sigh and shook his head. Gibbons waited for him to say something, but he just kept shaking his head. "So what's the story, Brant?"

Ivers frowned at him, then stared at Tozzi again. "Not very promising, Bert."

Gibbons flipped the Life Saver over on his tongue a few times. He hated his first name, Cuthbert, and any variation on it, but he rarely told anyone more than once that he preferred to be called by his last name. If you really knew him, you knew not to call him by his first name. That's how he knew who his real friends were.

"So what did the labs come up with on the two bodies?" Tozzi asked. Gibbons had told him to just shut up and listen, but Tozzi was too antsy to listen. He never listened. Go ahead and act like a pistol, goombah. That's just what Ivers is waiting for. An excuse to stick you back in the File Room. What a genius.

Ivers glanced back at Gibbons. He seemed unwilling to address Tozzi directly. Afraid he might bite maybe. "Well, as I assume you know, the two victims found in the Volkswagen were a male and a female. Bone analysis determined that they were in their late teens, early twenties. From their facial features, they think these two were either Korean or Japanese, but that's really just a guess. We've found no missing-persons reports on file that fits their description. The computer came up empty on their fingerprints, so we may assume that they were foreign nationals. We'll try to get Japanese and Korean authorities to run a check on the prints for us, but from past experience, Washington tells me cooperation on international investigations isn't very high on their agendas in the East."

"Were the cuts the cause of death?" Tozzi asked.

Ivers shook his head and shuffled through the reports carefully until he found what he was looking for. He didn't seem to want to look at Tozzi either. Probably reminded him that the two of them had made him eat crow not too long ago, forcing him to take Tozzi back. Who knows? Maybe Ivers was still embarrassed with himself.

"Shattered vertebrae in the necks of both victims indicate bludgeoning with a heavy object of some sort. The torso wounds were postmortem."

Tozzi pulled on his bottom lip and stared out the window. Gibbons knew the look. He was already putting together one of his famous theories. Gibbons swore to God he'd kick him in the teeth if he brought up devil cults again.

"Did the lab come up with anything special on the wounds?" The Life Saver rattled against his molars.

"They say the wounds were made by a long, single-edged, razor-sharp blade. Very likely a curved blade of some kind. Our people confirm the ME's opinion that both wounds were inflicted by a single stroke." Ivers drew in a sharp breath. Gibbons knew this was all for effect. With Ivers, most of it was. "One of the lab techs added a note of her own. She thinks the weapon could possibly have been a . . . *katana*, if that's how you pronounce it. A Japanese samurai sword. Apparently there are dozens of martial-arts retailers around the country who sell them mail-order. Washington is putting together a list for us."

Gibbons shifted the Life Saver to the other side of his mouth. "Does the modus match anyone we have on file?" Besides Jack the Ripper.

Ivers shook his head. "The computer came up with plenty of postmortem mutilations. But specifically, nothing like this."

Tozzi chewed his bottom lip and looked over at Gibbons. "Maybe it's some kind of ritual thing?"

Nice going, Tozzi. Go ahead, show the man that you're back out in yoyo-land.

Ivers finally looked Tozzi in the eye. He took off his glasses and held them in both hands. "We're considering that, Mike. Research is looking into it." He put the glasses back on.

Oh, Jesus.

"What about the blows that broke their necks?" Tozzi asked. "Any idea what that weapon was?"

"Skin wasn't broken on either of their necks. It could've been any of several things: a sap, a rubber truncheon, a rounded metal object of some sort, maybe something wrapped in cloth."

Gibbons was getting impatient. "They find anything else? How about in the car?"

"The car was pretty clean, I believe," Ivers said, checking the report to make sure. "But they did find some interesting things in the clothes. Synthetic fibers were found on the corduroy pants the man was wearing, fibers that match the carpeting used in certain Japanese cars currently in production."

"These fibers weren't from the Bug?" Gibbons asked.

"No. The Volkswagen had no carpeting. Volkswagen didn't offer it in those old models." Ivers flipped a page. "There were also substantial traces of chicken blood on his pants."

"A Satanic cult," Tozzi said right away. "They sacrifice chickens."

Gibbons glared at his partner and bit down hard on the Life Saver.

"In the female's pants pocket," Ivers continued, reading from the report, "they found a small set of shears. These." Ivers showed them an eight-by-ten black and white of an odd-looking set of shears, short, pointy blades with large rabbit-ear handles. "Research says that these particular kind of shears are commonly used to prune bonsai trees. This pair were made in Japan."

Tozzi's knee was bouncing all over the place. He was raring to go. Gibbons crunched down on the last slivers of his Life Saver.

Ivers took off his glasses and threw them down on top of the report. "And that's basically what we've got."

"It's better than nothing," Tozzi said. "We'll need a list of all the cars that have that kind of synthetic carpeting. The shears don't seem to fit. One of us will have to do some checking around, go someplace where they sell bonsai trees to see what we can pick up. Maybe those kind of shears are used for something else. The cult angle will have to be checked out, too. If there's nothing on file, I'll poke around that occult bookstore on Nineteenth Street, see if anything clicks. In the meantime—"

"Hold on, Tozzi." Ivers didn't look pleased. "There are a few issues we have to air before we go any further here."

Gibbons smirked. Told you to shut your yap, goombah.

"I'm not entirely comfortable with the idea of you out in the field on your own, Tozzi. Since this isn't a high-priority case, I think it best that you and Gibbons work together very closely on this. Do you understand what I'm saying?"

"Hey, wait a minute, Ivers. I didn't come out of retirement to baby-sit this guy."

"I don't want you to baby-sit anyone, Bert. I just think Tozzi should ease his way back into the routine."

Tozzi looked him in the eye. "Why?"

Ivers eyeballed him right back. "Because the Bureau does not applaud individual efforts, Tozzi, and that seems to be your proclivity. Just because we hushed up your renegade episode, doesn't mean it's been forgotten. If you intend to continue as a special agent, you have to get back to doing things the FBI way."

"I'm back in the fold. I told you." Tozzi was forcing a smile, trying very hard not to tell the SAC to go fuck himself.

"Let me just refresh your memory on some of the basics. All FBI operations must meet three requirements before confronting criminal suspects: superior manpower, superior weapons, and the element of surprise. We work as a *team* here, Tozzi. Remember that."

Tozzi rolled his tongue around in his cheek before he responded. "Right."

"I've ordered Jimmy down in Technical Services not to issue you any equipment without my signed okay. No spur of the moment buggings or any of that. I want to know what you're doing *before* you do it."

"I'll keep you very informed."

"And another thing, Tozzi. Leave your personal arsenal at home. In case you forgot, the special-agent issue weapon is a .357 Magnum revolver. If you intend to remain a special agent, that's the gun you'll carry. Understood?"

"Yes." Tozzi was seething.

Gibbons rubbed the sides of his mouth and watched this little drama unfold. Ivers was merciless, going for the guns like that. Tozzi was very particular about his choice of weapon, and he'd never been comfortable with any single handgun. He always said he was waiting for someone to make the perfect gun—that's why he switched off so often. He didn't like the .357 Magnum. Too clunky, he said. He was right about that. Gibbons suddenly became aware of Excalibur, his trusty .38, in the shoulder holster under his armpit.

Ivers turned to Gibbons now. "Do you have anything to add, Bert?"

"Nope." Gibbons stood up to leave. I don't want any part of this blanket party, Ivers.

"All right then. You can pick up copies of these reports from my assistant. And remember. I want to be kept apprised of everything. Daily."

Gibbons nodded as Tozzi got out of his seat and marched across the expensive wine-red Bokhara rug.

"Yes sir," Tozzi said. "You will be kept informed."

"Be sure I am."

Gibbons went out the door first.

"Fuck," Tozzi grumbled under his breath as he gripped the doorknob.

Gibbons caught the ugly look on Tozzi's face as the door swung back. He caught the heavy door before it slammed and closed it with a gentle click.

Gibbons tipped the last few drops of beer in the bottle into his glass. Tozzi was sitting sideways on the other side of the booth, looking out at the bar. He was twirling his bottle of Rolling Rock absently on the tabletop. There was this real knockout with long, straight blond hair and incredible legs standing at the bar, sharing a pitcher of frozen blue margaritas with her doggy girlfriends. Gibbons knew Tozzi was checking her out, the horny bastard. So was he.

"You gonna listen to him?" Gibbons said, staring at the blonde's legs. "About the Magnum, I mean."

"No."

"He'll bust your balls if he finds out."

"He won't find out." Tozzi took a swig. His eyes didn't leave the girl. It certainly was nice to see miniskirts back in style.

"What if you have to discharge your weapon and ballistics comes up with the nonapproved slug?"

Tozzi shrugged. "I'll tell him something."

One of the dogs refilled the blonde's glass and spilled some on the floor. The blonde wiggled up onto her stool and crossed her legs, giving them a nice stretch of thigh to look at. Gibbons wondered what blue margaritas tasted like. He had a feeling he probably wouldn't like them. He was actually surprised they made them here at the Auld Sod. He was surprised they got girls like that in here now. They never used to.

"Why don't you go over and talk to her?" he asked.

"I'm thinking about it," Tozzi said. He seemed hypnotized. "I could use a woman."

Gibbons laughed. "Who couldn't?"

Tozzi took another swig. "I need a wife."

"What?"

"I don't mean to marry. Just someone to pose as my wife. This apartment in Hoboken I told you about? I have to meet the landlord. He only rents to couples and I told the real estate agent I was married. I need a wife by Friday."

"Oh." Gibbons watched the blonde run her fingers through her hair. Her nails were long and purple, and she was wearing three earrings in one ear. "Forget it. Try one of her friends. They look like wives. She doesn't."

"Hmmm . . . I have a feeling she wouldn't buy my story anyway. She'd just think it was a come-on."

"It's a good come-on."

"Yeah . . . But if you were a landlord, would you rent to a woman who looked like that?"

"If I lived in the building, sure."

"I dunno . . ." Tozzi took another swig. "I don't think so."

Gibbons gulped down the rest of his glass. "So how's that going? You, ah . . . getting things back together all right?" He didn't know quite how to phrase it without making Tozzi sound like a mental patient. Tozzi was just coming out of a pretty shaky state, though. The guy went underground for chrissake, had to look over his shoulder every two minutes, people chasing him day and night from all directions—it must've done something to his head.

"Yeah, it's coming along," Tozzi said. "It's pretty weird, though. Everything I have now is new. Very weird. Of course, I guess you don't have much choice when you whittle your life down to three handguns and a suitcase full of dirty laundry."

Gibbons rubbed his nose and grimaced. Tozzi was going to get maudlin now, start crying in his beer. It was the guinea in him. He reached for his second bottle of Rolling Rock, tilted his glass, and poured. He usually ordered beers two at a time. It saved time waiting for service.

Tozzi suddenly took his eyes off the blonde and glanced at Gibbons. "Tell me, how're things with Lorraine?" He asked in that tone of voice that made it plain he already knew, so don't bother to lie. "I talked to her the other night. She's pretty upset that you decided to come out of retirement and go back to work."

Gibbons stared hard at the blonde. What was he, Lorraine's goddamn agent? Does Tozzi think he can start busting balls just because he's her cousin? Shit. He and Lorraine Bernstein had been an item long before he even knew Tozzi existed. Sure, they've been having fights. Big fights. But that was none of Tozzi's goddamn business.

"She says she's mad because you made a 'unilateral decision.' That's how she put it. She's hurt that you didn't at least discuss it with her first."

"We're not married, Toz." Gibbons sipped his beer. I don't have to explain anything to anyone. Including you.

"Why don't you just talk to her? You know, explain your side of it. She'll understand . . . eventually."

The blonde dropped her purse then. She got off the bar stool to pick it up, bending over from the waist and pointing her fanny to the crowd. Half the guys in the room went to heaven.

"Just talk to her, Gib. That's all. Just talk to her."

Gibbons glared at him. "Mind your own fucking business, Tozzi."

Tozzi nodded. "I knew you'd understand."

When Gibbons looked back, the blonde was heading for the door. Damn.

7

Restless flames shot out of tall oil-refinery smoke stacks and licked the black night over Elizabeth and Linden. In the distance, hundreds, maybe thousands of naked light bulbs outlined the nebulous pipework grids below those big lit candles. Closer, the roar of incoming jets made the corrugated aluminum door vibrate in his hand as the red and green lights of the departing flights filled the sky with artificial stars. A chill wind threatened frost. It reminded Nagai of home.

Nagai shut the warehouse door and threw the bolt. The greenish fluorescent lights inside made him blink as he walked through the maze of aisles formed by pallets stacked high with boxes of canned food. Del Monte Fruit Cocktail, Campbell's Pork'n'Beans, Heinz Sweet Gherkins, S&W Creamed Corn, Hershey's Chocolate Syrup, Bumblebee Chunk Light Tuna, V8. He wondered whether this place was still safe. He'd been careful about finding it, but Antonelli's family controlled East Newark and Hamabuchi's men moved like shadows. They certainly could've found it by now. He hoped not. Mashiro needed his own *dojo*.

Coming around a stack of Progresso Lentil Soup, he saw his samurai carrying two metal folding chairs into the center of his space. He stopped and watched Mashiro set up the chairs side by side, then fetch a glass jar of something he couldn't quite make out and a white porcelain rice bowl, setting these down on one of the chairs. Nagai noticed the white futon in one corner of the gray concrete floor and the hot-plate next to the antique stained cherry-wood weapons box. Nothing else in the way of comforts. This was how Mashiro wanted it. A secluded place to practice in is a samurai's paradise. Every morning he packs his things and stows them in the trunk of his car, then sets up again in the evening, like setting up camp. He noticed that Mashiro had already hung his ancestor's armor on the wall as he always did before practicing. It was his inspiration. Nagai watched the samurai taking off his shoes and socks and thought how cold the concrete floor must be. Mashiro's life was simple and purposeful. In a way, Nagai envied him.

Mashiro finally acknowledged his lord's presence with a curt bow, then went for his *katana* laid out on the futon and slipped it into the black belt that held his white *gi* jacket together. He then fixed the short sword, the *wakizashi*, so that it sat laterally over his belly. When he was ready, he looked to his lord and nodded.

Nagai returned the nod and went to the two folding chairs where he found a jar of Partytime Maraschino Cherries inside the rice bowl. He sat down in the empty chair, opened the jar, and dumped the cherries into the bowl. They were neon red under the fluorescent lights. He popped one in his mouth and immediately wished he had a whiskey sour.

"Ready?" he asked Mashiro in Japanese.

The samurai nodded and pulled his sword an inch out of its scabbard. A dark-crusted scar covered the cap of what was left of his right pinkie. Nagai saw a glint of metal where Mashiro had pulled the sword out. That was the place where the blade met the hilt, the place where the ancient characters were engraved. "Cut through cleanly—four bodies—in the hands of Yamashita of Kinki." He knew that Mashiro hoped to add a similar inscription of his own someday.

Nagai picked out a cherry by its stem, twirled it between his fingers for a moment, then abruptly flicked it at Mashiro. The samurai instantly drew his sword and slashed down all in one blurred motion. Nagai could see one half of the cherry a few feet from Mashiro's foot. The other half had disappeared someplace.

"Very good," Nagai said.

Mashiro returned the *katana* to its black leather scabbard. "Please continue," he said in Japanese. His goal was perfection, not praise. Nagai admired his discipline. He thought about telling Mashiro about D'Urso's offer—he'd been thinking about it all day and he still couldn't decide whether it would be a smart move or not. He wondered how Mashiro would react to it. Would he follow his "lord's" wishes without question? Or would the samurai think less of him for betraying *his* lord?

Nagai selected another cherry and tossed it in a high arc. It started to fall short of Mashiro's position, but the samurai rushed forward quickly and the blade slashed right to left, severing the target in two.

"Your finger doesn't bother you?" he asked. "It doesn't seem to have affected your swordsmanship."

"I'm learning to compensate," Mashiro replied. "The weakened hand must remind me of my error."

Nagai nodded thoughtfully. Mashiro lived by the book. There had to be some resentment, though. Nagai certainly resented Hamabuchi each time he'd been punished. "I'm sorry, Mashiro, but it had to be done."

Mashiro looked puzzled. "Why apologize? This is the way of the yakuza. This is how it must be. That's all."

Nagai flicked another cherry off his thumb as if he were shooting a marble. It made a line drive right for Mashiro's face. The sword waited over the samurai's head, then cut down vertically, greeting the cherry right in front of the samurai's nose. The two halves dropped at his feet.

Mashiro sheathed his sword. "You seem unsettled by this, my lord. Have you lived in America so long that you've forgotten our ways?"

Nagai twirled another cherry between his fingers as he stared at his samurai. Mashiro understood him. He could talk to Mashiro. They were fellow outcasts, after all. "Maybe I have been here too long," Nagai finally said. "But life is comfortable here. I like it here now. In many ways I like it better than back home." He stared at the spinning cherry in his hand. "But if I like it so much, why do I always think about returning? Is it just to be with my kids again? Or is it really something else?"

"Your confusion is smoke. It will blow off. Your aim is to see Japan again, be with your children, and most importantly, regain your former place of honor within the Fugukai." In

Japanese Mashiro's words were eloquently blunt. He spoke with absolute certainty. Nagai wished he could be so certain about things.

"Yes . . . I suppose." He put the cherry on his tongue, pulled out the stem, and rolled it around in his cheek.

"But you are worried about Reiko," Mashiro went on. "You would like to take your woman back to Japan with you."

Nagai nodded. Mashiro knew him very well. "To live honorably in Japan with Reiko, with my children . . . that would be paradise." It was beginning to sound like a foolish dream.

Mashiro shook his head. "There is no paradise. Only struggle."

"Winning is paradise."

Mashiro frowned and tilted his head, considering the statement. "Yes . . . you might say that."

Nagai took a cherry in each hand and suddenly pitched them underhand at the samurai. Mashiro made a choppy figure eight with his blade, cutting both targets. A lopsided half rolled back and collided with the pointy black toe of Nagai's alligator shoe.

"What about you, Mashiro? Do you want to go back to Japan?"

"If you want me to."

Nagai grinned. "But you don't really want to."

Mashiro shook his head. "No. Here is better for me. They want me badly over there. If I went back, I'd be an animal on the run again." He glanced up at the armor on the wall. "I'd rather not repeat Yamashita's fate."

Nagai stared into the pattern of the ancient armor, tiny, dull brass plates tightly knotted into an intricate weave of dark green, brown, and black leather thongs. He knew the story of Mashiro's ancestor who wore that armor, Yamashita, the illegitimate son of Japan's most famous samurai, Musashi Miyamoto—or so Mashiro claimed since Musashi supposedly had no children. According to Mashiro, Yamashita's lord Nagai was killed in battle, and all of his samurai were forced to become *ronin*, wandering warriors, exiled to a life of endless migration and marauding because of their lordless status. Despite his reputation as a fierce swordsman, Yamashita died like a peasant, the result of a trivial vendetta. His throat was slit from behind while he was humping some local woman. The murderer was a ninja hired by a Chinese silk merchant who lost his favorite horse to Yamashita in a dice game. Very dishonorable to kill a man while he's making love, but a typical ninja tactic, according to Mashiro. Nagai wondered if Mashiro would consider him a *ronin* if he betrayed Hamabuchi for D'Urso. Did samurai ever switch sides?

Nagai took two more cherries and lobbed them far to either side of Mashiro. The samurai drew the long sword in his right hand, the short sword in his left, and spread his arms like a bird of prey. He moved fast to the right, then lunged left. The *katana* sliced through one cherry, but the *wakizashi* only succeeded in batting the other one across the room and into a stack of boxes. Mashiro scowled and grumbled to himself.

Nagai was chewing another cherry. "Tell me something," he said. "What do you think of D'Urso? Really."

Mashiro raised an eyebrow. "How do you mean?"

"Should I trust him?"

"You've trusted him this far."

"So."

Mashiro rested his hands on the hilt of the long sword in his belt. "Something is bothering you. What? What has D'Urso done?"

Nagai considered telling him then, but suddenly changed his mind. "There's nothing that he's done in particular. I just have a bad feeling about him sometimes. I always find myself wanting to know what he's really feeling. On the surface he seems fine, but there always seems to be a nasty undercurrent, especially whenever Francione is around. I just don't feel right around them."

Mashiro scratched his neck. "I know little of feelings. Only actions." Nagai knew he'd say something like that. You're a big help.

"I get the impression that D'Urso has some big ideas, ideas that could wreck our partnership with the Mafia. I couldn't let that happen."

Mashiro shrugged. "What difference does it make who we sell our slaves to?"

"Hamabuchi wants us to do business with Antonelli's family. You know how he is about Antonelli, his old friend from the days after the war."

"Everything is war, all the time. Which war?"

"The one we lost." Wise guy. Is this how your ancestor spoke to his lord? "Hamabuchi told me right out. If our partnership with Antonelli's family falls apart, he'll blame me. He's already said as much. That's a lot of money he'd be losing." Nagai then held up his hand, fingers spread to show Mashiro his two stumpy fingers. "Another finger won't satisfy him if this deal is blown. I'm in exile as it is. The only punishment left is . . ."

"Death." Mashiro nodded like a horse. Who the hell's side was he on anyway?

The samurai got down on his knees then and bowed to his lord. "I will stand by you, no matter what. You have my pledge."

Nagai grinned wearily. Mashiro was a good man and tough, too. But come on, he was only one guy. And could D'Urso's Mafia boys really protect him from Hamabuchi's revenge? Not if they were all like that joke Francione. "Hamabuchi has a lot of men over here watching us," he said. "We've got sixty with us, but I know there're more here than that. The guys in our crew, the ones who supposedly take orders from us, they really get their orders directly from him. I *know* it. I'm living with assassins all around me." Nagai threw another cherry into his mouth, then spit it out. What the hell was he eating these things for?

Mashiro got to his feet and gestured with his head toward the bowl of cherries. Didn't he hear any of this, goddamn him? Nagai grabbed a handful of cherries in disgust and threw them at him.

Mashiro drew both swords. Flashing steel surrounded him like an evil mist. He was a goddamn human food processor, sending specks of neon red flying in every direction. His final slash was with the short sword. A cherry half flew straight up into the air. When it came down, he caught it on the flat of his blade. "There will be no trouble with D'Urso and no trouble with Hamabuchi. You will be happy. I am dedicating myself to it. Please do not worry." He flipped the sword up and tossed the cherry into his mouth. He bowed, grinned, and chewed.

Nagai forced a smile. Maybe he could switch sides and pull it off. Maybe Mashiro really was a one-man army. Musashi Miyamota apparently was. If Mashiro could keep him alive long enough for him to establish a power base here with D'Urso, it just might work out after all. It was possible. Nagai picked out another cherry from the bowl and popped it into his mouth. Life just might be okay after all.

8

It was almost seven when the PATH train from the World Trade Center rumbled into the Hoboken station. Tozzi's car was packed shoulder-to-shoulder. Lots of oxblood leather briefcases, Burberry raincoats, tortoise-shell glasses, and panty-hose legs in white Reeboks, and they were all getting off here. Standing in line to get through the turnstiles, Tozzi wondered if Hoboken was really the place for him. He climbed the stairs up to the street with the crowd and crossed the wide cobblestone street. As he approached the curb on the other side, he saw himself in the reflection of a plate-glass window in a fern bar. The light gray suit and the black Italian loafers were too new; they weren't him yet. He took a good look and was a little disappointed with what he saw. He didn't look that different from the rest of the crowd. Maybe he did belong here.

He'd promised the lady at Elysian Fields Realty that he'd be there at seven. He figured he may as well start looking for another apartment because there was no way he was going to be approved for the one on Adams Street that Mrs. Carlson had showed him. No wife, no good. He considered going to that meeting with the landlord on Friday anyway and telling them his wife had died unexpectedly, a brain tumor or something like that. Maybe the landlord would take him out of pity. But that was too stupid, he decided. Everything was stupid.

He'd spent the whole day trying to make a concrete con-

nection between the "Death Bug" murders, cult killers, and
swords, and he came up with absolutely nothing. He'd somehow forgotten how frustrating it can be poring through files,
cross-checking possibilities on the computer, spending hours
and hours trying to make the facts work the way you want
them to, then finally realizing that what you thought was a
brilliant hunch wasn't worth shit. The deep cuts on the two
bodies weren't quite like anything on file in the National
Crime Information Center database. The labs kept insisting
that the cuts were done simultaneously with a single blade,
and there was nothing like that in the computer. Tozzi had
found it hard to swallow when he first heard it, and he was
still skeptical. It sounded physically impossible. The ME had
to be wrong about that.

It was getting cold. The wind was beginning to bite. Tozzi
shoved his hands in his pockets, wishing he had his trench
coat with him, then remembered he didn't have that coat anymore. He'd have to get a new one. Shit. That was a nice coat,
too.

Walking up Washington Street, he noticed the paper jack-
o'-lanterns taped to the window of a very fancy Italian deli.
There was a whole rack of designer pastas just inside the door
and a freezer case next to it filled with a variety of frozen
sauces. In his family, they called it "macaroni" not "pasta,"
and "sauce" was "gravy." He didn't care much for these nou-
velle salumerias that specialized in sun-dried tomatoes and
porcini mushrooms. He liked the older places down on the
sidestreets where you could get a big ham and mozzarell'
sandwich with sweet red peppers, where they make the mozzarell' fresh in the back, where you can put a ten-spot on a
horse if they know you in some of them. Admittedly, he liked
the kinds of places wiseguys liked. Except he wasn't a
wiseguy. He was a fed.

Elysian Fields Realty was on the next block. Tozzi walked
briskly, anxious to get in out of the cold, anxious to find a
home. But then his eye caught a small, hand-painted sign
hanging over a doorway: HOBOKEN COOPERATIVE SCHOOL OF
SELF-DEFENSE. There were a bunch of Japanese or Chinese
characters written under the words. Tozzi backed up to the
curb and looked up to the second floor of the building over
the florist shop on the ground floor. The windows were all

brightly lit. He could see several figures in white uniforms moving around up there. Tozzi suddenly thought about the dead couple and the violent blows to the neck that killed them. He glanced down the street at the Elysian Fields Realty storefront. That could wait. This was more important. He opened the door and went upstairs.

There was no one in the small, cheaply furnished waiting room so he poked his head into the studio. It was a big space, just about the entire length of the building, paint peeling off the ceiling, brightly lit. The wood floor was almost entirely covered with big blue mats. There were about a dozen or so people on the mats, mostly guys, four women, a pretty even mix of white belts, orange belts, blue belts, and brown. They were paired off, practicing some kind of move that involved throwing an attacker grabbing you in a choke hold from behind. The teacher—the *sensei* as Tozzi remembered—was a mellow-looking guy with a full, reddish-brown beard and a receding hairline. He weaved through the pairs, watching them, frequently stopping to correct their mistakes. He was wearing what looked like a pair of full-length, pleated black skirt-pants over his white *gi* uniform. Tozzi had taken some karate at Quantico as part of his FBI training, a very condensed version modified exclusively for police work. He remembered his *sensei* only wearing his black belt. These skirt-pants were something new to him.

As he watched the *sensei* instruct the class, he soon realized that this wasn't karate, unless it was one of the more obscure forms. He doubted it, though, because it seemed nothing like karate. There were no kicks or chops. Everyone seemed very calm and poised. Whenever they paired off to practice, the person who initiated the attack invariably lost, usually winding up flat on his back or tumbling headfirst across the mat. The brown belts and some of the blue belts in particular seemed to exert very little effort when they threw their opponents. It almost didn't seem real. Tozzi was intrigued. He leaned up against the doorway and watched as the *sensei* called for an end to the practice of this technique. The partners stopped, bowed to each other, then rushed to kneel in a line facing their teacher.

The *sensei* then called on the biggest person in the class, a black guy who was built like a wide receiver. He handed the black guy a wooden sword and announced the Japanese name of the technique he was going to demonstrate. They faced off then, the black guy holding the sword in both hands. Suddenly he raised the sword over his head, lunged forward, and attacked as if he intended to slice the *sensei* right down the middle. Tozzi swore the guy was going to split his teacher's head open, but the *sensei* simply stepped to the side, grabbed the hilt of the sword over the black guy's big hands, apparently pumped up and down once, and flipped the big guy over head first. Holy shit! The floor shook when the black guy hit the mat. The *sensei* just stood there calmly with the wooden sword in his hand. Tozzi was impressed. It was just like something out of a kung-fu movie. When the black guy got back to his feet, the *sensei* presented him with the sword again. They did the same move a few more times. The black guy attacked a little more viciously each time, and each time he hit the mat a little harder. It almost looked fake to Tozzi.

"*Shomen Uchi Kokyu Nage,*" the *sensei* repeated. "Also known as the 'sledgehammer throw.' With motion this time. For demonstration," he added with a little smile.

The *sensei* nodded to his partner, then turned and started to run with the black guy in hot pursuit. Tozzi was surprised to see him running away instead of taking a stand and fighting. There was no doubt that the black guy was going to catch him, given the length of the guy's legs. The *sensei* was quick, though, and the black guy had to hustle to catch up and get within striking distance. Suddenly the *sensei* changed directions. The black guy followed, but when they got to the middle of the mat again, the *sensei* turned and faced the swordsman rushing at him full-tilt. The sword came down in a loud *whoosh.* He stepped to the side and grabbed the hilt, made that little pump-move, and the poor black guy was really flying now. Tozzi winced. The black guy hit the mat *real* hard this time. He took his time getting up. The *sensei* stood there calm and erect with the sword in his hand.

When the black guy was ready again, the *sensei* gave back the sword and they repeated the technique slowly as he explained the fine points to the class. Finally he and the black guy knelt down and bowed to each other. "*Shomen Uchi Kokyu Nage,*" he said. "Please practice in two lines. *Without* motion, please." A few people laughed.

Tozzi was curious. He'd never seen anything like this before. It looked fake, but he had a feeling it wasn't. He stayed for the rest of the class.

When class broke up, he waited for the students to disperse before he went over to the *sensei* who had stepped out of those skirt-pants of his and was busy folding them on the mat. It seemed like a very involved procedure.

"Hi," he said. He hunkered down in order to be eye level with the *sensei*.

The man stared at his feet. "No shoes on the mat, please."

Tozzi immediately stood up and took off his loafers, embarrassed. He should've known better. "Sorry. Tell me, this wasn't karate you were just doing here, was it?"

The *sensei* smoothed the pleats of his pants and shook his head. "Adult karate classes meet on Thursday and Saturday."

The guy wasn't unfriendly, but he had that sort of affable evasiveness a lot of people had in the sixties. You ask a question, he answers it, but you don't feel that you've gotten any information. "So what was this class?" Tozzi had to ask.

"Aikido."

"Aikido." Tozzi nodded. He'd heard of it, but he didn't know anything about it. "So tell me, what's aikido?"

The *sensei* stopped and looked up at him. He seemed to be sizing up Tozzi, trying to figure out what kind of answer he could handle. "Aikido is a Japanese martial art. It's based on harmonizing with the force of an attack and redirecting the attacker's momentum against him."

Tozzi nodded again. "I liked that move you did with the big guy. The one with the sword?"

The *sensei* smiled and continued to fold his pants, smoothing the wrinkles out of the sashes before folding them. *"Shomen Uchi Kokyu Nage."* He looked up at Tozzi. "With motion?"

"Yeah, with motion. That must really take some doing, throwing someone that big. You really made it look easy."

"That's one of the things we aim for, minimal effort."

"You're saying it *was* easy?"

He shrugged. "It wasn't hard."

Harder than talking to you? "Listen, my name's Mike Tozzi." He pulled out his FBI ID and showed it to him. "I'm a special agent with the Federal Bureau of Investigation." He paused for a second, suddenly realizing that this was the first time he'd gone through this routine since he'd come back. "I'd like to ask you a few questions. About the martial arts in general. You're not the target of this investigation, by the way. So don't worry."

"I wasn't." The *sensei* picked up his black pants, now folded in a neat bundle, and stood up. He extended his hand to Tozzi. "Neil Chaney."

Tozzi put his loafers in his other hand and shook the guy's hand. Standing together, he realized how small Chaney really was. Somehow he looked bigger, more formidable when he was doing aikido.

"I'm investigating a double homicide in which the victims died from a single blow to the neck that fatally damaged the spinal column. It appears that this was done with a blunt, heavy object of some kind, but we're not ruling anything out at this point." Tozzi hated the way he sounded. He sounded like all those starched-collar, three-piece polyester-suit feds he couldn't stand. He wondered if he'd always come off this way. He hoped to hell not. He consciously tried to relax his face before he posed his question. "Could someone who knew a martial art—like aikido, say—be able to do something like this?"

Chaney frowned, considering the question. "A direct blow to the neck? No, not aikido."

"Why not?"

"Aikido is a purely self-defensive martial art. In aikido, you don't initiate an attack. You react to being attacked and you use the force of the attacker's aggression back against him. What you're describing is more in line with full-contact karate, tae kwon do, wu shu, the hard martial arts. Someone accomplished in one of the hard arts would probably have the ability to kill."

"But an aikido black belt couldn't kill, even if he really wanted to?"

Chaney shrugged. "Depends on the situation. But the basic philosophy behind aikido is peaceful, so killing shouldn't even be in the person's mind. If you absolutely have to fight, then neutralizing your opponent is the goal. Make the aggressor impotent by virtue of his own aggression. Inflicting pain isn't the point."

"But aikido can cause pain."

"It can, but like I said, that's not the point."

"What is the point?"

Chaney smiled. "In twenty-five words or less?" He shook his head, still smiling. "Impossible to put into words. You're looking for a nice three-line dictionary answer. I wouldn't know where to begin."

"Try."

"Well . . . let's just say that the point of aikido isn't how to cream the other guy. It's how to fix the guy within yourself so that you'll always be able to handle the other guy. It's learning how to stay calm and relaxed but still strong, even when you're under attack. And this can apply to everything in your life, not just a fight."

Tozzi nodded. He wasn't sure whether this guy was a flake or not. It sounded just a little bit too New Age. But he had seen Chaney disarm the big black guy and flip him over. There had to be something to this.

Chaney smiled knowingly. "You kinda sorta don't believe any of this, right? Well, you can't really describe what aikido is all about. You just have to do it to understand it. If you're really interested, you're welcome to come sit in on a few classes. You live around here?"

"Ah, yeah. I'll be moving in soon." I hope.

"Good. Maybe you'll even like it enough to sign up. We can always use new white belts to throw around."

Tozzi thought about it for a moment. The idea of being calm and relaxed appealed to him. He couldn't remember the last time he was really calm and relaxed. He was also intrigued by the idea of reacting to an attack and using the attacker's momentum against him. He'd been in plenty of fistfights in his life and he understood how committing yourself to a punch could put you in deep shit sometimes. Besides, suppose the "Death Bug" killer actually was some kind of martial arts specialist. It wouldn't hurt to put himself in the killer's mindset, which he might get out of coming to Chaney's *dojo* a few times. "Yeah, maybe I will give it a try," Tozzi said. "When do you have classes?"

"We meet at eight on Mondays and Wednesdays, and four on Saturdays. I hope to see you around . . ." Chaney tapped his forehead with his finger. "I'm sorry. What did you say your name was?"

"Mike."

"Right. Mike. See ya around, Mike." Chaney went to the edge of the mat, bowed, slipped on a pair of tan rubber flip-flops, and walked over to a bank of second-hand gym lockers against the back wall.

Tozzi looked at his watch. It was twenty of eight. Shit. He wondered if the lady at Elysian Fields Realty was still waiting for him. He hoped she was. This apartment search had been dragging on too long. He was sick of living like a gypsy. He needed to find a place of his own, soon. He hopped into his shoes and headed for the door.

Maybe tonight, he thought as he rushed down the rickety steps. Maybe I'll get lucky. Who knows?

9

Gibbons was dubious as he stared at the huge freighter looming over the edge of the dock, its mottled gray-green hull the color of dinosaur hide. What the hell was he supposed to find here? The reasoning for coming down here to the docks was shaky, but Tozzi had insisted. The fibers on the dead kid's corduroy pants were from a new kind of synthetic carpeting found only in this year's Hondas and Nissans. So what? Just go down and check it out, Tozzi kept saying. Asian Automotive Importers, port of entry for all Japanese cars in this area, go check it out. For what? I dunno, Tozzi says, giving him the dumb immigrant shrug, look around, pop a few trunks, maybe you'll see something. Gibbons frowned and shook his head. The only thing he was going to see here were cars. What a ballbuster this guy is.

The freighter started to lumber out into the bay with the help of a few tugs. The thing was so big and hulking from this distance it felt like the land was doing the moving, not the ship. Gibbons watched it through the cyclone fence that surrounded the endless lot crammed with brand-new import cars right off the boat from Japan. He stared at the freighter's stern where HONDA was painted perpendicular to a vertical line of Japanese characters. He scanned the long lines of Honda roofs. All the little baby Godzillas just delivered from the belly of the big mama-*san*. Gibbons took out his handkerchief and blew his nose. Well, I'm here now, he thought. Might as well go in and take a look. Satisfied, Tozzi?

He shoved his hands into the pockets of his black raincoat and headed for the guard posted at the entrance of the lot, a young black kid in a rent-a-cop uniform who'd been giving him the hairy eyeball ever since he got out of his car. As Gibbons approached his booth, the kid put on a pair of mirrored sunglasses. Gibbons smirked and shook his head.

"You can't come in, sir," the guard yelled before Gibbons even got near his booth. "Employees only."

Gibbons nodded and kept walking.

"I said you cannot come in," the guard yelled.

Gibbons ignored him and just walked right up to the booth. The kid held his hand threateningly on the holster of his pistol, but the holster was snapped shut. You do a real quick draw with the holster closed, genius.

"Who's the supervisor here?" Gibbons asked.

"You can't buy no cars here. You can't come in."

Gibbons's face was stone as he stared into the kid's mirrored shades. Two malevolent Aztec deities stared back at him. "I don't want to buy a car. Get on the phone and call whoever's in charge here."

"I'm sorry, sir, but you cannot—"

"Tone down the drill-sergeant routine, palie. I can hear you. Just get on the phone and tell your supervisor that there's a special agent from the FBI here to see him."

The kid's face froze. His nostrils flared and raised his glasses. He didn't believe it.

Gibbons pulled out his ID and held it in front of the kid's face. "Does this make you happy?"

The kid stared at it for a long time.

"It's not a fucking book, genius."

"What?"

"Never mind." Gibbons started to walk around the yellow-and-black-striped lift gate.

"Hey, come back here! I told you you can't go in there." He rushed out of his booth, but Gibbons turned and squared off, his hands ominously in his coat pockets. The kid was still holding onto his holster. He might as well have been holding his dick.

"Don't sweat it, kid. I'll tell your boss you put up a good fight. I'll tell him it was just like the Alamo."

"The what?"

Gibbons scowled and turned away, disgusted. Everyone knows the goddamn Alamo. If they don't, they should.

The kid rushed back to his booth, obviously anxious to call in before his boss spotted the intruder wandering around by himself. Gibbons started walking toward the concrete-block bunker at the far end of the lot down by the water. It must've been at least a quarter mile from the front gate. As he walked, he noticed closed-circuit TV cameras on the lampposts, scanning the lot. Whoever was in the bunker already knew he was coming.

Somebody came out of the bunker then and started toward him in a big hurry. As the figure got closer, Gibbons could see that it was a guy with a big belly and a stumpy stogy in his mouth, struggling to make tracks. The way he ran it looked like he was trying to get around his big gut, but it was a pesky obstacle. He didn't look like he ran very often.

"Hey, hey, hey, what's going on here, what's going on? What can I do for you there, pal?"

The guy was all out of breath, panting through his teeth clenched onto that stogy. He unzipped the front of his green thermal sweat jacket and uncovered that behemoth belly of his. The buttons of his brown plaid flannel shirt were in agony, straining to stay together. He was a real sketch, this guy. He had to be somebody's brother-in-law, somebody who had some pull with the union. That's how these kinds of guys get these kinds of cushy jobs, which is how they get these kinds of bellies.

Gibbons didn't say anything; he just held up his ID. The guy looked at it, blinking. He was holding onto his belly like a beach ball, massaging it with fingers spread as he blinked at the ID.

" 'Special Agent C. Gibson,' " the fat guy read aloud. "What's the *C* stand for?" he asked.

Gibbons glared at him. "It's Gibbons, not Gibson, and don't worry about the *C*." Nitwit.

"Okay, okay, okay." The fat guy started blinking like crazy now. "So what can I do for you, Mr. Gibson? What can I do for you?"

Gibbons shut his eyes. It wasn't worth the effort. "I want to look around."

"Uh-huh." There was a long pause. "Look around for what?"

Gibbons gave him the stare. Another long pause. "I'm not at liberty to say, Mr . . . ?"

"Gianella. Joe, call me Joe." He smiled and rubbed his belly. When he smiled, his eyes disappeared in his fat face. "Lookin' for somethin', huh? So whatta ya lookin' for? Jimmy Hoffa?"

"You know where he is?"

"No, no, course not. That was just a joke. You know, a joke." Joe looked nervous.

"Look, Joe, let me lay it all out for you, okay? I'm FBI, you're not. That puts you at a disadvantage because if you don't get away from me and let me do my business, I can have you charged with obstruction of justice and arrest you as a suspected accomplice in whatever it is I'm investigating that I already told you I can't tell you about. So you bust my balls now and I'll really bust yours later. Do we understand each other?"

Joe started nodding like a marionette, jerking his head and shoulders up and down as he kept saying "Uh-huh, uh-huh, uh-huh . . ." Gibbons wanted to punch him in the eye because he knew the fat slob was just trying to stall him.

"You know, Mr. Gibson, I do believe you are what you say you are. But let's just suppose you ain't. I mean for all I know you could be some kind of corporate spy, you know? I mean, other car companies try to sabotage the competition all the time. Put pin holes in the brake lines, a little bit of sugar in the gas tanks to gum up the valves. You know what I'm talking about?"

Gibbons wanted to coldcock this guy in the worst way, but he knew better. They'd file charges against the Bureau that could invalidate any evidence he might find here. Oh, for the good ole days when J. Edgar ran things, when the law didn't get in the way of justice. He bit his tongue and reached for his wallet, pulling out a printed business card. "Here. Call this number. It's the FBI field office in Manhattan." Gibbons pointed toward the World Trade Center towering over the horizon. Joe looked like the type who needed visual aids. "Ask them for verification."

Joe took the card and blinked at it.

"Go ahead," Gibbons ordered. "Make the call. I'll wait right here. Hurry up."

Joe did that Howdy Doody nod again. "Yeah, good, okay. I'll do that. Be right back. Just hang on, Mr. Gibson." Gradually he turned and headed back to the bunker, studying the card as he walked.

Gibbons kneaded the back of his neck and glanced at the guard booth. He couldn't see the kid's head, only his feet propped up on the little counter in the booth. He was probably dozing. A regular Marshal Dillon, that one. He looked back toward the bunker and saw the Human Beach Ball huffing and puffing to make the quarter mile, running a few steps, then walking, then running a few more steps, then walking again. Gibbons glanced up at the video camera on the light pole staring down at him. He'd have to work fast.

He went into his pants pocket and came up with a bunch of keys on a ring, universals he'd brought from the field office. He headed for the nearest line of cars, four-door Accords, and quickly found the Honda key in his bunch. He glanced at the feet in the guard booth and fatso in the distance. He quickly turned the key in the trunk of a maroon sedan, knowing he didn't have much time. The Human Beach Ball would be back in the bunker in a minute. Gibbons imagined him collapsing into a squeaky desk chair at a cluttered metal desk, picking up the phone and starting to make the call, then looking up at the bank of black-and-white monitors right in front of him and seeing the pain-in-the-ass fed searching trunks.

Gibbons jiggled the key and finally got the trunk open. He scanned it quickly, lifted the mat and checked the tire well, slammed it shut, and moved on to the next car, a smoke-gray one. He knew this was an illegal search, but he didn't give a shit. Getting a warrant was a pain in the ass—by the time you finally get a judge to sign one, nine times out of ten either what you're looking for isn't there anymore or the investigation has taken you in another direction. Gibbons preferred one-stop shopping.

"Shit." The trunk of the smoke-gray Accord was empty, too. He skipped a few cars down the line and tried a silver job. Joe hadn't made it to the bunker yet. He was trying to maintain a fast walk now. Gibbons kept seeing himself on those monitors, multiple images from different angles. Maybe he should've gotten a warrant.

He popped the trunk and his eyes narrowed when he spotted a balled up thermal blanket and one of those crinkly plastic bags. The bag was full. Quickly rifling through the top, he found aluminum foil, plastic wrap, cellophane, and a couple of empty Coke cans. He didn't notice anything unusual at first because the cans looked like ordinary red-and-white Coke cans. Then he looked at the fine print on the side of one of them. It was written in Japanese characters.

Gibbons chewed on the inside of his cheek. Maybe those Jap auto workers aren't as perfect as they always make them out to be on TV. Maybe they goof off just like everybody else in the world, except they do it in the trunks of the cars.

But then he spotted something else. A white plastic hose wedged between the wall and the floor of the trunk. It didn't have any fittings on the end and had no apparent purpose that he could see. He took a closer look and saw that the end of the hose was pretty chewed up. He grabbed the hose and pushed it back toward its source. It moved freely. He shut the trunk halfway, looked through the back windshield, and moved the hose again. As he suspected, the other end jutted in and out of the crease in the backseat.

He walked around to the driver's side of the car and inspected the dash through the window. On the climate control panel, the vent switch was on "Fresh." He cupped his hand over the window of the next car and saw that the vent lever was on "Recirculate." The vents in the silver car were apparently left open so fresh air could get in and feed this air hose. It looked like somebody had spent some time in this trunk. Rents weren't that high in Japan.

Gibbons went back to the trunk, yanked out the hose, wound it around his hand, and shoved it in the pocket of his raincoat. He picked up one of the Coke cans, wrapping some tin foil around it to preserve any possible fingerprints, and put it in his other pocket. He shut the lid and put the keys back in his pants pocket, then wandered back into the aisle to wait for Joe, wondering whether the fat ass had spotted him on a monitor with his head in the trunk of that car.

* * *

Inside the bunker, Joe was panting, trying to catch his breath, pointing to the business card in his hand. "F . . . BI," he rasped. "Jesus . . ."

John D'Urso sat on the edge of the cluttered metal desk, gently patting the steel-gray hair at the back of his head as he stared up at the monitors. There were eight of them, two horizontal rows of four, each one a fish-eye panorama of cars, cars, and more cars. All except for the second from the right on the top row. That monitor was focused down on the nosy old guy in the awful-looking, single-breasted black raincoat, the guy who just shoved a hose and a soda can into his pockets.

He glanced over at the skinny yak in the horrible madras sports jacket leaning against the wall. He was staring up at the monitor, too. He already had his gun out.

"Take it easy there, brother," he said to the young yakuza hitter, waving his hand in front of the man's gaze and motioning for him to stay where he was. The yak narrowed his eyes to imperceptible slits and stared at him, clutching his gun in both hands. "It's okay. Put your piece away." D'Urso mimed putting an imaginary gun under his jacket. Reluctantly the kid put his gun away. The yaks didn't like taking orders from him.

"Mr. D'Urso, this guy says he's FBI. Jesus Christ, what're we gonna do, Mr. D'Urso?" Joe was still panting, sweat running down his face.

"You calm down, too, okay?" D'Urso reached for the control panel and turned a knob. The camera zoomed in fast, and the monitor went gray and out of focus, the picture lost in Gibbons's coat. D'Urso pulled back and focused on Gibbons's head. Just then Gibbons looked straight up and stared into the camera. "Thank you very much," D'Urso said with a smile. He looked down at the Panasonic VCR on a shelf under the monitors, adjusting his tie as he watched the blue numbers mounting steadily on the counter.

"He gave me this, Mr. D'Urso." Joe showed him the business card. "He said I should call his office to see that he's okay. What should I do, Mr. D'Urso?"

The yak was moving toward the door. He had that goddamn gun out again.

"Hey, you, sit down, I said." D'Urso shook his head and muttered to Joe, "Christ, you gotta put these goddamn people on leashes."

The yak resumed his position against the wall, staring up at the monitor with his arms folded over his chest, the muzzle of his piece poking out of his armpit.

"Take it easy before you have another heart attack, Joe." Joe was sweating like a pig, his face like a ripe tomato. D'Urso ran a fingernail between his teeth as he thought this through. FBI, huh? So what does he know? Maybe nothing. Maybe a lot. This could be good though, if he's on to the slaves. Maybe we can finagle it so that Antonelli and Hamabuchi take the rap for this. Get rid of the competition and clear the way for me. Depends on what this guy's here for. Gotta wait it out a little and see.

"Joe, listen to me. Get on the phone and call that number, just like he told you to." D'Urso pointed to Gibbons on the monitor. "If this guy finds out you didn't make the call, he'll know something's up and he'll just come back. Call 'em and get mad, be real indignant. Think like he's stepping on your rights. You understand me? After you make the call, go back out and cooperate with him. Be real nice. If he wants to look inside any cars, though, you tell him you don't have the keys and you can't get them today. Be polite about it and just tell him to come back tomorrow. Tell him he can see anything he wants tomorrow. Okay? Now make the call."

Joe wiped his face with his sleeve and picked up the phone. As he dialed the number, D'Urso took the card and read the name on it. "Mr. C. Gibbons, huh?" He glanced at the monitor and saw the old guy rotating his head on his shoulders. "What do you want, Mr. Gibbons? What is it you want?"

Joe was on the line now, complaining to someone about being hassled by some guy who said he was an FBI agent. He demanded to know if this guy "Gibson" was for real and what the hell this was all about anyway. D'Urso grinned and nodded encouragingly. Joe was pretty convincing.

D'Urso glanced down at the VCR again, then looked at the yak to make sure he was sitting still. The kid hadn't moved, but the gun was still poking out from under his armpit. In the shadows it looked like a snake head. He looked up at Gibbons who was cracking his knuckles now, and stroked the hair on the back of his neck. He was thinking of different angles, thinking hard.

10

D'Urso's office was big, but Nagai felt closed in here. He lit a cigarette, took a couple of puffs, then put it out in a big red venetian glass ash tray on the chrome and smoked glass coffeetable. He felt like throwing up. What the hell was wrong with D'Urso? How could he just let this happen? The FBI man was right there and he just let him go! Everytime Nagai thought about it his stomach tightened and he felt worse. Hamabuchi wasn't going to blame D'Urso for this; he was going to blame him. The kid was there, he saw everything, so Hamabuchi probably knows all about it already. Nagai gulped air to keep from heaving. That goddamn smell from downstairs wasn't helping. He could hear the conveyer belts grinding on the floor below, and he could picture all those slimy carcasses parading through the plant. Chicken shit out back, chicken blood and chicken guts everywhere else. He felt green. He folded his arms over his chest, pinched his nose, and sat very very still, staring straight ahead at the TV set, watching that man in the black raincoat breaking into car trunks again. It was the third time he'd seen the tape. What the hell had D'Urso been thinking about when he let this guy go? Is this how he thinks they're going to run things when they go out on their own? The hell they are!

D'Urso was sitting to his left on the gray velvet sofa, his fingers linked over his crossed knee. Francione sat on the arm of the sofa, hovering over his brother-in-law. They looked like they were watching a goddamn movie, as if this didn't concern them. What the hell are we supposed to do with a stupid video? The kid had been ready to take care of it right there and then, but D'Urso stopped him. Stupid asshole. The kid shouldn't have listened to D'Urso. He should've killed the FBI man. But Hamabuchi isn't going to blame this kid he sent me and he isn't going to blame Antonelli's people either. No, he's going to blame me, and that's going to cause problems. Goddamn them all.

Nagai glanced over at D'Urso. No reaction. What the fuck is wrong with him? On the TV, the FBI man scratched his head and stretched, then stared right up into the camera and wrinkled his ugly face. Damn him. He should be dead now. Dead.

"His name is C. Gibbons," D'Urso said. "That's what it says here on his card." D'Urso showed him the business card the FBI man gave fat Joe.

Nagai looked at the card, then stared up at D'Urso. "I still don't understand why you didn't kill him. You had the chance. My man was ready. Why did you stop him?" He wanted to scream at D'Urso, but the way he felt, he didn't have the energy.

"I've been trying to tell you, Nagai, but you're not listening to me. I had this crazy idea that we could frame Antonelli, have the FBI pin him with the slave thing, which would eliminate the competition for us when we get started. But then I thought about it. It wouldn't work. I'm too directly involved. They'd grab me long before they got to him. It was a nice idea, but totally unworkable."

"So why are we sitting here looking at television?" Nagai threw his hand out at the twenty-five-inch Sony. "Let's go find this guy and get rid of him before he talks."

Francione started laughing like a hissing radiator, his shoulders bobbing up and down. "Hey, Nagai, I don't know how you do things over in Japan, but here you don't go shooting federal agents like it's nothing. Shooting cops is not smart. They get very upset when you shoot one of their own. And that's when they start busting balls."

Mr. He-knows-it-all. Stupid punk. *We're* not afraid to shoot cops. "I'd like to have *you* shot, punk," Nagai muttered in Japanese.

D'Urso uncrossed his legs and sat forward, gesturing with

his palms up. "I know you're mad, Nagai, but listen to me. We couldn't have done the guy there anyway."

"Why not?"

"You think that guy's office didn't know where he was? If he was missing for a day or two, they'd start retracing his steps right back to the car lot. Then we'd really have trouble."

"We really have trouble now! I say it would've been simpler to kill him then. If anyone came looking for him, you could've had that fat ass Joe tell them yes, their friend Gibbons was there but he left. Simple as that." Nagai could feel the heat in his cheeks.

"You don't know what these guys are like, Nagai. You think the FBI is gonna just go away because some fat slob down at the lot tells 'em their man left. Not very likely." D'Urso was smiling. At what, goddamn it?

Spasms rippled across Nagai's gut. The FBI was going to expose the slave trade, and Hamabuchi was going to blame him. D'Urso keeps talking about how great their partnership will be, but they've got nothing set up yet. They can't protect him from Hamabuchi. Everything should've been running smoothly before they turned on their bosses. He wanted to have the chance to smuggle his kids out of Japan before they made their move. Nagai got that gagging feeling at the back of his throat again. Now he'll never see his kids. Hamabuchi would see to it. In his mind he could see the picture of Hatsu, Kenji, and the baby that he kept in his wallet. No . . . he couldn't let that happen . . . not if he could help it.

D'Urso sat back and extended his hands. "Look, Nagai, I can see that you're making yourself sick over this, but the only thing we can do right now is ride this thing out."

"I don't understand you. You're not even worried."

"Sure, I'm worried, but we can't overreact. You're assuming that this guy Gibbons knows all about the slaves. But what has he got? A piece of hose and a Coke can. What's that? Nothing. I really don't think we have anything to worry about right now. If he comes back asking more questions, pointing fingers . . . well, then we'll have to figure something out." He looked up at his brother-in-law. "Won't we, Bobby?"

Francione smirked, his eyes half-closed. "Don't worry, Nagie. I'll take care of this Gibbons guy if it comes to that."

Nagai's eyes shot open. "Him?" He pointed at the idiot brother-in-law. "You're not serious, are you?"

Francione pointed right back at him and started yelling. "Hey, look, Nagie, you ever wonder why the hell that fed was down at the docks in the first place? You ever think maybe it was because of that VW they found in the river? Maybe that's what he was investigating. If you and Mishmosh had gotten rid of those two bodies the way you were supposed to, we wouldn't be in this situation now. Maybe it's *your* fault that this Gibbons guy was snooping around."

"Well, maybe you're right. Maybe it is my fault." Nagai stood up, went over to the VCR, and ejected the video tape. "If it's my fault, then I'll fix it. *My way.* It's the only honorable thing to do." He brandished the tape in Francione's face like a knife.

"Hey, come on, sit down, Nagai," D'Urso said. "We'll handle this. Don't—"

"No, no, no. *I* will take care of this." He headed for the door with the tape in his hand. The idiot brother-in-law started to get up to stop him, but he shoved the punk back down as he passed by. The nausea had settled down. It was his head that was throbbing now. When the time was right, Mashiro would take care of the brother-in-law, too. D'Urso would never have to know.

Francione yelled after him. "Leave that tape here. You fucking hear me, Nagai? I'm telling you."

"Nagai," D'Urso called to him. "Come back and sit down. Can't we just discuss this like rational people?"

Nagai paused out in the hallway. "Let him go, John," he heard Francione say. "How's he think he's gonna find this guy Gibbons? Call up the FBI and ask for his address? Stupid fuck."

Nagai heard Francione's snide laugh as he headed for the stairway. Asshole. He thinks he knows everything. He'll see.

The smell was overpowering when he got to the first floor. The noise was deafening, the shuffle of the slaves' feet combined with the machinery as they hustled all those dead chickens through the plant. He felt like he was going to puke again. Walking fast toward the back door, he glanced to his right and saw a procession of whole plucked chickens hanging from stainless-steel hooks dipping down one after the other into a murky bath. Standing over the vat was a slave, staring dead-eyed at him. Half the slave's face was purple with bruises, one eye puffy and closed. It was that kid who burst into the back room the other day, Takayuki, the one Mashiro beat up. Ballsy son of a bitch.

"What're you looking at?" Nagai snapped.

Takayuki kept working, washing those stinking chickens, staring at him with his good eye.

Nagai couldn't take the smell. He turned away and rushed out before he started gagging.

Mashiro sat on his knees on the concrete floor, candlelight flickering over his back, his sword in his belt. Nagai rubbed his cold hands and peered over the samurai's shoulder. A wooden board was laid out in front of him, a jar of Welch's Grape Jelly off to the side. A dark line of jelly had been painted down the length of the board. Mashiro, Mashiro. Nagai shook his head. The samurai was testing his own patience as well as his accuracy with the *katana*. He was waiting for cockroaches, perfectly calm and perfectly still in the cold, darkened warehouse. Nagai stepped closer and could make out the broken bodies of two cockroaches stuck to the jelly. He knew Mashiro could keep this vigil for hours, waiting endlessly for the cautious insects to feel secure enough to come scuttling out again and take the sweet bait.

Nagai quietly found a seat off to the side on a box of Dole Canned Crushed Pineapple and held the camcorder he'd brought in his lap. Two hungry bugs were testing the edges of the board. Mashiro was stone. The roaches climbed the board and stopped, their antennae twitching and twirling. Mashiro was the darkness. The first roach found the jelly, took a reading, and stepped right into it. The second one paused a moment, then dashed for the sugar. They dipped into the jelly like deer at a stream. Suddenly the sword flashed and flashed again. Two more hacked bodies littered the board.

"Very good," Nagai said in Japanese.

Mashiro didn't turn around. "Never good enough," he said in a soft grunt.

"Good enough for me. More than good enough." Mashiro had to be. He was the only one he could turn to now.

Nagai looked into the viewfinder of the camcorder. The FBI man was in there. Like a cockroach in a box. If only the nosy bastard really were in there, dammit. He pressed the rewind/search button and Gibbons started moving jerkily, rushing backward to the Honda, skittering around it like a bug. He went to the trunk, pulled the air hose out of his pocket, and put it back in. Nagai ran the tape back to the point where Gibbons used his keys to open the trunk.

"Mashiro."

"*Hai.*" Mashiro stood up and walked over to his lord. No sign of pain or stiffness in his legs. And he was three years older than him. Remarkable.

"Here, look at this." He hit the play button and handed the camcorder to Mashiro who took it and peered into the viewfinder. "That man is a cop, a federal government agent, FBI."

Mashiro nodded with the camcorder stuck to his face, his other eye squeezed shut. "He's taking an air hose out. He knows about the slaves?"

"He must suspect something."

Nagai watched Mashiro watching the tape for a few moments. Then Mashiro started nodding again. "Interesting . . ."

"What?"

"This FBI man is not so young. Surprising."

Nagai shrugged. He thought of Reiko. What's old? What's young?

"Why are you showing me this?" Mashiro asked.

"Study his face. I want you to do something."

"Kill him?"

"No. According to D'Urso and the punk, it's a bad idea to kill cops in America, especially federal cops."

Mashiro put down the camcorder and scowled. "A poor excuse for cowardice, I think."

Nagai shrugged. "Perhaps."

"D'Urso's people are supposed to take care of the police. That's their part of the bargain."

"I know, I know, but he doesn't want to do this one. He says killing him would make things worse for us."

"Do you believe that?"

"I'm not sure."

"Then why shouldn't I kill this man? Just to make sure."

Nagai thought about it. "They might be right, I don't know. It's their country, they should know."

"So if you don't want me to kill this man, why are you showing me this?" Mashiro was so up-front, so matter-of-fact. He was beautiful.

"I want you to find this FBI man and hurt him in such a way that he will never be able to testify in court as to what he found at the docks."

Mashiro shrugged. "I could cut out his tongue."

"No. No blades. Hands. Can you do something to him that will incapacitate him without killing him? You know, like a permanent coma."

Mashiro nodded once.

Nagai was ashamed to be skeptical, but he had to know what Mashiro had in mind. He had to know that it would work. "What can you do?"

Mashiro held out his hand in the karate blade-hand position and looked at his lord. Then without a word, he walked to the back wall of the warehouse where his ancestor's armor hung. Nagai hadn't noticed it when he came in. It loomed in the flickering candlelight like a ghost. Mashiro gathered up an armful of boards from the floor, clear pine about two feet long and a half-inch thick, just like the one he'd smeared the jelly on. He set them up on two cinder blocks, laying them down one by one. "Ten," he finally said, pointing to the neat stack.

Nagai went closer and Mashiro took his stance behind the boards, feet apart, slowly taking aim with his blade-hand, touching the top one and raising his hand, touching and raising, touching and raising until he was ready.

"*Haaaiii!*"

His hand smashed down on the stack . . . and nothing happened.

Panic shot through Nagai's gut. It was the first time he'd ever seen his samurai fail. Fear grabbed him around the neck. "What—?"

Mashiro calmly held up one finger, then proceeded to dismantle the stack of boards, one by one, examining each one. They were all solid, untouched. Nagai felt sick.

Then Mashiro picked up the bottom board. One end dangled at a right angle from the other it was cracked so badly. Splinters jutted from the break. He'd broken the bottom one but left all the others intact. How the hell—? Nagai's smile hurt he was so relieved.

"When I worked for Toyota, there was a young tiger in my division making aggressive maneuvers for rapid career advancement. He rose quickly, and in no time I found him over my shoulder, eyeing the job I was in line for. Our boss liked this young man very much. I had a bad feeling that I would be passed over. One night after work I followed him to a bar and watched him drinking with his young associates. When he went to the bathroom, I followed. He was standing there taking a piss when I delivered this same blow to his neck. For some reason, I was afraid to kill back then. I could do it easily, but I was afraid to. I don't know why. So I practiced, calibrated my attack so that my hand would fall just short of death. The young tiger became a vegetable. As far as I know, he still lies in a back room in his parents' home, permanently asleep. Four years now. He will never recover. His parents punish themselves needlessly by keeping him. I will silence the FBI man the same way," Mashiro said. "No killing. No problem."

Nagai grinned. His throat ached so much he couldn't speak. He knew all along that Mashiro could do it for him. Mashiro could do anything, anything. Who needs the fucking Mafia? Who needs Hamabuchi's fucking hitters? Who needs any of them? A tear squeezed out of the corner of Nagai's eye as he laughed.

"Do you know where I can find this FBI man?" Mashiro asked.

Nagai reached into the pocket of his jacket. "Our man down at the docks that day was smart enough to follow him home. Here's his address." He handed him a slip of paper.

"Gib-*bons*," Mashiro pronounced, staring at the paper.

"That's his name. Gibbons."

Mashiro nodded, looking at the address, sizing up his task. He bowed to Nagai, then turned on his heel and bowed to the shadowy armor hovering over them. "Gib-*bons* . . . *hai*."

Nagai swallowed over the hard lump in his throat, closed his eyes, and let out his breath. *Sayonara*, Gib-*bons*.

11

Lorraine was at the stove putting the kettle on. Gibbons watched her from the living room. As he zeroed in on her backside, he suddenly remembered that knockout blonde he saw at the Auld Sod the other day with Tozzi. That girl was something, yeah, but she didn't have anything on Lorraine. Not really. Lorraine still had a nice figure, and when she wore her hair down—long, dark, and loose—she was a Renaissance dream. The blonde would be very lucky if she looked this good at fifty-one. Lorraine's hair was tied back tight now, though. She was still pissed at him.

"What's this?" Lorraine said as she pulled down a box from the kitchen cabinet shelf where the Lipton tea bags usually were. Gibbons came in from the living room and looked at the box in her hand. There was a picture of a Mandarin prince on the front. The prince had long, curling fingernails and a thin, curlicue mustache. Lorraine narrowed her eyes skeptically. "Oolong?"

"Yeah, oolong." The fluorescent bulb under the counter buzzed softly.

"But this is commie tea. You told me you don't buy commie products."

"*You* like commie tea. It's not for me. It's for you." He put the last of the dirty dishes in the sink and went back into the living room. Damn. He was just trying to be nice, thinking of what she likes for a change. Suspicious of everything, these damn Italians.

The water in the kettle started to simmer. She took down two mugs and made tea for them—oolong for her, Lipton for him—then cut a few slices of the zucchini bread she'd brought from home and laid them on a plate. She was still mad at him for going back to work. She said she wanted to at least be a part of the "decision-making process." What she meant was that she wanted to have the veto. You're no kid for God's sake, she kept reminding him, you really shouldn't be working out in the field anymore. It's too dangerous. You can't keep up with Michael. It was the friendly reminders like these that made him ignore her and opt for the unilateral decision. She dunked the tea bags a few more times and tossed them into the sink. That's why he was getting the cold shoulder now.

She came into the living room, balancing the plate of zucchini bread on top of her mug of oolong. Gibbons was sitting on the couch, looking through the book she'd brought him, a scholarly study of the function of the centurion in the Roman army between 450 BC and 350 AD. He liked books about the Roman empire, but she'd made it clear that this wasn't a peace offering. She'd explained that it was a complimentary copy sent from the publisher courtesy of the author, a tweedy Boston Brahmin now teaching at UCLA who always brings some exotic liqueur to the Classical and Medieval History Society convention each year in the hope of luring her back to his hotel room. Last year it was a green potion from the Abruzzi region of Italy called Cent'Erbe, she said. The year before it was a rare Spanish armagnac. He was good-looking in a waspy sort of way, but she'd never taken him up on his standing invitation. This little slice of academic life was her way of getting back at him. He watched her set down his tea on the coffee table. If the convention were tomorrow, bet she'd go to bed with the jerk for a can of Bud just to fix him.

"So how's the case going?" Her voice was very frosty. Very out of character for her.

Gibbons flipped to the table of contents in the book. "Slow." He didn't look up from the page.

"No leads?" More frost.

"Not really. You want to go out to a movie tonight?" Better than sitting here in the meat locker.

"You hate going to movies."

He looked up at her. "You don't."

"I don't think so. There's nothing I'm dying to see."

Can't butter you up, huh? "Oh. Okay." He went back to the book.

"Ivers must be getting antsy. He hates bad press, doesn't he? You once told me that ritual murders that aren't solved quickly create very bad publicity for the Bureau."

He looked up at her. Since when do you care about bad publicity for the Bureau? "Who said anything about ritual murders?"

"Well, the way the killer cut them . . . It certainly seems ritualistic. That's what Michael says."

He shut the book, tossed it on the coffee table, and reached for his tea. "That was yesterday's theory. Now he's hot on karate killers."

"I take it from your tone of voice that you don't agree."

Gibbons shook his head. "The problem with Tozzi is that whatever comes into his head goes out his mouth. Tomorrow it'll be something else."

She broke off a piece of zucchini bread. "If you don't try out different theories, how else do you solve the case? Don't you have to consider every possibility, no matter how strange it may seem?"

"That's Tozzi's usual style. He's gotta jerk around for a while with the tangential stuff before he gets down to business."

"You don't jerk around?"

He looked at her. "No."

"Never?"

"Come on, let's go to a movie." He started to get up.

"I said I didn't want to go." She crossed her arms over her chest.

Gibbons sighed. He could see it coming. "Why not?"

"Do you really think street punks are capable of this kind of carnage? Or was it the Mafia? You always like to blame the Mafia. That's *your* thing." She was getting testy. "But how many people would have the intestinal fortitude to make incisions like that, then pick up the bodies and put them in a car? It had to have been some extraordinary fiend. Even professional hit men do it quickly and get away fast. You told me that yourself."

"What do you do, take notes when I say things?"

"Well? *Do* you think the Mafia is responsible?"

Gibbons shrugged. "Could be."

"Do you *really* think the murderer was some guy acting on orders from his boss? It seems to me that it would take a hell of a lot of loyalty to kill like this. No, you're wrong. I don't think it was the Mafia." She was gloating.

Gibbons shook his head slowly. "Who's more dedicated to their bosses than Mafia guys? They'll put you through a meat grinder and make hamburger if their boss tells them to. They're as vicious as they come. Believe me. I've seen."

She looked him in the eye. "So why the hell did you go back to all that?"

The play of moonlight and shadow on the cobblestones turned the alley into the knotted armor on a giant samurai's chest. Mashiro stood in the shadows and felt his ancestor's presence under his feet. He counted the floors of the building across the way. There were lights on in the apartment. He crumpled the note with the address written on it and threw it away, then reached into his pocket for a handful of salt. He mumbled a prayer to the venerable Yamashita and tossed the salt onto the cobblestones.

"Let me tell you something." Gibbons was on the edge of the couch, pointing his finger at her. "You've got a bug up your ass because I went back to work. You think there's something wrong with me because you think I get off on this kind of violent shit."

"Well, don't you."

"No, I don't. Maybe Tozzi does. But I don't."

"We're not talking about Michael."

"You know, you and your cousin are two of a kind. You have to blow everything way out of proportion. Well, put this in your notes. The motives for murder are almost always very simple ones. Hate, greed, revenge. One guy sees another guy scratching his new car in a parking lot and he goes nuts, bashes the other guy's head in with a tire iron. That's a typical murder."

"Are you telling me these two kids were slaughtered and mutilated because they scratched the wrong man's car?"

"Don't act so stupid, will ya? The point I'm trying to make is that in a murder investigation you've got to concentrate on the motivation for the murders, not how it was done. *That's* how you investigate a homicide. Once you get bogged down in all kinds of irrelevant crap, you end up chasing your own tail."

"Maybe *you're* the one missing the point. Thirty years as a special agent doesn't necessarily make you an expert on every crime, past, present, and future. I think you're being too close-minded about this. It's a strange world and it gets stranger every day. You have to admit this was no ordinary killer. This was done by a killing machine."

Gibbons chewed his upper lip and squinted at her. He was getting heartburn. "You sure you don't want to go to a movie?"

"Yes, I'm sure."

Come on, maybe *Jaws* is playing somewhere.

Looking down at the cobblestone alley from the fire escape, Mashiro could see his ancestor's body, a giant warrior lying in state, noble in death. He bowed his head in reverence, then mounted the next step of the iron stairs, treading carefully. He stared up at the lighted windows three floors above and thought about the young tiger who challenged him at Toyota, remembering the tingle along the edge of his hand as he watched the young man sprawled out on the bathroom floor in that bar. He thought about his promise to his lord Nagai, then proceeded toward his mission.

"I never thought you had such a limited imagination," she said, shaking her head. "I'm really disappointed in you. You insist on the most mundane plausibilities. Maybe this killer is a psychopath. A psychopath who thinks he's a . . ."—her eye caught the book on the coffee table—"a Roman centurion, let's say. You would never consider that, would you?"

"You're all wet. Psycho killers are a whole different ball-game."

"No, no, just listen to me for a minute. Here's this individual, well-read in the history of ancient Rome, someone who gets a real charge out of wearing a short sword and a breast plate. But then one day he snaps, and because he's so entrenched in the lore of the Roman campaigns, he starts to believe that he's a centurion. But the thing about the centurions is that they lived only for the army, they were born to take orders. So what does our killer need to complete his reincarnation as a true centurion? A Caesar, right? Now let's suppose some villain enters his life, someone who sees that he can use this poor demented soul for his own evil ends if he just plays along and tells the guy he's his general. *Think about it.*"

"I'm thinking about having you committed. Can we change the subject now?" He started to put his arm around her.

"No." She pushed his arm away. "You're not listening to me. That's your whole goddamn problem. You don't consider anyone else's point of view. How can you ever solve a crime if you can't acknowledge someone else's reality? Maybe you could before, but you can't now. Face it, you can't do it." She grabbed her mug and gulped tea with her eyes closed. She was trying not to cry.

That awful, gut-wrenching silence stuffed the room then. He felt like a real turd. His going back to work upset her a lot more than he thought. He really was a shit-head sometimes. "I know you're pissed as hell at me," he finally said. "I'm sorry. We should've talked about it first, I guess."

She slammed down the mug on the coffeetable and splashed tea. "Saying 'I'm sorry' isn't an eraser. It doesn't make it all disappear."

"I'm apologizing. What else can I—"

"It's not enough. It doesn't make up for the past. You always do this to me. You shut me out all the time. You never think in terms of *us.*"

He let out a long sigh. "I hate these conversations. What am I supposed to do here? Cry? Sorry, I don't cry. You want me to say something, but I don't know what it is. If I thought my going back to work was going to get you all bent out of shape like this—"

"It's not that you went back to the Bureau. It's the fact that you didn't tell me what you intended to do."

"Well, what the hell did you think I intended to do? After thirty years with the FBI, what am I going to do? Become a florist?"

She laughed through her tears and shook her head. "You'll never change, will you?"

He hooked his hand around her neck and drew her closer. He felt awful seeing her cry over him. "Look, I don't know what to say to you. I love you, but—"

"Okay, shut up. That's all I wanted to hear. Just make me one promise and I'll be happy."

"What?"

"Be more careful from now on. No more derring-do. My heart can't take it. You're not invincible, no one is. Cut the risks. Stick with Michael when it gets dangerous. Promise me that. I don't want to get old alone."

Gibbons swallowed hard. "Okay . . . I promise. I'll be more careful."

She hugged him close, pressing her lips to his, smothering a sob. She ground her mouth against his and reached into his shirt, rubbing the hair on his chest. He held her tight. He didn't want to let go. She might see a teary eye if he did. She started to unbuckle his belt then.

He turned his head to disengage for a moment. "Hey, you sure you don't want to see a movie now?"

She sniffed and laughed, a real laugh. "Just lie back and relax, Gibbons."

She unzipped his pants and went for him, squeezing tight until he was even harder than he already had been. He unbuttoned her blouse and fumbled with the bra hook in the front. Impatient, she unhooked it herself and quickly threw off the blouse and bra in one motion. He caressed one soft breast in his thick, callused hand as she twisted to kick off her slacks. His other hand smoothed the panties over her ass and outlined the seam around the edge of her pubic hair. She smiled through a kiss and tasted his tongue. Hers was delicious.

Suddenly she pulled away and arched her head back. "I just thought of something."

"What'd I do now?"

"Not about you. About the killer."

"Oh, shit . . ."

"Maybe he's not a centurion. Maybe he's a Russian cossack. Those guys were really sword crazy." She grinned down at him slyly.

"Give it a rest, Bernstein."

"You've got to consider the possibilities. Otherwise you get stale." She was laughing softly as she leaned down and started

nibbling his earlobe while he feather-stroked the crease
where her thigh met her crotch. He grinned and groaned low
like a horny bear.

Outside the living room window, the stout dark figure
peered in at them. Mashiro glanced down through the iron
grid under his feet at the moonlit cobblestones and frowned.
Very dishonorable to attack a man making love to his woman.
He turned and headed down the fire escape as silently as he
came, trying to ignore the sounds of pleasure coming from
inside.

12

The dusty smells of lawn fertilizer and weed control brought back memories—not entirely pleasant memories. When he was a teenager, Tozzi worked summers with a gardener from his neighborhood, busting his hump mowing lawns six days a week from seven till sundown, pushing those goddamn mowers back and forth, up terraces, down ravines, across lawns as big as outfields, his fingers itching with the constant vibration, going deaf from the noise of the motor, sweating buckets in the noonday sun. He could remember how much he hated those big expensive houses in Short Hills, Milburn, South Orange, West Orange, Livingston. You rarely saw any people living in them. The only signs of life were the rumbling central air-conditioning units, which he always took as a snub. Ha-ha, you're hot, we're not. He still had something of an automatic prejudice against rich people. Sure, he realized now that if those rich people hadn't hired their gardeners, kids like him wouldn't have had summer jobs. Still, when you're pushing a lawnmower back and forth, back and forth, back and forth, and it's ninety-six degrees, humid as hell, and you know there are people somewhere in those air-conditioned houses because the Caddy's in the drive, you tend to think in terms of plantations, white-suited Kentucky colonels, and chain gangs.

He stared through the hot-house windows in the front of the nursery and watched a green dump truck backing up to the loading dock. As soon as the truck stopped, the gardener jumped out of the cab and started yelling at his men to hurry up and load bags of fertilizer onto the truck. He was a foxy-looking guy with a thick Italian accent who spoke with the kind of operatic expansiveness that made everything he said sound like bullshit. Freeman, the owner of this nursery, eyeballed him skeptically through black horn-rimmed, Coke-bottle glasses, shifting his big cigar from one side of his mouth to the other. He filled out the gardener's receipt on a clipboard that rested on his big belly. He was about six-five, at least 280 pounds. The skinny Italian jabbered away at the big man, gesturing with his arms, grabbing his crotch and laughing. Tozzi wasn't sure, but it seemed like the gardener was telling Freeman a dirty joke. Freeman wasn't laughing, though. He reminded Tozzi of the dim-witted Cyclops in an old Jason and the Argonauts movie he remembered watching as a kid on "The Million Dollar Movie." He imagined the gardener intentionally distracting Freeman as his men got a pointy log ready to stick in the giant's eye.

Tozzi took a second look at the gardener's two helpers then. He went closer to the window to get a better look. They were both Asian, most likely Koreans, which surprised him. These Italian-immigrant gardeners usually hired other Italians or Hispanics. Tozzi had worked with a Bolivian and a couple of Uruguayans in his time, but he'd never seen any Asian help. He always thought the Koreans were too clannish to work for anyone else. Of course, it seemed like they had cornered the market on produce stands in the New York area. Maybe gardening was just a logical extension of their thing with plants.

The truck pulled away from the loading dock and Freeman lumbered back inside. "Sorry to keep you waiting," he growled.

"No problem," Tozzi said, walking back to the counter.

"That guy's a real pain in my ass. Always in a big fucking hurry. Treats his men like shit, too. Never thought I'd ever feel sorry for slopes." He scratched the stubble on top of his crew-cut head and rolled the cigar to the other side of his mouth where he had several teeth missing on the bottom. The cigar rested nicely in that space. "Now, you said you're from the FBI? A real FBI agent, huh?"

Tozzi nodded and smiled patiently. He'd seen this reaction before.

"Damn. Never thought I'd ever meet a damn FBI agent. So what can I do for you?"

"Well—"

Freeman's face suddenly turned uglier. His magnified eyes bugged out under his glasses. "You're not investigating me, are you?"

"No sir. I think I mentioned before we were interrupted that you are not the target of this investigation."

"Is it my wife?" The cigar rolled around in his mouth, then went back to its space.

"No sir. Not your wife either."

"Too bad. I wish somebody'd put her away for ten, twenty years. Do me a favor."

Tozzi smiled obligingly, but he had a feeling this wasn't a joke. "Marital problems?"

"Fuck no. Business problems. I shoulda never agreed to let her come in here and do her thing. House plants and all that shit." He pulled out his cigar and spit on the floor. "Plants belong outside, goddammit. And those frickin' bonsai trees. Ridiculous, spending all that time and trouble to keep a tree small like that. It's unnatural. Look at this place. I used to have a nice dirty place here. Now it looks like some kind of boutique, these rich bitches trooping in and out of here all the time. If the old lady wasn't making so much goddamn money on those stupid little things, I'd boot her and those damn weeds of hers the hell out of here."

"Ah-hah." Tozzi nodded. "Well, I came because your ad in the yellow pages said you specialized in bonsai trees. Maybe I should talk to your wife."

Freeman rubbed his nose with the back of his index finger and glared at him. It was clear that the big man was reforming his opinion of the FBI agent now that he knew Tozzi was here for goddamn bonsai trees. "She ain't here today. She's at some bonsai tree convention in New York."

Tozzi opened a manila envelope and pulled out the eight-by-ten photo of the shears that were found on the female victim. He laid it on the counter. "What can you tell me about these?"

"What do you want to know?" The Cyclops was getting belligerent.

"These are the kind of shears they use to prune bonsai trees, right?"

"Yeah."

"Do you sell shears like this?"

The Cyclops scowled down at the photo as if Tozzi had just put dogshit there. "Yeah, she sells these things."

"These were made in Japan. See the inscription on the blade? The ones you sell, are they made in Japan?"

"They better not be, goddamn it. Too damn expensive. We'd be stuck with 'em. Order the cheap ones from Taiwan, I told her. Her lady friends won't know the difference. I told her, you order those Jap ones and I'll stick your head in the chipper, goddamn it. For once, she listened to me." The cigar bobbed up and down in its resting place.

Tozzi nodded, wondering how serious he was about putting his wife's head into a wood chipper. It wouldn't be a first. Not that long ago some guy out in the boonies in upstate New York killed his wife with an ax, then put her in the chipper to get rid of the body. He might've pulled it off, except that her pelvis kept jamming up the machine. He kept trying it and eventually she stripped the gears. At his trial, he referred to her the same way, both alive and dead, as "that goddamn cunt."

"You know of anyone around here who does sell the Japanese ones?" Tozzi asked.

"Nope. Ask the wife, though. She'd know. She'll be back tomorrow."

"Okay. Tell her I'll give her a call. Thanks for your help."

He garbled something Tozzi couldn't understand. As Tozzi headed for the door, an obviously well-to-do suburban matron came in. She was a real sketch. Henna red hair, jade-green eye shadow, killer nails in mauve, white fur jacket. Tozzi glanced back at Cyclops behind the counter and wondered if he kept the chipper out back.

Outside, Tozzi noticed a white Mercedes wagon parked next to his car. There were three people in the backseat: a toddler in a car seat, a little girl who looked about kindergarten age, and a dark-haired woman. Tozzi assumed she was the baby-sitter because she was sitting in the back with the kids, her head bent over a stack of construction paper on her lap. Opening his car door, he noticed that the baby-sitter was making animals out of folded pieces of construction paper. She was just finishing one up, a yellow rhinoceros. The little girl was clapping her hands and making giddy squeals. The toddler was fast asleep. As he turned the ignition key and started his engine, the baby-sitter was suddenly startled. She jerked her head around and stared at Tozzi, a look of terror and anxiety on her face. Tozzi instantly thought of war victims—World War II, Vietnam—noticing for the first time that she was Asian. Another Asian. He forced a smile to calm the girl down as he backed out of his space and left the nursery, wondering whether seeing three Asians in a row was just a coincidence. Maybe it was one of those things like when you buy a new Chevy and all of a sudden all you see are Chevys on the road. Maybe it was just cosmic irony. Who knows? He threw it into drive and pulled out of the parking lot without giving it another thought.

After leaving Freeman's Nursery, Tozzi drove into the center of town to grab a sandwich. The only coffee shop in Milburn was one of those Fifth Avenue-type places where rich old ladies pay six bucks for a scoop of cottage cheese and a half a canned peach on lettuce with melba toast on the side. The sight of that much blue hair and mink gave him the creeps, so he got his tuna on rye to go and ate it outside on one of the park benches that were artfully set among the meticulous rock-garden beds that lined this stretch of Milburn Avenue in front of the kind of shops he'd never dream of going into.

But as he ate his lunch, he began to notice something very peculiar. It wasn't unusual to see young women pushing baby carriages and strollers through the center of any town, but of the eight he spotted in the course of eating the first half of his sandwich, five of them were Asian. One of them was pushing a baby carriage so he couldn't see the baby—it could've been hers, though she seemed too young and too humble to live in a town like Milburn—but the others were all pushing white kids. They all seemed very young, late teens, early twenties. Same age as the two kids who bought it in the VW. Seemed like more than just a coincidence.

He dumped the rest of his coffee into the begonias, packed up his trash, and went back into the coffee shop. As he walked to the back, his nose was assaulted by an onslaught of overpowering perfumes. He breathed through his mouth and made his way back to the pay phone, happy to see that they had a phone book. This kind of place would. He poked around through the yellow pages, looking up "Baby-sitters," "Nannies," and "Children." Under "Child Care," he found several day-care centers, one employment agency called Domestics Unlimited that provided live-in au pairs as well as cooks, maids, and chauffeurs, and the Eastlake Academy, a school for nannies that specialized in providing "trained nannies in the British tradition for discerning parents." The school was in Maplewood, the next town over. Tozzi glanced at his watch and grinned to himself. Time to pay a visit on the Eastlake Academy.

Pip, pip, major.

As Tozzi dug into his pocket for change for the meter, he looked across the tiny park next to the post office at the old Erie-Lakawanna railroad station where a train was just pulling out. Maplewood Village, as it was called, actually sort of felt like an English village. Quaint but not obnoxious about it. Before he took the depressing rented room he was living in now in Weehawken as a temporary solution, he'd considered getting an apartment here, but ultimately he decided it wasn't his kind of place, which suddenly reminded him that he better call Mrs. Carlson and cancel that meeting tonight with the landlord who "prefers married tenants." He'd call her later and make up some excuse. Too bad, he liked that place on Adams Street. It was gritty but clean.

Maplewood Village was really the perfect place for a nanny school in "the British tradition," he thought, as he walked past the Christian Science Reading Room and the stationery store to the doorway marked "49." It was a two-story yellow-brick building with stores on the first floor, offices on the second. The Eastlake Academy was in Room 22. Tozzi went upstairs and followed the arrows to Room 22, smiling nostalgically as he suddenly recalled dumpy Miss Frances on "Ding-Dong School." That's probably the kind of ladies who come out of the Eastlake Academy. Older, gray, kindly but proper, firm and correct. Miss Frances with an accent.

But when Tozzi pushed the buzzer on Room 22 and opened the door, what he saw was something else again. She was standing beside the reception desk, holding the phone to her ear. She had legs, incredible legs. Tall. Padded shoulders. Nice shape. Early thirties. Dark red hair. Small, Oriental-looking eyes, laughing eyes. She flipped her hair behind her ear and looked over at him. She smiled cordially. There was a slight space between her teeth. He almost dropped dead.

". . . yes, Mrs. Danzig, yes. I *assure* you. All our nannies have been thoroughly trained in child care. Our women have completed courses in pre-school psychology and first aid as well as the traditional nanny curriculum . . . Well, they will bathe the children, of course . . . Only if there's an emergency. If the baby spills his milk, nanny will clean it . . . No, I'm afraid our nannies don't do floors and windows . . . No . . . No, I'm afraid not . . . Very well, I'm sorry we couldn't accommodate your needs, Mrs. Danzig. Good-bye." She hung up the phone and smiled at Tozzi again. "Hello. Can I help you?"

She was very British. Welcoming but still stiff upper lip considering that she had apparently just lost a client. "Well," he said, "I'm interested in hiring a . . . nanny."

"Well, you've come to the right place." She walked toward him and extended her hand.

Tozzi's heart kicked. He wanted to grab her and kiss her. Was she ever nice.

"I'm Roxanne Eastlake," she said, shaking his hand. "I'm afraid my secretary is out to lunch right now." She rolled her eyes back toward the reception desk. They were light brown, dark gold. "Please come into my office, Mr . . . ?"

"Uh . . . Tozzi. Mike Tozzi."

"This way, Mr. Tozzi." She pronounced the z's like s's. So what. She had a beautiful ass. And that space between her teeth . . . ooo-la-la.

Her office was all brass and burgundy leather. A lot of women decorate their offices like powder rooms. This office was very classy, no silk flowers but no high-tech black-lacquer-and-chrome power shit either. He liked it. He liked her.

"Now," she said, lacing her fingers on top of her blotter, "tell me what you're looking for in a nanny, Mr. Tozzi."

"Well"—it was hard not to stare at her—"I have a daughter—"

"How old?"

"Uh, two."

"Ah-hah." She nodded and smiled, encouraging him to go on. Oh, that space! It was so sexy.

"Well, you see, Ms. Eastlake, I'm on the road a lot. Business. And—"

"And your wife works?"

"No . . . she's dead."

"Oh . . . I'm terribly sorry, Mr. Tozzi."

"No, no, it's okay. It was a long time ago."

She furrowed her brows. "But you said your daughter is just two."

Tozzi nodded, trying to think of an answer. "It seems like a long time ago. We were separated . . . I never really liked her."

Ms. Eastlake smiled tolerantly as if she were listening to a mental patient. "So I take it you need a full-time live-in nanny?"

"Yes. Actually I was thinking about one of these Asian girls everybody seems to have. I have a neighbor who—"

"The nannies I represent, Mr. Tozzi, are thoroughly trained in all aspects of child care. Young American women trained in this country by former British nannies. They are the state of the art, if you will, the best. However, I have to tell you that I do not have any Asian women on my roster. And I must point out to you in all candor that, professionally speaking, as far as I've seen, these Japanese girls who've become all the craze are far inferior to my people."

"Well, everyone seems to have them."

Her nostrils flared. "If your neighbor leapt off the Empire State Building, Mr. Tozzi, would you follow?"

Tozzi suppressed a grin. If you were the neighbor, Ms. Eastlake. "So you're saying you don't have any Japanese nannies."

"Indeed not. And please don't credit them with the title of nanny. What they are, in fact, are cleaning women who also watch the kids."

He noticed that the angrier she got the more her accent faded. "Well, if you don't represent these Japanese girls, who does?"

"I'm sorry, Mr. Tozzi, but I'll be damned if I'll act as a referral service for them. I just lost a very good client because the nanny I supplied wouldn't wash the floor. The woman told me her sister-in-law's Japanese girl washed floors and even did windows. Cleaning windows is not child care, Mr. Tozzi. Child care is caring for children, period. I've lost a lot of business thanks to these Nips. They're cut-rate, to be truthful. If you want to go cheap with your child's well-being, then get yourself a Nip girl. But if you truly care about your daughter, as I suspect you do, you'll opt for a properly trained nanny."

Her choice of words seemed odd. Maybe she'd been in America for a long time. The mix of the accent with the American phrasing was very sexy, though. She was something. "Ms. Eastlake, I have to come clean with you. I'm not really in the market for a nanny."

"Pardon?" Her eyes became slits. She was about to become quite furious.

He pulled out his ID. "I'm with the Federal Bureau of Investigation. I'm gathering information on a case."

She glared at the ID, then glared at him. "What the hell *do* you want? Why the ruse?"

He regretted telling her the truth. She looked like she didn't like him at all now.

"You know, just because my phone isn't ringing off the hook, that doesn't mean my time is yours to waste. I have enough to do to keep this business afloat, I don't need government interference. I don't need this aggravation. I really do care about children. I care about their needs, particularly the ones who're neglected by parents who're too damned busy to be bothered with them. I'm sure you don't understand any of this, but I do and I think it's important. That's why I can't believe that you'd have the gall to come in here and feed me this cock-and-bull story, blithering on about the Jap—"

"Whoa." He held up his hands in surrender. "I'm sorry about the story, but it was necessary until I knew you were all right."

"Oh . . . and am I 'all right'?" Very sarcastic now.

"Just fine."

"You know, you've been eyeing me like a dog eyeing a steak since you arrived. You're not very subtle for an FBI agent. I caught you staring at my fingers, looking for a wedding band.

I don't need some sex-starved cloak-and-dagger man invading my office just to harass me."

The idea suddenly popped into his head. He spoke before he could talk himself out of it. "Would you consider doing me a very big favor?" he said, cutting her off before she started up again.

Her eyes shot open in disbelief. "What utter gall," she whispered venomously. "You are some piece of work, Mr. Tozzi."

"You know, I may be able to help you with your Japanese competition," he said, having no idea what he could do for her. "This all relates to the case I'm working on. We can discuss it now and then go out to dinner tonight. My way of apologizing for the intrusion. How's that sound to you?"

The corners of her lips turned up. She was curious. Tozzi was delirious. "And what about this favor?" she asked, eyeing him with a wry grin. "What is it?"

"Oh, it's nothing much. We can take care of it on the way to dinner."

She leaned back in her chair and folded her arms over her chest. She sized him up, taking her sweet time about it, lording that wry grin over him. Then she suddenly broke out into a full-fledged smile and showed him that space between her teeth again. "Explain yourself, Mr. Tozzi. I just might be intrigued."

Tozzi's cheeks felt hot. It was a very inviting space.

13

"So what do you think, Mrs. Tozzi? Is it everything your husband told you it would be?" The overhead light glinted off Mrs. Carlson's oversized glasses, making her seem even more bizarre than she already was.

"Indeed, Mrs. Carlson. It's all that and more." Roxanne stepped back a half-step to maintain the personal space this henlike real estate agent persisted in invading.

Tozzi just stood there on the bare floor, watching Roxanne play "Mrs. Tozzi." She was doing a good job, better than he ever expected. She must've been an actress once. He hoped he was just as convincing as "the husband."

"Michael, darling, I want to show you something in the bedroom." She extended her hand to Tozzi. "I have an idea about the bed."

He raised an eyebrow as he stepped toward her. What bed? I don't have a bed, dammit.

Roxanne smiled at Mrs. Carlson. "You'll excuse us for a moment, won't you, Mrs. Carlson?"

"Oh, of course, of course."

She took Tozzi's arm and led him into the empty bedroom. "You're a lousy actor, Tozzi," she whispered when they were out of earshot. "I wouldn't have taken the part if I knew you'd be such a stiff. Loosen up."

Tozzi shrugged. "Gee, I thought I was doing okay."

"Why don't you act like you know me, at least?" Out of the corner of his eye he could see Mrs. Carlson loitering down the hall. Suddenly he felt Roxanne's hand caressing his cheek. "See, you're blushing now, Tozzi. A man doesn't blush with his wife."

Tozzi coughed. "I can't help it. I mean, we just met this afternoon."

"Listen," she said, "we both know you have the hots for me, so there's nothing to be embarrassed about. You're being ridiculous now, and you're well on your way to losing this apartment. Any idiot can see right through you. Mr. Halbasian isn't going to buy our little act."

He took her hand from his cheek and held it in both of his. "Why not? Mrs. Carlson believes we're married."

"She'd believe we were Chuck and Di if we told her so. Her commission's at stake."

He wrapped his arms around her waist and grinned. "Okay, okay, you're right. I'll be cool. I'm getting into it. See?" He pulled her close.

She gave him that wry grin of hers. "Yes, I see." She took his hand then and pulled him over to the place where she thought the bed should go, against the wall between the windows. Tozzi objected mildly, saying what he thought a husband who knew he'd ultimately be overruled would say. He waited for her reply, but she was lost in thought, staring out the back window at the dark settling on the backyard. It looked ominous out there, and it wasn't even night yet.

"Maybe Halbasian will be doing you a favor if he rejects you," she said, still staring out the window. "Why the hell do you want to live here anyway? I wouldn't live here if you *paid* me eight-fifty a month. It looks like Beirut for God's sake."

Tozzi glanced back at Mrs. Carlson who was still loitering. He put his arm around Roxanne's shoulder for appearances. He really liked this husband and wife routine. "What're you talking about, Beirut? Everybody wants to live in Hoboken. It's chic, it's goddamn yuppie heaven. And it has history, too. I didn't tell you. Frank Sinatra used to live in this building."

"So why didn't he stay?"

He looked her in the eye, nose to nose. "You really know how to bust *cogliones*, Ms. Eastlake."

"Uh-uh. Call me Roxanne, darling." She kissed the end of her finger and touched his nose. "It's more convincing."

He could smell her she was so close, the real her, not the cologne. She smelled very nice. He had an incredible hard-on.

"Mr. Halbasian's here," Mrs. Carlson crooned from the hallway.

Roxanne took Tozzi's elbow and led him out to meet their prospective landlord. His underwear was constricting him he was so hard. He forced himself to walk straight as they headed for the living room, expecting to see a bald, grizzly fat man in a polyester suit and a polo shirt. But the guy standing in the living room with Mrs. Carlson didn't look old enough to shave.

Mrs. Carlson threw her arms open like a game-show hostess. "Mr. and Mrs. Tozzi, this is Jeffrey Halbasian."

Everyone shook hands and exchanged pleasantries. Tozzi was leery of him, though. It was hard enough taking Dennis the Menace in a Botany 500 suit seriously, but having him as your landlord? There was something basically wrong about that.

"Sorry, I'm late," the kid said. "Hectic day on The Street. Lot of flux on the Dow all afternoon."

"Ummm." Tozzi nodded and grunted.

Roxanne bugged her eyes out at him as if he'd done something wrong again. Was his prejudice against money-people that obvious? He worked up a warm smile for the kid to recover the fumble.

Roxanne started bubbling. "That's quite all right, Mr. Halbasian. We haven't been waiting long." She started pouring on the Brit, probably figured young Halbasian would eat it up with a spoon. Most Americans with pretensions to wealth and power did. That's what she'd told him in the car on the way over here. They always thought it was so classy, so "Masterpiece Theatre," she said. Hell, if it would help him get this damn apartment, pour it on thick.

She'd moved a step closer to the Menace. "I must tell you, Mr. Halbasian, we're absolutely in love with the apartment. The renovations are so well-done. I think the place is just *sup-ah.*"

Young Halbasian's face brightened like Tiny Tim's on Christmas morning. He took the hook, the little guppy. Tozzi loved it.

Young Halbasian clasped his hands behind his back and

stuck out his chest. "I'm so glad you like it, Mrs. Tozzi. A lot of work went into renovating this building. But I tend to think that a restoration isn't complete until the tenants have been selected. I'm very big on ambience. I think it's very, very important. We want people who will maintain the ambience that the new Hoboken is striving for."

Was this little shit coming on to her or what? What was he, crazy? Goddamn. That was the whole problem with giving kids adult responsibilities. They don't pick up on the subtleties, like the jaw muscles Tozzi felt flexing in his face right now. This is how kids get hurt.

"Tell me something, Mr. Halbasian," Tozzi cut in. "By ambience, do you mean that you basically rent to white, upwardly mobile types? Or do you actually try to mix up your tenants—black, white, Hispanic, Indian, rich, poor—for a more bohemian ambience?"

"I don't think I follow you, Mr. Tozzi."

"Well, there aren't too many people who can afford these kinds of rents. It seems to me that your 'ambience' would have to be pretty much yuppie for you to get these . . . kinds of rents."

The tense silence indicated that they all knew what Tozzi was driving at. Halbasian glanced at Roxanne and Mrs. Carlson, then glared at Tozzi. He looked very cross, like the little kid who'd been embarrassed in front of the teacher he had a crush on. Well, what do you want from me? Tozzi thought. I didn't tell you to grow up to be a rent gouger and a racist.

Seeing her commission evaporating before her eyes, Mrs. Carlson decided to break the silence. "I understand your concerns, Mr. Tozzi, and I assure you that neither Mr. Halbasian nor my company would ever tolerate discrimination on any level. It's illegal, and we abide by the law. As for the rents that are charged, all rents in Hoboken are regulated by the city's Rent Leveling Board. You're free to go to city hall to check the history of this unit, and I'm sure you'll see that Mr. Halbasian has priced this apartment within the board's guidelines."

"Ummmm." Tozzi nodded, looking down at young Halbasian, deliberately accentuating the difference in their heights. Roxanne was giving him the bug-eyes again. He didn't care about the apartment now. He was having too much fun busting balls.

"Nothing personal, Mr. Halbasian, but because of my job as a federal law-enforcement employee, I'm obligated to ask these things. You see, it would reflect badly on me if I rented under anything other than legal circumstances. I'm sure you can understand that." He looked down patronizingly on Halbasian.

"Oh, no problem. I entirely understand your position." The kid was frying. It was clear from his face that he hated Tozzi's guts now.

All of a sudden Tozzi had second thoughts. What the hell was he doing? He wanted this apartment, for chrissake. He *needed* this apartment. Couldn't invite a woman like Roxanne back to that shitty rented room he's got now. Maybe Ivers was right, maybe he did have problems with authority figures. Maybe it wasn't too late to make up, though. He put on the warmest smile he could muster and started complimenting the renovations. Roxanne picked up on her cue and chimed in, but Halbasian didn't look happy. He looked like he was going to pick up his ball and go home.

Mrs. Carlson piped up, desperate to salvage the situation. "Mrs. Tozzi works in Washington. A lobbyist, you said?"

"Yes. I do lobby work for several British concerns." She left it simple. Let young Halbasian's imagination fill in the blanks. Very smart.

Mrs. Carlson clucked down at Halbasian, keeping him close under her wing and away from Tozzi. "They keep an apartment in Washington. Mrs. Tozzi stays there most of the time, and Mr. Tozzi's work brings him to the capital frequently."

"How much time would you actually be spending here?" Halbasian asked Tozzi. The little piss-off wasn't too good at hiding his feelings.

Tozzi opened his mouth to answer, but Roxanne cut him off before he did any more damage. "Well, besides being stationed in DC, I do travel quite a bit. As does my husband, sporadically, as he's needed. It's hard to say how much time we'd be spending here in Hoboken." She looked at Tozzi, begging him with her eyes not to blow it. "Maybe two weeks a month?"

He shrugged. "Sometimes more, sometimes less. It depends on work."

Young Halbasian nodded, squinting at Tozzi. Either he was trying to figure out how he could get rid of him and just take her, or he was wondering how he could rent out the apartment on the sly for the weeks they wouldn't be there, the money-grubbing little shit.

"The apartment really is su-pah," Roxanne suddenly gushed to Tozzi. "I saw some wonderful Laura Ashley prints that would go nicely with the Persian rug. And don't you think that scrubbed pine cupboard we saw at Dillingham's would be perfect for the dining area? Over there?"

Halbasian twitched his pointy mouse nose and raised an eyebrow. He smelled fine English cheddar. He was going for the bait again. Tozzi covered his mouth with his fingers and grinned.

"And the portrait of grandfather over the mantel? With the two tufted leather armchairs on either side." She turned to Halbasian and started gushing directly at him. "You'll have to come for tea once we've set up. A proper English tea by the fire. I bake the yummiest scones, Mr. Halbasian."

The grubby little mouse relaxed his face. He was thinking of Alistair Cooke with the roaring fire behind him. The scones did it. She was right. A real sucker for the Brit pedigree baloney.

He glanced at Tozzi quickly, then settled his gaze on her. His expression was liquid, like someone who'd just taken a terrific crap. "What can I say, Mrs. Tozzi? You're perfect. I'll have the leases sent to Mrs. Carlton's office by Monday."

"Su-pah!"

"Wonderful!" Mrs. Carlson said with unconcealed relief.

"I know you'll like it here," Halbasian said. He shook Roxanne's hand, then reluctantly offered to shake Tozzi's.

Tozzi smiled and pumped his hand. "Just one thing, Mr. Halbasian. That junk in the backyard—when will it be cleaned up?" He wasn't letting go of young Halbasian's hand. He couldn't help himself.

"Soon."

"How soon?"

"Very soon."

"I hope so." Tozzi finally let go. Halbasian wasn't about to wince in front of them, but his fingers did look a bit red.

They were playing the "Tarantella" now, which was a blessing because it had no words. When the skinny guitar player sang, he ended all his phrases by sliding around the note before settling on it, sort of like a warped Dean Martin record. His guitar was also a little out of tune, and he paid absolutely no attention to the rhythm machine clicking out a fast samba beat. His partner, the accordion player, looked just like Dom DeLuise. He was the better musician, but he was too damn loud. Tozzi's cousin Sal took accordion lessons when they were kids. When Sal was twelve, they bought him an amp. Lady of Spain, I adore you for the whole neighborhood. Amplified accordions should've been included in the Geneva Convention.

Across the table, Roxanne picked the meat out of a mussel and discarded the shell in the empty plate between them. "Halbasian's going to change his mind. He doesn't like you."

Tozzi glanced at the plastic grapes and the Chianti bottles hanging on the wall. The bottles were vibrating dangerously, thanks to the accordion. "Yeah, I know Halbasian hates me, but he *loves* you." He took another mussel from the big bowl. He really wanted to dunk a piece of bread in the sauce, but he was afraid she'd think he was a pig. "As soon as he heard your accent, I knew we were in."

"Is that the only reason why you asked me to do this? Because I'm British?"

"No. I'm not that calculating."

"Yeah, I'll bet."

"Anyway, you're not completely British."

She stopped chewing and stared at him. "You really are a sleuth, aren't you? How did you know?"

"Your accent isn't always so strong. It slacks off when you're off guard. Your choice of words gives you away, too. For instance, most of the time you say things are 'great,' but with Mighty Mouse everything was '*supah.*' " Tozzi reached for a piece of bread and thought about dunking again, then put it down on the side of his plate.

"Well, now that the jig's up, I guess I have to fess up." She speared another mussel, chewed, and swallowed before she continued. "I was born in America—right here in Jersey, in fact, in Trenton. My father's British. He was working at a research lab in Princeton back then."

"So where did you get the accent?"

"We moved back to England when I was four. He got bored with what he was doing here so he decided to go home and teach. We lived in London until I was twelve."

"Then what?"

"Oddly enough, we moved back to Princeton. Dad received a lifetime fellowship from the Foundation for Advanced Scholarship."

"Isn't that the place where people get paid just to sit around and think?"

She grinned. "That's one way of putting it." She tore off a piece of bread and dunked it in the sauce. Tozzi smiled. She was okay.

Tozzi dunked his bread then and was careful not to get any sauce on his shirt. "Now, as long as I'm playing Sherlock Holmes," he said, wiping his mouth with his napkin, "I'd say your mother wasn't English. You're too good-looking to be one hundred percent Brit."

"Heavens!" she said with heavy irony. "You mean my gypsy blood is *that* evident?"

"Gypsy?"

"Russian gypsy. From the Ukraine."

Tozzi chewed another piece of bread and nodded. Gypsy blood . . . He felt a little guilty thinking what he was thinking, but he couldn't help it.

The duo suddenly got much louder as they finished the "Tarantella" with a dramatic crescendo, the accordion making the silverware rattle. The Chianti bottles were trembling. Tozzi felt like he was at an Italian wedding.

"What is this, an Italian wedding?" she said over the noise.

Tozzi shrugged. She really was all right.

"We're gonna take a break right now," the guitar player said with his mouth right on the mike, "but we'll be back in a little while to do a whole set dedicated to Mr. Sinatra. Okay?"

A few people applauded. An old guy sitting behind a golden-fried mountain of calamari banged his knife against his water glass.

"I can't wait," she said, rolling her eyes to the ceiling.

Too bad. Tozzi actually liked Sinatra, but these two guys might change that. "I apologize for the lounge act. It's the food I come here for."

She sipped her wine. "No need to apologize. I know how it is. The tackier the restaurant, the better the food. I know a few places in Trenton just like this."

The tough-looking waiter came by then to take their plates and leave their salads. He looked like he could've been related to the accordion player. "Everything okay?" he asked.

Tozzi nodded. "Fine."

"You got any requests for the band? After the Sinatra set, that is."

"Do they know 'When the Moon Hits Your Eye Like a Big Pizza Pie'?" Roxanne asked.

"Why su'." The waiter smiled like a bulldog. Apparently he thought she was okay, too. He picked up their bowl of mussel shells and left.

"That one they should do well," she said with a conspirator's twinkle in her eye.

Tozzi sipped his wine and remembered the real name for that song, "That's *Amore.*" He decided not to go looking for signs and symbols, not yet. "So, Roxanne, now that you've been good enough to be my wife for the interview, I'd like to return the favor and help you with your Japanese nanny problem, if I can."

She sighed deeply and dropped her cheek on her fist. "I don't know what to do. I can't last another quarter the way things are going."

"Tell me about it."

"There's not much to tell. I'm being undercut. I don't know exactly what the Japs are charging, but it has to be less than we are because they're stealing all the business."

"Where do they come from?"

She shrugged. "I'd like to know. There are only a handful of nanny schools in this country, and I represent all of them."

"You mean the Eastlake Academy doesn't really train nannies. You're the agent for these schools."

"Exactly. Calling my business an academy is a bit of bullshit, but it's the kind of cachet you need to bring in customers. People like Mr. Halbasian would be impressed by something called the Eastlake Academy." She turned up the Brit accent as she said this, then laughed, but it was forced. "My guess is that the Japanese girls are all illegal aliens."

"Could be. But are they free agents cashing in on a good thing, or is there some kind of organization behind them?"

"Oh, no, they have an agency . . . of sorts. One of my ditzier ex-clients had to tell me all about them when she called to cancel the nanny I got for her. The woman blithered on about a Mrs. D'Urso from Short Hills and how she'd supplied her with a wonderful little Japanese girl who does absolutely everything for her—short of satisfying her poor husband, I suppose. From what I understood, this Mrs. D'Urso is running a real backroom operation out of her home—no advertising, no listing in the Yellow Pages, all word of mouth. Doesn't pay her taxes either, I'll bet. She's the one who apparently started this whole Japanese fad, and from what I've heard, she's marvelous at convincing these snotty nouveau-riche ladies that they simply must have one of her girls. These ladies have been my bread and butter, but this year I've been losing them in droves."

Tozzi speared a forkful of arugula and thought about telling her, then decided he better not. He could be wrong. But if his hunch was right, her competition was tougher than she ever imagined. He knew of a D'Urso who lived in Short Hills, John D'Urso, the most aggressive *capo* in the Antonelli family. But if this Mrs. D'Urso was John D'Urso's wife, what the hell would she be doing running a nanny service of all things? He wondered if her nannies were all Japanese. He wondered if the girl who was killed in the Death Bug had been one of her girls. There was a lot to wonder about.

"I take it from your silence that my problem is pretty hopeless," she said.

He shook his head. "No . . . not necessarily. Could you get me this Mrs. D'Urso's address? I can pass it on to Immigration and Naturalization. They may be interested in checking these girls for green cards."

"I'm sure I can get it for you. I'll chat up that ex-client of mine. She has a very big mouth." Roxanne looked happier already. Tozzi felt a little light-headed. He really wanted to help her.

He ate some more arugula and gave her an encouraging smile, but he had no intention of alerting Immigration and

Naturalization. They love to pull those infamous raids of theirs, which might be good for them, but not for him. His concern was a double murder, and they'd most likely fuck things up for him. They could have theirs later.

The duo returned to their instruments then. Tozzi hoped the guitar player would tune his guitar, but it didn't look like he was going to. He just adjusted the strap on his shoulder, grinning into the mike, as his partner cranked up the rhythm machine and picked a beat.

Suddenly the accordion swept through the room like a tornado with the intro to "Strangers in the Night." The Chianti bottles rattled. The skinny guitar player started to sing. Tozzi looked into her eyes. She gazed back into his. Her eyes were like melting chocolates. Her lips parted moistly. Their fingers entwined across the table. Then they both started laughing uncontrollably. It was all so cornball. He loved it. She was great.

"Let me ask you something, Roxanne."

"Ask me something." She looked sly and giddy.

"Would you be interested in coming over to the apartment as soon as I move in, just to make some decorating suggestions?"

She gazed at him over the rim of her wineglass. "To work on the 'ambience'?" She really did have laughing eyes.

"No, seriously, I'd just like to get a woman's opinion on what I should do with the place." He couldn't keep a straight face either.

"My, aren't we cheeky."

And horny, too.

The accordion swelled. The bottles chimed. She was terrific. Tozzi felt great.

14

Tozzi felt stupid. He felt sore and stupid. His hands were blistered, his back hurt, and he couldn't keep his attention focused on Neil Chaney as he demonstrated aikido techniques, which made him feel even more stupid each time he had to pair off with one of the people in the class to practice. It didn't help that Neil referred to each technique by its Japanese name, which just confused Tozzi. And it didn't help that he was constantly being corrected by the others in the class. He knew they meant well, but he wasn't in the mood to be told that he stood the wrong way, sat the wrong way, stretched the wrong way, fell down the wrong way, attacked the wrong way, and even punched the wrong way. He'd been in how many fistfights in his life?—too many to count—and now he had to be told by an eighteen-year-old girl that he didn't punch the right way? Rationally he knew she was right, that they had a certain way of doing things in aikido, that he was a beginner and that he just had to learn. But he wasn't feeling very rational right now, and everything was pissing him off.

He wished to God he had some of Gibbons's patience. Gibbons knew how to work an investigation, how to let the facts gestate, how to go over the same territory again and again until he found what was hidden there. Tozzi was like a kid. He needed instant gratification. You get a lead, you follow it, you uncover the crucial evidence, *bang!* you solve the case— *bing-bing-bing*, just like that. Rationally he knew that wasn't the way it went in the real world. But being rational was never one of his strong suits. He preferred swinging down on a rope, causing confusion, making things happen. Or at least that's the way he liked to think of himself.

Neil Sensei, as everyone called him once they were on the mats, was demonstrating a technique with one of the other black belts, a big-boned, pasty-faced guy. The black belt was aiming some pretty vicious-looking punches at Neil Sensei's midsection. Neil Sensei would step out of the way, gently grab the big guy's wrist, cover his hand with his own, point the guy's fingers at the floor, and force him to fall flat on his back. Simple.

Ha! Tozzi knew better. Things were never that simple in aikido. Not only did you have to get the move right, including the footwork, you had to keep the four basic principles of aikido in mind while you did it. A sign on the wall reminded you in case you forgot: Keep one point, Relax completely, Keep weight underside, Extend *ki*. Tozzi had learned that evening that one point was somewhere below your belly button, and being aware of it was supposed to keep you strong and balanced and do something for your energy flow. Keeping weight underside vaguely made sense to him in terms of balance—better to be bottom-heavy than top-heavy. Relaxing completely was a nice idea, but somehow Tozzi had a hard time relaxing when he knew someone was about to punch him in the gut. (Neil Sensei kept telling him his tension stemmed from the fact that he wasn't keeping his one point, which he thought he was, sort of. It was a vicious circle.) And as for *ki*, well, the best explanation he'd gotten so far was from some spaced-out grad student from Stevens Tech who told him that it was "sorta like projecting this spirit, this feeling, this aura that's kinda like your phazer set a little higher than just stun."

Right. Beam me up, Scottie.

How the hell were you supposed to keep all this in mind and get the moves down right to learn the damn technique? And how the hell could you learn anything sitting on your knees all the time in *seiza*? Everyone else in the class could sit like this indefinitely, even look comfortable doing it. But he had to keep shifting his weight so he could tolerate the pain, forcing himself not to think about the spasms he knew were just waiting to grip his thighs and ankles. Damn.

He'd hoped this class would help him work off some tension, not add to it. The pain in his legs and the feeling of hopeless ineptitude wasn't what he needed right now, having spent the whole day at John D'Urso's house, cultivating his fucking endless flower beds and picking every last stray leaf out from under the goddamn shrubs. It was Roxanne's fault. She'd worked too fast and gotten D'Urso's address for him early that morning. He'd hoped to spend the day with her, maybe take a drive somewhere, but duty called. Dammit. He really wanted to see her. Instead, Tozzi went right over to D'Urso's and arrived just in time to see the gardener's truck pulling out of the driveway of D'Urso's big pseudo-French chateau. The gardener's name was painted on the doors of the truck: NICK PARISI, LANDSCAPE CONTRACTOR. That gave him the idea. He was already dressed pretty sloppy in jeans, a sweatshirt, and a jeans jacket, so he ran over to Freeman's Nursery in Milburn and picked up a three-prong cultivating hook and a flat-edged spade, then went back to Short Hills and parked around the corner from D'Urso's. He pulled the tools out of the trunk and walked back to the D'Urso house.

He went straight to the backyard, which was surrounded by an eight-foot, black iron-bar fence. It felt like he was in the lion's cage at the circus. There was a wooden swing set with a built-in tree house on the lawn behind the kidney-shaped pool. The swing set made him feel a little better. Wiseguys probably won't shoot if their kids are around. Posing as one of the gardener's helpers should be pretty safe, though, he figured. Just as long as Nick doesn't come back.

He started working on the beds, pulling weeds, digging up fresh soil and smoothing it out with the hook, then cutting a nice neat edge all around with the spade. He kept glancing back at the house, hoping to see something suspicious—like a bunch of Japanese girls running around the place—something he could take to Ivers so he would authorize a formal electronic surveillance. Good ole Ivers and his goddamn daily reports. Tozzi'd love to have a real report ready for him first thing Monday morning, something worthwhile, something he could shove up Ivers's ass. Tozzi was grinning meanly to himself when the glass patio doors suddenly slid open and this young guy in a purple sweater and baggy, pleated, gray plaid pants came out.

"Hey! What're you doing over there?" He kept his head cocked to one side—to keep that faggy-looking piece of hair out of his eyes, Tozzi figured. He definitely had the wiseguy attitude even if he didn't have the look. One of D'Urso's crew no doubt.

"I said what are you doing?" The guy enunciated every syllable. He probably assumed Tozzi was an immigrant.

"I'm doing the beds," Tozzi said.

"What's-his-name, the gardener, he just left a little while ago. What're *you* still doing here?"

"Nick left me here to do the beds. It's about time, too. Look at that." Tozzi pointed to the beds. "These roots need to breathe. Gotta break up the soil, let the air in." He was right. The beds hadn't been touched all season. Nick was a shitty gardener. Gradually the punk nodded in agreement.

"You gonna be here long?"

Tozzi shrugged. "As long as it takes. There's a lotta work here. Look at those hemlocks, look how straggly they are. They have to be trimmed. That's a big job. I won't finish all this today. No way." He figured he'd pave the way just in case he had to come back.

"Yeah, the place does look pretty bad." The punk nodded and pushed up the sleeves of his purple sweater. "Do a nice job, okay?"

"Oh, yeah. Of course. That's all I know how to do." Tozzi kept smiling until the punk went back inside. Now he had to work, dammit. He always hated digging beds. To him it was worse than mowing grass in the heat of August. After that last summer he'd worked for a gardener, the one between his senior year of high school and his freshman year of college, he swore he'd never do this kind of work again. Who'd of thought eighteen years later he'd be digging beds again? Never say never, they say.

He worked there from ten-thirty to almost three, and in all that time he didn't see a goddamn thing. No one came in or out except for the punk who left around noon in D'Urso's black Mercedes. No stream of illegal aliens, no giggling gei-sha girls, no sign of John D'Urso or his wife. Only a little girl who stared at him for a while from behind the sliding glass doors up on the deck, and a glimpse at the Japanese woman who pulled her away from the window. From the brief look he got, this woman seemed a little older than the girl who'd been murdered, mid-to-late twenties, maybe. She was also quite a looker. Tozzi kept thinking of these nannies as homely girls. Of course, he'd also expected to find some old bag running the Eastlake Academy, and Roxanne turned out to be something else. Something else indeed. As he worked, he kept hoping the Japanese woman would come out with the kid so he could talk to her, but that didn't happen. He thought maybe if he could get inside, he could corner her. After the punk left, he rang the doorbell and asked to use the toilet. The Hispanic maid answered and showed him to the john in the basement. She also waited outside the door so she could escort him right back out. Shit. He kept trying to come up with some other ploy to get to the baby-sitter, but in the end all he could do was work and watch and wait for something to come his way. As the day stretched on, it became obvious that he was going to have to come back and work on those hemlocks on Monday. Shit. At quarter of three, he picked up his tools and headed back to his car.

Driving back to his rented room in Weehawken, Tozzi couldn't stop thinking about the Japanese woman at D'Urso's house. Why would a Mafia guy let his wife get involved with a nanny business? And why Japanese nannies? Was it just to give the wife something to do, to get her out of his hair? Possibly. But even assuming the business was legitimate, why let her work out of the house? These guys never like to draw attention to themselves, and their homes are their castles, literally. Didn't it occur to him that a home business like this might make the IRS or Immigration a little curious? And why just Japanese girls? It didn't make sense. On Friday Gibbons had told him about the air hose he found in the Honda. Assuming that D'Urso was smuggling Japanese workers into the country, why go to all that trouble? Down at the Mexican border, you can get illegal aliens from Central America by the truckload. And they get themselves into the country. That had to be cheaper than shipping them one by one from Japan. Anyway Roxanne thought D'Urso's wife was undercutting her price. What kind of profit margin could they have with these Japanese nannies? D'Urso would never get involved in any kind of operation that didn't leave him with a healthy cut. It just didn't make sense.

He kept thinking about the D'Urso's nanny, forcing himself to remember her face. There was something different about her expression, more world-weary than those other Asian nannies he'd seen around Milburn. None of that *Teahouse of the August Moon* happy-happy innocence. She looked like she knew more than she'd ever tell.

Tozzi took the exit off the Parkway and looped onto Route 3 East, shaking his head at himself. He was doing it again. Christ, he'd only seen her for twenty seconds. He was doing a whole character study based on a twenty-second look from thirty feet away through a plate-glass door? Pretty flimsy. He was making up stories again, bending reality to make it be the way he wanted it to be. That's how he got into trouble before. That's the kind of shit Gibbons always warned him about. Well, maybe Gibbons was right.

As he drove down the highway, he started thinking about the two dead kids and the cuts on their bodies and karate chops to the neck, and suddenly he remembered that there was an aikido class in Hoboken this afternoon at four. He glanced at his watch and decided he had just enough time to clean up, grab some sweats, and get over there. He decided throwing people around the mats might be a good way to work off some of this edginess he always seemed to have. Yeah, work off some of the frustration. Just what he needed after a wasted day like this.

He was wrong.

Neil Sensei finished his demonstration and bowed to the pasty-faced black belt, then instructed the class to pair off and practice. The spacey grad student from Stevens tapped him on the shoulder. "Shall we dance?" he asked.

"Sure." Tozzi noticed that he was a blue belt, one of the middle ranks. Good. Tozzi figured the guy was experienced enough to teach him something, but not so good as to make him look bad.

"My name's Chris. You're . . . ?"

"Mike."

He took off his glasses and adjusted the elastic strap. "Is this your first time here?"

"My first time actually practicing, yeah."

Chris smiled and nodded as he put his glasses back on. "Thought so. You look a little confused. No problem. It took me about six months before I stopped feeling stupid."

"Six months, huh?" Great, just what I need, a six-month inferiority complex.

"Okay, this technique is called *Tsuki Kote Gaeshi*, which roughly means a wrist twist from a punch attack. You punch me. Aim for somewhere around here." Chris pointed to his sternum. "We'll go slow."

Tozzi took his position, standing in *hanmi* with his front foot at a ninety-degree angle to his back foot. He clenched his fist, palm up, the way he'd seen the black belt do it, and thought about how the guy had punched Neil Sensei during the demonstration, twisting his fist and giving it some snap, karate fashion. After being criticized twice today for his imprecise attacks, he was determined to deliver at least one good punch. Chris looked him in the eye and nodded. Tozzi took a breath, stepped forward decisively, and punched . . . at air. Chris had turned sideways to avoid the blow, which left Tozzi's arm extended right in front of him, Tozzi off-balance. Chris quickly took advantage of Tozzi's weakness, grabbing his wrist and twisting it back so that Tozzi had no choice but to slam down onto his back.

Tozzi forgot to fold his leg back behind him to control the fall the way he'd been taught. He hit the mat hard and felt it in his kidneys.

Chris stood over him, fiddling with his glasses. "I guess nobody told you, Mike. The force of your attack always determines the force of the throw. That's why I said go slow."

Tozzi nodded as he got to his feet. "Right."

"Okay, let's try the other side."

Tozzi knew this meant he was supposed to switch his feet and punch with the other hand. This time he punched in slow motion, and Chris threw him nice and easy.

When it was Tozzi's turn to throw, Chris patiently talked him through all the steps, giving him pointers as he began to get it. They went back and forth like this, Chris throwing twice, then Tozzi throwing twice. When Tozzi threw, Chris slapped the mat hard as he fell, something all the experienced people did. It was meant to stop the momentum of the fall. The resounding boom of Chris slapping the mat made Tozzi feel good, even though he knew it was really more like a pro wrestler pounding the hollow floor of the ring for effect, not him hammering Chris to the mat.

They practiced like this, repeating the technique again and again, and after a while Tozzi actually began to feel that he was getting it. He was getting out of the way, most of the time, and a couple of times he sort of felt semi-competent, throwing Chris without exerting a lot of energy, just using the force of Chris's attack against him.

"Now how about punching a little more realistically?" Chris said. "Make like you're really pissed at me. Like you really want to hit me."

"Okay," Tozzi said. He took his position, determined not to hold back this time. Chris knew what he was doing. He'd get out of the way. This one would be for real.

Tozzi stepped forward, light on his feet. He looked Chris in the eye, nodded, and rammed his fist right at Chris's gut. Once again Chris got out of the way, caught Tozzi's balance, grabbed his wrist, and twisted hard. Tozzi fell back and slammed against the mat, and even though he got his leg under him, he still hit hard enough to rattle his ribs.

Chris stood over him, shaking his head.

"What'sa matter?" Tozzi asked.

"That didn't feel right. Can we try it again? Same side."

"Didn't feel right . . . Okay. Whatever you say."

Tozzi got back up and delivered the same punch. Chris threw him down with a loud thud. This time might have been a little bit harder.

"Better?" Tozzi groaned, getting up on his elbows.

"Yeah, that did feel better." Chris looked content. "Your turn."

Tozzi climbed to his feet slowly, determined to do the best fucking *Kote Gaeshi* anyone had ever seen from a beginner. He really thought he had it now. He could do the whole technique without getting hung up on the mechanics of each little move. He took his position, standing in *hanmi*, waiting for Chris to throw his punch. Chris made a fist. Tozzi was ready. Chris started to move forward. Tozzi could already hear him hitting the mat. Come on. Now—

"*Hai,*" Neil Sensei called out from the front of the room.

Chris immediately stopped his attack and bowed to Tozzi. "Thank you, Mike."

"Ah . . . yes, thank you." Tozzi felt like he'd been robbed.

Everyone rushed back to their places, sitting *seiza* in two lines, waiting for Neil Sensei to begin the next technique. Tozzi glanced at Chris and frowned. He'd been ready. He felt he could've done it right this time. He'd been robbed, goddamn it.

Tozzi sat down slowly on his knees. He could've done it, goddammit. Next time. He rested his weight on his heels, and immediately his thighs started to ache. Neil started his demonstration. Next time. Then he felt the charley horse mounting in his calf. Shit. He got his legs out from under him and sat on his butt as he quickly started to massage the cramp. Yeah . . . maybe next time.

15

"No Sweet'n Low?" D'Urso said. "No more Sweet'n Low, Michelle?"

"I'll get it," she said and went back inside the house.

They were all up on the deck, having coffee. Tozzi recognized D'Urso right away from pictures he'd seen in FBI files. Perfect steel gray hair, the granite-block build, the slick, continental clothes—he was unmistakable.

The punk who tried to hassle him on Saturday was up there having coffee, too. Tozzi overheard D'Urso and his wife calling him Bobby. Today he was wearing a very trendy-looking baggy tobacco-brown suit. He also wore his shirt buttoned at the collar without a tie. A real Mr. Groovy, this Bobby whoever-he-was.

Mrs. D'Urso was a nervous-looking woman, petite with thin little wrists that looked like they'd break easily. She had big hair, honey blond, and she was made-up for the ball first thing in the morning. She almost looked like one of those sultry bitches on the prime-time soaps, the ones who're always pulling everybody else's strings and making all the other characters miserable, except that behind all the mascara, she had these real scared-rabbit eyes. Tozzi suddenly wondered whether the rabbits they use for mascara tests ended up looking like Michelle D'Urso.

From where he was now, on his knees in the beds that lined the back of the house, Tozzi couldn't see much through the shrubs, but he could hear them pretty well. This would've been a hell of a lot easier, though, if he could just plant a bug under the deck and go back to the car to eavesdrop. But Tozzi couldn't sign out equipment without Ivers's say-so, and he knew Ivers would never go for it on this one. He'd go ape if Tozzi told him about the Japanese nannies. It was so nice having a boss you could talk to.

Tozzi crawled a little closer so he'd be right under the deck. There were plenty of dead leaves stuck under the shrubs. If anybody came by, he'd start pulling them out by hand so he'd look busy doing the cleanup.

"She's still busting you about this, that sister of mine." Tozzi recognized Mr. Groovy's voice. "Thick head just like her ole lady."

"She just gets nervous, that's all. Don't worry about her." D'Urso had a surprisingly mellow voice.

"I don't know what the hell she's got to squawk about. Shit, she'll be sitting pretty too when you get through."

D'Urso didn't answer, and Tozzi wondered why. Maybe he'd answered with a gesture, or maybe he didn't want to talk about whatever it was that his wife was giving him a hard time about.

Just then he heard Michelle D'Urso's high heels banging across the wooden planks of the deck. She pulled up a chair, but there was a moment of awkward silence.

"John," she finally said, "I don't mean to be a pain about this—I really don't—but I just don't understand why we have to change now. It doesn't make sense when we've been doing so well with them. It seems very risky to me."

"Oh, for chris—"

"Shut up, Bobby." D'Urso curbed him like a dog. "It isn't risky, Michelle. It's good business sense. Just look at the car business. Japanese cars used to be real cheap in this country, but then they got wise over there and raised their prices. So what happened?"

"I don't know, John. What?"

"Dealers started bringing in cheaper cars from Korea. See, you gotta go with the market, honey. Get the best price."

"But, John," she whined, "we're not talking about cars."

"Listen, let me explain it just in terms of your end, the nannies. These girls are costing us twenty-five grand a piece now, right? This means we've got to place each girl in a home and have her on the job for fourteen months before we earn back our initial investment. Now, if we can get girls cheaper, we can shorten the turn-around time and show a profit that much sooner."

"Yeah but, John, you don't understand." Her whine got worse. "The Japanese girls have cachet. People want them in their homes, they're the in thing. But grown-up war babies from Vietnam, Laos, Cambodia? Come on, John. They won't be so easy to sell. They're no substitute for Japanese girls."

"Why do these ladies come to you, Michelle? For Japanese decorations or for nannies? Believe me. You offer them a good price, and they'll take the war babies."

"I don't know, John. I've got my hands full with these Japanese girls just trying to keep them under control. Who knows what these new girls will be like? It's just going to add to the headache. Maybe we should wait awhile before we make the change."

"You worry too much about everything, Michelle." Mr. Groovy had to throw his two cents in. "You think the yaks are the only ones who can keep your girls in line? Fuck 'em. We don't need them. Your girls won't run away on you—believe me—because even after the yaks are out of the picture, our guys will keep everybody in line real nice."

"Bobby," she said, "they're not stupid. Some of them are beginning to think they're getting a raw deal. All the girls have plenty of opportunity to take off. It's not like they're in chains or anything. They've got some money—"

"The pocket money you give them? Where they gonna go on that? Even if they hoarded it, how far do you think one of these kids could get without a green card and a passport? Wake up, Michelle. Anyway, most of your girls are still basically happy. It's the factory guys who give us the trouble."

"Really. Maybe you forgot that it was one of my girls who ran off with her boyfriend and was killed by your friend Mashiro."

Tozzi stopped breathing. Say his name again, dammit.

"He ain't no friend of mine."

"I still have nightmares thinking about that headline about the 'Death Bug.' I keep wondering when the papers are gonna run a picture of her. Then what am I supposed to say to the family she worked for, huh? It's giving me an ulcer, for God's sake."

"Honey, I keep telling you the papers are not going to run any pictures of your girl," D'Urso said. "If they had one, they would've used it by now."

"How the hell can you two be so goddamn calm?" she whined. "You act like this is nothing. I'm worried!"

No one said anything for a moment. "I know you're worried," D'Urso said quietly. "But it's really the old man you're worried about, right?"

"Of course, I'm worried about the old man," she said in a loud whisper. "You went against his direct order, John. He told you not to use the girls for hookers, but you went ahead and did it anyway. What if he finds out about your whorehouse in Atlantic City?"

"So what if he does?"

"He told you not to use them as hookers, John! He's the boss, John. He told you and you disobeyed him."

"Oh, Christ Almighty," Bobby said, raising his voice. "They're goddamn slaves. We'll do what the hell we want with them."

She lashed right back at him. "Carmine Antonelli only looks like a nice old grandpa, Bobby. He'll cut your heart out and eat it for breakfast if you cross him, and you know it. He'll kill us all. He will. And what about my baby? Oh, God! Amanda! Her too, Bobby! Antonelli doesn't care! He'd have her killed, too!"

Tozzi's mouth was dry. It was hard to believe what he'd just heard, but the punk came right out and said it. The Mafia was in the slave business. Jesus Christ. Tozzi decided to creep out of the beds and get out of there before they spotted him lying in the dirt. They'd just assume he was eavesdropping, and guys like D'Urso aren't very good about giving people the benefit of the doubt. Tozzi crawled around the corner of the house as D'Urso tried to get his hysterical wife to calm down. From what he could hear, it wasn't working.

D'Urso sat by himself out on the deck. Michelle was inside washing her face. Bobby had gone in, too, to take a crap or something. He stared down at the sun gleaming off the water in the pool and suddenly wondered when the hell the pool guys were gonna come and empty it. It was October, for chrissake. Why hadn't Michelle called them? What the hell's wrong with her? Doesn't she see anything? He was about to go in and yell at her when he caught himself. She was crazy enough now. Better leave her alone. He was reaching across the table for the coffeepot to pour himself another half a cup when he heard the glass doors sliding open behind him.

"Daddy!"

"Hey! Here's my girl."

D'Urso's three-year-old daughter, Amanda, ran over and leapt into his lap. She threw her arms around his neck, puckered her lips tightly, and gave him a loud kiss on his nose. D'Urso hugged her tight and rubbed her back. She was wearing sweat pants again today. Why the hell didn't Michelle ever put a dress on her once in a while?

Then he noticed Reiko standing there in the doorway with all that beautiful hair hanging down her back. Some of these Jap broads were unbelievable. Reiko was one of the best-looking ones he'd seen. Bet she's as good as the Jap *braciole* he'd had at Hamabuchi's place in New York. He wouldn't mind finding out. She'd go good down in Atlantic City.

"Reiko," he said, stroking his daughter's hair. "You wanna cup of coffee?"

She furrowed her brow in confusion. No speakee English. That could be a problem. She could learn, though.

"Coffee," he repeated, picking up the pot. "You want coffee?"

"It's okay, Reiko," Amanda said, settling into her father's lap and reaching for an anisette toast. "You can have some."

"Sure she can," D'Urso said. He poured a cup for the woman. "You want milk, sugar, Sweet'n Low?" He looked up at her and pointed to the items. "How about me?" He was grinning.

Reiko whipped her head to move her hair over her shoulder as she took a tentative step forward. She pointed to the silver sugar bowl and indicated a little bit with her fingers.

Just then Michelle came out. She'd fixed her makeup, but she still looked pretty washed out.

"Mommy." Amanda jumped down from her father's lap and ran to her mother. She took Michelle's hand and led her to a chair. "Here. You sit down here, Mommy. You be sick and I'll be the doctor. You sit down and I'll make you all better." She took another anisette toast and started to crumble it on the table. "I'll make some pills for you, okay, Mommy?"

When she saw what the child was doing, Reiko went to stop her, but Michelle waved Reiko off. "It's okay, Reiko," she said, nodding her head affirmatively. "Imaginative play is good for her at this age."

D'Urso snickered. "Whatta you telling her that for? She doesn't understand English."

"Well, how else is she going to learn unless someone talks to her?"

D'Urso shrugged and smoothed his tie. She was still touchy.

"Sit down, Reiko." Michelle made hand signals toward the deck's built-in bench. "Have a seat."

Reiko just stood there, holding the cup and saucer until Amanda went over and led her to the bench by the hand. "You can help me make the pills," the little girl said. She went back to the table for another cookie, then started to crumble it on the bench. Reiko swept up the crumbs and put them in her saucer, then placed the saucer under the child's hands so the crumbs wouldn't get all over the place.

D'Urso sipped his coffee, studying his wife, trying to figure out how he should approach this. "Listen," he said, "you got any good girls? As good as Reiko, I mean."

"What do you mean 'good'?"

"Good with kids. What else do you think I mean?"

"Well, yeah, there are a few outstanding girls. At least that's what the families they work for tell me."

"You think you could get one of them back? You know, do a substitute thing."

"Why?" Michelle already looked suspicious.

"I want us to have a good nanny for Amanda. I've got something else planned for Reiko."

Michelle stared at him, her eyes narrowing. Fuck. Here we go again. "No way, John. No. We've already gone through this. You are not going to turn this girl into a whore. Do you understand me?"

"Don't tell me what I'm gonna do. I said I'm taking Reiko, and that's it."

"You can't take her. Amanda loves her." She was whining again. "It would be too disruptive. God, all the books say this is such a critical stage in a child's development. No, no, you can't do this to your own daughter."

"Come on, will ya, Michelle? Two days with a new girl and she won't even remember the old one." He glanced at Reiko sitting on the bench. She was helping Amanda crumble the anisette toasts. Her hair had fallen down over her face like a shiny black curtain. God, she must be incredible.

"You have no respect for child care, do you, John? You think it's easy, anyone can do it. You think it's like putting someone on the assembly line down at the chicken plant. Well, it's not like that at all. You have to know what you're doing with kids. You have to build up a rapport with them. Reiko and Amanda have that kind of relationship. We can't destroy it just because you need another hooker."

"You know, I'm gonna throw out all those goddamn kid books you got. You don't have any common sense anymore. Did your mother need a million books to tell her how to bring up a kid? My mother didn't."

She glared at him. "Don't get me started on your mother."

"What about my mother?" Little bitch.

"Nothing." She wouldn't look at him.

"Whatta you mean 'nothing'? Go ahead. Say what's on your mind."

She looked up at the sky, clenched her fist, and bit her bottom lip. "Look, John, I don't want to fight with you. I didn't mean anything about your mother. I'm just nervous."

"Nervous about what?"

"Everything—the whorehouse, you taking Reiko away, Mr. Antonelli. It's too many changes, John." She was starting to cry again. Jesus Christ.

"But why does that make you nervous?" He was struggling to hold his temper. As his grandpa used to say about his grandma, what she needed was a good slap and a big shut-up.

She started sobbing like a baby. "Antonelli's gonna get good and mad at you. He's gonna think you're getting too wise for your own good. I'm afraid of him, John, afraid of what he'll do to us."

"What's the matter, Mommy? Why are you crying?" Amanda looked like she was going to start bawling herself.

D'Urso rubbed his face. "Stop crying, Michelle. You're up-
setting Amanda. Stop crying and just listen to me. You won't
have to worry about the old man much longer."

She stopped crying. Her eyes widened. It looked like she'd
stopped breathing. "What are you saying, John?" Her voice
was a desperate whisper.

He hadn't meant to tell her, but it was too late now. She
knew. It wasn't hard to figure out, though. "I've made up my
mind," he said. "The old man's gotta go."

She tried to get the words out but she couldn't. She was
hyperventilating. She put her hand over her mouth and
looked at Amanda.

He grabbed both her wrists and gently made her face him.
"Don't throw a fit now. Just listen to me for a minute."

"You're crazy!" she hissed. "You're crazy! If he ever finds
out you put a hit on him, he'll kiss us all."

"Michelle, five years ago I might've agreed with you. Antonelli was a real boss back then, but he's too old now. He's lost
it. He's weak, he's out of touch with reality. Half the crews in
the family do whatever the hell they want, and he doesn't
even know it. He's bringing the whole family down."

Mascara was running down her cheeks. She looked like that
guy Alice Cooper now. "The man is a *boss*, John. You kill him
and you'll start a war between the crews. You don't want that,
do you?"

"Thank you, Michelle, thanks a lot. It's so wonderful to
have a supportive wife." He threw her wrists back at her.

She stopped crying and wiped her eyes with a napkin.
"This is wrong, John. This is a big mistake you're making."

He slammed his fist down on the table. A cup fell off the
edge and smashed on the deck. "The old man is keeping us
from making this slave thing really take off. He says we can't
do this, we can't do that, but he still wants his fucking forty
percent off the top. How does he expect me to pay his cut and
make a decent profit if he won't let me have a few girls turning tricks on the side? That's not asking much. But he says no,
you can't do that. It's not honorable. If you ask me, he and his
buddy Hamabuchi are two cuckoo birds with this honor crap.
The man's just gotta die. He's lived long enough already." He
stood up and buttoned his double-breasted suit coat.

He suddenly noticed that Reiko was staring at him. She did

that shrug again to flip the hair over her shoulder. He brushed his lapel and pursed his lips to contain the grin. Yeah, I like you too, honey babes. One of these days, Reiko. Very soon. I promise.

Amanda hopped down off the bench and carried the saucer of crumbs over to Michelle. "Here you go, Mommy. Here's your pills. You eat these up and you'll be all better."

"Thank you, honey," Michelle said with a sniff and started eating the crumbs. She was bent over the saucer like it was lobster she was eating, swiping at her eyes with that grimy, mascara-smeared napkin, making believe everything was all right for the kid. Stupid. She never used to be this stupid. Having kids makes women batty. It ruins them.

"I'll see you later," he said to his wife. "Bye, Amanda."

"Bye-bye, Daddy."

As he turned to go, he caught Reiko's eye again. He grinned at her and winked. Yeah, one of these days, Reiko. One of these days.

16

Reiko always did this when they made love. Straddling his hips, riding him slowly, steadily, teasingly, she'd tilt her head back and let her long, silky hair sweep his balls as she traced his tattoos with a light fingertip. First she'd do the green dragon on his left shoulder, outlining the teeth, dotting the scarlet eyes, scalloping the scales, following the curls in the beast's tail right into his armpit. Then she'd go to the dragon on his right shoulder and do the same to him.

From there she'd move on to the left devil mask over his ribs, always tracing the tongue first, then the long blue penis nose. The right devil always came next, in the same order as the left: tongue, nose, mouth, eyes.

Then she'd go on to the fat black *fugu* in the center of his chest, starting with the blowfish's blubbery lips, traveling over his dumb brow, up and over his back, swooping down and out to form the tail, stopping to outline the membranes of the tail, then returning to his form, following the dip of his fat belly before rising to his chin and twisting her finger over his bulging yellow eye to complete the fish.

Finally she'd concentrate on the medallion superimposed on the fish's flank, the medallion of the *Fugukai*, meticulously writing out the characters that formed their organization's name. Nagai always wondered why she followed this painstaking ritual, especially when they only saw each other once a week at most. It wasn't particularly erotic anymore. It was actually Reiko's long hair tickling his balls that turned him on. That's why he told her never to cut it, no matter what.

She finished her tracing and twisted her hips, screwing her moist folds around him. They linked fingers and she continued her twisting, bouncing a little. But her hair didn't quite reach his balls now, dammit, and that suddenly made him impatient. He was full, ready to explode. He locked his elbows and lifted her off him, then rolled her over onto the squeaky mattress. She fell into her own hair like a princess dropped from heaven. He found her silky wetness again and slipped in, gyrating his hips to make his presence felt. He wanted to tease and stroke her, but he was anxious and impatient. She liked it prolonged. She said making love slowly made time stop. Sometimes sex was like that for him, but not often. Not since he'd come to America. It was hard to make time stop when you had Mashiro and two of Hamabuchi's kids waiting for you in the parking lot of this crummy motel, waiting to escort you to a meeting in New York at noon with another one of Hamabuchi's goddamn contacts.

Shit. He was losing it, getting limp thinking about work. He had to hurry before he lost it completely. Nagai started to thrust, picking up the rhythm, arousing himself so he wouldn't be embarrassed by failing to come. Sweat beaded his brow. He was working hard now, pounding, trying to hold himself together. He pumped and pumped and pumped and worked his hands under her, kneading her ass with all that lovely black hair tangled between his fingers. He thought of Reiko in a room in a nice house in the country, her hair so long it filled the room with deep piles against the rice-paper walls. She lived there naked, only for him. Her hair was her clothes, their furniture, their bed. Sun came through the windows and made the coils of her hair shine. All of a sudden he started to come. Yes. That one always worked.

When he opened his eyes again, Reiko's head was resting on his bicep. She was pouting. "You do it like an American," she said in Japanese.

He looked up at the painting hanging on the wall over the bed. Red carnations in a Chinese vase painted on black velvet. The flowers were upside down. He wanted to sleep. "How do you know how Americans do it?"

"I've seen the videos they bring home. I have to make believe I don't understand. Blush at the sex scenes and all that crap. D'Urso thinks it's very funny." Her contempt for the D'Urso family rose to the surface easily. He wondered if she was as good an actress as she thought. That worried him.

"So how do Americans fuck?"

"Fast. Like rape, except at the end they always say 'I love you.' Real crap. Have you ever seen *From Here to Eternity*? A classic, dear Michelle tells me. She owns her own copy. Burt Lancaster on the beach on top of that blonde. Real fast. Awful."

"Who's Burt Lancaster?" He grinned. He knew who Burt Lancaster was.

She pouted and turned away, resting her cheek on the right dragon's back. My princess.

"I'm sorry," he finally said. "Sometimes I get . . . nervous, edgy. It's hard to relax sometimes."

"I know." He could feel her sighing breath on his bare chest. "That's why I never tell you anything until we've finished. But that doesn't seem to matter anymore. You're always this way."

Shit. Don't pull this shit on me now. Please. "I'm sorry. Sometimes I can't help myself. Things will get better. Soon, I hope."

"No they won't." She pushed herself up and glowered at him. There were bitter tears brimming in her eyes.

She was so dramatic. She just liked to see him get upset. For some reason, women like to see their men get rattled now and then. Stupid. "Well, what is it? Talk to me."

"Do you want the bad news or the worse news?"

He frowned. "I don't like these games."

"D'Urso told his wife he's going to kill Antonelli."

She settled down on her elbow, waiting for his angry reaction. He wasn't going to give her the satisfaction. Instead he looked up at the carnations. Fuck.

"You're not surprised?"

He stared at the carnations and wondered how you paint on velvet. "D'Urso told me he had something big planned. I guess this is what he was talking about. I thought the bastard was smarter than that." He pulled Reiko's head back down onto his chest and stroked her hair as he pondered how this would affect him and his defection from the Fugukai to a

partnership with D'Urso. If D'Urso was strong enough to
pull this off, it would be great for the slave business. The
competition from Antonelli and Hamabuchi would be elimi-
nated. They'd be the only game in town. But if D'Urso tried
to get rid of his boss and failed, he could get caught in the
crossfire of Antonelli's retribution. Nagai tugged on his earlobe. Maybe it would be better for him if he remained uncom-
mitted to D'Urso until this power play was settled. It's never
smart to be caught backing the loser in one of these things.

"Does D'Urso have any support within the family?" he
asked, recalling his own attempt to have Hamabuchi killed
and the supposed supporters he thought he had.

"I've heard D'Urso and Bobby discussing their friends in
the family. Some of them are 'real good guys,' they say. They
seem to imply that these men are more loyal to D'Urso than
to Antonelli. They mention names, but I can't remember
them. Italian names all sound alike to me. *Ip-pee, del-lee, roh-
loh, roh-lee.*" She wrinkled her face in disgust.

"Did D'Urso say how he was going to kill Antonelli?"

Reiko shook her head. "He never discusses details with his
wife. Dear Michelle usually gets hysterical enough with what
little he tells her. I thought she was going to have a fit when
he told her about this. She turned white. Later she warned
Bobby that someone named Vincent would kill them first."

Nagai nodded. Ah, yes . . . Vincent. Quite formidable,
supposedly. Mashiro could take care of this Vincent for
D'Urso. If Nagai decided to go over to D'Urso's side. If . . .

Nagai sank down into the pillows and stared at the red
carnations. But why was D'Urso even considering it? Hadn't
he learned anything from Nagai's own big blunder? Still, part
of him wanted to advise D'Urso so he could re-enact his own
attempt on Hamabuchi and prove that it could have worked.
But the Mafia practices a hard art: Force is met with equal
force, automatically. Antonelli won't play the wise old master
with D'Urso the way Hamabuchi had with him. No. This
wasn't smart.

"I told you there was more bad news," Reiko said, breaking
into his thoughts. "Don't you want to hear it? You don't seem
very concerned." She didn't hide her annoyance with him.
She hadn't always been this bold and testy with him. It was

only after she started spying for him that she started talking back like this.

He stared her in the eye and considered a hard slap across the face to remind her where her place was. "I'm listening. Speak."

"D'Urso and Michelle had a fight over me. He wants to take me out of the house and make me a prostitute in his whorehouse." She said it like a threat.

"Have they told you to pack your things yet?"

"No. She wants me to stay with the child. But he's determined and he always gets his way. I'm telling you right now, though. I am not going to be a prostitute! I'll run away first."

He stared at her. He didn't like this belligerent pushiness of hers. She'd picked that up in D'Urso's house. "You're not there yet. Don't worry about it until it happens." He wondered if he could change her mind. Having a spy down at the whorehouse in Atlantic City could be advantageous. It wasn't as if she'd never done it before. Maybe he could convince her, make her a few promises. Not now, though. Later. After she cools down.

"He likes me, you know. I always catch him staring at me, saying little suggestive things to me."

Nagai frowned his brow. "Who?"

"D'Urso! He wants to fuck me. One of these days when Michelle is out shopping, he's going to do it. He's going to rape me." She didn't sound worried. Just more of that threatening defiance in her voice.

"You never told me this about him."

"Well, I'm telling you now. It's true. He wants me very badly." She sounded like a little spoiled brat.

"If you let him," he said slowly, "consider yourself just another slave. That's a promise."

She pouted and whined. "But what if I can't stop him?"

"That's your problem." Her face was on the verge of crumpling into tears. She knew he meant it.

He looked up at the branching cracks in the ceiling. They didn't look like anything in particular. He shut his eyes. He could've drifted right off, but he knew she'd wake him up as soon as he did.

He heard her sniffing back her tears. "What are you going to do?" she demanded. "This is serious."

He opened his eyes and stared at her, annoyed with her badgering. "I'll decide what to do and when to do it."

"But you—"

"But nothing. Everything is under control for the time being. You're not in the whorehouse yet, and I happen to know that Antonelli is in Florida right now. D'Urso won't try a hit on unfamiliar territory."

"How can you be sure of that?"

"I know." I was there. D'Urso wants revenge. He wants to see it, at least be near enough to feel it. Another mistake.

Reiko sat up and hugged her knees. "I don't see how you can say everything is under control. You haven't done a thing yet."

"I don't have to do anything. If D'Urso tries to move you out of the house, we'll deal with that then. But as it stands, no one's bothering us. As Mashiro always says, let the attackers come to you, don't go chasing them. Until they bother us, we won't bother them." But if I ever find out D'Urso is getting it on with you . . .

She reached across his chest and took a cigarette from his pack of Marlboros on the nighttable. "This sounds like the spiritual bullshit the karate teachers used to hand us in school. You going zen on me now?" She lit the cigarette, then tossed his lighter back onto the nighttable. It bounced off and hit the floor. She didn't bother to pick it up.

When she mentioned school, Nagai thought of that slave at the chicken factory, Takayuki, the one she went to school with. Had she been a ball-buster like this when the poor bastard tried to win her affections with English tutoring? She could be cruel when she wanted to be.

He glanced at his lighter on the cheap blue shag rug. "I'm not zen, just smart. A little strategic thinking works in these situations. Ask Mashiro about it sometime."

She blew smoke out of the side of her mouth. "No thanks."

"There's a lot to be learned from him."

She didn't answer. He knew that she thought of Mashiro as just another thug in the gang, someone definitely below her status and unworthy of her consideration. But is a good woman worth more than a loyal man? A man of Mashiro's abilities? He didn't have to wonder. Mashiro didn't talk back.

She was pouting again, still hugging her knees, watching

the smoke rise from the tip of the cigarette in her hand. He took the cigarette from her and stuck it in his mouth as he picked out a strand of her hair and slid it through his fingers, making a small noose with the end. Squinting through the rising smoke, he looped the noose over her nipple and tightened it until she brushed him away. He laughed softly. Suddenly she threw her arms around him, burying her head in his chest and covering his tattoos with all that ebony hair. He smiled. This was what he liked to see.

"I love you, Nagai. All I want is for us to be happy together. That's all I want."

He felt the tears on his skin, and he hugged her, sliding his fingers through all that hair. His smile faded. I love you. Just like the Americans in the movies, he thought. Burt Lancaster and the blonde on the beach . . . getting it on . . . getting sand in their bathing suits . . . just before Pearl Harbor.

He stroked her hair, looking at his cigarette lighter on the floor, listening to the traffic outside the drawn curtains. It must be getting late. Mashiro was waiting. D'Urso's wife would be expecting her home from her "walk" soon. It was time to go.

17

———————

"Where's the Russian?" Tozzi looked pissed.

Gibbons slathered mustard on the two halves of his pastrami on pumpernickel as Tozzi made faces at his sandwich. Now what the hell was bothering him? "What's the matter?"

Tozzi didn't answer. He was staring at their waitress, trying to get her attention, but Rudy's Deli, like every other halfway decent place to eat in Lower Manhattan, was always mobbed at lunchtime, and she was busy taking orders at another booth.

"I must come here at least twice a week," Tozzi grumbled, "and nine times out of ten I order the same thing, turkey on rye with coleslaw and Russian *on the sandwich*. And every time they get it wrong. They always forget to put the coleslaw on the sandwich, but today it's something new. Today they forget the Russian." The waitress was rushing over to the sandwich counter now. Tozzi started waving to her. "Selma! Over here!"

"Normal people eat coleslaw on the side," Gibbons said, considering the sandwich half in his hand. "Why do you have to have it on the sandwich? You special?"

"Because that's the way I like it, and that's the way I goddamn ordered it. Selma!"

Gibbons bit into his pastrami, wishing Tozzi'd just shut up and eat his goddamn sandwich the way it was. Who the hell wanted to hear Selma now? She was the reason he didn't come here all that often. That sick cow face and the dramatic sighs and the breast beating as she cried on your shoulder with that same old story of hers. Jesus.

Gibbons ate as Tozzi kept waving and eventually Selma came waddling over, jiggling her D-cups, pencils stuck out of either side of the lacquered red hairdo that didn't move. "What can I do for you, hon?"

Tozzi explained his big problem in great detail. He sounded like some old lady complaining down at the Social Security office. Gibbons kept eating, trying not to pay attention, hoping he could ignore what he knew was going to come next, the sad tale of Lydia and Morris.

When Tozzi finished with his complaint, Selma shook her head slowly and clucked, pulling the sick cow face. She sighed and squeezed into the booth next to Tozzi, shoving him over with her hip. Shit. Here we go.

"You know Rudy never used to make these kind of mistakes," she said with another long, dramatic sigh. "You have to forgive him. He hasn't been the same since Lydia left him."

Gibbons looked over at the short guy with the bad toupee making sandwiches behind the counter. He didn't look so bad.

She sighed again, paused, then started her story. "That Lydia—a beautiful woman, I can't deny that—but trouble from the word go. Never wanted to work here in the deli. She thought it was beneath her. Not even hostessing she would do. 'It's okay,' I told Rudy at the time. 'We can manage.' I mean, who needed her, the Jezebel? She couldn't pour a cup of coffee without spilling to save her life. And the few times she did work here, she just flirted with anyone who'd pay attention to her—and believe me, everybody paid attention to Lydia. Even my Morris, the schnook."

Selma looked up at the ceiling now and rapped her knuckles on her chest a few times. "Six days a week my brother and I ride the Long Island Expressway at the crack of dawn to open this place up. Four-twenty in the morning, every morning, Rudy picks me up. For twenty-two years we've been doing this. So how were we supposed to know that back in Hempstead, my sister-in-law Lydia was keeping the sheets warm for that son-of-a-bitch husband of mine? Come to find out they'd been doing it for years, practically from the day that bitch—excuse my language—stood under the *chuppah* with my poor brother. Can you imagine? We don't know nothing, Rudy and me. We're busy working here. Then one day the two of them troop in here just before the lunch rush and tell us that they're in love and that they're leaving together. Rudy's stunned, he can't work for the rest of the day. Me, I want to kill her. One of the dishwashers had to stop me, actually physically had to stop me. I had the bread knife right here in my hand. I was going to slice her up like a *challah*, the *farshtinkener* bitch."

Selma paused to shake her head and sigh again. "There it was, ten to twelve, and I'm watching the two of them get into our Chrysler—which, by the way, had just seven payments left on it, most of which was paid for by yours truly—and I see them drive off, heading for who the hell knows where. Never saw them again, the both of them. The car either. And it was a nice car, too. I hope she made his life miserable." She sighed again and stared off into space.

"That's awful," Tozzi said. He looked uncomfortable. Probably felt guilty for bothering a woman with such troubles for something as trivial as Russian dressing. The sap.

Gibbons bit into his pastrami and stared at her as he chewed. "How long ago did that happen, Selma?"

She focused her eyes on Gibbons's and narrowed them with vengeance. "I'll never forget. It was a nice sunny Friday in April. Nineteen-seventy-two."

Gibbons nodded. "Life is tough, Selma." He still had a hairline in '72. So did Rudy, probably. He glanced over at Tozzi who was trying to look sympathetic when he was really wishing she'd just go away and let them eat. You satisfied, asshole?

"Rudy never got over it, huh?" Tozzi's concern sounded lame.

Selma suddenly whipped her head around and nearly put Tozzi's eye out with one of her pencils. "Could *you* get over something like that?" she said. "How could you? My brother deserved better than her. He was a good-looking man. He could've done better."

"Say, Selma," Gibbons said, finally fed up with the soap opera, "how about a refill on the coffee when you get a chance?"

Suddenly she seemed to come back to her senses. "Oh, sure,

hon, I'm sorry. It's just that I get carried away when I talk about—"

"Yeah, I know." He cut her off before she got started again. She struggled out of the brown vinyl-upholstered booth and stood up, patting the back of her hairdo. "I'll be right back with a fresh pot."

"And will you bring this guy some Russian for his sandwich?" Gibbons called after her. "Before he has a conniption fit," he added under his breath.

"You're a real sweet guy, Gib. The lady's pouring her heart out and all you're worried about is your coffee."

"I've heard the story before. Anyway you're the one who called her over because you didn't get your goddamn Russian."

Selma returned then with a Pyrex pot of coffee and a paper cup of Russian dressing for Tozzi. "There you go, boys. Everything hunky-dory now?"

Gibbons looked up at her. "Yeah, hunky-dory."

"Thanks, Selma," Tozzi said nicely, trying to make up for his partner's rude behavior.

"Okee-doke." She turned and waddled down to the next booth to peddle her refills.

"Now," Gibbons said, tearing the foil off a little plastic cup of half and half and dumping it into his cup, "fly that cock-and-bull story by me once more, the one you were trying to sell me before you had to have your little Russian incident."

Tozzi frowned. "Look, I know you think this is bullshit, but I heard them talking about it. I was right there lying on my stomach under the shrubs. D'Urso is importing slaves from Japan."

Gibbons sipped his coffee. "I don't buy it, Toz."

"Why not? Christ, I saw Japanese nannies all over Milburn. Roxanne Eastlake, the woman at the nanny agency I told you about, told me it's D'Urso's wife who's handling them. Also, I overheard them talking about the 'yaks.' They could've been referring to the yakuza, the Japanese Mafia."

Gibbons closed his eyes and shook his head. Here he goes again. First it's a devil cult, then it's a karate killer, now it's the yakuza. Gibbons decided not even to comment on it. "I still don't buy this Japanese slave-trade shit. It doesn't make sense."

"Why not?"

"Because Japan is a rich country and everything is expensive over there. If you were gonna buy slaves, you'd buy them cheap, right? Get them from some dirt-poor third-world country, right? Not from a country where a steak costs you eighty bucks. Am I right?"

Tozzi rubbed his mouth. He was getting frustrated. Logic that didn't jibe with his version of reality had a way of doing that to him. "All I know is what I heard."

"So why don't you go tell Ivers."

Tozzi was glaring at him now. Gibbons smiled like a crocodile. He knew why. "Well, you can't say the man didn't warn you, Toz. If you had reason to believe there was something going on at D'Urso's house, why didn't you ask for a wiretap? He's gonna be real happy to hear about you sneaking through the bushes, eavesdropping on D'Urso with nothing on tape, nothing we can use against him in court. I swear to God, Tozzi, you get smarter everyday."

"Okay, fine. Now that we've established that I'm the fuckup here, and you've gotten your licks in, how about if we decide how we're gonna proceed with this?"

"What do you mean 'we'?"

"We're partners on this case. Remember?"

"Unfortunately, I do."

"Good, I'm glad to see the Alzheimer's hasn't set in too badly yet."

Gibbons sipped his coffee and ignored the comment. "What have you got in mind, Sherlock? I can't wait to hear."

"I want you to go to D'Urso's chicken processing plant in Harrison and check it out. It's called Farm-Fresh Poultry, and it's supposed to be one of his legit fronts, but from what they were saying on his deck the other day, I have a feeling he may be using slave workers there."

"So why don't *you* go? You got something against chickens?"

"His brother-in-law knows my face. He thinks I work for the gardener."

"Who the hell is this brother-in-law? What are you worrying about him for?"

"His name is Bobby Francione. He's on file in the computer. Just got out of Rahway a little while ago. He was into stealing cars for a high-ticket chop shop up in Bergen County. Only German cars—Mercedes, Audis, and BMWs. His file says he was little more than a gofer, but I have a feeling he's got big ambitions now. He seems pretty tight with D'Urso."

Gibbons propped his face on his hand and looked at Tozzi sideways. "Why should *I* have to go to Harrison? Why not get someone from the Newark office to check out the chickens?"

"You know why. Because I'd have to go through Ivers who would want to know why I suspect D'Urso and how I arrived at those suspicions, et cetera, et cetera."

"And you don't want to tell him you've been moonlighting with a gardener for purposes of unlawful surveillance."

Tozzi nodded as he finally took a big bite out of his sandwich. The coleslaw inside dripped out the bottom and through his fingers. He seemed satisfied. Gibbons wondered if this was what they meant by "hog heaven."

"Besides," Tozzi said with his mouth full, "Newark operates like the Keystone Kops. They think they're the Untouchables over there. Very unsubtle."

"I've never heard that." In fact, he had.

"Come on, Gib. I was hoping you could get in and out of there without showing your ID. Just look around, see how many slanty eyes you can count. If you find a few, then we'll have something to work with, something we can go to Ivers with."

"And what will I tell him when he asks what the hell I was doing out of our jurisdiction?"

"Don't worry about it. We'll cook something up. Just go check out the chicken shack. Please."

Gibbons rubbed his nose with the back of his finger. Goddamn Tozzi. Always had to go through the back door first. Slaves. From Japan. With the yakuza. He was fucking crazy. How about a simple, illegal alien shakedown, just like the kind of shit that goes down every day on the Mexican border? Someone knew those two kids were sneaking into the country. They were easy prey. They were probably robbed and killed for whatever money they had on them. Simple as that. The only twist was that they came from Japan, not Central America, and it happened somewhere in New York Harbor, not down in Texas or out in California. That's what *he* thought this was all about. But Tozzi didn't want to hear about that. It was too logical.

"So will you do it?" Tozzi persisted. "Will you check out the chicken shack?"

Gibbons just stared at him. If he didn't go, Tozzi wouldn't stop bothering him with this slave shit. He might even go over there himself, risk being recognized by this brother-in-law and getting his head blown off. He was that stupid. It would be easier to just go, prove him wrong, and get this stupidity over with. Then maybe they could get down to a more realistic investigation.

"Are you going to do it or not?" Tozzi insisted as he stuffed his face. "Tell me now."

Gibbons reached over and stole the pickle from Tozzi's plate. They were the kind he liked—crunchy, not too sour. He bit off half of it and chewed slowly. "I'll think about it."

Tozzi looked disgruntled. Gibbons knew he liked these kind of pickles, too. "I didn't say you could have that."

Gibbons took another bite. "Sorry."

This was damn weird. Gibbons hated to admit that Tozzi might be right, but something was very wrong here. He was standing in the middle of the processing floor at the Farm-Fresh Poultry factory, watching chicken carcasses hung on a conveyer line shuttling from station to station. One after another, they were submerged in big vats of bloody water, then some were detoured to stainless-steel tables where they were cut into parts, others sent whole to a machine that wrapped them in plastic and spit them out onto a conveyer belt. The clack and rumble of the machines was the only noise in the place because the people who worked here didn't say "boo," not to him, not to each other. They worked fast and steady, like the rest of the machinery, eyes down, no expression on their faces whatsoever. And goddamn it, there wasn't a round eye in the house. Every last one of them was Oriental.

Whether they were Japanese or not, he had no idea. And if they were slaves, they sure as hell weren't saying. They sure worked like slaves, but the doors weren't locked. He'd walked right in. But if these guys were slaves, where were the overseers? Who was in charge here? There were no cars in the front lot, and aside from a few trucks at the loading dock, there was just a sad-looking white Dodge parked out back, a traveling salesman's kind of car, definitely not the kind of vehicle Mafia guys like.

Gibbons walked over to one of the vats where six of these young guys, three on each side, were washing chickens. One of them had a nasty black-and-blue mark on the side of his face. Globs of chicken fat floated on the briny pink water, and it smelled worse than it looked. How could you ever eat chicken again after smelling this?

"Hey, fellas, where can I find the boss?"

They kept scrubbing those damn chickens, eyes down.

"The boss," he repeated, raising his voice over the noise. "Where's the boss?"

It was as if he wasn't there.

"Anybody speak English? Do you understand me? English?"

He stared into each face one by one, trying to make some eye contact. Nothing.

He didn't like this at all. Even if they'd been warned not to talk to strangers, these poor schlumps wouldn't even look at him, didn't acknowledge his presence in any way. Other than retards and robots, only people with something serious to fear behave this way. It made Gibbons nervous.

"Okay, this is your last chance, boys." He pulled out his ID and waved it at them, hoping something that looked official might goose them a little. "Special Agent Gibbons of the Federal Bureau of Investigation. Like the police but better. Savvy? So if any of you knows English, speak now or forever hold your peace."

The one with the bruised face looked up, then looked away quickly when Gibbons made eye contact. "You got something to tell me?"

No response.

Gibbons put his ID back into his pocket. "Thanks a lot," he muttered as he turned away and walked toward the iron gridwork stairs that led to the second floor. The offices must be up there, he figured.

Gibbons started to mount the steps when he noticed a couple of guys at another vat staring at something on the other side of the room. He turned around and saw another Oriental guy standing in the doorway by the front entrance, just standing there staring at him. The guy was as wide as he was tall. He looked like a beetle standing up on its hind legs, wearing a loud black-and-white houndstooth sports jacket.

"You in charge here?" Gibbons called over to him.

The beetle nodded and started walking toward him, no expression on his face.

"I want to ask you a few questions," Gibbons said. He came down off the steps to meet the nodding beetle. "Listen, I—"

Suddenly the beetle took a giant leap and was airborne, one foot extended, aimed directly at Gibbons's face. Gibbons tried to get out of the way, but there was no time. The foot caught him in the shoulder. He fell flat on his back, hit hard, and slid a few feet on the wet sawdust that littered the tile floor. The fall knocked the wind out of him, but he managed to reach into his jacket and pull his gun. He held it on the big beetle who was standing over him, staring down at Excalibur with contempt.

Takayuki stopped breathing when he saw the gun emerge. He froze where he stood with his hands in the cold greasy water of the vat. He should have said something. He should have warned the policeman about Mashiro.

"Back off, Tojo," the policeman shouted, but Takayuki already guessed what Mashiro's next move would be. It happened so fast all he saw was the gun skittling across the floor and hitting the wall, and Mashiro's foot snapping back after he kicked the man's hand.

The policeman scrambled to get to his feet then. He got to one knee, but Mashiro's lightning fist caught him square in the chest and knocked him back onto his haunches. He rolled over onto his side and clutched his chest, wincing and gasping for breath. Takayuki immediately feared that the man was having a heart attack. He could feel the pain radiating through the poor man's torso. He knew from experience.

Mashiro stood back, waiting. The policeman tried to focus his blurry vision on the samurai, but then he looked over at Takayuki's work station. Takayuki panicked. He was looking right at him.

* * *

Lorraine . . . I promised her this wouldn't happen . . . I said I wouldn't get hurt . . . fuck . . . help me, boys . . . I can't get hurt . . . she'll kill me. . . .

"Hey . . ." He winced and forced out a grunt. "How about giving me a hand, boys?" It hurt to breathe. "No, huh. For Lorraine?—*oooph!*"

Mashiro's foot found that same spot in the middle of his chest. The man was writhing in the sawdust now. God, he wished he could stop this. Maybe if they all rushed the samurai at once? Takayuki glanced around the room at the pale, scared faces of his companions and knew they'd never do it. They'd all seen the devastating power of Mashiro's skills. They were as scared as he was.

Cold sweat covered his face. The stupid man was on his hands and knees now, struggling for breath with his forehead on the filthy floor. Stay down, fool. Fake it.

Mashiro was hovering over the policeman, his legs wide apart, testing the distance between his open hand and the man's neck, the same way a karate master sizes up a stack of boards. Takayuki's breath was short. He knew what was coming.

Looking all around him, wishing there was something he could do, Takayuki reached for the only weapon available, a plucked chicken hanging right over his face on the conveyer line. He grabbed it by the legs and flung it fast. The chicken soared and hit the hump of Mashiro's back just as his hand was reaching its target. The policeman collapsed on the dirty floor flat on his belly. He wasn't moving.

Mashiro whipped around, crouched to confront his attacker, but all he found was the yellow-skinned chicken lying at his feet. He glared at them all one by one, searching each face for a sign of guilt. When he came to Takayuki, he stopped.

Takayuki felt faint. He thought his legs were going to buckle under him they were shaking so badly. Mashiro knew it was him. He already had a black mark against him for going to D'Urso and demanding to know what happened to his cousin. In an instant he considered dozens of impossible retaliations against the samurai's inevitable attack, even though in his heart he knew that nothing he could ever do would hinder this madman. Takayuki clenched his teeth and braced himself for the slaughter.

But when Mashiro suddenly turned away and went over to pick up the policeman's gun, Takayuki's pulse raced even faster. He watched Mashiro put the gun in his pocket as he walked back, then the samurai hunkered down over the policeman's still body and put his fingers to the man's neck. He rolled back the man's eyelids, then slowly rotated his head, feeling the back of his neck. Finally Mashiro nodded and muttered something that ended with a short laugh. The samurai took the man's lifeless arm and hauled him up, getting under his limp body and carrying him out to the loading dock over his shoulder.

After Mashiro had passed through the plastic strips that hung over the loading dock bay, Takayuki listened to the silence as he stared at the chicken on the floor, sawdust clinging to its skin. It was quiet for only a moment, though, as his companions went right back to work as if nothing had happened. He scanned the groups of animated bodies, continuous motion under the harsh fluorescent lights, and wondered if they were human anymore. Then he went back to work, too.

18

The elevator lurched to a stop. Tozzi's stomach was jumpy enough. "Come on, come on," he said, impatient for the doors to open.

Roxanne stood next to him, looking uncomfortable. "Maybe I should wait for you down in the lobby."

"No, stay with me." He was looking up at the lighted number "9" over the elevator doors, the floor Gibbons was on. Nine was Tozzi's lucky number. He hoped it was lucky for Gib, too. The elevator doors parted then. The first thing he saw was Brant Ivers standing by the nurses' station talking to a stocky doctor in a white lab coat. The doctor had a big bushy beard and wore wire-rim glasses. He looked like one of the Grateful Dead. Tozzi hoped he wasn't Gibbons's doctor. Gibbons would hate him.

"Mike." Ivers extended his arm and drew Tozzi into their conversation. He clasped Tozzi's shoulder firmly, brothers-in-arms, as if he actually liked him. Asshole.

"How is he?" Tozzi asked.

"We don't know yet," Ivers answered before the doctor could get a word out. "We're waiting for his CAT scan results right now."

"Is he awake?"

"Well—" the doctor started, but Ivers cut him off.

"He seemed to be coming out of it about two hours ago, but then he fell back into the coma."

"Not a coma, technically," the doctor corrected. He seemed remarkably patient with Iver's horning in on his territory.

"Anyway he's unconscious now," Ivers said. "They're doing the best they can for him." He pressed his lips together, touched the doctor's shoulder, and smiled encouragingly at him.

A born leader, that Ivers. Tozzi wondered where the hell guys like Ivers learn this stuff.

"Your cousin is here, Mike." Ivers nodded down the hall. "Go see her. She's by herself. I'll let you know as soon as we know anything."

Oh, God, Lorraine. She must be a mess. Tozzi nodded and started heading down the hall, then remembered Roxanne was there. He grabbed her hand and dragged her along with him.

"This may be awkward, Mike. You sure I shouldn't wait downstairs?"

"No, stay. Please."

As they entered the visitors' lounge, he spotted Lorraine right away. She was sitting by herself with her legs tucked under her on an apple-green vinyl couch, a collection of paper coffee cups on the coffeetable in front of her. She was wearing one of her "school marm" outfits, a light brown suit with a lacy blouse and a string tie. Gibbons always complained about her "school marm" clothes. She must've come straight from class. She was staring out into space.

"Lorraine. How you doing?"

Lorraine blinked and looked up. She looked at Roxanne first and frowned. Then she saw him. "Oh, Michael. It's you." She took his hand and pulled him down next to her on the couch. Roxanne stood there, looking like she'd rather be somewhere else.

"Lorraine, this is a friend of mine. Roxanne Eastlake."

Lorraine worked up a smile and a nod.

Roxanne sat down in the orange vinyl armchair on the other side of the white Formica coffeetable. "I'm sorry to hear about—"

"Please," Lorraine raised her hand, "no more condolences. I've heard enough of that already. He's not dead yet."

Roxanne pursed her lips and looked at Tozzi.

He shrugged. The woman was under pressure. Can't expect her to be polite under these circumstances.

Lorraine let out a long sigh then. "I'm sorry if I was sharp," she said to Roxanne. "I'm sorry . . ."

"It's okay," Roxanne murmured.

Tozzi started cracking his knuckles before he realized what he was doing. Maybe Rox should've waited downstairs. "How is he?" he asked his cousin. "What're they saying?"

Lorraine pushed the hair out of her face and shrugged. "There's a blonde nurse who keeps coming out on the hour, telling me not to worry, he'll be all right. But the surgeon made me feel like I should go out and start pricing tombstones. The doctor with the beard said something about a concussion and a terrible bruise on his chest. Everytime I ask him for an update, he keeps saying we have to wait for all the test results to come in before they can determine anything for certain. I'm all confused."

"What happened? They didn't have any details when I called in at the office."

"All I know is what your boss Mr. Ivers told me. The people down in the Emergency Room this afternoon say that a heavyset Asian man carried Gibbons in, set him down on an empty gurney, took Excalibur out of his pocket, returned it to Gibbons's holster, and then walked right out. Apparently this Asian man had driven Gibbons's car here because it was found abandoned with the keys in the ignition in an ambulance bay. There are FBI people examining the car and his gun for fingerprints and whatever else they look for. There's a forensics man—I forget his name—conferring with the doctors. That's all I know about it." Lorraine shut her eyes and squeezed out a tear. "He promised me he'd take care of himself, Michael. He said he wouldn't let this happen. Damn him."

Tozzi nodded. It's never a matter of *not* letting it happen. It just happens. You have to deal with it as best you can when it does. He looked at Roxanne who was sitting with her hands in her lap like a kid waiting in the principal's office.

"Why do you guys hate him so much?" Lorraine suddenly asked.

"Who?"

"Ivers."

"He's an asshole."

"He seemed nice enough to me."

"Yeah, well, maybe Ivers isn't that bad." Tozzi wasn't going to get into this with Lorraine, not now.

"Of course, there is something about him—I can't put my finger on it. I imagine if you had to deal with him on a regular basis, he could get under your skin."

Yeah, like herpes.

"Mike?" Ivers was standing twenty feet away in the doorway, waving him over. Tozzi could see the Grateful Dead doctor walking down the hallway the other way. "Can I see you for a minute?"

"Sure." Tozzi stood up and looked at Roxanne. Lorraine was still hanging onto his hand. "I'll be right back," he whispered to them. "He must want me for some FBI bullshit. I'll be right back." He let go of Lorraine's hand and raised his eyebrows at Roxanne as he turned to see what Ivers wanted.

Lorraine stared at her cousin walking over to his boss. Ivers pulled him out into the hallway where they huddled, brows furrowed, one talking, the other nodding, both very serious. She shook her head and started to laugh bitterly. "They always do this, the two of them."

"Pardon?" Roxanne said.

"Michael and Gibbons. They have a way of denigrating what's topmost in their minds. Just 'some FBI bullshit.' Ha! God, they live and breathe for the Bureau. I don't know what they'd do without it." Lorraine leaned forward and picked up her paper coffeecup. She looked down at the cold coffee, considered it, then put it back down.

"Would you like a fresh cup?" Roxanne said. "I'll see if I can find one for you."

Michael's girlfriend was uncomfortable. She was looking for an excuse to escape. Lorraine remembered feeling that way when her father was in the hospital, dying of cancer. It seemed like he was on the verge of death for months. She dreaded going to the hospital and was always eager to run any errand for anyone just to get out of that damned pink waiting room. "No, that's okay. I've had too much coffee already."

"It's no bother. Really."

Lorraine listened to her accent and for the first time took a good look at her. British? Not Michael's type. Lorraine scowled at herself. Christ, I sound just like my mother.

"It must be awful waiting here like this, not knowing anything." Roxanne was trying to be cheery. She didn't know what else to say.

"It's pretty awful . . . not much fun."

"Yes . . . I can imagine."

Could she? She was very pretty. Michael's a sucker for a pretty face. That's what Gibbons always told her.

Roxanne flashed another cheery smile. She was trying, she really was, but what the hell can you say to someone who's been sitting on a plastic couch all day waiting to hear if the man she loves is going to live, die, or be a cripple? What do you say?

Lorraine looked at the ceiling and blinked back the new tears. Christ, this was so self-indulgent. Enough already.

"Roxanne," she started, wiping her eyes, "are you . . . are you and Michael . . . seeing each other?"

"Well, yes . . . sort of. But I don't think you want to discuss—"

"I hope you haven't fallen in love with him yet," she murmured.

"Pardon?"

Lorraine blushed. She hadn't meant to say that out loud. "I'm sorry. That must've sounded very hostile. I didn't mean it that way."

"You're putting me in your position, aren't you?" Roxanne's eager smile faded. So did her accent. She was pretty when she smiled; handsome when she didn't. A very unconventional beauty.

Lorraine sighed. "All day I've been thinking about what it must be like to be a cop's wife, but being married to a special agent has to be worse. It doesn't end at the end of a shift. They're always on the job, it seems, in mortal danger eighty percent of the time. That's the way it seems to me. It's not easy to love a man like that."

"Is Gibbons particularly . . . exuberant about his job?"

"Exuberant? No. He gripes about it all the time. He's dedicated, yes. Tenacious. Obsessed, too. But exuberant? No, that's Michael, I think. It was him I used to worry about more than Gibbons."

"Why?" Roxanne looked surprised. She must not know him very well.

"He's reckless, a daredevil. And hard-headed, too. God, some of the things he's done, you can't even begin to imagine." She stopped short and caught herself. She shouldn't be telling her all this. It must sound awful.

"I may be taking you the wrong way, Lorraine, but somehow this sounds like a warning."

Lorraine looked down at the coffeetable. "This is all premature, Roxanne. You two just met. I shouldn't be scaring you like this."

"You're not scaring me. I think you're just concerned. And worried."

Lorraine looked her in the eye and saw Roxanne in her shoes. She may not think so now, but it could happen to her, too. God forbid. Lorraine pushed the hair out of her face. She knew she looked like a wreck, but from Roxanne's point of view, maybe she seemed more like the ghost of Jacob Marley dragging his chains. Good. Roxanne needed a healthy dose of fear and reality. Nothing against Michael and his budding prospects, but she should be warned. No woman deserves to go through this.

Lorraine then noticed the doctor with the beard standing out in the hall with Michael and Ivers. He was talking and they were listening. She couldn't read his expression through the beard and glasses. Her stomach clenched, then cramped. She couldn't move. He's dead. That's what he's telling them. Michael's going to come over and tell her Gibbons is dead.

Michael was nodding to the doctor. She crossed her arms and pressed her forearms against her stomach. He turned away from the two men and came into the room. She wanted to double over, but she was petrified.

"Lorraine," he said softly.

Always the gentle, soothing voice breaking the bad news. He reached out for her hand, but she couldn't move. He sat down next to her and touched her knee. No, don't say it!

"Lorraine, the doctor just told us. He woke up. He's gonna be all right. He's out of the woods."

She closed her eyes and felt it all drain out of her until she was limp and empty, a spent balloon on the ground. He's going to be all right. Dear God. "He's going to be all right," she repeated in a whisper.

19

The streets were deserted as Tozzi drove down Harrison Avenue. He saw a yellow light up ahead and sped through it, then immediately let up on the accelerator and brought it back down to forty. He didn't want to give a cop on the graveyard shift something to do, but it was a struggle to stay off the pedal. It seemed calm outside his windshield, but inside his head he was ready to explode. Roxanne said she could see it in his face when he came back from seeing Gibbons after he woke up. She kept looking at him funny every time he gunned across an intersection on their way back to her apartment. She invited him to come in for awhile, asking him not to go yet. She knew he was crazy, and she was afraid he'd do something crazy. But she hadn't seen Gibbons's swollen face bursting out of the plastic neck brace, or the black-and-blue mark with the knuckle prints on his chest. She hadn't heard him mumbling and rambling, barely coherent he was so doped up with painkillers. Tozzi knew he was crazy, that he was liable to do something he'd regret, but she didn't understand. This was *Gibbons* they tried to kill, *Gibbons.*

What Gibbons had been able to tell him, he already knew or just assumed. He'd been attacked at the chicken factory by a stocky Asian man wearing a loud black-and-white check sports jacket over a black knit shirt. Gibbons also said something about a lot of Oriental guys just hanging around and watching. Tozzi figured these were probably slaves—unless they were yakuza. Tozzi asked him to describe them, but Gibbons was too out of it to answer.

Either way he knew he had to check the place out for himself. He knew going there alone wasn't the smartest thing in the world, but at two in the morning, D'Urso's troops weren't going to be in full force. Anyway, part of him wanted somebody to start something with him, give him an excuse to go wild. His nerves were jangling, and he was itching to pay somebody back for what happened to Gibbons because that was no ordinary assault. It was vicious and brutal . . . and it was Gibbons.

Tozzi was trembling deep in his chest he was so mad. He knew it was wrong, but he wanted revenge and he wanted it badly. It was the kind of self-righteous thinking that had gotten him into trouble before, but that just didn't seem to relate now. He tried to control this fury, he even tried to use things he'd learned at aikido class to get himself under control—keep one point, relax completely, never do anything out of anger. But as much sense as that made in class, he couldn't apply it to himself, not now. Japanese wisdom had no appeal, not when it was a Japanese hitman who'd beaten the shit out of his partner.

The tires squealed as he turned left off Harrison Avenue onto Queenstown Street, following it out until the road went from asphalt to cobblestones and the streetlights became scarcer between the prefab warehouses and the grim brick factories. Farm-Fresh Poultry was at the end of this dead-end on the left, a dingy brick factory dating from the twenties surrounded by a high cyclone fence. There were no lights on inside as far as he could see. Tozzi cruised by and made a U-turn at the end of the street, which was stupid, he realized as he did it. If someone was in there, the sweeping headlights may have already alerted him. It wasn't the kind of street where cars just happen to get lost in the middle of a week night. But as he made his turn and his lights beamed into the lot behind the building, he noticed something odd. He stopped and backed up a few feet to get a better look.

There were three pathetic-looking truck trailers parked in the corner of the lot. One was bashed in on top; another was listing to one side on a flat tire. Judging from the height of the weeds that had grown up around them, they hadn't been on the road in some time. But the peculiar thing was that there were power lines running from the factory to each of the trailers. And on top of each one there was a refrigeration unit of some kind, which looked odd to him. Refrigeration units were usually on the front of the trailer, right over the cab of the tractor. They could've been keeping frozen chickens in those trailers, but somehow Tozzi didn't think so. They seemed too makeshift for that.

He pulled up to the curb, switched off his lights, and cut the engine. Moonlight beamed off the coils of razor wire on top of the cyclone fence. Pretty mean-looking stuff just to keep chickens in.

Tozzi got out and fetched the bolt cutters out of the trunk. He went to the section of fence where the shadows were darkest and quickly snipped as many links as he thought he'd need to squeeze through. Maybe they wouldn't notice a small hole right away, he thought, tossing the cutters back into the trunk. He pried open the flaps in the fence and forced his way through. Gouging himself on the sharp ends, he wished he'd cut a few more links. Too late now.

He walked around the perimeter of the fence, staying as far as possible from the spread of the floodlights attached to the corners of the factory. As he approached the trailers, he could hear the drone of those refrigeration units, which up close seemed more like the kind of central air-conditioning units you see tucked behind the shrubs in the suburbs. The first thing he thought of was an afterhours gambling joint, but there were no cars in the lot. When he walked up to the nearest trailer, he noticed a shiny new padlock in the rusty door hasp. He put his ear to the cold gray metal, but all he could hear was the vibrations of the droning air-conditioner on top. He reached into his pocket for his Pik-Ez set and went to work on the lock. It popped open easily enough. Opening the door was going to be the hard part. Tozzi pulled the .44 Special Bulldog out of his belt clip, not knowing what the hell to expect.

The rusty hasp sounded like fingernails on a blackboard as he moved the handle and threw open one of the doors. The floodlights cast weird shadows inside the dark compartment, shadows with eyes that shined back at him, a lot of eyes.

Jesus, Mary, and Joseph. He was afraid he'd find something like this.

Tozzi climbed in slowly, his gun pointed up but at the ready. Despite the noisy air-conditioners, the air was hot and wet in there, the stink overpowering, like a combination of BO and artificial roses.

Light from the parking lot angled into the trailer. Metal-frame bunk beds lining the walls on both sides, three high. As his eyes adjusted to the dim light in there, he could make out a few of the sallow faces peering at him. He took a step forward and suddenly heard an agitated voice coming from the shadows in the back. He could barely hear it over the noisy vent in the ceiling.

"Anyone speak English here?"

The complainer continued to jabber in what Tozzi guessed was Japanese as he stepped out of the shadows. Tozzi was surprised to see how young he was, just a teenager. He was also surprised when he realized that the kid wasn't talking to him. He was harping at one of his buddies in a bottom bunk. "*Takayuki! Takayuki!*" he kept repeating, then he turned to Tozzi. "This Takayuki," he said in broken English, pointing down at the bunk. "He talk."

The kid hunkered down next to the bunk and jabbered even more insistently now, this Takayuki guy in the bunk replying in what seemed like one-word answers. Finally Takayuki rolled out of the shadows and stood up in the aisle, facing Tozzi. He was a kid too, and he had a nasty bruise that covered one side of his face like an unlucky birthmark. It was hard to tell in the dim light, but Tozzi guessed from the gray-yellow color of the bruise that the beating had been several days ago.

"We will not work now," he said to Tozzi in very good English.

"What?"

"No more night work. That was not in our agreement. We must refuse."

Tozzi fingered the gun in his hand and suddenly realized that these poor bastards probably thought he was one of D'Urso's goons here to drag them back to the factory. He stared at Takayuki's bruised face and felt for him. He was making a stand but his tone was so weary and resigned. It was as if he were just saying this because he felt he had to, not because he thought it would do any good.

Tozzi put his gun away. "I'm not one of D'Urso's men. I'm with the FBI."

No reaction.

"I'm a federal law-enforcement agent . . . a policeman. Do you understand what I'm saying? I'm rescuing you guys." Tozzi smiled and nodded his head to reassure them.

Takayuki shook his head. He looked even sadder now. "Thank you for coming, but please leave now. And please lock the door behind you. Thank you."

"What?"

"You don't understand. If the lock is not secured, they will think we tried to escape. The consequences for that are severe."

"Who's 'they'? D'Urso?"

"Yes, D'Urso," he said tentatively. "But it's usually Nagai's men who do the actual punishment."

"Nagai?"

"Yes. Nagai. Who else? The Fugukai enforces the rules. They were the ones who brought us here. Surely you must know this . . ." Takayuki's eyes widened as his voice trailed off.

The names started to register with Tozzi. D'Urso, his wife, and her brother had mentioned Nagai and the Fugukai on the deck the other day. There was another guy they talked about, too. What the hell was his name? "Do you know someone called . . . Mashiro?"

The inside of the trailer suddenly went dead silent. The vent kept sucking like a mechanical blow-hole. "Tell me," Tozzi finally said. "I can help you."

Takayuki hunkered down next to his bunk, lifted the thin mattress, and pulled out a worn newspaper. Tozzi recognized it right away. It was a copy of the *Post* from last week. He remembered the headline. DEATH BUG FOUND IN HARBOR.

Takayuki held up the newspaper for Tozzi to see. "We steal newspapers from the truck drivers so we can know what's going on in the world. These two people who were killed? My cousin and his fiancée. They tried to escape, but Mashiro found them. This was their punishment."

"Do you know this for sure? Are you certain Mashiro killed them?"

"I'm sure. Mashiro handles all the punishments." Takayuki turned his face to the light and ran his index finger along his bruised cheek. It was worse than Tozzi thought. "The work of the yakuza samurai," Takayuki said bitterly. "Pain and death are his purpose for being."

Tozzi looked around at the scared faces. "A friend of mine came here to the factory yesterday. An older man, gray hair, about my height—"

Takayuki was already nodding. "Yes, Mashiro did that, too. Is your friend still alive?"

Tozzi was put off by the presumptive question. Why did he automatically assume that Gibbons was dead? Was Mashiro that bad? "Yeah, he's alive. He's in the hospital, but he'll be all right."

"That's good. I am relieved. I apologize for not doing more to help your friend, but interfering with Mashiro often means death. He was going to break your friend's neck, but I threw a chicken at him. I hoped it would break his concentration."

"His concentration?"

"Karate. It's one of Mashiro's deadly arts. He was attempting to break your friend's neck with his bare hand."

Tozzi closed his eyes. His head was beginning to pound. He wanted to hit something, break something. This fat-ass Mashiro in his stupid check jacket was settling into the crosshairs of his anger. "Explain something to me," he said, forcing himself to breathe evenly so he could calm down enough to talk. "How did this happen to you? Were you all kidnapped? How did you get here?"

"In the trunk of a Toyota Corolla. Very tight."

"You mean they smuggled you people into the country in the trunks of new cars?"

Takayuki nodded. "On cargo ships from Japan. They put us in trunks the night before the ship was loaded. We remained hidden until we were far out at sea. As we approached America, we had to go back into the trunks again. Sometimes many days lying in one position, in the dark, breathing through an air hose. Very—what's the word in English?—claustrophobia. When I came over, unloading took longer than anticipated. I had consumed all my food and drink. I went without for, I think, two whole days."

"How the hell could they do this to you? It's . . . unbelievable."

Takayuki shrugged. "It was bad. But not as bad as living under the oppression of Mashiro and the Fugukai."

"How . . . how did they do it? Were you all kidnapped?"

"No, we were not kidnapped. We agreed to come."

"You *agreed* to come?"

"Yes, of course. We all signed contracts with the Fugukai."

Takayuki turned back to his companions and said something in Japanese. Several of them rustled through their belongings and pulled out folded sheets of paper to show Tozzi. Their contracts.

Tozzi just shook his head in disbelief. "The Fugukai is a yakuza gang, right?"

"Yes. The Blow Fish Gang in English."

"Why the hell would you sign any kind of deal with the yakuza? They're criminals. Do you know that? What made you think you could trust them? What did you think you were going to get out of this deal?"

"We got it. Passage to America, the land of opportunity."

Tozzi rolled his eyes. "I'm caught in a fucking time warp," he muttered under his breath. "I don't understand."

"I will explain. The Fugukai offered to get us to America in exchange for our services. We were led to believe that we would have good jobs in the fields of our interests. Obviously they lied to us about that. But you see, we wanted to come to America so we could succeed in life and regain our lost honor. In Japan we are labeled failures because we did not score high enough on our university entrance exams. If we had stayed in Japan, we would have only qualified for jobs as clerks, secretaries, assistant store managers, postal employees."

Tozzi's Uncle Frank, Lorraine's father, had been a mailman. "So what's wrong with that?"

"Failure is disgrace. How can you face your friends and family when they know you are a person without honor?"

"Come on, there's more to life than school. Can't you get ahead on the job in Japan?"

"Very difficult. The jobs we could get pay very little

money, and everything in Japan is very expensive. Japan is a prosperous country, yes, but prosperity is only for the prosperous. The salaries we could earn would only pay for the bare necessities: a small one-room apartment, two, maybe three hours commuting time from Tokyo, a very tiny car, enough food but nothing special, a small stereo and a television but none of the elaborate electronic equipment our country proudly exports to the world. Not easy for a failure to get ahead in our country." Takayuki coughed out a humorless laugh. "We did not want to be slaves to menial jobs. The Fugukai told us that in America the system was different. Desire and diligence counted for more here. We could succeed here, regain our honor, make our parents proud of us again. That's what they told us and we believed them."

"How did you kids get involved with the yakuza in the first place? You were students for chrissake."

"With *shabu*."

Tozzi shrugged. "What's *shabu*?"

Takayuki turned to his friends and had a short conference. "*Shabu* means 'white diamonds.' That's what we call it at home. I believe you call it 'speed' here."

"You mean 'speed' as in drugs? As in amphetamines?"

Takayuki nodded. "Yes, drugs." He didn't seem at all ashamed to admit to it.

"Are you telling me you guys are all speed freaks? Drug addicts?"

Takayuki furrowed his brow and shook his head. "No. All serious students in Japan take *shabu* so that we can stay awake to study at night, especially during exam hell."

"What's 'exam hell'?"

"This is what we call the time in February and March when they give the important exams, the ones that determine whether you advance to the next level or not. Always a very crucial time for us."

Tozzi rubbed the back of his neck. Jesus, what a mess. "How many of you are there? Here in America, I mean."

Takayuki shrugged. "Hard to tell. There are sixty-two of us here at the chicken factory. There were at least three-hundred students on the ship I came over on, and there have been several other such shipments that we know of."

Jesus Christ. That asshole Ivers was going to demand to

know what the hell he was doing here tonight, how he got in and all that. But that was all inconsequential bullshit right now. This went beyond legal procedure and Bureau rules. These guys were being held against their will as slaves for chrissake.

"Okay," he announced to all of them, "the nightmare is over. I'm going to unlock the other two trailers and, Takayuki, I want you to explain everything to them. You stay put right here until I can put something together. I'll go call for help and we'll have buses here in a few hours to—"

A desperate hand suddenly gripped Tozzi's forearm. "We cannot go with you," Takayuki whispered frantically. "Mashiro will hunt us down. He will kill us the way he killed the others. His sword will find us. You cannot do this to us!"

"Take it easy now." Tozzi held his shoulder. "We can protect you. I promise. You won't have to worry about him anymore."

"Your protection is useless against Mashiro. He is a samurai, a *real* samurai. He has dedicated his life to killing. His yakuzas will find us, then they will call him. That's how they keep us under their domination. If we go with you, Mashiro will find us. He will kill us, all of us. I know this. Please go now and lock us in again. Please, you have stayed too long already."

"But—"

"Please! Go!"

Tozzi looked into his eyes and saw the liquid terror. Then that hot, cloying smell came up again. It was suddenly overpowering. It took him a moment to realize that this was the smell of fear. He could feel it creeping up around him like rising flood waters, cold and murky. He took in a deep breath and felt for the gun under his jacket for reassurance.

He searched their pale faces for some sign of encouragement, for just one of them who'd be willing to save himself. But there was no one. The faces just hung there in the dark like helpless fruit on a doomed tree. He considered alternatives. He could contact Immigration and Naturalization, let them spring a raid on the chicken plant. But what about all the other slaves D'Urso imported? Who knew how many others there were? Hundreds, thousands? D'Urso sure as hell wouldn't tell them where they were. And would one raid really affect this slave trade? Sure, they could put D'Urso away, but then someone else in the Antonelli family would be assigned the job. The slaves would just keep on coming.

All of a sudden he could hear Ivers's warning about the Bureau frowning down on individual efforts. He should report this, but knowing Ivers, it would do a lot more harm than good. Ivers would notify the Newark office and together they'd call out the heavy artillery, bust D'Urso, and hang him up on a hook like a dead shark for the cameras. Ivers wouldn't want to hear anything about other slaves. If something's wrong, just take care of it. That's the way he thought. He never wanted to know anything about the big picture.

Tozzi glanced around the trailer at all those pleading, terrified faces staring back at him, and that's when he made up his mind. Fear like this has to be respected. He turned to Takayuki. "Okay. Have it your way."

He hopped down out of the trailer and slowly closed the door. He heard the annoying squeak of the rusty hasp, but it didn't affect him now. Hooking the lock into the hasp, he held it in his hand for a long moment before he finally pushed it closed. Slowly he started to walk backward into the flood-lit lot, staring at the three trailers, still stunned by what he'd just seen and heard, wondering what the hell kind of monster could inspire this kind of terror in these poor people. He glanced up at the black power lines over the trailers, then noticed the red warning lights slowly flashing on a row of giant oil tanks in the distance by the river. He pictured Godzilla tearing Tokyo apart.

A monster called Mashiro, he thought. That's what kind of monster.

He stared at the blinking lights, wondering what in the hell he was going to do now.

20

Nagai turned away from the noise and the action up on stage when the fish arrived at their table, the waitress bowing as she set the ugly thing in front of Hamabuchi. The fat fish lay tilted on its belly like a tugboat run aground, one dead eye staring in Nagai's direction. Nagai stared back at the fish and sighed to himself. He never really cared for *fugu* and this whole ceremony was a bore. Sure, the first couple of times it was dangerous and exciting, the ultimate test of a man's loyalty, the essence of the Fugukai. But ever since his exile to America, Nagai had abandoned the ritual himself, though he never told Hamabuchi. It wasn't that he'd forgotten how to cut the fish or that his men were too cowardly to eat the potentially fatal flesh served up by their boss. It was just that the only blowfish you can get in America isn't poisonous. The whole thing about making your men watch as you carefully remove the deadly liver and ovaries to test their trust and loyalty to you just doesn't make any sense with American *fugu*. They don't have the juice. What good is the ceremony if there's no risk of dropping dead at the table? But with Hamabuchi it was different. The old boss always managed to have the real thing imported for his ceremonies, no matter where he was. Lucky him.

Nagai glanced back at the stage where two young women wearing only the traditional sumo-wrestler's loin knot were ramming into each other as the small crowd of respectable businessmen from his country raucously cheered them on.

He wondered what their respectable American business associates would think if they knew about this place. A little bit of the Ginza tucked away in the middle of Manhattan. Everybody needs a little fun and relaxation now and then, even respectable bastards. Nagai turned his attention back to the two combatants smashing into each other, each trying to push the other out of the white circle painted on the stage. These couldn't be Japanese girls, he thought. Not with those tits. He glanced back at the waitress for comparison, but her tits, if she had any, were hidden under the folds of her kimono. No, Japanese tits are nothing like those things up on stage. They don't bobble and jiggle like that. Nagai smiled as the girls collided once more and shook flesh. Tits like *fugu*.

"Are you certain you don't want us to prepare the fish for you?" the waitress asked Hamabuchi sweetly in Japanese. "One of our chefs is licensed."

Hamabuchi waved her offer away with the heavy-duty black rubber gloves. "In Japan, a chef may need a license from the government to cut *fugu*, but I need no such license." He gave her that funny little smile of his, the one that could be taken as either fatherly benevolence or utter contempt. He started to put the gloves on then, leaving her with nothing to do but leave. Nagai could tell from her stiff smile that she thought he was an asshole.

Nagai considered telling him now but then decided he better wait until Hamabuchi was finished. The old man was getting up there, and he didn't want to upset him before he cut out the poison parts. Just a tiny nick to the liver could taint the whole fish, and it was he, not Hamabuchi, who had to take the first bite. He sneaked a look back at the sumo girls. The one with the short hair and the big lips was very aggressive, but the other one was prettier. The old man was steadying the fish now, probing with the knife for the right place on the back of its head to start cutting. Nagai watched him make the first two deep cuts into the *fugu*'s neck, severing the backbone. He dug his fingers into the incision, felt around, then pulled out the backbone all in one piece which turned the fish inside out. He flipped the whole thing over and yanked on the prickly skin until it hung loose around the tail like a man with his pants down around his ankles. The old man looked over at him then to make sure he was watching. This was the delicate part; Nagai knew he was supposed to look. Hamabu-chi took off the gloves and went searching through the messy entrails for the liver and the ovaries, which he proceeded to cut out much too quickly for Nagai's comfort. But of course he always did it this way. It was part of the test. Hamabuchi picked out the poison organs on the tip of his knife and laid them out in a small saucer. He cleaned the knife in a bowl of hot salt water, then went to work cutting the white flesh into thin, translucent slices, arranging them on two wooden trays. Hamabuchi set down the knife and washed his fingers in a second bowl, then presented one of the trays to Nagai with a bow of his head. He had that smile again.

Nagai took his chopsticks, picked up a slice of *fugu*, and dipped it in his saucer of tangy *ponzu* sauce. The businessmen started shouting and cheering wildly as he brought the fish to his mouth, but he resisted the impulse to turn and see if the pretty one was winning. Well, down the hatch as they say here.

He started to chew, staring up under his brows at Hamabu-chi, waiting. If it didn't happen in fifteen seconds, it wouldn't happen at all. He swallowed, grinned, and bowed his head to his boss. The ceremony was completed. Satisfied now, old man?

"So," Hamabuchi said, dipping a piece of fish for himself, "any new developments since I was last here?"

Hang on to your hat. "Yes. D'Urso is planning to have Antonelli killed."

Hamabuchi's eyes started blinking, the *fugu* poised in front of his open mouth. Nagai had seen this reaction before. The old man wasn't happy. "When? How? Have you warned An-tonelli-*san*?"

Nagai shook his head. "I just found out yesterday. I don't have any details. I considered going directly to Antonelli to warn him, but I didn't think it was my place to do that. I felt you should know first."

"Antonelli is my brother," the old man pronounced grimly. "He cannot be betrayed this way." He sounded like one of those old fart warlords from the samurai movies.

Nagai nodded to reassure him. "I've sent a few men to watch D'Urso and his hot-head brother-in-law. If it looks like they're getting ready to make their move, we'll know about it right away. If you want, I can send Mashiro to kill them both." He was still unsure about going into business with D'Urso. If D'Urso sent Antonelli to heaven and got away with it, then Nagai would commit himself. In the meantime, he'd go through the motions to keep Hamabuchi from becoming suspicious.

"No, stay out of their way. We can't interfere in their affairs. That would ruin things between us. It would mean the end of our joint venture, despite my friendship with Carmine."

"How would that ruin things if we save Antonelli's life?"

Hamabuchi seemed annoyed with his question. "How would we react if the Mafia started meddling in our private business? We're sailing on rough waters here. It should not be us who capsizes the boat."

Thanks for the vivid imagery. "Will you tell Antonelli?"

Hamabuchi was frowning like a bulldog. His eyebrows twitched as he considered the question. "I don't know . . . I don't think so."

"Why not? He's your friend."

"Friends don't spy on each other. If I tell him, I'll have to tell him how I know. Naturally he'll think I don't trust him and never have trusted him. It will destroy our relationship . . . and a very lucrative partnership. No, I can't tell him."

Some friend. Maybe D'Urso *will* be able to pull this off. Hmmm . . . Yes, but what if Hamabuchi goes ahead and tells Antonelli anyway? The old man was crafty; he might do anything. Nagai had to be sure. "Why don't you tell Antonelli about D'Urso and tell him *I* did the spying? Blame me."

Hamabuchi glared at him. He looked like a mean, bug-eyed frog now. "You have been in America too long, Nagai. *I'm* responsible for anything my men do. I *am* the Fugukai. *My* honor rests on *your* deeds."

Here we go with the Kurosawa crap again. "Then what do we do?"

"We make sure this execution doesn't happen. Make sure D'Urso does not accomplish his goal, just don't show your hand. Business must continue uninterrupted." Hamabuchi paused to eat his *fugu*. "I'm sure you can put yourself in D'Urso's frame of mind." He was looking down at his saucer as he swirled another piece of fish in the sauce. "Do whatever is necessary to discourage him." He cast his eyes meaningfully at Nagai.

How subtle you are. Bastard. Sic the failed assassin on the would-be assassin. How fucking clever. Won't you be surprised when D'Urso succeeds and we take over the slave trade for ourselves? Nagai dipped another piece of *fugu* and tossed it into his mouth. This really was very good, better than he remembered. "Don't worry. I'll handle D'Urso," he said.

Hamabuchi nodded resolutely and looked down at his *fugu*, dipping another slice. "Be sure you do, Nagai."

Nagai nodded as he took a slice of *fugu*.

"It used to be so much easier to keep loyal men." Hamabuchi swirled his piece of fish around and around in the sauce. "Tradition was incentive enough at one time. But times have changed. A boss must use management techniques with his people." He kept moving that piece of fish in the dark sauce. "By the way, Hatsu sends her love to you."

"What's that?"

Hamabuchi looked up and raised his bushy eyebrows. "Hatsu. Your daughter. Have you forgotten her? Kenji swings a good bat now. Your boy may grow up to be the next Sadaharu Oh. And the little one—I think of her as my own granddaughter." He chuckled gently and put the fish in his mouth.

"You've seen them recently?"

"Yes, of course. Didn't they write you? They're living at my country house now."

"Which country house? You have several, don't you?"

Hamabuchi just smiled and swirled another slice of fish. "You will see that no harm comes to my friend Antonelli, won't you?"

Nagai's mouth was tingling from the *fugu*. The sauce was sour in his throat.

Suddenly the businessmen started cheering again. Nagai looked up just in time to see the short-haired girl shove the pretty one down right on her ass outside the circle. She hit the floor hard, her tits flopping, and she winced in defeat. She looked like she was going to cry.

"Nagai?"

He turned back to that damned little smile. He pictured the kids, tried to remember where all the old man's country

houses were. It was useless. Hamabuchi could have them anywhere.

"Nagai, you haven't answered me. Will you protect Antonelli? With your life?"

Nagai set down his chopsticks and wiped his mouth with
his napkin. His throat was sore. He pictured Hatsu's face,
Kenji in a baseball uniform, the baby . . . then he held his
breath and bowed to his boss. "*Hai.*"

The old man smiled.

Nagai watched Mashiro's profile as the samurai pulled the
Cadillac up to the loading dock behind the factory. He
glanced at the three kids in the backseat, tough and quiet, all
narrow eyes and moody lips, the three of them. He looked
like that himself once upon a time. The old man had personally recommended these three. They worked well together,
he said. Toshio, Hideo, and Ikki. Moe, Larry, and Curly. Initiated into the Fugukai by working as the old man's personal
house slaves for an entire year, the same way he came up. But
that was a long time ago.

Mashiro turned off the engine. The inside of the car was
suddenly silent. Nagai could feel the kids looking at him,
waiting for his order. He still wasn't one hundred percent
convinced that this was the way to handle this, but he
couldn't think of any other way. He'd let D'Urso know that
he knew what he was planning. Just look him in the eye and
leave it at that. Keep the warning unstated. Let him do all the
wondering about who else knows. Maybe that would change
his mind.

He reached for the door handle and instantly the kids
rushed out of the car to cover him. They moved swift and
silent. Mashiro got out then, at his own pace. He wondered if
Mashiro felt displaced by the presence of the kids. After all,
the samurai was the only force he'd ever needed before. The
kids were for show, that's all. He hoped Mashiro realized
that.

The kids mounted the stairs to the loading dock and waited
for him, Mashiro lagging behind to watch his back. Just then
Francione pushed through the hanging plastic strips that covered the open bay. Instinctively the kids fanned out around
him, just in case. They were good.

Francione made believe they weren't even there. He jerked his head to flip that stupid hair out of his eye, the cocky bastard. "You're just the man I want to see, Nagai. We've got a problem in here." He jerked his thumb back inside. "Come fix it."

Hideo and Ikki held the plastic drapes open as Francione led the way into that back room where Mashiro had sacrificed his finger. Nagai caught a glimpse of Mashiro's hand. The end of the finger was still bandaged.

Two of D'Urso's lumpy greaseballs in their tight suits were holding two of the chicken slaves with their arms pinned behind them. One of the slaves looked like he was going to shit his pants, the other looked angry and indignant. He recognized the indignant one right away. It was Takayuki, the little big mouth, the one Mashiro had to set straight. Apparently one taste of Mashiro's hand wasn't enough.

D'Urso was standing off to the side with his hands clasped behind his back. Unlike his brother-in-law, he seemed unruffled by whatever the trouble was.

Nagai looked at D'Urso. "What's going on?"

D'Urso just shrugged and nodded toward the two slaves. He was going to let Francione do the talking. He seemed to be giving the punk more responsibility these days, preparing Bobby for a bigger job once he becomes boss. Fat chance now, my friend.

Francione pointed to the scared slave. "This guy has been dragging his ass all day. When I told him to get moving, he just started giving me lip. Three times I told him to shape up and he still didn't listen, so I decided to beat a little sense into him. But when we pulled him off the line, this other guy follows us in here like Mighty Mouse to save the day. These guys are getting way out of hand, Nagai. Now are *you* gonna do something about it or do *we* have to? Huh?"

Where the hell did the little punk get off talking to him this way? Nagai looked at D'Urso who seemed unconcerned. Was this what D'Urso really thought of him? Did D'Urso think he was supposed to take shit from this little asshole when they went out on their own? Fuck that.

"Discipline is my responsibility," Nagai said to D'Urso with deliberate calm. "We'll take care of them." He gave the kids instructions in Japanese.

But when the kids went to take the slaves from the greaseballs, Takayuki started struggling, shouting in Japanese. "No! Stop! No more beatings. No more stinking chickens. We quit."

"What's he saying?" Francione pulled a sour face. "What's his problem?"

Nagai looked at Mashiro who nodded back. He knew what to do.

"No!" Takayuki screamed in Japanese. "Another step closer and I tell them about the federal agent Mashiro tried to kill right here in the factory. I know about Reiko, too, how she spies for you. I've seen her here with D'Urso's wife and daughter, pretending to be one of us. I'll tell them all about her."

God, no! "Mashiro! *Sugu Yatchimae!*"

The samurai's leg became an instant blur, a peacock tail of motion, as he pivoted, extended, and hammered his heel down onto the side of Takayuki's neck. Blood spurted where the heel of his shoe ruptured flesh, splattering the other slave and the greaseball who held him. Takayuki crumpled as the greaseball reached into his jacket and pulled a gun. Instantly Ikki lunged, threw the greaseball's gunhand up, kneed him in the nuts, and cracked him over the head with his elbow. The greaseball dropped to his knees and grabbed his head for protection. Ikki took a step back and stood over him, the greaseball's gun in his hand. Hideo and Toshio were already in position in case anyone else panicked.

Mashiro looked grim, deliberately unimpressed. These kids were all right, though. Moe, Larry, and Curly. Nagai grinned at D'Urso, waiting for his heart to stop pounding, searching the man's face until he was convinced that D'Urso hadn't recognized Reiko's name in Takayuki's outburst.

Nagai glanced down at Takayuki's body, then looked at the idiot brother-in-law. "Your problem is solved."

"The fuck it is," Francione yelled. "I want a replacement for him."

Nagai nodded slowly and walked past him. "Sure, whatever you want. As soon as the next shipment comes in."

He walked over to D'Urso then and stared him in the face. "I heard a rumor that you're considering a plan for rapid career advancement. It's not a very good idea. I *strongly* suggest you rethink your plans."

D'Urso's nostrils flared. "What're you saying?" For the first time since he'd met him, D'Urso looked angry. Very angry.

"And also," Nagai said before D'Urso could get another word in, "I've considered your offer, but I have to say no thanks. Things are better for me as they are." He turned his back on D'Urso and headed for the doorway with Mashiro and the kids in tow.

"Hey, hold on, Nagai!" D'Urso reached out to grab Nagai's arm, but Mashiro's hand locked onto his wrist before he touched him.

"There's nothing to discuss, D'Urso. You know where I stand." He pushed through the plastic drapes into the cold air. The sun sparkled off the chrome on the big black Caddy's long fins as his entourage followed him down the steps of the loading dock. He could feel D'Urso glaring at him from inside the loading dock with his fists clenched in his suit coat pockets. The man was burning up inside. The world was shattering around him. Nagai knew the feeling.

As Ikki opened the car door for him, Nagai stared up at D'Urso. Be smart, my friend. Put it out of your mind.

He got into the car, and Mashiro put it in reverse and started to back away from the loading dock. Through the windshield, he watched D'Urso standing there glaring at him, his expensive blue suit shining in the cold sun.

21

D'Urso peered through the heavily tinted windows as Bobby squeezed the Mercedes between a double-parked cement truck on the right and a dumpster on the left. Clusters of tenements on both sides of the street were being renovated for condos. Hoboken—the whole fucking town was always under construction, but as far as he was concerned, it was still ugly.

The revolving drum of the cement truck had pink polka dots painted on it. As they passed by, D'Urso could hear the cement in the drum rumble and ping. He watched the polka dots glide up and disappear over the top, and he thought how nice it would be to stick Nagai in a cement truck with fucking pink polka dots, the son of a bitch.

Clearing the truck and the dumpster, Bobby hung a right onto an even narrower one-way street made worse by cars carelessly parked bumper-to-bumper along both curbs. At the next corner, he turned right again onto Adams where cars were double-parked solid in front of Farinelli's Italian Specialties, so Bobby just stopped in the middle of the road. Farinelli's jerky-looking kid was standing outside in front of the window where all the provolones and the salamis were hung, waiting there like a mamaluke, holding the bag. Look at that, will ya. Long dirty hair, earring, black Bon Jovi T-shirt. What a jerk.

Bobby hit the button and his window rolled down. "Hey,

Cheese," he called out to the kid. "You get the order right today or what?"

"I always get it right," Cheese said with a sniff as he walked into the street. "It's my old man who fucks up, not me."

"Oh, yeah? Did you remember to make the sandwiches with prosciuttine and not plain ham this time?"

"Yeah."

"And what kind of peppers did you put on? Hot or sweet?"

"Sweet."

"And is the mozzarell' fresh?"

"Yeah."

"You lie."

"I swear to God."

"Ask him about the marinated mushrooms," D'Urso said.

"Yeah, the marinated mushrooms, Cheese. They in there?"

"It's in there, it's in there."

"Yeah? And what's to drink?"

"Orangina and a Diet Coke. Okay?"

A tinny car horn let out a blast just then, and D'Urso turned around in his seat to see where it was coming from. A little yellow Volkswagen Bug was on their ass, a Puerto Rican guy behind the wheel leaning on his horn. The car reminded him of the orange VW and Mashiro's big screwup. D'Urso scowled. If he could just get rid of the two of them, Mishmosh and his boss, oh, how happy his life would be. Damn them.

The Puerto Rican guy leaned on his horn again. "Hey, shut up, okay?" Farinelli's kid yelled.

"Pay the kid and let's get out of here," D'Urso said, taking an envelope out of his inside pocket and handing it to Bobby.

"Here." Bobby passed the envelope to the kid, took the bag, and laid it on the seat between them. "I'm telling you now, Cheese, this better be right."

"Don't worry about it," the kid whined. "It's right, it's right."

"Okay. I'll take your word for it."

"Yeah, you do that."

Bobby's window glided up as the Mercedes started to pull away. D'Urso turned around and looked at the Bug again. "Go uptown and park where the factories are. We'll eat there."

Bobby glanced over at him again as he drove, as if he were checking to see if he was all right. He'd been doing that off and on all morning, and D'Urso wished the hell he'd stop. "What's on your mind, Bobby? Just say it."

Bobby drove through the next intersection and cruised up the next block of renovated tenements. "What's on my mind? I'm worried about what's on *your* mind. That's what's on my mind."

"Yeah? And what am I worried about?"

"That the Jap knows. Christ, he could be telling Antonelli right now. Except you don't look too worried about it, John. That's what I don't like."

D'Urso smoothed his tie, running his fingers along the silver-gray silk. "Don't worry about Nagai. I don't think he'll do anything." He was struggling to stay calm. You panic and you're sunk. There was still a way to pull this off. Just be like the fucking Japs—stay calm.

"I dunno about that, John. I'm not so sure about him. Nagai's a rat. He won't just sit on what he knows for nothing."

"I think he will."

"The hell he will."

"Listen to me, Bobby. The Japs don't play that way. If he ratted on us, it would be very dishonorable. And that's one thing these Japs are cuckoo about. The worse thing a Jap can do is lose his honor, you know, lose face. You saw Mishmosh cut the end of his own finger off. That's what that was all about." He kept stroking his tie, staring straight ahead out the windshield. He hoped the hell he was right.

Bobby kept driving. The next block had regular poor-people tenements. The one after that started the factory district. Not so many cars up here.

"Go to the next block and park over there, on the right," D'Urso said.

As Bobby parked the car, D'Urso reached under his seat for the towel. Before he even saw it, he could feel that it wasn't one of the good ones. He pulled it out and unfolded it. Some stupid-looking, cockeyed blue thing was printed on it.

"What the hell is this?"

"Cookie Monster," Bobby said as he cut the engine.

"Who?"

"Cookie Monster. Sorry, it's Amanda's. It was the only clean towel I could find this morning."

D'Urso smiled as he thought about his daughter. "Cookie Monster, huh?" He laughed sarcastically through his nose. "Think he's related to Mishmosh?"

"This isn't funny, John." Bobby was twisting that piece of hair in front of his face around his finger. He wasn't being calm.

D'Urso spread the towel over his silver-blue pants, then reached for the bag. He looked in, then took out the sandwiches and the sodas. Unwrapping one of the sandwiches on the seat, he picked up a half of the twelve-inch sub, leaned forward over his knees, and took a bite. He nodded as he chewed. "Good."

Bobby took the bottle of Orangina off the dash, twisted the cap off, and took a swig. "How can you eat, John? My stomach's all in knots. These guys're gonna get us killed and you're eating."

D'Urso chewed. He popped the tab on the Diet Coke and took a sip. "Don't get nervous, Bobby. I talked to the Filipinos last night."

"What'd they say?"

"I talked to the new big man over there in Manila. Quirino. He used to work for President Marcos. He says we don't need Nagai to get new slaves over here. He told me he's got a solid connection in Taiwan for shipping them, and it can all go through him. He'll be our man in the East. He says the yakuza mean shit in the countries where the new slaves will come from. So fuck Nagai. We don't need him."

"Hey, great!" Bobby tore the paper off his sandwich and bit into it. He ate like he thought someone was going to take it away from him. "This is great, right? Now we can just whack him and get it over with."

"Yeah, except you're forgetting something."

"What?"

"Mishmosh. You want to go try to whack Nagai with Mishmosh around?"

"No thanks."

"That's what I thought."

"So what do we do?"

"We get rid of Mishmosh first."

Bobby stopped chewing. He looked a little pale all of a sudden.

"Take it easy. I don't want *you* to go after him."

"No disrespect, John, but I'd have to refuse that one. Mishmosh is one dangerous motherfucker."

"Right. That's why we're gonna let the feds do it."

"Wha'?"

D'Urso nodded. "You heard right, the feds. After I talked to Quirino, I sent an anonymous letter to the FBI in the city. Gave them a lot of juicy info about Mishmosh. Told them it was him who did the two stiffs in the Volkswagen."

"Jesus, John, isn't that a little risky? What if they take him and he starts talking? If he's gonna rat on anybody, it'll be us, not the yaks."

"Do you think Mishmosh is the kind of guy who's gonna sit still to plea-bargain with them? Of course not. When they corner him, he's gonna try to fight it out. And when those guys make an arrest, they always come in packs like they're going to war or something. Shotguns, M-16s, all that shit." Again, he hoped he was right.

Bobby took another quick swig of his soda. "Yeah, okay. So Mishmosh becomes a memory. What about Nagai?"

D'Urso bit off another chunk of his sandwich. "While we're waiting for the feds to find Mishmosh, we're gonna put a little pressure on Nagai to give him something to think about." He took a drink, then swallowed. "There's a shipment from Japan due in today. I'm fixing it with the union boys to go out on strike right after the boat docks and the captain transfers the car keys to the dock boss. That ship will have to stay put right where it is with Nagai's merchandise locked up tight in their trunks."

"What if the captain just tells his men to break the locks and let 'em out?"

"I told Fat Joe to send some guys on board with a message for the captain. They start popping trunks, we start popping heads. They won't try it." D'Urso took another sip of his soda. "I can see the strike going on for a few days. The kids'll be trapped where they are. They'll start going nuts . . . then they'll start dying. If the goods perish on board, I know Nagai will have to answer to Hamabuchi for it, and that's a lot of damaged goods to answer for. Nagai won't want that to happen so when he hears about the strike, he'll think twice before he starts sticking his nose in my business." D'Urso ripped off another hunk and smiled as he chewed.

"Won't the old man suspect something when he hears you called a strike?"

D'Urso frowned. "When has Antonelli been so concerned about what the crews do? He doesn't care about anything anymore. That's his whole problem, right?"

"Yeah . . . right."

D'Urso reached into the paper bag again and pulled out a gun.

Bobby started to choke. "What the hell?"

"The 'marinated mushrooms.' That Cheese is a good boy. He got it right."

D'Urso handed the gun to Bobby who beamed at it like a kid with a new toy. It was a gawky-looking thing, but Cheese's old man assured him it was as good as an Uzi or an M-10. It was a Wilkinson "Linda" 9mm autopistol with a thirty-one round clip. Good as an Uzi, he said. Some guns look sharp, but this wasn't one of those. A heavy son of a bitch, a foot long, gawky-looking. But so what if it was clunky? It'll do the job. Only, who the hell ever heard of a gun named "Linda"?

Bobby was grinning, staring down at "Linda," working her safety back and forth.

"Get ready, Bobby. Very soon."

"Yeah. Very soon. And Nagai can go fuck himself." Bobby pointed the gun at the floor. "*Bada-bing, bada-bing, bada-bing!!!* Carmine Antonelli . . . sleeps with the fishes."

D'Urso laughed and squeezed his sandwich as he ripped off another hunk. Yeah . . . sleeping with the fishes . . . very soon . . . if it all works out.

22

Tozzi sat on his knees in his new living room, trying to get used to sitting *seiza*. Neil Sensei had told him that sitting *seiza* properly would center the body, coordinate it with his mind, and bring on a state of calm alertness. But for Tozzi, sitting *seiza* only brought on a state of pain. His thighs and ankles were killing him, but he tried to stick it out, willing to accept Neil's promise that this would pass with time and practice. There was one nice thing about the torture of sitting *seiza*, though. That pain distracted him from the other pain in his lower back that he got from sleeping on the couch. Thank God they were delivering the bed today.

He sighed, staring straight ahead at the blank beige wall between the two front windows. He wished to hell sitting *seiza would* bring him a little calm. He'd been up half the night, tossing and turning, hoping those faces in the shadows would go away for a while so he could get some sleep, but he just couldn't get those Japanese guys locked up in the trailer out of his mind. He hadn't told anyone about it, and that was bothering him. If Ivers knew he was sitting on this information, he'd go ape. It was just the kind of thing Ivers had warned him not to do. He really wanted to tell Gibbons first, but the guy was still in the hospital, for chrissake. It didn't seem right to aggravate him while he was still recuperating. Anyway, last night Lorraine told him that Gib was supposed to be released today. He'd tell Gibbons all about the slaves when he picked him up at the hospital later today. Gibbons will hit the ceiling when he tells him that he hasn't told Ivers, but deep down Gibbons knows how Ivers always fucks things up. What they should do is figure out how to handle this on their own first, at least present Ivers with a definite strategy in order to keep him from coming up with one of his own. Tozzi breathed a little more relaxed now. They would tell Ivers—soon but not now.

Tozzi was starting to relax, staring at the blank wall, when the doorbell suddenly rang and he jumped. Roxanne. Tozzi got up off his sore legs and hobbled over to the intercom.

"Hello?"

"It's me. Princess Di."

Tozzi frowned. It took him a moment to realize she was referring to British royalty. His first thought was Princess *Die*. Wonderful frame of mind he was in today. He shook his head and buzzed her in.

He opened the door and looked down the stairwell, listening to her steps. "How's it going, Your Majesty?"

She didn't answer until she could see him from the landing below. "Elevators are wonderful inventions," she said sarcastically. "So are parking spaces. Too bad this neighborhood has neither. I must like you to put up with this."

He watched her climb the last flight. "Hi. How ya doin'?" he said as she walked up to him.

"Honey, I've missed you." She threw herself into his arms and kissed him just the way he'd wanted to kiss her when he took her home after dinner the other night. He wished he could forget about the slaves for a little while, but thinking that made him feel guilty.

"Well . . . hello," he said when she let him up for air.

"Got to keep up the ruse," she whispered. "You know, hubby and wifey. Can't let the neighbors get suspicious. And you never know. The landlord might have a private detective working for him."

"A detective?"

"Very common these days. Landlords spy on their tenants to make sure they're on the up-and-up. Make sure there are no after-hours sex clubs on the premises, no outlawed pets, no illegal aliens packed into their apartments." She flashed that sly smile of hers. "I read all about it in *New York* magazine."

Tozzi forced a smile for her. Illegal aliens. She had to mention that. He hadn't told her about the slaves either.

"Why don't you come in out of the noonday sun . . . dear?" He led her into the apartment and shut the door.

"Is anything wrong?" she asked as she threw her suede jacket on the couch. "You look a little washed-out."

"No, I'm okay." He stared at her legs. She looked nice in jeans. "You know, I really do appreciate your doing this for me. You sure it's not a big imposition."

"Oh, it's a terrible imposition," she said. "As you know, clients are breaking down my door. Taking today off could be disastrous for the Eastlake Academy. It's a big risk, but I'm prepared to take it."

"We're funny today, aren't we?"

She shrugged. "It's no problem, Mike, really. My office is a crypt. I'm glad to get out frankly. Besides, you need a bed."

He took that last line the way he normally would've liked it. But why was this happening now, dammit? "Well, I'd wait for the bed myself, but something's come up that can't wait. I called the place where I bought it and they said it would be delivered sometime between ten and six. The lady said she couldn't be more specific than that. Sorry."

"I told you. It's no problem. I brought a book."

"I may be back late. You don't have to stay."

"Wait a minute! You promised dinner for this little favor. I'm staying put until I collect."

"Fine."

"Anyway, be late. I don't care. The Miss Galaxy Pageant is on TV tonight."

"You want to watch the Miss Galaxy Pageant?"

"I love beauty pageants. All those totally repulsive girls demeaning themselves on national television. Does wonders for my superiority complex. It's better than *The Gong Show.* Better than the Westminster Kennel Club competition."

"Right." She was in such a good mood. He wished he could join her.

Her smile faded. She looked concerned now. "Are you sure you're okay?"

He stared at her and sighed. Should he tell her about it? She was involved after all. And wasn't this how he always got himself into trouble in the past, keeping things all bottled up, mulling it over in his head again and again until it became *his* version of reality? Maybe it would be better to get someone else's opinion. It would certainly be a relief to tell her, just to get it off his chest. Besides, she'd be a neutral listener. Gibbons sure as hell wouldn't be.

"I've found out some things in the past few days." He sat down on the couch. "Not very pleasant. It's been bothering me."

She sat down next to him, staring into his eyes. "Tell me."

"The Japanese nannies? You want to know why they're putting you out of business? They're slaves."

"What do you mean slaves?"

"Slaves. As in 'way-down-yonder-in-the-land-o'-cotton.' It's hard to believe, but it's true. I met a bunch of them."

She bit her bottom lip and laid her hand on his knee. God, he wished she wouldn't do that now. She looked so good, but it wouldn't be right, given the conversation and all.

"You mean they're forced to work and . . . and beaten if they don't?"

Tozzi nodded. "Two were killed for trying to escape. Two that I know of."

"When is the FBI going to rescue these people?"

Tozzi looked at her hand on his knee, then shook his head. "The FBI doesn't know anything about it. I haven't told anyone yet."

"Why not, for God's sake?"

"Because the slave I talked to said there are hundreds of them here. Maybe thousands. Sure, we can rescue the ones I found, but what about the others? How will we find them? Once it gets out that the authorities are looking for them, they'll be that much harder to find."

"But, Mike, you have to tell somebody." The sunlight shimmered through her hair. The color was indescribable, like red gold. She looked so sad and pained. He wanted to comfort her, hold her, touch her. It wouldn't be right, though. She'd think he was an animal. He'd feel like an animal. "You have to tell somebody, Mike," she repeated.

"I told *you.*"

"You know what I mean."

"I'm picking up Gibbons at the hospital this afternoon. I want to discuss it with him first."

"How's he doing?"

"Okay. The doctor wants him to take a month off to rest, though. Lorraine wants me to convince him to stay down at her place until he's well. I know what he's gonna say to that."

"Any progress in finding the squat Jap fellow who beat him up?"

"I got a call from the office a little while ago. Someone apparently dropped a dime on our man."

"Say again."

"Dropped a dime. It means we got an anonymous tip on the guy. An unsigned letter with a lot of choice details about him. It could be a prank or it could be real. I don't know yet." He looked at his watch. "I told them I'd be in this morning to check it out." He glanced at his watch again. It was getting late.

"Oh . . . well, you better get going then, I guess." She took her hand off his knee.

"Yeah, I guess." She had that look like she really didn't want to be left alone. He didn't want to leave her.

He nodded. She nodded. He looked at his watch again. "Well, I don't have to rush. I've got a little time."

She turned away so that he saw her profile in the bright sunlight. "Please don't think me insensitive or uncaring, but I . . . I . . ." She turned and faced him again, tilting her head to one side as she hooked her hand around the back of his neck and pulled him close, slowly pressing her lips against his.

He tasted her lips, ran his hand down her ribs, felt her tongue with his. When he happened to find the space between her teeth, his dick started to throb.

She tugged on his necktie and started to unbutton his shirt. He reached under her sweater and unhooked her bra, palming a breast and circling her nipple with his thumb.

"Oh, Mike, I'm sorry, but I just couldn't wait," she breathed into his ear.

"I know how you feel."

She pulled the lilac sweater over her head, and her falling hair filtered the sun. He went for her belt. She undid his, then fumbled with the pants button with one hand as she rubbed him through the material.

His shoulder dug into the couch pillows as he shifted his

weight to help her get his pants off. He couldn't believe they were doing this. For a moment he wasn't sure he wanted it to happen. Not now. Not when he had so much on his mind. She buried her head in his chest then, which made him even harder. Of course, she was the one who started it . . . No, maybe they shouldn't wait. He unbuttoned the pants himself.

He kicked his pants off and ran his hand over her ass, then followed the seam of her panties with his fingers, playing around where the inside of her soft thigh met her crotch. She licked her fingers and rolled the tip of his dick between her thumb and index finger. He stroked her lightly with his middle finger, back and forth, slow and steady. She twisted her hips to get more of his finger and he felt her moistness. She moaned. He closed his eyes and let himself get lightheaded.

"Oh, Mike . . ."

"Rox—"

The doorbell rang. It echoed through the empty rooms.

Tozzi bolted up, his heart pounding. His face was drenched. He saw those faces in the shadows behind his closed eyes. No. This wasn't right.

She glared at the intercom. "The bed, I take it."

He looked at his watch. "Listen, Roxanne—you're gonna think I'm crazy, but how about if we continue this later? When my head is a little clearer."

The doorbell rang again.

"Sure . . . of course. You've got a lot on your mind. I understand." She looked disappointed.

Tozzi felt awful. He didn't think she did understand. Not really.

She got up and leaned into the intercom. She was only wearing panties. Blue cotton ones with little ducks marching across the ass. "Yes?" she said.

"We got a bed here for Tozzi?"

"Yes, that's right." She hit the buzzer to unlock the door downstairs, then rushed back to the couch to get dressed. Tozzi was sitting on the edge of the couch, pulling his pants on. His dick ached. He felt like a balloon with a slow leak. He knew he'd have this pent-up feeling for the rest of the day.

After she got her sweater back on, she hugged him sideways and whispered in his ear. "Come home as soon as you can. I'll have the bed set up."

There was a pounding on the door then.

"Be right there," Tozzi yelled. He kissed her quickly, then stood up to put his shirttails in. "Keep your pants on," he muttered under his breath. He looked at her zipping up her jeans. He hoped she did understand.

23

Gibbons ripped open the Velcro straps on the foam-rubber neck brace around his neck and loosened it a little. He'd been fooling around with it all day, but nothing felt right. Tozzi's dramatic revelation didn't do much for his comfort level either. He re-did the straps, but the collar still didn't feel right. Fucking Tozzi. Can't even let a man be miserable in peace.

"You *looking* for trouble or what, Tozzi? When the hell are you gonna wise up? Why didn't you tell Ivers?" Gibbons glared up at Tozzi from where he sat, but the damn brace made looking up uncomfortable. He got up out of the chair so he could look his partner in the eye, but Tozzi decided to sit on the edge of the bed then. What a pain in the ass this guy was.

"Look, you know how it is with Ivers. He'll call out the heavy artillery to liberate those guys at the chicken shack just to get his face on the six o'clock news. If that happens, we can forget about finding the rest of them. D'Urso and his yakuza friends will move those guys so fast, it'll be a fucking disappearing act. We'll never find them."

"I still don't buy this yakuza business. Sounds too much like one of your usual fairy tales." He leaned up flat against the wall. His neck was killing him. He hated those goddamn painkillers, though. Stupid things made you dopey.

Tozzi started looking around the room, bouncing his knee. He was nervous. He usually did stupid things when he was nervous. "You know a guy named Bob Chen?" he asked. "He's a special agent with the Honolulu office."

"I think I may have heard of him, yeah." Gibbons was determined not to let Tozzi softsoap him into one of his crazy schemes. Not this time. From now on, it was by the book.

"I gave him a call this afternoon. He's the Bureau's unofficial expert on the yakuza. He told me they're all over Hawaii and California, and he says there's some strong evidence that they're beginning to set up camp on the East Coast."

"There's a lot of competition around here. Why would they move into an already glutted market?"

"Why do they all come here, Gib? The money. LA may be groovy, but New York is where the real money is."

"Tokyo isn't exactly poor." Gibbons shifted his hips, but nothing seemed to help. It felt like someone had just pounded a few two-inch finishing nails into his neck and shoulders.

"Too much competition in Japan. In terms of manpower, the Mafia is like the Mickey Mouse Club compared to the yakuza. They've got over a dozen major families. Sixty thousand made members, forty-something-thousand associates. Their biggest family is bigger than all the American Mafia families combined. And Japan has only half the population we have. To survive, these guys have to spread out."

Tozzi was great with facts and figures when he wanted something. It wasn't going to work this time, though. "Ivers isn't going to buy this. He'll say the chicken factory is an isolated case. Yakuza, slavery—it's too farfetched for him." Gibbons tried tilting his head back a little to relieve the pain. That seemed to help.

"Yeah, but when you think about it, Gib, slavery is a natural for this area. The yakuza have been into slavery for a long time. It's not that uncommon in the East. But America is a virgin market for that product. It only makes sense that they'd try to bring it here. Even Ivers can follow that logic."

"Don't count on it. Even if I did think this was a yakuza-Mafia operation, my word doesn't count for a whole lot with him." He rolled his eyes toward his partner. "And yours is worth shit. Just tell him and let them raid the chicken factory. Maybe some of those guys can help us find the other slaves."

"No, they don't know anything." Tozzi looked disgusted with him. "We can't tell Ivers yet."

"Then when? Tell me. When?" he shouted. Goddamn, that hurt. Maybe he could just take half a pill.

"When we know more about the slave business, that's when. How big it is, who this guy Nagai is, who's buying the slaves—"

"And how the hell are we gonna investigate all that without Ivers wondering what the hell we're doing?"

"I'll do all the legwork. You just run interference for me with Ivers."

Gibbons grit his teeth. Jesus Christ Almighty. Tozzi was pounding those nails in a little farther. He tried not to wince, though. He didn't want Tozzi to see how much pain he really was in. "This is how you got into trouble the last time, asshole. You thought you knew better than the whole Bureau, so you went renegade. And this is the same reasoning you used to get me to help you last time. You remember?"

Tozzi pulled that defensive guinea look of his. "I don't need the history lesson, Gib. All I'm asking is that we sit on the information for a little while until we can come up with some concrete evidence that Ivers can't ignore. Something that'll prove to him that this is a very big operation that can't be shut down with a one-shot raid."

Gibbons squeezed his eyes shut and rotated his head ever so slightly. It hurt like a bastard. "All right, all right. We'll sit on this for a little while, but unless you come up with something by the middle of next week, we go to Ivers. Okay?" He didn't feel like arguing right now.

"You all right? You don't look good."

Fuck you. "I'm fine. I'm okay." He lowered himself back down into the lounge chair beside the bed and rested his head against the high back. That seemed to hold the pain down to a dull ache. Tozzi was looking at him with that same wet-eyed long face of concern that Lorraine had been wearing lately. He wished to hell they'd both shape up. He wasn't a cripple, for chrissake.

"Did I tell you about the letter?" Tozzi said.

"What letter?"

"A tipster sent a letter to the field office, unsigned of course. He knew all about the two kids in the VW. According to the letter, the guy who did it is a Japanese named Gozo Mashiro. There was a complete description of him, the kind of car he drives, and a couple of places where he hangs out. Ivers sent McFadden and Brenner out to locate him. This Mashiro was the one the slave told me about that night at the chicken factory, the one they're all so afraid of. According to that slave, he's also the one who beat you up."

"Gogo" Mashiro. Sounds like a guinea legbreaker, almost. The goddamn son of a bitch. "Anybody run a check on him?"

"Yeah. There was nothing in our files on him, so Ivers put in a request to the Japanese National Police Agency for information on him. He told me not to expect much because the Japanese usually aren't very generous about sharing information, but this time the telex was like a slot machine that hit the jackpot. It turns out that Mashiro has been on their most wanted list over there for about eight years now."

"Yeah? For what?" Gibbons was beginning to taste revenge. No one had ever kicked his ass this badly.

"The report said Mashiro was a middle-management executive for Toyota, a bachelor, good worker but nothing outstanding about him. In October of eighty-one, he was passed over for a promotion. The next day he shows up for work with a samurai sword and goes berserk. Killed his boss and the personnel director, then wounded eight others. Hacked off one lady's arm just above the elbow. He was last seen running off into the woods behind the Toyota offices in Nagoya. When the police started investigating, they found out that he had spent several years at the"—Tozzi went into the pocket of his jacket and pulled out a small green notepad—"the Tenshin Shoden Katori Shinto Ryu. You got that?"

Gibbons shrugged and regretted it as soon as he did it. The fucking nails again. Jap bastard.

"This is a school just outside Tokyo that still teaches the old samurai fighting arts, including classical sword technique. The school has been in operation since the fifteenth century."

"Is this where they train their killers over there?"

"No, it's all very spiritual now, sort of like going into the priesthood. But apparently no one ever explained that to Mashiro."

"How about that? I was beat up by a trained samurai. Better than being taken out by some ordinary little punk, I suppose." Gibbons imagined sticking Excalibur down the bastard's throat and seeing what the fuck he'd do then.

"That's not all, though. Mashiro has also studied several of the martial arts, including Shuri-te, which I found out is the hardest of the hard-ass schools of karate. When he went off his rocker, he was a fifth-degree black belt."

"Oh, I feel better already." *Bastard!*

"The interesting thing is that when Mashiro disappeared, he had no yakuza connections. The National Police think he might've hooked up with a gang while he was on the run, and they've been helping him hide out all this time."

"Sounds like a convenient excuse for not catching him." I'll catch him.

"Well, they claim that any yakuza boss would love to have a guy like Mashiro in his gang. Sort of like a Mafia capo here recruiting Andre the Giant into his crew."

"Who?"

"Never mind."

Gibbons almost shrugged again, but he caught himself this time.

"I wish there was some way I could telex the NPA in Japan without Ivers finding out and ask them about the Fugukai and this guy Nagai." Tozzi scratched his neck under his chin which immediately gave Gibbons an itch in the same place. Goddamn him.

He started to shake his head, but that hurt, too. "Forget about that. International requests have to go through headquarters. You're out of luck. Unless you're ready to tell Ivers about crawling through D'Urso's flower beds and breaking into that trailer."

"Hmmm. That's what I figured. Damn." He kept scratching his neck, the bastard.

Tozzi got quiet then. He was trying to figure out how to circumvent the system and telex Japan without anyone in the Bureau knowing about it. Stubborn son of a bitch. Gibbons kept thinking about Mashiro, reconstructing the scene in the chicken factory. He replayed the whole thing in his head, trying to figure out what he'd do differently. He'd *kill* the son of a bitch, that's what he'd do differently. Put a fucking bullet in his head. Splatter his brains all over the goddamn—

Gibbons caught himself then. Vendetta, revenge, getting even. He was thinking like Tozzi now, for chrissake. He sighed and looked down at his suitcase on the floor. Where the hell was that goddamn doctor? He wanted to get out of here.

"Mr. Gibbons. How are you feeling?"

Gibbons knew that chesty contralto all too well. He rolled his eyes toward the doorway. There she was. The two-ton buttercup.

"I feel like a bag of shit, Fay. How're you?"

Fay had long blond Alice-in-Wonderland hair and tits like bowling balls. She was the first person he saw when he woke up from the coma, and his first thought was what the hell kind of material is that nurse's uniform made of that it can take that much stress without splitting. She steamed into the room, stopped dead, bounced her fists onto her hips, and glared at Tozzi sitting on the bed.

"Are you a patient, sir?"

"No."

"Then please get off the bed."

"It's already messed up," Tozzi said.

"Hospital policy, sir. Only admitted patients belong in the beds. Our insurance doesn't cover visitors falling out of hospital beds. Please take a chair." After Tozzi got up, she turned back to him and switched her lipstick smile back on again. Fifty nurses work this floor, a few of them real knockouts. Gibbons couldn't figure out why the brutal-looking ones always liked him.

"Did you take your pills after lunch, Mr. Gibbons?"

"Yes." It took three flushes to get the damn things to go down the toilet.

"Good. Here's your prescription." She handed him a little brown plastic bottle. The dopey painkillers.

"Where's the doctor? I thought he was supposed to see me off."

"Dr. Lipscomb was called away, but don't worry. He's already signed your discharge papers." That big red smile hovered over him like a pterodactyl.

He smiled back, with his teeth.

"Now you can take the painkillers whenever you're in discomfort, but don't take more than four a day and at least four hours apart. Okay?"

"Right."

"And also, you shouldn't drive while you're taking these. Or operate any heavy machinery."

"Right." Excalibur only weighs about two pounds.

"Now let's see here." She flipped through papers on her clipboard. "Billing has all your Blue Cross/Blue Shield information. Good. So all you have to do is sign here . . . and here, and you'll be all set."

Gibbons took the ballpoint from her chubby, ruby-nailed fingers, scribbled his name next to the two x's, and gave back the clipboard.

"Good. Now I want you to rest. Lie down as much as you can, take it easy, and keep that brace on whenever you're standing or sitting up. The best thing to do would be to just stay in bed and prop yourself up nicely with pillows. Always give your poor neck as much support as possible. We don't want to see you back in here now, do we?" She oozed like a melting hot fudge sundae. "An orderly will be right in to see you out. Bye-bye now." She twiddled her fingers like Oliver Hardy and steamed back out the door.

"An orderly? For what?"

"To take you downstairs in a wheelchair," Tozzi said. "It's an insurance thing. So you don't fall down and break your neck while you're still in the building."

"Fuck that. Come on, let's go." Gibbons started to haul himself out of the chair.

"So, ah . . . where we going?" Tozzi wasn't making any moves to go.

"Home. Where the hell else am I going to go?"

"Oh . . ." Tozzi started nodding at nothing. "Okay. I just thought—"

"You thought what?"

"Well, I was talking to Lorraine last night and she was kind of hoping you'd go down to her place for a couple of days at least. You know, to recuperate. I could drive you down right now. I've got the time."

"Recuperate, huh? Is that what she said? Retire is what she means."

"No, that's not—"

"You know, you burn me up, the two of you. A concussion and a few bruised vertebrae and all of a sudden I'm scrap metal. Every time she's come in here, she's had that face, that oh-you-poor-old-dog face. And she's always hinting around that maybe I should go back into retirement. Now she's got you working for her cause. Well, if you think I'm through, Tozzi, fuck you, too."

"Hey, I'm not telling you to retire. But I think you should take Lorraine into consideration for a change. She loves you, you stupid asshole. She's worried about you. Just spend the weekend down there. Make her happy."

"She's turning into an old lady with all this worrying shit. But if she thinks she's gonna make an old man out of me, she better think again."

"Okay, granted, she's been kind of a pain in the ass about this, but she's also been worried sick about you. She knows what a pig head you are. She knows you're not gonna take care of yourself. She just wants you to get better, that's all."

"I am better, right now, and I'm going back to work. To-morrow."

"Don't be stupid. Take it easy for a few days."

"The discussion is over. I don't want to talk about it any-more. Case closed." Gibbons bent down to get his suitcase and felt those nails again.

"Put that down. I'll carry it."

"I can do it."

"*Madonn'*, what a hardhead!"

"Can the guinea dramatics, will ya? Let's go."

"Hold on a minute. Tomorrow's Saturday. Where are you gonna go back to work?"

"I'm not stupid, Tozzi. I know I'm not working on all cyl-inders. I'm not gonna push it."

"So what are you gonna do?"

Gibbons sighed in annoyance. "I'm gonna sit in my car with a pair of binoculars and watch D'Urso's house, that's what I'm gonna do. I'll have my collar, I'll bring some pillows —it'll be just like being home on the couch. Given all that you've told me, I think there's a certain degree of urgency here and someone ought to make at least a token effort to check out the domicile of the guy who's got sixty slaves locked up behind his factory. Wouldn't you say so?"

"I agree one hundred percent. I think we *should* put a plant on D'Urso's place."

"Not *we*, Tozzi. *Me*."

"Pick me up at eight. I'll buy coffee."

"If you intend to get something to bring to Ivers by next week, you better get your ass in gear and start looking. Forget about keeping me company."

Tozzi grinned. "What better place to start looking than D'Urso's house? Just blow the horn when you get to my place. I'll be right down."

Gibbons hated it when Tozzi kept his cool. Actually it wouldn't be so bad having some company tomorrow, and anyway he might not feel like driving the whole day. Tozzi could come. As long as he shut up about Lorraine.

"I'll spring for the donuts, too," Tozzi said. "Honey-dips, that's what you like, right?"

Gibbons finally exhaled in resignation. "You're a real pain in my ass, Tozzi. Be ready at seven. And I don't like goddamn honey-dips. Get cinnamon crullers."

"Right."

"And remember the deal. If you don't track down anything new on the slave thing by Wednesday, we take it to Ivers as is."

Tozzi closed his eyes and nodded.

Just then a short little guy with round, wire-rim glasses came into the room pushing a wheelchair. "Okay, Mr. Gibbons. Time to go. Hop on."

Gibbons pivoted on one foot and turned around stiff-legged, like Frankenstein. He looked down at the orderly, the neck brace pushing the flesh up around his jowls. "Get out of my way before I throw you *and* that wheelchair out the window."

The orderly froze, mouth open, glasses glimmering.

Gibbons stepped around him and Tozzi followed, snickering behind his fist.

"But, Mr. Gibbons . . ." the orderly called after him weakly.

Gibbons kept walking, swinging the suitcase by his side. "Don't sweat it, pal. I'll be okay. And have a real nice fucking day."

24

Tozzi moved the phone to the other end of the bed and sat with his back up against the wall. "Lorraine, listen to me." He shifted the phone to his other ear. "I told you. I tried to convince him, but he didn't want to hear anything about it." He glanced at his watch. They'd been on the phone for twenty minutes now.

"But you promised me, Michael. You told me you would get him to come down here."

"I'm telling you I tried, but you've got to understand he's very touchy right now. He doesn't want to be treated like an invalid, and frankly I don't blame him."

"I'm not treating him like an invalid. I just want him to rest, goddamn it. He has to give this time—the doctor said so."

"Yeah, I know all that, but Gib has been a special agent his whole life. This is a guy who's never once had desk duty. He works the streets, that's what he knows, that's what he does. He's worried that he might not be able to do that much longer."

"Did he say that?"

"No, but I know him. That's what he's thinking. He doesn't want to make his exit before his time."

"What is it with you two? You're two of a kind. Stubborn and proud, and all for what? The greater glory of the FBI?"

"No, no, you don't understand." Tozzi pulled the phone away from his ear. Now this one was getting sweaty. "He

thinks you want him to retire. That's what's bothering him."
Why was he telling her all this? Gibbons should be having
this conversation, not him. Gibbons should've told her this a
long time ago. Part of him thought his cousin was absolutely
right, for chrissake. So why the hell was he arguing Gibbons's
case? Shit.

"I gave up hoping that he'd ever retire a long time ago. All
I want him to do is recover before he re-injures himself. And
would it really be such a tragedy if he sat this one out? Tell
me the truth. If that karate nut finds out Gibbons is out walking around, won't he try to finish the job he started?"

"I'm not a psychic. I can't read minds, Lorraine."

There was testy silence on the line for a moment. Tozzi
could hear his own breathing in the phone.

"Answer me this, Michael. Are we in agreement that he
should rest, that he shouldn't be working at least until the
doctor says it's okay?"

"Yes, I think he should rest." He wasn't going to say for
how long. They'd already gotten into it over how long Gibbons should recuperate, a few days versus a few months.

"Then if we agree that he should rest, *why the hell are you
taking him out on a stakeout tomorrow?*"

"You don't have to yell, Lorraine. I can hear you." Why are
you busting my balls with this? I'm just trying to keep the
two of you happy.

"*Why, Michael? Tell me why you are taking him to work one day
after his release from the hospital.*"

He couldn't believe how much she sounded like her mother
when she got mad. It was just like talking to Aunt Philomena,
another real ball-buster. "First of all, Lorraine, the plant on
D'Urso's house was his idea, not mine. I invited myself to
come along so that I could watch him and make *you* happy.
Okay?" As if I have nothing better to do.

"Well, I'm *not* happy."

"Listen to me. All we're going to do is sit in his car and
watch this Mafia guy's house, that's all. He'll be wearing his
neck brace, he'll bring pillows. He can lie down in the backseat if he gets tired. It'll be the same thing as sitting home on
the couch."

"That's bullshit, Michael, and you know it. You're going to

be down in some god-awful neighborhood in Newark or wherever, looking for trouble."

"Not true. We'll be in a nice wealthy suburban neighborhood where you don't even see people walking their dogs it's so ritzy. Believe me, nothing will happen to him. I guarantee it."

"How can you guarantee anything? You promised to get him down here and you didn't do that."

Yes, Aunt Phil.

"Where exactly will you be tomorrow?" she continued. "I want to know."

"You know I can't tell you that."

"Goddamn you, Michael. How can you be this way to me? I used to change your shitty diapers, for God sake. Why are you doing this to me?"

I don't know, Aunt Phil. I must be just plain bad.

"I blame *you* for this, Michael. If it weren't for you, he wouldn't have all these reckless macho ideas. He's trying to keep up with you. You realize that, don't you? But at his age he shouldn't be working out in the field at all."

I dare you to tell him that to his face. "Lorraine, I think you're blowing this way out of proportion."

"I'm done talking, Michael. I've done all I can. All I can say is that if he gets hurt tomorrow, I'm going to hold *you* responsible. That's all."

Wonderful. "Don't worry, Lorraine. He'll be okay."

"I'd really like to believe that. I really would." She hung up the phone.

He stared at the receiver and sighed. "Good night, Aunt Phil."

Great. Now they were both mad at him. Gibbons thought he agreed with Lorraine about taking some time off to recover and reconsider retirement. Lorraine thought he didn't give a shit about Gibbons's health, that all he was concerned about was playing cops and robbers again with his old buddy. You try to be a good guy and you end up the bad guy. Shit.

He laid back on the new bed, staring up at the ceiling. It was nice and firm, but it smelled new. He was really getting sick of that new smell. He looked at his watch. It was just six-thirty. Roxanne went back to her office after the bed arrived. She'd left a note inviting him to come over to her place this

evening to watch the Miss Galaxy Pageant. He called her up
to say he'd pass on Miss Galaxy but promised to pick her up
around eleven and take her out for a sandwich or something.
He still couldn't believe she was into watching beauty pageants.

He stared at the shadowy walls and stretched his feet until
he heard his ankles crack. His ankles were still sore from
sitting *seiza*. Some people can sit that way indefinitely. Neil
Chaney could. This guy Mashiro probably could, too, and on
a bare floor, no doubt. That's probably what he does when he
practices his sword techniques or whatever. A real hard-ass,
this guy. Gibbons never takes shit from anyone, but Mashiro
apparently made short work of him. Tozzi looked at the
growing darkness outside his window and wondered what
he'd do if he had to take on Mashiro. Shoot the bastard, of
course. But Gibbons didn't get a chance to shoot him.
Mashiro took his gun away first. How could you beat this guy
if you had to fight him one-on-one, no weapons? He thought
about Gibbons's pale, lifeless face as he lay semi-conscious in
the hospital, the monitor beeping over the bed. Tozzi could
feel it then, in the pit of his stomach, like a small invading
virus entering his system. Fear. He wasn't used to the feeling
and he didn't like it being there. He looked at his watch again,
then sat up and reached for his loafers on the floor. He decided to go for a walk.

Tozzi recognized the lone pair of tan rubber sandals at the
edge of the mat as soon as he walked into the *dojo*. Neil Chaney was there, practicing alone with his wooden sword, the
bokken, standing in one spot, turning in all directions as he
sliced down with his sword. Tozzi realized this was similar to
another exercise they did in aikido where you thrust your
hands up, then dropped them to your side, repeating this motion as you faced eight different directions. He'd heard the
Japanese name for this exercise but he couldn't remember it.

Tozzi couldn't tell whether Neil noticed him standing
there in the doorway because he didn't stop what he was
doing. Instead he picked up his pace, calling out the eight-
count faster and faster until he was just a blur of chopping
motion. It almost seemed unnatural, the speed he was doing

this, but Tozzi knew it came from staying relaxed. At least that's what he'd been told.

When Neil finally stopped, Tozzi walked over to the edge of the mat before he had a chance to start up again. "Hi. I'm not disturbing you, am I?"

Neil shook his head and just looked at him as if he were waiting for him to explain himself. Tozzi had observed that Neil only talked as much as he had to and often left long awkward pauses, just like this one. He was weird like that. Maybe this was all part of being *sensei*. Or maybe he was just weird. It was hard to tell.

"I saw the lights on," Tozzi explained. "I was sort of hoping I'd find you here."

Neil nodded, a funny little half-smile on his face.

"Well—I told you I was in law enforcement, didn't I?"

Neil nodded.

"Well . . ." Tozzi wasn't sure how to word this. "There's this person I'm investigating. He's pretty aggressive and very dangerous, and I . . . I have a feeling I'm going to meet up with him sooner or later. I was, ah, thinking that maybe you could show me a few moves that I could use on him. Nothing esoteric, just some basic practical aikido."

Neil closed his eyes and shook his head.

"Look, I realize this must sound pretty offensive to you. Here I am, a beginner, I've only taken two classes so far, and I'm asking you for shortcuts. That's stupid, I know. But I really need your help." *If you saw what Mashiro did to Gibbons, you'd understand.*

Neil shook his head.

"You don't know what I'm up against, man. This guy is a . . . a samurai when you come right down to it. He's a fifth-degree karate black belt and a formally trained swordsman. He's already hurt my partner, and I have this gut feeling that it's only a matter of time before he finds me. I need something if I'm going to go up against this guy." *Come on. Don't let me down. Please.*

Neil nodded thoughtfully. "How fast can you run, Mike?"

"Come on, I'm being serious here."

"So am I. Because unless you can run away from him, you haven't got a chance against a trained *bushi*."

"What's that?"

"A 'martial man.' A samurai."

"Isn't there *something* you can show me?"

Neil's face turned to stone. "You're insulting me, Mike. You're insulting anyone who practices a martial art. It would take years of dedicated study to hold your own against someone as accomplished as you say this samurai is. I'm a second *dan* black belt. I've been studying aikido for eight years. I'm not sure I could hold my own against this guy."

Tozzi pinched the bridge of his nose. Shit. After another awkward silence, he looked Neil in the eye. "I've had it out with plenty of people in the past. Gun fights, fistfights, knife fights, you name it. I've had to face killers, mobsters, drug runners, psychopaths, sociopaths. But you know something? This is the first time someone's ever spooked me before I even met him. I don't want to be an instant black belt. I just don't want to be scared when I meet up with this guy. Because if I am, I'm sunk. That's what I was hoping you could do for me. Just show me a few things that will make me believe it might possibly be an even match. Please, Neil, I'm asking you."

Neil rested the tip of the *bokken* on his shoulder and scratched his beard. "Aikido teaches you how to remain calm in the face of an attack. It shows you how to extend *ki,* how to use your attacker's aggressiveness back against him. It shows you how to be aware of everything around you, and how to anticipate your opponent's intentions. I could teach you some of that. But not tonight."

"Because that takes years," Tozzi said. Yeah, yeah, I know.

"That's right. You've got too many bad habits to break before aikido can work for you. Rule number one: You never fight in anger. In the West, that's the only time people ever fight. You have to learn how to be calm, how to center yourself, not just in a fight but all the time. I can tell just from the way you talk that you're very aggressive and combative. You want to cold-cock the son of a bitch before he even gets near you. That's not aikido. You have to wait, be patient, let your opponent commit himself first so you can use that first strike against him. This goes entirely against the grain of your natural instincts, doesn't it?"

Tozzi pressed his lips together and nodded. "But isn't there anything you can show me? Anything at all?"

Neil stared at him for a long moment. "How late can you stay tonight?"

Holy shit! Tozzi broke out into a smile. "As late as you want." He remembered his promise to Roxanne, but this was more important. He hoped she'd understand that.

"Basically I can begin to show you how to get out of the way. And we'll only be scratching the surface." Neil sounded doubtful.

"Great. Fine. Anything will be more than I have now." Tozzi didn't like the doubt in Neil's voice. He deliberately tried to ignore it to keep his hopes up. He had to prove to Neil that he was really interested, that he wanted to learn. "You couldn't also show me that technique where you throw the attacker who's chasing you with the *bokken*, could you?"

"Which one is that?"

"I don't know what it's called. It's the one where the guy is chasing you, trying to bop you over the head from behind and you turn quickly to face him. You get out of the way, and as the sword comes down, you somehow grab his hands and flip him over on his back and take the sword away, too. I saw you do it the first night I came here."

Neil looked unsure. He handed his *bokken* to Tozzi. "Show me what you mean." He turned and started to run across the mats.

Tozzi quickly kicked off his shoes and left them by the tan sandals, then immediately started to run after him, circling back around the mats until he managed to catch up and get within striking distance. "You remember this one?"

"Go ahead," Neil shouted. "Strike."

Tozzi raised the wooden sword over his head as he ran, hesitated a moment, then brought it down toward Neil's head. Suddenly Neil stopped short and faced him. The next thing Tozzi knew he was flat on his back staring up backwards at him. His eyes went out of focus for a second.

"*Shomen Uchi Kokyu Nage.* Is that the one you meant?"

"Yeah . . . that one." Ooow. Not bad.

Tozzi hauled himself to his feet, breathing hard but still smiling. "So . . . shall we get started?"

Neil shrugged and nodded. He had that funny little grin again.

Tozzi took a deep breath, prepared to put in a long night.

He felt better already, though, just standing here with someone who knew so much and was willing to share it. If he had
to face Mashiro when he walked out of here tonight, he'd still
be very very wary of the guy, but he wasn't going to let the
bastard scare him. No way.

25

Nagai leaned over the stack of Gatorade boxes and peered down at the tiny screen of Mashiro's Sony Watchman TV. The obnoxious emcee in the inflatable tuxedo stood in front of the line of finalists, smiling like a fool at the girls, tugging on his black bow tie with the microphone under his arm, acting like a rooster. The girls looked alike to Nagai—a solid wall of cleavage, sequins, ugly puffy hair, anxious eyebrows, and toothpaste smiles. The emcee continued to preen as he leered at the girls. He reminded Nagai of D'Urso, the son of a bitch.

Nagai glanced up from the TV at Mashiro sitting *seiza*, motionless in the shadows, doing his meditation. He looked at his watch and frowned. Come on, Mashiro. Hurry up. Johnny Carson is almost over on Channel 4. He scratched his scalp behind his ear and looked down at the TV again. Sometimes these fucking samurai rituals were a pain in the ass.

The emcee looked down at the envelopes in his hand. "Here we go, girls." Now he had a toothpaste smile, too. "Our third runner-up for the title of Miss Galaxy is . . . Miss Canada!"

Nagai grunted at the tiny moving figures. They were like the bugs on a Raid commercial.

The emcee opened another envelope. "Our second runner-up for the title of Miss Galaxy is . . . Miss Ecuador!"

More tears and commotion. Nagai glanced over at Mashiro

again. He hadn't moved in the last half-hour. Why must this take an eternity? Come on. He turned back to the TV.

The emcee turned sideways to the camera and faced the last two girls who stood shoulder to shoulder now, clutching each other's forearms. They looked like they were about to face death. "A little nervous?" the rooster asked with a stupid chuckle. The girls nodded like monkeys.

Hurry up, hurry up.

The orchestra held a note of suspense as the emcee opened the last envelope in his hand. He smiled, took a deep breath into the microphone, rolled his eyes at the girls. "Our first runner-up, whose duty it will be to carry on the title in the event that the reigning Miss Galaxy cannot continue to wear her crown, is . . . Miss Egypt!"

Panic and confusion. Like a bomb scare.

"Our new Miss Galaxy is *MISS HONG KONG!!!*"

The girls hugged and cried. Noise and more confusion. The other girls put a crown on Miss Hong Kong's head, a fur robe over her shoulders, roses in her arms. She cried and walked and waved.

Nagai smirked. Good choice. But he still wondered what happened to Miss Japan. He'd tuned in late.

As the music swelled and the credits rolled over teary Miss Hong Kong, Nagai noticed Mashiro stirring, the stone man coming to life. "Mashiro," he called to his samurai. "We've got trouble."

Mashiro got to his feet and pulled the ends of his black belt tight around his *gi* jacket. He approached Nagai and bowed his head. "What trouble?"

"Reiko called me tonight."

"From D'Urso's house?"

"Yes, from D'Urso's house." Nagai rubbed the back of his neck. "They're going to do it soon, she thinks."

Mashiro nodded. "You seem unsettled. Is there something else?"

"That punk Francione has a new gun. She says he threatened her with it. He was drunk, calling her Antonelli and pretending to shoot her. The son of a bitch."

"Did he hurt her?"

"She says no." Nagai was suspicious, though. D'Urso was dying to get into her pants. The punk probably wanted her too, just because his boss wanted her. Nagai wondered whether Reiko would tell him if they tried anything with her.

Mashiro walked over to his futon and picked up his sword. He cradled the weapon in his palms and bowed to his lord. "He has dishonored you. Shall I go kill him?"

Nagai considered it for a moment, then finally shook his head, disgusted. "She told me the drunken bastard was talking nonsense. In his craziness he said something about splattering brand-new cars with Antonelli's blood and watching it run down into the water. The new car lot down at the docks —that's what he was talking about. That's where they must be planning to shoot their boss."

"When are they going to do this? Did she say?"

Nagai shrugged. "He didn't say. Bastards. All she said was that Francione and D'Urso are both in the house now, sleeping."

"I can go right now. Dead in their beds by morning."

Nagai shook his head again. "We can't do that. It'll make *us* look bad. We can't operate like ninja. Hamabuchi would never let us get away with that."

Mashiro scowled. Nagai forgot. The samurai hated the sneaking, cowardly ninja and didn't like being compared to one.

"But we have to save Antonelli," Mashiro objected. "All your dreams sail on his pulse. If D'Urso succeeds, your hopes will sink. Let me kill them before they make their attempt."

Nagai was annoyed with Mashiro's fancy imagery. He sounded like Hamabuchi. "No, we can't kill them at home. We have to catch them in the act."

Mashiro dropped his sword to his side. "What do you want me to do then?"

Nagai reached into his pocket for a cigarette. His lighter flared in the dimness and he took a long, deep drag. "Be down at the docks before dawn. Stay out of sight and just be ready for anything. In the meantime, I'm going to try one more thing to persuade D'Urso to reconsider making his big move."

"Why are you being so nice to him? He doesn't deserve another chance."

Nagai sucked on the cigarette and made his lips pop. Smoke

filtered up to reveal a sly grin. "He may listen to me if he has something to lose. Something the son of a bitch cares about."

A small grin appeared on Mashiro's face. He could guess what Nagai had in mind.

"Get some rest," Nagai said. "If we're lucky, nothing will happen. But be there anyway, just in case. Perhaps the punk will do something stupid and give you a reason to introduce him to your blade."

"*Hai.*" Mashiro's grin stretched wider. He turned and gazed up at his ancestor's armor hanging on the wall. It was like a floating spirit in the shadows.

"In the days when my ancestor Yamashita fought for *his* lord Nagai," Mashiro pronounced, "a samurai made his lord powerful and powerful warlords made the shogun supreme. It was the magnificent invincible fabric of the greatest warrior society of all time." Mashiro's broad chest heaved as he took in a deep breath. "I am in that tradition. Your power will flow on like the river, my lord. I will not fail you."

Nagai dropped his cigarette on the floor and twisted his toe over it. "Right . . . I know I can depend on you." He never knew what to say when Mashiro gave him all this tradition stuff. "I'll see you tomorrow then, Mashiro."

He turned to go, then remembered the Watchman. "By the way, I left your TV on that stack of boxes over there."

Mashiro bowed and Nagai turned to go. His footsteps clicked on the concrete floor. He looked over his shoulder as he walked and saw Mashiro going over to retrieve his TV.

He stared at Yamashita hovering over the scene. The protecting spirit. Nagai shrugged and headed for the door. Who knows? Maybe he was.

As he passed the long dark aisles of palettes stacked high with boxes and crates, Nagai suddenly thought he heard something, a faint voice coming from behind. He stopped and listened, then glanced at his watch. Ten minutes to one. Yes, of course, who else would it be? Mashiro liked Letterman. Lots of good fools on that show, he always said.

26

Lorraine rushed down the incline of the sidewalk, a stiff wind pushing from behind and blowing her hair in her face as she looked for numbers on the storefronts, searching for #49. All around her there were people going about their suburban Saturday morning business, lots of activity around the supermarket and the hardware store. A pack of boys ran past her like banshees, the bunch of them pushing and shoving to get through the door of a small variety store up ahead where dozens of plastic and rubber Halloween masks hung in the window. She stopped and looked. Most of the characters were new to her, but she did recognize a few. Dracula, Fred Flintstone, Skeletor, the Smurfs, Charley Brown and Lucy . . .

Damn him.

She refocused on her own reflection in the glass. The wind blew strands of hair across her sagging face. Her eyes were rimmed, and she looked as tired as she felt. She was wearing a pair of baggy jeans that should've been washed last week, and her shoulders slumped with fatigue under the old black-and-white buffalo-plaid lumberjack shirt she just threw on this morning when she got the idea to come up here to Maplewood. She stared at her forlorn condition against the background of all those gruesome plastic faces, and she saw herself as the Wicked Witch of the West. If she was a witch, it was his fault. Gibbons was turning her into an old hag, the son of a bitch.

A little girl with short red braids came out of the store,

holding her father's hand. She was wearing a wide-brimmed, straw Chinese coolie hat, pressing it to her head against the breeze with her free hand. Lorraine couldn't see her face, only the braids. The girl was whining that the wind was going to blow her away, but her daddy reassured her that he wouldn't let that happen, just keep walking. They paid Lorraine no mind as they walked around her.

She looked across the street and gazed at the storefronts over there, looking for a number. She squinted at the Christian Science Reading Room and the stationery store next door, and then she spotted it, #49, on the glass door between the stores on the ground floor of that two-story yellow-brick building. She dug into the breast pocket of her lumberjack shirt and pulled out the scrap of paper with the information she'd scribbled down from the phone book: Eastlake Academy, 49 Main, Rm. 22.

Lorraine pushed the hair out of her face and dashed through traffic, heading for Room 22. She chewed her lip as she ran. Please be there.

She pushed through the glass door, climbed the stairs, and followed the arrows to the Eastlake Academy. When she got to the door, she could hear music inside. It sounded like a Vivaldi concerto, very bouncy and determined. She knocked on the door, waited, knocked again, then let herself in. She wasn't going to be put off anymore, not by anyone.

The waiting room was empty. She followed the music to the next room where Roxanne was sitting behind her desk, staring out the window with her feet up on the radiator. The music was coming from the stereo nestled in with the books on a high bookcase.

"Hello."

Roxanne's head whipped around, her eyes wide with alarm. She stared at Lorraine for a moment. It wasn't a very welcoming stare.

"God, you scared me." Roxanne got up and turned off the music. She looked like she wanted to be alone.

"I apologize for barging in on you like this, but as you can probably see, I'm at wit's end."

"Is there something wrong, Lorraine? Can I help?" There was chilly formality in Roxanne's voice, a kind of clipped detachment she must use with her clients. Not the tender doe Lorraine met at the hospital. Something was bothering her.

"I don't mean to bother you, Roxanne, but you're my last hope." Lorraine sat down on the edge of the burgundy leather sofa. She'd been up most of the night, and she was exhausted. "What's wrong?"

"Gibbons. He's the only thing that's ever wrong."

"I don't follow you." Roxanne sat down behind her desk. She sat very straight and proper, still very cold. Lorraine decided to ignore it. For the moment, she had her own problems to deal with.

"He was released from the hospital yesterday. Yesterday! He's supposed to be resting, for God's sake. But where do you think he is right now? Out on a plant with Michael."

"A plant?"

Lorraine sighed. Roxanne didn't know the jargon . . . yet. "That's what *they* call it. A stakeout. Michael told me last night on the phone."

"I talked to him this morning. I was supposed to see him last night, but he got tied up with something important, he said. He said he was going to be working this morning, but he didn't give me any details."

Oh, so that's why the cold shoulder. Michael stood her up last night. And Michael's cousin must be culpable by blood, no doubt. Lorraine sighed. She was tempted to say something to Roxanne, give her the voice of experience, but what good would it do? It's like the college professor telling the bright-eyed student that pursuing a career in academia might be a mistake, that there's no future in it. They already have their minds set. They never listen.

"They're like goddamn kids, those two," Lorraine said instead. "Daredevils hell-bent on getting themselves killed. The trouble with them is that Gibbons won't admit to himself how old he really is. He thinks he can keep up with Michael, and Michael does nothing to discourage him. Michael, on the other hand, feels he has to live up to the legend, Gibbons, the salty old dog of the Bureau. They feed off each other like that. They're incredible."

Roxanne sighed and shook her head, the frost melting away. "Yes, they certainly are incredible." She looked up at her bookcase and smirked. "You know, I've only known your cousin for a week. Seven days and one morning to be exact, and he's got me acting like a silly idiot. I think about him all the time. It's ridiculous. I haven't felt this way about a man since high school. I didn't think I'd ever feel that way again. So giddy, so . . . I mean, this simply is not adult behavior. After all, it's only been a week . . . and a morning."

Lorraine sighed. "Sounds like you're pretty much head over heels."

Roxanne just looked down at her blotter and shrugged.

A loud drone from outside filled the silence. A small airplane, Lorraine guessed. She hugged the flaps of her lumberjack shirt. It was cold in Roxanne's office. "I went to your apartment this morning, but you weren't home. I looked you up in the phone book. I had to find you because I need a favor."

"What is it?"

"I want you to give me that mobster's address. That's where they are. I want to talk some sense into Gibbons before he gets hurt again."

Roxanne started playing with the ring on her finger, a flat oval onyx in a beaded silver setting. "Well, I—"

"I know you know where it is. Gibbons told me it was you who put them on to this D'Urso character in the first place." Lorraine stared into her eyes. She was not going to be put off.

Roxanne seemed startled by her determination. "Well, yes, it's true that I told Mike about Mrs. D'Urso's pirate babysitter business, and one of my nosybody ex-clients did tell me where she lived. I've driven by the house, just out of curiosity, so I could take you there. But . . . well, Mike and Gibbons won't be very pleased to see us, will they? Interference from us . . . well, wouldn't that be some kind of crime? Technically, I mean. Like obstruction of justice, or something like that."

Lorraine stared hard at her. "Is it that you're so mad at Michael you don't want to see him, or does he have you that snowed with the FBI bullshit? He's got you thinking the same way Gibbons made me think all these years. You're making room for the FBI. You can't take the man without the Bureau. It's a package deal, no substitutes. I think having to live with a conniving battle-ax of a mother-in-law would've been better than this."

Roxanne was twisting that ring around her finger, around and around. "But do you really think going to find them would be wise? I mean, will Gibbons really listen to you if you just show up like this? He'll only be furious and more unreasonable, won't he?"

"I really don't care what he thinks. I'm tired of accommodating his feelings, cajoling him, stroking him, always trying to persuade him to see it my way. I'm worried about me now for a change and that's what I intend to tell him. If he really cares about me, he'll come home and rest the way he's supposed to. The doctor said he could do permanent neurological damage, maybe even paralysis, if he doesn't take it easy. So if he gives me this shit about having a job to do, then that's it. He can get himself shot for all I care because I don't want him on his terms anymore." She stuck her hands under her armpits. Her fingers were freezing. "So are you going to give me that address or not?"

Roxanne stopped playing with her ring. "I suppose if I were ever in your position, I wouldn't want to be put off. It could happen." She looked up at her bookcase again and sighed. "All right. I'll take you there."

"Just give me the directions. You don't have to come."

"Yes I do. Otherwise it'll be two against one." Roxanne flashed a knowing grin.

Lorraine shook her head and grinned back. Roxanne was all right. There was hope for her yet.

"Come on," Roxanne said, walking around the desk. "We'll take my car."

Seeing the shine of Roxanne's red hair as she stepped into the sunlight reminded Lorraine of that little girl with the red braids and the coolie hat. "Fine. We just have to make one quick stop first."

As she followed Roxanne out into the reception room, Lorraine snatched a Kleenex from the box on the desk and blew her nose. A united front. Two on two. Maybe she wouldn't be put off this time.

27

Gibbons shifted his butt and pressed his back into the passenger seat, then picked up the binoculars and scanned the property around D'Urso's house again. It was almost ten-thirty and still quiet. He stuck his finger in the neck brace to get the damn thing off his Adam's apple for a minute. The pain he felt yesterday had diminished considerably, but now he had a new pain. It felt like he had two bowling balls hanging off his shoulders and no matter what he did he couldn't shrug them off. He wondered if Nurse Fay, the two-ton buttercup, felt this way all the time.

"How's the neck feel?" Tozzi asked.

"Fine." Gibbons shot a sour look at his partner. "Why do you keep asking me that?"

"I have to," Tozzi said, gazing down at the *Daily News* open on the steering wheel. "I promised Lorraine I'd take care of you." Tozzi didn't look up but he had this shit-eating grin on his face.

"Fuck you, Tozzi." He scanned the house with the binoculars again.

"You're quite welcome, Gib."

Gibbons put down the binoculars. "This is useless. There's nothing to see here. Come on, let's go. We'll tell Ivers and let him do what he wants with it. At least it'll get things moving."

Tozzi shook his head. "You said we could sit on it until the middle of next week. You promised."

"So what?"

"You promised."

"I take it back then. Let's go."

Tozzi shook his head again. "See? Lorraine is right about you. You don't keep your promises."

"Eat shit."

"Why don't you just take the goddamn painkillers and sit still for a while?"

Gibbons didn't answer. He'd brought the pills, just in case. But Tozzi was just assuming he had them. Prick.

"If we don't see anything by lunchtime, we'll go. Okay?"

"Don't do me any fucking favors."

Tozzi went back to his newspaper, but Gibbons could feel him grinning, the bastard. Bad enough that he was letting Tozzi drive his car. He could drive it himself if he wanted to —he wasn't an invalid. It was just looking left and right when he came up to an intersection that was a problem. Sometimes he'd forget about his neck and turn his head instead of turning his shoulders. That hurt like a bitch. That's why he was letting Tozzi drive. Not because he couldn't. It was just to give himself a break. That's all. He lowered the binoculars and looked at Tozzi. He better realize that.

After a minute, Tozzi noticed that he was being stared at. "What're you looking at me like that for?"

"Like what?"

"Like Sister Theresa Ignatius, my fifth-grade teacher, that's what."

Gibbons didn't like being compared to a nun. "I don't know what you're talking about."

"You got this real pissy look on your face. What am I, putting fingerprints on your steering wheel? What?"

"Shut up and read your paper."

Tozzi looked down and flipped the page. "It's okay. I know what's bothering you."

"Oh, yeah? What?"

"Lorraine."

"Fuck you." He tried rotating his shoulders a little. The bowling balls had suddenly gotten heavier.

"Yeah, all right, fuck me." Tozzi snapped another page. "You been fighting with her all week, and now you want to take it out on me. Well, that's okay. Go ahead. I'll be the punching bag. I understand."

Gibbons could feel his face turning to stone. He wanted to smash Tozzi over his big guinea nose with the binoculars. Bastard. Of course it was Lorraine who was bothering him. What the hell did he think? Tozzi's too goddamn young, that's his problem. He sleeps with anything that moves and thinks it's love. In ten, fifteen years he'll change his tune. That's when he'll wish he had a good woman, not some bimbo, someone you can talk to, someone you can stand to be with more than ten minutes. That's his whole problem. He doesn't know what loving a woman is all about. Not really. No use explaining it to him, though. The guy's got a thick head. Always has to learn the hard way. Bastard.

Gibbons let out a long sigh that ended with a rumbling growl deep in his throat. "Come on. D'Urso's not here. We're wasting our time. Let's get out of here."

Tozzi kept looking at the paper and shook his head slowly. "Who was the one who always preached to me about being patient on a plant? About sitting tight and waiting it out until your ass went numb? About following proper procedure no matter how boring it got?"

"The place is too quiet," Gibbons overrode him. "If you weren't so damned interested in the paper, you'd see that. Christ, we've been here since eight and all I've seen is one goddamn dog pissing on D'Urso's lawn. I haven't seen a single person in this neighborhood. Not even a fucking jogger. D'Urso's not here, believe me."

Tozzi glanced down at the house over his paper. "I see a three-car garage, doors closed. How do you know D'Urso's Mercedes isn't in there?" Tozzi turned the page and went back to the paper. "Short Hills is a very rich community. Rich people don't jog on the street. They go to health clubs. A rich guy doesn't just go out for a stroll in the neighborhood. Rich people don't hang out on the corner to shoot the breeze either. Rich people don't like to be seen around their houses. Don't ask me why—that's just the way they are. Now as for the dog, I'm surprised he wasn't shot on sight. Piss burns are murder on a lawn, especially from female dogs. Only thing you can do is cut out the whole section with a linoleum knife, replace it with a patch of sod, and hope it takes."

"Are you through, Tozzi?" Gibbons wanted to break his nose in the worst way, the wise-ass.

"I'm just explaining why we have to sit here—"

"Hold on. What's this?" Gibbons lifted the binoculars and focused on the two figures walking up the road now, approaching D'Urso's corner lot. Two women, both wearing jeans and hats. He fine-tuned the focus to get a better look at the hats. That's what he thought they were, big straw coolie hats. Looking down from where they were parked high up on the hill, Gibbons couldn't see their faces. The hats covered them completely.

He handed the binoculars to Tozzi. "Couple of Jap broads coming up the road. From D'Urso's wife's baby-sitting crew, I'll bet."

Tozzi lifted the binoculars and took a look. "They aren't Japanese. Look at how they walk. That's an American walk."

Gibbons laughed. "Who're you bullshitting? American walk, my ass."

"And besides, those hats are Chinese, not Japanese."

"Oh, that's right, I forgot. You're the big expert on everything Japanese now that you're taking karate lessons."

Tozzi looked at him through slit eyes. "Not karate. Aikido. I knew I should never have mentioned it to you."

Gibbons smiled like a crocodile. "Noooo. I'm glad you told me. I mean, who wouldn't want to have Bruce Lee for a partner? God, I feel fucking safe as shit just sitting here next to you."

"I will never tell you anything again, Gibbons. I swear to God."

Gibbons pinched his nose and closed his eyes, trying to contain himself. He couldn't stop laughing, though, imagining Tozzi in one of those cheapie kung-fu movies. *Wham! Blam! Slap! Pow!* He'd be perfect. All this laughing hurt his shoulders, but he didn't care. He needed something to laugh about.

Tozzi tried to ignore him. "Those are two nice ladies from the neighborhood out taking a walk."

"I thought you said rich people don't take walks." He couldn't stop laughing.

"You're busting my balls, Gib."

"And what about the coolie hats, Toz? What do you make

of them?" He could tell from the tight look on Tozzi's face that he was getting under his skin. Good.

"I don't know, Gib. Let's see. Maybe they just got back from a trip to China. Maybe they're gardening hats. To keep the sun off their heads."

"It's October, genius. The sun's not that hot."

Tozzi ignored him and went back to the *Daily News*. Eventually Gibbons stopped snorting and chortling and went back to watching the house.

Nagai drove. Hideo sat next to him up front, Toshio in the back. Ikki was in the van up ahead with the others. He followed the van as it turned off South Orange Avenue and headed up the hill into Short Hills. They hadn't said a word since he'd given them their instructions that morning.

"Hideo," he suddenly said, breaking the silence, "what would you do if a man raped your woman?"

"Kill him," the young man said automatically.

"Toshio?"

"Rape *his* woman, then kill him."

"And what would Ikki do?"

Toshio spoke up after a moment. "Rape the man *and* his woman. Then kill him."

They all laughed, but it was tense.

Nagai couldn't stop thinking about Reiko, wondering what D'Urso and the punk had done to her, wondering why she wouldn't tell him last night. He imagined what she'd say if he pressed her for an answer. She'd scream, say it was his fault, say she told him they wanted to make her a whore. He tried not to think about it. There were more important things to worry about now. Anyway, if they *had* touched his woman, he'd have D'Urso's. Whatever they'd done to Reiko, he'd take an eye for an eye. The Mafia aren't the only ones with balls.

He steered the Caddy around a sharp curve, staying close to the van. He wondered how stupid D'Urso would be. Would he back down once they took his wife or would he keep playing the big man, daring them to do something? What D'Urso didn't know was that he was prepared to do anything he had to. Keeping Antonelli alive and Hamabuchi happy was all that mattered. If he had to kill the bastard and wipe out his whole family in the process, he'd do it. D'Urso would learn the hard way how the yakuza do business.

The van took a left and started climbing a steep hill. Nagai followed, the old Caddy's transmission clunking as it downshifted, the engine whining. D'Urso's house was on the next street on the right at the end of the block.

"You know what you have to do?" he asked the two kids.

"*Hai.*"

"*Hai.*"

"Good."

He would have liked to have Mashiro here, but he felt confident with Moe, Larry, and Curly. They were good. D'Urso and Francione weren't home, so there shouldn't be any problems. If there were, Hideo, Toshio, and Ikki would handle it. No problem. They were good.

As the van took the next corner, Nagai set his jaw and gripped the wheel tight, wondering what he'd say to Reiko when he saw her.

"Goddamn," Tozzi suddenly said.

Gibbons rolled his eyes at him. "What?"

"Wait a minute." Tozzi had his finger on an item in the newspaper.

"What is it?"

Tozzi put the paper on the dash and pointed to the article. "Says here that the Dockworkers Local called a wildcat strike against Asian Automotive Importers yesterday."

"Asian Automotive Importers is the car lot where I found the air hose and Japanese Coke can."

"Yeah, I know. Listen to this: 'A spokesman for Asian Automotive called the strike "unjustified and unexpected," adding that his company will sue the union for loss of profits if they do not return to work immediately. A freighter containing new Toyota automobiles from Japan has been docked at the company's Port Newark facilities since early Friday morning, waiting to be unloaded. The Greater New York Toyota Dealers Association is urging Asian Automotive to settle with the union quickly to avoid loss of sales due to lack of inventory. A union spokesman predicted that the strike would be "a long one" if their grievances were not addressed,' blah, blah, blah. The Antonelli family has been mixed up with those dock unions since the forties."

Gibbons nodded. "As I remember, about ten years ago one of Antonelli's people was implicated in some scam to buy controlling shares in a Vegas casino with money siphoned from the Dockworkers' pension fund. You think D'Urso's got something to do with this?"

"Sure, why not? Maybe he's trying to pressure his buddy Nagai."

"How?"

"That guy Takayuki? The one I talked to in the trailer behind the chicken shack? He told me about how they smuggle slaves in the trunks of new cars, how they take just enough food and water to last them until all the cars are unloaded and they can be let out after dark. He told me on his trip over they had to go hungry for a few days before they were unloaded. If there are people trapped in those Toyotas on that ship, they may be without food or water right now. It doesn't take that long to die of dehydration, does it? They could be in danger of dying. Hundreds of them."

"And there's no profit to be made on damaged goods. Who's gonna pay for a dead slave?"

Tozzi frowned. "You're so eloquent, I can't stand it."

"Hey, that's Mafia hardball. If D'Urso wanted to get something out of this Nagai character, this would be the way he'd do it. Grab him by the nuts and squeeze till he gives."

Tozzi reached for the key in the ignition and started the engine. "We better find a phone and call this in. Get Ivers to alert the Coast Guard. Have them board the freighter and open some trunks—"

"Hang on a minute." Gibbons was looking through the binoculars at the house. Those two broads in the coolie hats were still hanging out on the corner down there, but now a pair of vehicles was just pulling up in front of the house. A light metallic blue van and behind it a big old black Caddy. A Caddy with *fins*. Christ, Caddy's haven't had fins in—what?—twenty-five, thirty years.

"That's a sixty. I can tell from here," Tozzi said, spotting the car. "My old man had one just like it."

"Spare me the trip down Memory Lane," Gibbons muttered, still peering through the binoculars.

Four men got out of the van, two out of the Caddy. Damn if these guys didn't look Japanese. Three of them crossed the lawn and went around back. Three went to the front door and rang the bell. A Japanese woman with real long straight black hair opened the door and motioned frantically, pointing back inside. There was a lot of nodding, then the three who went around back returned dragging this little bleach-head blonde across the lawn.

"That's D'Urso's wife," Tozzi said. "What's going on?"

"Looks like retaliation to me." The three Japs who were at the front door suddenly cut through the bank of shrubs and trees that separated the lawn from the curb and surprised the two broads in the coolie hats who just happened to be in the wrong place at the wrong time. The Japs pinned their arms behind their backs and forced them over to the van where they'd already taken D'Urso's wife. "What're they bothering with them for? They're just out taking a walk."

"Nobody walks in this neighborhood," Tozzi said grimly.

Gibbons lifted the binoculars to his eyes again. One of the Japs was pointing vehemently at the two women, and D'Urso's wife kept shaking her head no. The women were struggling to break free, but it was useless. They fought so hard they knocked the coolie hats off their heads. Gibbons focused on their faces. The redhead looked familiar. But when he got a good look at the brunette, the bottom dropped out of his gut. "Oh, Jesus—"

Tozzi grabbed the binoculars out of his hand and looked. "That's Roxanne and Lorraine. What the fuck is going on?"

Gibbons wasn't listening. He strained to see what was going on in the distance, the figures disappearing into the van, thinking about Lorraine in that ridiculous hat silently screaming for help. He was pissed as hell at her, and he was paralyzed by the gruesome thoughts and possibilities that went through his mind so fast the only thing that really registered was the fear and anxiety of a world without Lorraine. He thrust his hand into his jacket, reaching for his gun, but he moved too fast and the pain that screamed through his shoulder instantly brought tears to his eyes. Goddamn! Lorraine needed him, but he was useless! He was a goddamn gimp!

Pinned against the seat by the pain, Gibbons blinked back

the tears and saw the Japs getting into the van and pulling away from the curb, hanging a right around that corner and racing off down the hill. The old black Caddy with the fins followed close behind like a guard shark.

Gibbons turned his head toward Tozzi. "Go, goddammit! Hurry up! Go!" He didn't realize that Tozzi already had it in gear, that his foot was on the accelerator, that the forest-green LTD had left a long pair of skid marks at the curb. He didn't even feel the pain now. All he could feel was this massive sense of dread about to roll over him, flatten him, ruin everything. That and the shame of realizing that he might not be able to do a damn thing to prevent his worst nightmare from happening.

Oh, Jesus . . . Lorraine. They've got Lorraine!

28

Antonelli sat on the edge of the limo's backseat with the door open, pointing that bony finger at D'Urso. The old man's face was red he was so mad. Even his scalp was red under the thin white hair. "What I want to know is where the hell you get off calling a strike on your own. Tell me, John. I want to know."

D'Urso shrugged and caught a glimpse of Vincent standing off to the side between the fenders of the limo and the Mercedes. Big Vincent looked nervous. He was the one who picked this end of the lot, but he still looked nervous. He kept looking back through the cyclone fence, at that rotten pier over the water and the abandoned rowboat turned over on its back by the fence.

D'Urso glanced at the razor wire coiled on top of the eight-foot fence. What the fuck did Vincent think? Some hitter's gonna jump out from under the boat with a machine gun and start shooting through the fence? Fucking dummy. Still, he liked to see Vincent sweat for a change. The big man scanned the long lines of these little shitty Jap cars all around them, glancing nervously at Bobby leaning on the fender of the Mercedes with his arms folded over his chest while trying to keep his eye on the old man the way he was supposed to. Vincent didn't know where the fuck to look. All he knew was that he'd fucked up and let the old man get into a bad situation. If a hit was on, it could come from anywhere out here. D'Urso was glad to see him worried.

"Are you listening to me, John? I want to know what the hell you were thinking about when you did this. Explain! Are you *trying* to ruin our relationship with Hamabuchi's people? Are you?!" The old man's raspy voice already sounded like a death rattle. The skin around his eyes and over his cheeks was so tight you could make out his skull. The old man was practically dead already.

"Take it easy, Mr. Antonelli," Vincent cut in. Probably worried that Antonelli was gonna have a heart attack.

The old man pointed two bony fingers at his ape and glared at him. Stay!

D'Urso puckered his lips so the old man wouldn't see the little grin. This was almost going to be too easy. He kept running it through in his mind, and it always came out pretty much the way he wanted. He scratches his cheek to give Bobby the signal. Bobby pulls that Linda gun and starts plugging the ape. By this time he has his own gun out of the ankle holster and he gets to put a few slugs into Vincent for good measure. Then he turns to the pathetic old man, who wouldn't have the strength to pull a trigger even if he did carry a piece, and takes him out point-blank in the head. Quick and neat.

"Goddamn it, John, you're not even paying attention to me! Answer me for chrissake! Why did you call a strike without coming to me first?"

"Well, Mr. Antonelli, to tell you the God's honest truth, I ordered the strike on my own because I thought it was necessary. But I knew you wouldn't see it that way so I went ahead and did it on my own."

The old man was burning up. His lips were sunken, his mouth shut tight like someone's ole granny. "I don't fucking believe—"

"No, no, wait," he interrupted. "I want you to hear me out first. These Japs have been jerking us around almost from the beginning. I been telling you this, but you just let it happen. Hamabuchi thinks he's the only game in town, but he's wrong. I've found new suppliers, cheaper slaves—"

"Bullshit, you have. I say we deal with Hama—"

"Just listen to me for a minute. I know how to make money with this operation, real money. You buy cheap and move volume. Triple what we've been doing. And you bring in more girls. Make the good-looking ones turn tricks—"

"You know damn well what I said about prostitution."

"Yeah, I know you don't want it, but you're wrong. I've been running a cathouse down the shore for a couple of months now. It's been very profitable. Let me tell you."

John glanced at Vincent as the old man sputtered. The ape looked *very* nervous. His hands were at his sides, ready to go for the gun under his jacket. It was time. You don't play games with guys like Vincent. D'Urso casually raised his hand and scratched his cheek.

Bobby rolled his eyes to Vincent, made sure he wasn't looking, then whipped the autopistol out from under his jacket and started shooting. The close explosion of automatic fire made D'Urso's ears pop. White-hot muzzle flashes brought his eye to the Linda gun in his brother-in-law's hand. Vincent had managed to pull his gun, but Bobby fired another burst into his chest then and he fell backward, his arms splayed out like a retard, his gun flying in the air over his head. D'Urso heard Vincent's gun hitting the cyclone fence, that springy clattering sound, like a wild pitch hitting the batter's cage.

The old man stared at the dead ape lying on the ground wedged between the two cars. He glanced up at D'Urso and hissed, "Bastard!"

Nagai glanced at Hideo and Toshio. They were silent. Hideo kept his gun on his lap. Nagai looked in the rearview mirror at the van. Ikki was staying close, keeping up. They had the women. Now all they had to do was find D'Urso before he killed Antonelli. Mashiro was there, but Nagai was still concerned. Mashiro's good, but he can't stop bullets. He should've thought of that last night.

He gunned through a yellow light under the soot-black iron structures of the Pulaski Skyway and headed for the Doremus Avenue exit. The Caddy rumbled over potholes. Nagai heard rattles in the car he'd never heard before. The goddamn road was like a battlefield. He looked in the rearview mirror again. The van was still behind him. At the top edge of his windshield he could see planes flying low on their approach to the airport. They were almost there. Five minutes. Five minutes, D'Urso. Just stay cool for five more min-

utes. Nagai stepped on the gas and held it to the floor. Fuck
the potholes.

The old man was pouting and sputtering in Italian. D'Urso
couldn't understand what the hell he was saying. But who
cares anymore what he has to say? Bobby stood there gripping the Linda tight, holding it on Antonelli. He looked very
serious. D'Urso leveled his gun on Antonelli's face and
smiled.

"Hey, hey, hey! Shut up and listen to me, Antonelli."

The old man kept sputtering, sitting there with the car
door open, throwing his hands out and gesturing at Vincent
like some old greenhorn just off the boat.

"Look, Antonelli, this is the end. As a boss, you lost it. You
have to go."

Antonelli scraped the underside of his chin with the back
of his hand and spit on the ground. The old Sicilian curse:
May you spit blood. Jesus, this guy was a goddamn fossil.

"Listen to me, Antonelli. I'm gonna make you a deal here.
You're gonna die—that's not the issue. Whether I make it
hurt or not is the issue. Now, you admit to my face that
you're a senile old fart, that you've fucked up the family so
bad I don't even know where to begin describing our problems, and that what this family really needs now is someone
capable, someone younger, aggressive, profit-motivated. In
other words I want to hear you *say* that *I* deserve to be the
new boss."

"Go fuck yourself!"

D'Urso cocked his gun. Come on, I want to hear it. "Because if you don't say it, I'm gonna start with your knees.
Then I'm gonna shoot out your elbows. Then I'm gonna give
it to you in the throat where it's gonna hurt like a—"

The roar of approaching engines drowned him out. D'Urso
looked over his shoulder to see a blue van speeding toward
them. It screeched around in a tight circle so that its tail end
was facing them. Right behind the van was the Batmobile,
Nagai's old black Caddy. Fuck!

He looked at Bobby who seemed very confused, almost like
he was afraid to take his attention away from the old man.
Wake up, asshole. Over the roof of the Mercedes, D'Urso saw
the back doors of the van fly open. Three broads were tied

back-to-back inside. Three of those slanty-eyed yak hitters were back there, too. They were holding guns on the broads as they kicked and shoved them to make them move to the edge and turn around. Then D'Urso realized why they were turning the broads around. So that he could see the little blonde who'd been facing inside. His fucking wife, that's who. Jesus Christ Almighty!

The doors of the Caddy opened. Two more hitters took cover behind the doors, more guns, pointed at them now. From the driver's side, Nagai poked his head over the roof.

"You're fucked, D'Urso," he shouted. "Throw your guns over here, you and Bobby."

"Fuck you, Nagai!"

"Are you blind? We've got your wife and her friends."

Nagai shouted something in Japanese to his men in the van, and they hauled the three women to their feet. D'Urso had no idea who the hell the other two were. Michelle didn't have any friends. What the hell was Nagai trying to pull here?

"Throw down your guns or we start shooting."

What does he think this is? *Bonanza?*

Nagai yelled something else in Japanese and one of the hitters in the van singled out the older broad, the one with the long dark hair. He grabbed her by the hair and stuck his automatic in her ear for everyone to see.

"She goes first," Nagai shouted. "Then the redhead. Then your wife. Want to see if I'm kidding? Do you?"

D'Urso looked over at Bobby who still looked confused.

"They got Michelle, man." Bobby looked like he was going to cry. He was too worried about his goddamn sister, the asshole. He wasn't paying attention.

"John!" Michelle screamed. "Bobby! Listen to him! Please!"

Shut the fuck up. God*damn* it!

"What the hell's going on here?" D'Urso turned toward the croaking voice. The old man was standing up now, leaning on the limo door.

"Mr. Antonelli," Nagai yelled. "He brought you here to kill you."

"Michelle!" Bobby yelled. He sounded like fucking Sylvester Stallone at the end of the first *Rocky* movie yelling for his girlfriend. Then he started shooting that damn gun off at the yaks.

D'Urso dropped to a crouch and got closer to the Mercedes for protection. "Watch out for your damn sister," he yelled, but Bobby couldn't hear him. Then he heard different shots, single shots, returning Bobby's fire. Yak slugs were zinging into the other side of his car. Fuck this, he said to himself and scrambled to his feet. A Mercedes is not enough protection against these nuts. He ran with his head down and lunged into Antonelli, propelling the two of them into the back of the limo. He quickly shut the door and peered out just in time to see Bobby's wild fire rattling one of the open doors of the van.

"Hey, Bobby! Watch out for your sister, ya jerk ya!"

The shooting stopped for a second and he could hear Michelle's high-pitched scream, yelling at her brother to stop it. But then he nearly jumped out of his skin as he felt the old man's bony hand on his backside, grabbing the flaps of his jacket, trying to pull himself up. He shuddered at the old bastard's touch and knocked his arm away. Antonelli fell back onto the floor, a weird, wet grunting sound coming out of him now.

The shots seemed to subside then, except for the crazy three-round blasts of Bobby's autopistol. When D'Urso got back up to the window, he saw why the yaks had stopped shooting. Crouched behind his nut brother-in-law was this guy who looked like a big fucking armadillo in a Darth Vadar helmet holding this evil-looking sword in both hands. Jesus! It was fucking Mashiro!

Michelle screamed. "Bobby, look out!"

But it was already too late. The sword jumped out of Bobby's stomach. Speared him right through like a goddamn hors d'oeuvre. Bobby's gun went off once more, shooting out the tire of the Mercedes right beside him. Mashiro propped his foot on Bobby's ass and yanked the sword out of him. Bobby turned in a corkscrew and landed on his back, a dark circle of blood on his gray shirt, that stupid curl hanging over his staring dead eyes.

"Don't do it, D'Urso," Nagai shouted. "I'm telling you." Nagai was right there now, right on the other side of the Mercedes. "You kill Antonelli, we kill you." He moved around the back end of the Mercedes, his gun leveled at the rear window of the limo.

D'Urso bit his bottom lip. Who the fuck does this guy think he is, standing there like that? Superman? What does he think, he's the only one with a gun? Stupid bastard. D'Urso switched the .38 to his left hand, wiped his sweaty palm on his pants, then switched the gun back to his right.

"Don't be stupid, D'Urso. Come out now. You've got nothing to gain."

D'Urso pulled the lever on the door and paused to make Nagai think he was giving up. "At least I've got the guts to kill *my* boss," he shouted, kicking the door open. "More than I can say for you."

D'Urso squeezed off two quick shots. Nagai lunged back behind the Mercedes as the giant armadillo ran into the line of fire. The idiot just stood there, protecting his boss. How fucking noble. D'Urso bit his lip and fired his last four shots at Mashiro. The fucking idiot just stood there gritting his teeth. Mashiro must've taken at least three slugs, his head twitching with each one. He was just standing there, that mean motherfucker expression frozen on his ugly face. It took half a minute before the stupid Jap finally stumbled back and tripped over Bobby's body.

"*John!*" Michelle was screaming and crying. She was still tied to the other two broads, at least two yaks that he could see crouched behind them. Then, beyond the van in the distance, D'Urso spotted a dark green sedan racing into the lot. The sedan screeched to a stop, and the driver got out and went to the trunk to get something. He shut the trunk and went around to the passenger side.

"*Oh, God! John! Help!*"

D'Urso looked over the seatback at the ignition. No keys. Shit. He crawled over the old man who was still stuck on the floor wheezing for breath, and went out the other door. Bullets zinged off the hood of the limo as he ran in a crouch to Vincent's body, squeezing under the limo's bumper, so he could search the dead man's pockets for the keys. He got lucky and found the ape's key ring right away in his jacket pocket. There was a gold horse-shoe charm on a chain hanging from the ring. Some fucking luck, Vincent.

"*John! Oh, God! John!*"

He ran back in to the limo, praying those yaks shot as bad as they spoke English, got behind the wheel, and stuck the key in the ignition. As soon as the big engine turned over, he gunned it.

"John! Help us! John! Oh, Jesus!"

The hell with you, Michelle.

He threw it in gear with the engine racing. The transmission balked. The limo threatened to stall, then suddenly it shot off. He steered blind, keeping his head down, veering around the end of a row of Corollas.

"John?! John!!"

He peered over the dash and put the accelerator to the floor, swerving down the aisle between two long lines of Corollas, passing that green sedan speeding down the next aisle in the opposite direction heading for the mess he didn't want any part of.

"John!!! John, come back!!!" Michelle D'Urso screamed at the departing limo. *"Fuck you, John! Do you hear me, John?! You're a real cocksucker, John!!!"*

Shut the fuck up, Michelle.

D'Urso wondered about that green sedan, who that was. He glanced at the side mirror on the passenger side and saw Nagai's face, his hair blowing all over the place. What the—? He turned around. Nagai was holding onto the rear door handle, his feet stuck to the outside of the door, hanging out there like fucking Spiderman! Son of a bitch!

D'Urso threw his arm over the seat as he drove, pointed his gun at the back window, and pulled the trigger.

Click. Empty. Fuck!

D'Urso spun the wheel right and left, swerving the limo and making it fishtail. But Nagai's determined face was still in the mirror. "Goddamn you, Nagai! God*damn!*"

D'Urso gripped the wheel and kept driving.

29

Gibbons hit the brakes hard and pulled the LTD up to the right side of D'Urso's black Mercedes, using it as a barrier between them and the guys in the van. He kept his eye on the Mercedes, Excalibur in hand, just in case someone was hiding inside it, while Tozzi got out and took up a position behind the rear fender of D'Urso's car with the shotgun.

"FBI," Tozzi shouted at the group in the van. "Lay down your weapons."

Gibbons strained to see if Lorraine was still in there. He could see figures inside the dark box, but he couldn't make her out. He recognized D'Urso's wife and Tozzi's girlfriend, though. Lorraine must be behind them. His throat was dry; he tried to swallow. Good that she was in back of them. Less chance of getting hit by stray fire, a distinct possibility with a 12-gauge shotgun in Tozzi's hot little hands. Oh, Jesus.

"Don't shoot!" the bleach-head screeched. "We're in here!"

Someone started yelling in Japanese, then a single shot suddenly shattered the rear window of the Mercedes. It came from behind the old Caddy parked next to the van.

Gibbons saw that look on Tozzi's face, the tight jaw, the cuckoo eyes. Oh, shit. Here we go.

"All right, asshole. Have it your way." Tozzi leveled the shotgun and let loose a cannon blast that blew out the Caddy's front passenger door window and made the body work look like a cheese grater. The blast reverberated over the lot. No return fire. That got their attention.

"I'm going after the limo," Gibbons yelled to Tozzi.

"Forget the limo," Tozzi yelled back, giving him that annoyed, don't-go-straining-yourself-now look.

Screw you, Tozzi. "Watch it with that thing," he said, nodding at the shotgun. "Don't shoot Lorraine."

"Yeah, don't worry about it."

Another shot from behind the Caddy shattered more glass. Tozzi immediately answered in kind, putting more holes in the Caddy and rocking it on its springs. Gibbons hesitated, looking into the van. He adjusted the rearview mirror and focused on the limo swerving down the next aisle with some nut hanging out the window, it looked like. Shit. He slumped down behind the wheel, threw it in gear, and drove off, screeching around the end of the row of Toyotas, then picking up speed on the straight-away. He glanced over at his partner holding the shotgun. Tozzi better be careful with that goddamn thing. If Lorraine gets hurt, he'll be one sorry asshole.

The limo was up ahead in the distance. Suddenly Gibbons saw the limo's white backup lights go on. The limo had run up to a dead end. It was a solid line of Toyotas on both sides right up to the fence. Gibbons smiled with his teeth. The limo was hemmed in.

Suddenly he heard the shotgun behind him again, two rapid shots. His heart stopped. Lorraine! He turned his head quickly to see if she was all right, and sharp pains stabbed the base of his neck. God*damn!* Unconsciously he let up on the accelerator as the pain thrummed. Then his attention was brought back into focus by an incredible bashing sound. Up ahead the long sleek limo was ramming its tail end into the line of little cars on the right, burning rubber in forward and reverse, desperately trying to make a hole in the line. The Toys didn't move that easily, though, and one pesky little devil decided to lock bumpers with the limo. The guy who'd been hanging out the window was on his belly on the hood now, hanging onto the windshield wipers for dear life.

Gibbons hit the gas and rushed toward the limo. He braked hard, waited, then gunned it again to time his move just right. The limo revved, burned more rubber, and pushed the stubborn Toy on its tail back into the line. Gibbons quickly pulled up to the limo, nosing right up to the limo's grillwork and kissing bumpers.

"FBI," he yelled out the window as he stomped on the parking brake.

The limo revved and lurched forward, jolting the LTD and crunching both their headlights. Gibbons's car rocked up and down violently, and the neck brace wasn't enough to cushion this action. Gibbons grit his teeth against the pain as he stepped on the brake with both feet and locked his knees in position. From the anguished sounds of squealing metal, he assumed the bumpers were locked. It felt like he was trying to capture wild game, *big* wild game.

Through the two windshields he could see John D'Urso behind the wheel, facing him. The Japanese guy on the hood was trying to steady himself on his knees. D'Urso's legendary, perfectly styled steel-gray hair wasn't so perfect now. His shiny silk tie was askew. Spider cracks in his windshield fractured the beefy face with the mean, frantic eyes. Steam and blue exhaust clouded the space between the windshields.

Gibbons switched Excalibur to his left hand and pointed it out the window. He could taste hot antifreeze in the back of his throat. *"You! Put your hands on your head,"* he shouted. *"D'Urso, shut off the engine and put your hands on the wheel where I can see them. You're both under arrest!"* But neither of them could possibly hear Gibbons over the deafening roar and piercing squeals of the limo's overheated engine. He started shouting again, but it was no use. His neck was throbbing.

"Give it up, D'Urso," the Japanese guy yelled. He was holding a gun against the windshield.

"Get out of my face, Nagai!"

Nagai fired his weapon point-blank through the glass. There was no way he could've missed.

Then Gibbons saw it, through the cracked windshield. A hand, an arm, a gun coming over the backseat.

"Get down!" he shouted as he ducked under his own dash. The explosion of three quick shots overrode the noise of the panicked limo. Another explosion followed a split-second later. Then one more. Gibbons waited until he heard the engine die down to a hissing idle. The limo stopped struggling, he could feel it in his brake pedal. When he looked up, he saw

the windshield now shattered in an intricate crystalline pattern interrupted by four random exit holes. Nagai was sprawled out on the hood. He wasn't moving. Blood gushed out of his mouth and nose and beaded up on the polished black metal. More blood oozed out of two small wounds in his chest. Gibbons looked at the holes in the windshield. There should've been five.

Gibbons took his feet off the brake to see if the parking brake would hold the idling limo. The LTD jerked back. She wouldn't hold.

"Shut off the engine and throw out the gun," he ordered. "FBI!"

A moment later the limo stopped struggling. Gibbons cut his engine, and the sudden quiet felt like cotton batting around his head. Then he saw the hand again, coming out of the rear side window, placing the revolver on the roof. The hand slid the gun forward so that it skidded over the roof, slid down the windshield, tripped over the windshield-wiper gutter, and landed in Nagai's crotch. It was a small gun, an automatic. Probably a .22.

The back door of the limo opened then, banging against the silver Toyota next to it, and the hands emerged, draping themselves over the top of the door. Old, bony, liver-spotted hands.

Gibbons opened his door, bumping it on a battered candy-apple red Corolla. He kept his gun trained on that rear door as he climbed over the wreckage with great difficulty, doing his best to deny those nails in his neck. Hopping down off the interlocked bumpers, he ripped off the neck brace and threw it away. The clammy flesh around his neck suddenly felt cold. He pulled his chin in gently and lowered his head very delicately. The pain wasn't so bad now. He walked toward that open door, careful to keep his body erect, more careful to keep the gun leveled at the dark-tinted window below those hands. When he peered over the top of the door, he found Carmine Antonelli sitting on the edge of the seat, his legs hanging out. Gibbons let out a long breath.

"Stand up," Gibbons said. The old man complied, a placid expression on his face as Gibbons frisked him, then started to read him his Miranda rights.

"Don't bother. I've heard it before," Antonelli rasped in a tired voice.

Gibbons finished the recitation anyway. He wished he had a pair of handcuffs on him, but then he took a good look at the feeble old guy. Couldn't run off if he wanted to. Gibbons opened the driver's door and peered into the front seat. Sunlight filtered through the blood-smeared windshield like a stained glass window. D'Urso's body was slumped over on its side. The plush gray upholstery was soaked with blood from a chest wound. The back of his head was gone, too. Little pieces of his brain were stuck to everything.

"You killed them both."

The old boss looked away and didn't answer.

"Why both of them?"

Antonelli looked him in the eye. "Self-defense. Okay? The Jap boy was after John." He nodded at D'Urso's body. "I have to protect my people."

Gibbons straightened up and adjusted his head until the pain was bearable. "So why'd you kill your boy, too?"

Antonelli spit on the ground. "He was a little bastard. He betrayed me."

Gibbons smirked. "Spare me the King Lear rap."

"You're not so young yourself."

"Yeah, I know. Come on, let's go." He took him by the elbow, but Antonelli didn't move. He was staring inside the limo.

"I couldn't let you guys have him. You'd just send him to jail. What's that? That's nothing. John dishonored the *family*. What he did demanded justice, *our* kind of justice."

"Yeah, right. Very noble of you. They ought to make a movie about your life. Come on, move." Gibbons pulled him away from the car and gave him no choice but to walk. He walked very slowly, leaning on Gibbons's arm.

"I need a phone," he croaked out through his wheezing. "Get me to a phone."

"You gonna call off the strike?"

"None of your fucking business. Get me to a phone."

"Don't worry about it. You'll get your call."

Two more shotgun blasts echoed across the lot then. Gibbons tightened his grip on Antonelli's elbow and strained to see what was going on by the silver-blue van. Goddamn that

Tozzi. His Ithaca 37 Police Special held eight rounds, and
Tozzi had extra shells in his pocket. A pump-action twelve
gauge. Not the kind of gun Tozzi should have. He didn't
know what kind of gun Tozzi should have, the trigger-happy
son of a bitch. The jerk never watched out for civilians. If
anything happens to her, I'll kill him. I'll kill somebody.

"Hey, easy with the arm," the old boss complained. "You're
hurting me."

Gibbons ignored him. In the distance he could see guys
hightailing it across the lot on foot. Tozzi must've finally
scared them off with the cannon.

"Slow down!" Antonelli rasped. "I can't go so fast."

Gibbons resented having to walk at the old guy's pace.
Made him seem old. He wasn't old. Just hurt a little. His neck
was beginning to hurt real bad now.

The shotgun went off again, making a couple of gulls flying
overhead scream in fright. One of the doors of the van fell off
its hinges and clattered to the pavement.

"Goddamn you, Tozzi!" he yelled. "Watch it!"

"What'sa matter?" the old man asked.

"Shut up!"

The pain was cutting into his shoulders as if there were an
ax buried in each one. He couldn't walk much faster than
Antonelli now. For the first time in his life, he did feel old.
Anxiety suddenly clutched his gut, anxiety, regret, and fear.
An old man all alone without Lorraine. His legs wanted to
move faster, but the pain weighed him down. He had to get to
the van, though. He had to see her, had to make sure she was
all right, had to make things right with her, apologize. He had
to hold her. Lorraine.

Gibbons's throat was tight. He couldn't swallow. Still, he
tried to yell. "You hit her, Tozzi, and I'll kill you! I swear to
Christ I will!"

"Wha'?"

"Shut up and move!" They walked on, the old man shuffling at a snail's pace.

"Come on! Move, damn you!"

But the old man couldn't.

"Hurry up!"

He tried to hurry Antonelli along, but he couldn't do it.

"Come on, come on! Go!"

Then Gibbons stopped and almost lost control of the tears he was holding back as he realized that it was him who was leaning on Antonelli. Like an old man.

30

Tozzi peered over the trunk of the Mercedes, the shotgun ready in his hands. The trashed Caddy looked like a dead shark. The van was comparatively untouched, the women still sitting back-to-back inside the shadows. He could hear water lapping the rocky shore of the bay. It was quiet now. Tozzi was suspicious.

"They're gone. Please come untie us." It was Roxanne's voice.

She didn't sound overly distressed, thank God. But then he wondered if one of the yaks might still be in the shadows in the back of the van with them, holding a gun on her, forcing her to tell him the coast was clear. That might be a little paranoid, though, considering the language barrier. Anyway, if there was a guy in there hiding behind their skirts, he'd just sit tight and wait. He's already got the hostages. Why rush it and eliminate the element of surprise? He rubbed the sweaty stock of the shotgun. He wanted to go to her, see if she and Lorraine were all right, but he didn't dare, not without a backup. Where the hell was Gibbons? He didn't like being out here all alone.

He scanned the area for movement behind any one of the dozens of cars in his line of vision. He stared at the three bodies sprawled out on the pavement on the other side of the Mercedes: some big guy half-under the car, the punk Francione, and another guy who was flat on his back with his legs on Francione's chest. That one had to be Mashiro. The guy was actually dressed in feudal Japanese samurai armor. From where he stood he could see the glint of the sword lying on the ground next to the bodies. Unbelievable.

A gull landed on the pavement next to the bodies and cocked his head to one side, then the other, considering the punk. The bird pecked at his shirtfront a few times, then flew off.

Tozzi stood up slowly, braced for a shot from anywhere. He circled round the back end of the Mercedes, quickly crossed the open battle ground, and went directly to the back of the Cadillac for cover. He pointed the shotgun at the cab of the van. The driver's door was open. He moved around slowly until he was sure that the cab was empty. He got down on his knees then and looked for feet under the van, figuring someone might be waiting on the other side. No feet. He relaxed a bit as he stood up with the shotgun cradled in one arm. The Caddy's pointy fin was right in front of him. He couldn't resist running his hand over it, recalling the Cadillac his father had when he was a kid. He put both hands back on the shotgun right away, though. There were too many hiding places around here. This was no time for nostalgia. He looked around the lot. And what the hell happened to Gibbons?

Tozzi went over to the back of the van and squinted into the shadows.

"Well, if it isn't the Lone Ranger?" He recognized Roxanne's sarcastic tone. She was sitting Indian-style, her hands tied behind her back, trying to spit stray pieces of hair out of the corner of her mouth.

"Michael, where the hell have you been? Help us for God's sake." He recognized Lorraine's scolding, same as when she used to baby-sit for him. She was sitting the same way, wincing as she struggled in vain to get free.

"Who're you? You a cop or what?" He even recognized Michelle D'Urso's nervous-Nelly chirp. She made little faces every time she was jostled by Lorraine's struggling.

"Calm down, calm down," he said wearily, stepping up into the van. With this much attitude, maybe he should leave them this way.

"Come on, Mike. My wrists are killing me."

"Yes, mine too."

"Yeah, me too."

Why didn't they gag them, too? "Take it easy. I'm here."
He touched Roxanne's cheek, then reached over and laid his
hand on his cousin's shoulder. "Everybody all right?"

"No, we're not all right!" Roxanne snapped back. "Get us
out of these things."

Their wrists were bound behind their backs, arms interlocked to keep them together. The yaks had used those stupid
plastic-strip handcuffs. Leave it to the Japs to go high-tech.
Why couldn't they just use rope like your average criminal
element? Shit.

He set down the shotgun and tried to undo Roxanne's
cuffs, but they were on too tight. Shit. "Anybody got a knife,
a pair of scissors, something like that?"

Michelle D'Urso rolled her eyes. "Are you for real?"

"Don't be ridiculous, Michael."

"This isn't funny, Mike."

"Hang on, hang on." He dug into his pants pockets for his
key ring which had a nail clipper attached to it. He started
working on Roxanne's cuffs, chewing through that tough
plastic with the clipper. It took some doing, but he eventually
got through it.

"Thank you," she said, massaging her wrists, still with the
attitude.

"You're welcome." He didn't like that look she was giving
him, as if *he'd* done something wrong. He went to work on
Lorraine's cuffs.

"Where's Gibbons?" Lorraine asked as soon as she was free.
"Is he all right?"

Tozzi frowned. This is gratitude. "He's around here someplace." Jesus.

"Hey, what about me?" Michelle whined.

"You sit still," he said. "You're under arrest."

"What?!"

He ignored her, reaching into his shoulder holster and pulling out his revolver. "Lorraine, take this." He handed it to his
cousin. She held the gun as if it were radioactive.

"Gibbons ever show you how to work a safety? This
thing." He worked it on and off to show her.

"Uh . . . I don't know, Michael."

"Take it, Lorraine," he ordered. "The three of you stay

right here until I come back. If anyone shows up to bother you, use it. You hear me? Use it. Just make some noise." He looked down at the big gun in her slender trembling hands. It'll make noise all right. A .357 Magnum makes a lot of noise. He wondered whether he was making a mistake. Shit, he had no choice. He was alone out here. Gibbons could be in trouble. He should also call for help, have those yaks on the run picked up.

He picked up the shotgun and stood up. Roxanne was rubbing her wrists, still looking at him with that pissy, accusatory face. When he talked to her this morning, he had a feeling she was mad about last night. Clearly he was right. Christ. He didn't need this shit now. He leapt down out of the back of the van, avoiding her gaze. "Sit tight, gang. I'll be back."

He shaded his eyes from the sun and scanned the lot. He spotted Gibbons way in the distance across the lot with some little skinny guy, taking their goddamn time about getting here. What the hell is this? The old age home? Then it occurred to him that maybe Gibbons was hurt. He was walking, though. If he was hurt, it probably wasn't that bad. Tozzi looked around the big lot. They needed help. He had to get to a phone. He spotted a concrete bunker at the other end of the lot, but that was at least a hundred-fifty yards away. The guard booth at the entrance was even farther. He didn't like the idea of leaving the three of them here alone, Magnum or no Magnum. Then he spotted D'Urso's shot-up Mercedes. A car phone. Maybe he's got a car phone in there.

He trotted over toward the black Mercedes, confident that D'Urso was the type to have a car phone, but when he came up to the bodies, he paused to check. The samurai was on his back, his black helmet skewed over most of his face. He stared at Francione's body and couldn't help feeling glad that he was gone. That guy was trouble, pure and simple. If he stuck around, he'd just get worse. Better off dead. Tozzi stared at the coagulated blood soaking his groovy shirt and wondered who did the honors. Forensics will figure it out. He craned his neck to get a better look at the big guy over by the Mercedes, maybe recognize—

Suddenly he felt metal hitting metal as the shotgun whipped out of his hand. He saw it scuttle and clatter over the asphalt and disappear under the black Caddy Then he saw the blade glimmering right in front of his face like a cobra ready to strike. He leapt back out of range. The corpse was up on his elbow, moving—the samurai. The sword was in his hand. Instinctively Tozzi reached into his empty holster. Shit. He glanced over at the van. Mashiro was on his feet now. There was blood flowing down his sweaty face inside the helmet. There was a lot of blood all over the front of his braided armor. He stunk like something gone rotten. The expression on his face was mean. The eyes were empty black slits. All of a sudden Tozzi thought of that tongue-twister from when he was a kid: The big black bug bled black blood. Say it three times, fast. Shit.

Behind him, he could hear Roxanne and Lorraine in the van getting hyper, debating what they should do, no doubt. Lorraine didn't know how to use a gun. Did Roxanne? Not likely. If Lorraine started shooting, though, maybe it would distract this nut. Maybe she'd even get lucky and hit the son of a bitch. Of course, she might hit him, too. No. Don't shoot, Lorraine. No, don't.

Mashiro gripped the sword in both hands and held it high over his head, sort of like a batter at the plate. He stalked Tozzi slowly, his knees bent, his stance wide. His breathing was wet and hoarse. Tozzi backstepped, trying to keep himself from staring at the shiny blade. He vaguely remembered Neil Chaney saying something at their all-night aikido session about keeping the proper distance from an opponent and being aware of the whole man, not focusing on any single part of him.

He then remembered something else Neil had said about the martial arts in general. Whenever at all possible, avoid a fight. Run away if you have to. Better that than having to use your skills.

What skills?

Tozzi was sweating. His throat was dry. His eyes stung.

He thought about running, pretty confident that he could get away. Mashiro had short legs, and besides he was wounded. He'd lost blood; he couldn't be very steady on his legs. But then he remembered Roxanne and Lorraine inside the van. And Michelle D'Urso, still handcuffed. He couldn't leave them here with this psycho. He couldn't just run away. He'd have to keep Mashiro occupied at least until Gibbons

got here, until Gibbons could shoot this mother in the head
and finish the job. Come on, Gib. Make it snappy.

Tozzi backpedalled to put more distance between them, but
Mashiro rushed him unexpectedly to keep the same distance.
He moved amazingly fast, with this peculiar bow-legged step,
like a scorpion on the attack. Damn. So much for the bad legs
theory.

Mashiro started mumbling bitterly in Japanese. Tozzi
could guess what he was saying—the same thing he'd be saying if he had a couple of slugs in him and was crazy for
revenge. His stomach started to cramp as he kept moving
back slowly, maintaining that distance between them as he
wondered what the hell he was going to do when this guy
finally made his move. The Bureau didn't offer much in the
way of sword defense when he was in training at Quantico.
The only sword experience he had was the little bit he'd done
in aikido class with the wooden practice sword, the *bokken*.
Well, you use what you've got, right? He just wished he had a
little more faith in what Neil had shown him. This was no
time for doubt.

Tozzi kept backstepping, considering other possibilities,
considering faking left and right, hoping the samurai would
show a weakness he could take advantage of, a sore knee,
anything he could—

But suddenly Mashiro attacked, rushing him head on, the
sword held high. Tozzi had no time to think. He just acted,
doing exactly what he did last night each time Neil attacked
him that way with the wooden sword. *He got out of the way.*
Not by stepping back, but by stepping into the attack and
staying close to Mashiro, too close for the long blade to be a
threat, facing him as he passed. Tozzi turned around completely as Mashiro rushed by and backstepped away quickly
as Mashiro spun around and countered with a horizontal
waist-high swipe. Mashiro yelled something in anger, but the
swoosh of the lightning blade cutting the air was the only
sound Tozzi really heard.

It worked! Damn, it worked! Tozzi wiped the sweat from
his brow and immediately corrected his posture, forcing himself to stand relaxed in front of the samurai, shoulders square,
presenting a big chest, giving his opponent "a big target," as
Neil always said.

Mashiro rushed him again, holding the sword as if he were planning to lop Tozzi's head off, and again Tozzi avoided the sword by stepping into the attack, then moving out of range behind his opponent.

It worked again! Tozzi was in heaven. This was great! There really was something to this aikido stuff. He felt guilty that he'd doubted.

Mashiro's grumbling got a little louder now. He peppered it with short, abrupt shouts, like an angry dog barking at an intruder. Suddenly, in mid-bark, he attacked once more, the sword held high over his head again as if he aimed to split Tozzi right down the middle. Stay calm, stay calm, Tozzi repeated to himself. He forced himself to wait, wait, wait— until Mashiro had committed his balance, until he couldn't reverse his attack—then he spun out to the side, actually nudging shoulders with the mad Jap as the polished blade whooshed through the space where Tozzi had been, struck the ground, and sunk into the blacktop. Mashiro screamed in fury and yanked out the sword, then turned and immediately positioned himself for another pass.

Shit. Tozzi realized he could have done something that time. If he'd been quicker, he could've tackled him from the side while the sword was stuck in the pavement and gotten Mashiro away from his weapon. Or he could've punched him in the kidneys. Or grabbed him from behind and tied him up in a full-nelson. He knew what Neil had preached about resisting the natural urge to fight with your emotions and revert to ingrained streetfighting methods. He remembered all that stuff about the dangers of losing your one point and getting unsettled. But this was ridiculous. He knew how to streetfight. He didn't know aikido. Anyway, all he had to do was keep Mashiro busy until Gibbons got there. He glanced over his shoulder. Goddamn Gibbons who was still fifty yards away, taking his everloving sweet time getting here with that old crony of his, whoever the hell he was.

The sun beamed off the samurai's black helmet. The small brass plates on his armored chest shimmered. Mashiro was shouting nonstop now, ranting at Tozzi. He was breathing heavily, and the tracks of his sweat marbleized the bloodstains on his face. He smelled awful.

Come on, man. Do it again. Same move. Come on, you ugly
mother. Do me a favor.

An inhuman guttural scream erupted from the samurai as
he rushed again, sword held high over his head.

Tozzi grinned. Goddamn! He was doing it again! The same
move!

He steadied himself, forcing his legs to stay still until the
right moment, waiting for the sword to begin its downward
arc, waiting for the moment, anticipating his counterattack.

Tozzi waited, waited, then moved, spinning out to the side,
bringing himself shoulder to shoulder with Mashiro as the
blade sliced the space where he'd been. Now! He stepped
behind Mashiro and reached under his elbows, visualizing his
hands slipping under Mashiro's armpits, his fingers linking
behind the samurai's sweaty neck under the helmet. He could
feel himself bearing down fast and hard, forcing him to drop
the sword.

His mind was there before his hands were, though, and it
didn't happen the way he envisioned it.

As Tozzi reached out and committed himself to his attack,
Mashiro suddenly wheeled around and struck, cutting Tozzi
just above the elbow with the part of the blade closest to the
hilt. The shock of being cut made everything go black for a
microsecond. Then Tozzi heard one of the women screaming,
and instinctively he grabbed the wound with his other hand
and backpedalled the hell out of the way before the killing
blow came.

Mashiro was growling and laughing. Tozzi looked down at
his arm. His jacket and shirt were neatly sliced; blood was
seeping through his fingers. That goddamn thing was sharp
as a razor. Tozzi suddenly felt guilty. This was his punishment for disregarding Neil's instruction. Catholic school
logic.

"Shoot him! Shoot him!"

The samurai turned his attention to the voice screaming
from the van.

"Shoot him!"

Roxanne was yelling at Lorraine who was clutching the
revolver in both hands, squinting and wincing, trying to
track Mashiro who was stalking them now, moving evasively
right and left as he approached the van with that scorpion

scuttle of his. His grunting was cocky and menacing, spider-and-the-fly menacing. It was obvious to him too that Lorraine had never fired a gun.

"Hey, asshole!" Tozzi shouted. "Come finish me off! Come on, you bastard, don't leave me like this! Finish the job, you dishonorable son of a bitch you!"

Mashiro paid him no mind, intent on doing his sidewinder dance toward the women.

Roxanne was going crazy up there. Shit! Leave them alone, you thick-headed bastard. Tozzi ran on the balls of his feet, ran right up behind Mashiro, and kicked him in the seat of his pants.

Mashiro erupted, turning and slashing repeatedly, enraged.

Tozzi jumped back out of range, gripping his wound, trying to ignore his own lightheadedness. "Me, asshole! You deal with me first!"

Mashiro broke into an awkward, hobbled run. Tozzi turned quickly and ran, too, sprinting away from the samurai. But then Tozzi heard an unearthly roar behind him, and he slowed down to look over his shoulder. Mashiro was just standing there in position, his sword up in the batter's stance again, waiting for Tozzi to answer his challenge. Tozzi glanced at the van, then turned and faced him. He wasn't going to be afraid.

Mashiro charged quickly and attacked. Tozzi ducked, the blade whirring over his head. Mashiro stumbled with the force of his own swing, and Tozzi kicked him in the butt again, then started to run back the other way.

"Come on, ugly! Catch me!" He glanced ahead at the van and caught the terror in Roxanne's face. He looked back over his shoulder as he ran. Mashiro thrust his sword into a brown Corolla's headlight and let loose with that gravelly shout again, the samurai war cry. He broke into a wild run, chasing Tozzi for all he was worth, following as Tozzi zigzagged down the aisle, taunting him, circling around and dodging him. Tozzi wondered who was going to run out of steam first. Up ahead, Tozzi could see the rear end of the black Caddy, Roxanne and Lorraine standing on the tailgate of the van just beyond. Panting for breath, he felt weak and faint, but Mashiro's plodding footsteps were right behind him now. He couldn't think now, just do. Adrenaline worked his legs as the presence behind him got closer. He glanced back quickly and saw the threatening shimmer of the blade. He kept running, pushing. Go, go, don't stop. Then he suddenly remembered something from last night. The sword was moving toward his head now, he could feel it coming. No time to think. Just do. And he did.

Tozzi stopped abruptly and turned to face Mashiro, the way Neil had shown him. As the sword descended just inches from Tozzi's face, he grabbed Mashiro's hands on the hilt, braced the samurai's elbow, pumped down once to take his balance, then once more with feeling to do the throw. Mashiro flipped over in a flash. Tozzi blinked and panicked, suddenly remembering that he was supposed to take the sword away, too. Mashiro still had the goddamn sword. But when he looked up, he saw the samurai's body suspended in mid-air, upside-down, jerking violently. Tozzi blinked. He was confused. This wasn't right. The sword slipped from Mashiro's fingers then and clattered onto the pavement. Tozzi felt dizzy. He couldn't figure out what the hell—

But then the blood dripped off the chrome point of the Caddy's tailfin and it glinted in the sun, sticking out of Mashiro's chest, and Tozzi finally realized that the samurai was impaled there. Like a Japanese beetle stuck on a pin.

"Madonna mia!"

Tozzi turned toward the raspy voice and was surprised to see that the old geezer hanging on Gibbons's arm was Carmine Antonelli.

"Quiet." Gibbons scowled down at the old don, then looked over at Tozzi who was prodding his wound.

"You hurt bad?" Gibbons asked.

Tozzi gasped for air and coughed. "I dunno. I don't think so."

"Put your arm up over your head. Higher than your heart," Antonelli said. "It'll control the bleeding."

Gibbons glared at him. "You a doctor now?"

Antonelli shrugged. "Just trying to help."

"Just try to shut up."

Antonelli shrugged again and looked away.

Gibbons took a look at the wound. "He's right. Put your arm up. By the way, I take back what I said about whatever it is you're studying. Aikido, right? Nice move. I'm impressed."

Tozzi made a face and shook his head at the dangling samurai. "I don't know," he muttered. "It worked, I guess, but it didn't feel right—"

"Jesus, you're a violent son of a bitch. You never told me this about yourself." Roxanne came around from behind him and pulled his arm down so she could look at it. Without asking, she helped him out of his jacket, then ripped the torn sleeve off his shirt and made a tourniquet out of it. Her eyes were soft and caring. The touch of her hands made him feel even more lightheaded. Maybe she wasn't mad anymore.

"Aren't you going to say 'thank you' for the rescue?" he asked.

"I wasn't planning on it."

"No?" Shit.

She smiled slyly then and showed that incredible space between her teeth. "But if it'll make you feel better—"

"No, no, no . . . it's okay." Tozzi grinned. "Just tell me one thing. How the hell did you get mixed up with—?"

Tozzi suddenly became aware of Lorraine standing beside him. She stood there like a zombie, her arms hanging limp, her hair wild. She stared at his wound as Roxanne wrapped it, tears brimming in her eyes.

"Here," she said, suddenly sticking his gun into his holster.

"What's wrong, Lorraine? Are you hurt?" Tozzi knew what was wrong, but he didn't know what to say to her. He looked at Gibbons. Don't be a jerk. Say something.

Lorraine's eyes flashed like a death ray as she glared at Gibbons. "No. I'm not hurt." Her voice was like ice. Tozzi'd never heard her sound so vengeful.

Tozzi looked at Gibbons who was just staring at Lorraine. Gibbons let out a long sigh, but he didn't say anything. What the hell was he waiting for?

She turned abruptly and stomped off. Tozzi waited for Gibbons to say something, to stop her, to go to her, but the asshole didn't. He felt for them both really, but maybe a little more for her. Aw, come on, Gib. I know it's hard, but don't be a jerk. Don't do this to her.

Antonelli started coughing and wheezing then, and Gibbons glared at him as if he'd done something wrong. Lorraine was already in the next aisle, still walking. Gibbons kept looking down at the little old man. He kept *not* looking at Lorraine. What the hell's wrong with you, man?

A chill wind suddenly blew in off the bay, pushing the gliding gulls sideways across the sunny sky. Tozzi sighed and shook his head. Roxanne wasn't smiling anymore. She knew what was going on. He let out a long, disgusted sigh and stared at the dead samurai impaled on the fin of the old black Caddy that was just like the one his father used to have. The sun was bright and hot for this time of year. A stream of very red blood was snaking its way across the black asphalt from the dark puddle that had collected under the shadow of the chrome bumper. Tozzi sniffed and wiped the sweat off his face. The big black bug bled black blood.

31

Ivers had that constipated look again. His lips were thin and tight, and his brow was furrowed. He sat there behind his big mahogany desk in that awful shit-brown suit of his, making faces at the letters on his desk, trying to maintain some semblance of being the Special Agent in Charge of this field office. Gibbons almost felt for the guy. This one must've been a bitch to explain to the Director.

Tozzi was in the other chair across from Ivers, both feet on the floor, both hands on the arms. He looked calm and composed, his face relaxed. He claimed he was learning how to keep his "one point," whatever the fuck that was. Somewhere under his belly button, he said. What a whack. This aikido shit is going to his head. He's going fucking zen now. Jesus.

Ivers's chair creaked, and he started huffing and puffing again, blowing air out his nose loud enough for his secretary outside to hear. The Big Bad Wolf was going to give it another try.

"You're originals, you two." He picked up one of the letters on his desk. "This one is from Amnesty International. You'll be getting letters of commendation from them for your work in freeing the slaves." Ivers shook his head. "FBI agents getting kudos from Amnesty International. This has to be a first."

Ivers picked up another letter. "The Japanese ambassador has invited you two to a luncheon. They want to give you medals or some such shit for your"—he looked down at the letter—"your 'heroic efforts in single-handedly rescuing Japanese citizens victimized by an international criminal conspiracy.'" He looked at them over his half-glasses. "Nice."

Gibbons's stomach went sour as he thought about raw fish. "Forget it. I'm not eating sushi."

"You ever try it?" Tozzi said. "It's not bad."

Ivers glared at them. "*Everybody* loves you. The whole world thinks you're both just wonderful. Thanks to all the news coverage over the weekend, even the President has inquired about you two. The Director ended up having to do a fancy little tap dance in the Oval Office this morning, answering a lot of questions he really didn't have good answers for. He got on the horn with me right afterwards and put my balls in the vise. What the hell's going on up here? he wants to know. An international slave trade in the United States and he knows nothing about it? Two special agents from the New York office playing Batman and Robin against a yakuza-Mafia coalition, but he doesn't know a goddamn thing about it. All *I* know is what I read in the papers, since you guys apparently think filing regular reports is beneath you. But I can't very well tell him that, can I? No, I have to do a fancy little tap dance of my own. That's what *I* had to do."

Gibbons scratched his nose. He didn't need this bullshit. "Sorry for your trouble." Asshole.

"You know, everybody else may think you're heroes, but I don't. I think you're hotdogs. Disruptive, insubordinate hotdogs. You're a mockery of everything the Bureau stands for."

Gibbons saw red. "Listen, pal, I was out in the field catching lead when you were still wearing short pants in prep school. Don't tell *me* what the Bureau stands for. It stands for catching bad guys and bringing them to justice, not creating paperwork in the office and not watching your ass all the time just so you can worm your way up to the next promotion."

Ivers slapped the desk. "You're out of line, Gibbons."

Gibbons pounded the desk. He'd been dying to tell this guy off. "Three-hundred-and-twelve people were trapped on that ship, fifty-nine had already gone into shock from dehydration when the Coast Guard started popping trunks. Mrs. D'Urso was so shook up on the scene, Tozzi was able to get her to tell us where her husband kept his records, and as a result, twelve-hundred more slaves were located and freed this week-end. Carmine Antonelli was arrested on a charge that'll probably stick for a change. John D'Urso didn't get to kill his boss, which you can bet would've set off the kind of gang war this town hasn't seen since Lucky Luciano was around. And on top of all that, the yakuza doesn't have a foothold in New York anymore. Is all this the result of your able leadership, Ivers? Not on your fucking life. All *you* know how to do is suck up to the Director and write reports. *We* know how to get results."

"Easy, Gib," Tozzi said.

"Yes, you got results," Ivers shouted back. "But not by the book. Not our book. You withheld vital information from the Bureau while you conducted the investigation your way."

"It all came down so fast," Tozzi cut in. "There wasn't a whole lot of time for writing up reports. We took the only sensible course of action."

"Cut the bullshit, Tozzi. You guys endangered hundreds of lives doing things your way. It wasn't sensible. It was bull-shit."

Gibbons was sorely tempted to say it right there and then, but he still wasn't sure yet. Instead he looked past Ivers, out the window. "Oh, go scratch, will ya?" he muttered.

Ivers pointed his finger in Gibbons's face. "You know, the only reason you're so goddamn arrogant, Gibbons, is that you're riding high with all this hoopla. You know we can't touch you right now. God forbid if the two big heroes were ever disciplined. I can hear the editorials now if we tried it. It's like goddamn blackmail. And this isn't the first time you've done this to me."

That's it. Gibbons sat forward on the edge of his seat and stuck *his* finger in *Ivers's* face. "Well, if I'm such a goddamn thorn in your side, maybe I should quit. How about that? I'll quit and you can go back to fucking things up your own way. That okay with you, Ivers? Will that make you happy?"

Ivers was seething. "That would make me *very* happy."

"Fine." Gibbons got up and knocked his chair over as he did. He walked out the door and slammed it behind him.

Tozzi looked at the door in shock. Gibbons, the black of shoe, the white of shirt, the straight of arrow, mouthing off to a SAC? He never thought he'd see the day. He looked at Ivers.

"Ah, maybe we should continue this later when we're all a little cooler."

"Oh, don't worry about that, Tozzi. We certainly will continue this later. You can count on it." Ivers's tone was sarcastic and ominous. He started shuffling through files, making himself busy all of a sudden, which was obviously Tozzi's cue to get lost. He *was* an asshole.

Tozzi left Ivers's office and went directly to Gibbons's cubicle where he found his partner sitting with his feet up on his desk and his fingers linked over his mouth as if he were praying. Tozzi expected him to be fuming. Actually he looked more sad than mad.

"Hey, Gib, you're not serious about quitting, are you?" Tozzi pulled up a chair and sat down.

Gibbons rolled his eyes at Tozzi, then blinked and sighed. Tozzi didn't like the implication of his not answering.

"Ivers is an asshole. Putting up with his crap is just part of the job. You know that."

"Yeah . . . I know that."

Gibbons was almost whispering he was so subdued. This wasn't like him. Normally he'd be cussing Ivers up and down. What the hell was with him? "Listen, let Ivers cool down a little, then I'll go back and talk to him. We'll go in together later this afternoon, listen to his crap, make nice, and be done with it. What the hell, just make him feel like he's on top. That's all he wants—"

"How's your girlfriend, Toz?"

"What?"

"Roxanne. How is she?"

"She's okay. But what's she got to do with anything?"

Gibbons nodded behind his folded hands. "She's a nice girl. Don't be stupid. Be nice to her."

"What're you talking about?"

"Just listen to me. Be nice to her. Don't ever hurt her. You'll regret it."

Tozzi sighed. Now he knew what this was all about. "My dear cousin Lorraine. She's on your ass again about retiring, right?"

Gibbons let out a long sigh. "I haven't talked to her since she walked off the car lot the other day. She's not answering the phone." He picked up a ball-point pen off his desk and clicked it a few times. "She's right to be pissed off at me. I don't blame her."

"So you're gonna quit the Bureau to keep her happy? Come on, Gib. That's crazy."

"You know, when I was laid up in the hospital, I gave some pretty serious thought to getting married. I gave it a *lot* of thought. We need some stability, something more permanent. We're not getting any younger. Me especially. What am I gonna do when I get out of this job? What if I got real sick, bedridden like I was? Who's gonna take care of me? Who'd take care of Lorraine, for that matter? You?"

"You're getting maudlin, Gib. Either that or senile."

"Go ahead, make jokes, Tozzi. You can laugh 'cause you're still young." He started clicking the pen again. It was beginning to aggravate Tozzi.

"What are you saying here? You want to retire now? Go settle down in some leisure village with my cousin? Is that what you're thinking?"

He looked Tozzi in the eye. "I don't want to lose her."

"You mean she gave you an ultimatum? If you don't quit the Bureau, she walks out of your life forever?"

Gibbons shut his eyes and shook his head solemnly. "No, I told you. I haven't talked to her about this at all. This is what *I'm* thinking."

Tozzi's heart was beating fast. He didn't want to lose his partner. "You better go see a doctor. You're definitely not yourself."

Gibbons put his feet on the floor and threw the pen on the desk. Tozzi waited for the nasty remark. It didn't come. What the hell's gotten into him?

"Just give me a straight answer, Gib. Just tell me. Are you quitting or not? I have to know."

Gibbons smiled like a crocodile, a born-again crocodile, a crocodile holding onto new wisdom, a crocodile who'd seen the light . . . a crocodile with no fucking bite. "Later," he said, moving around his desk. "I gotta go to the john."

He walked out and left Tozzi sitting alone in his cubicle. Tozzi's brow was furrowed. There was a hollow feeling in the pit of his stomach, and it wasn't because it was almost lunchtime. He picked up the pen from Gibbons's desk and started to click it.

BONUS EXCERPT
from the new Gibbons and Tozzi thriller BAD LUCK,
on sale in July 1990 from Delacorte Press

Chapter One

The steel I-beam sailed through the clear blue sky, so nice, like a bird. Sal Immordino stood there facing the yellow-beige aluminum wall of the trailer, looking straight up at the towering crane and the rust-colored I-beam on the end of its cable, pleased to see that something so big and heavy could be so graceful. He followed the long metal beam's flight high over the construction site, grinning a little as he pulled down his zipper and fished around in his underwear.

"Hey! Whattaya doing over there?"

"Leave him alone, Mike."

Aaaahhhhh . . . A dark blot spread through the sand on the ground. It made a nice sound, Sal thought, the steady stream hitting the sand. Sorta plopped when you poured it. He stared up at the sky, smelled the salt air on the breeze, and ignored the two stupid bodyguards standing over by the trailer door.

"Go use the Porta Pottie, for chrissake."

"Shut up, Mike."

"Whattaya mean, shut up? He's out in the open, peeing against the wall, for crying out loud. That's not right."

"Just shut up, Mike."

"What? You think he understands me? Lemme tell you. That guy's not right in the head. He's a friggin' dummy. He doesn't understand what you say. That's why he's standing there with his thing hanging out, doing it like nobody can see him."

"Mike, *shut up.*"

"Hey, what's he gonna do, beat me up?"

"Shut up, will ya? He's gonna hear you."

"I'm supposed to be afraid of him because he's big, because he used to be a pro boxer, a heavyweight? I don't give a shit. Look at him. He's all fat. He must weigh two sixty, two seventy. At least."

Two fifty-five, Sal thought, shaking himself off. Two fifty-five and six foot four, asshole.

"I don't get it. What the hell could Mr. Nashe want with this big jerk? I mean, look at the way he's dressed. Mr. Nashe doesn't even let the janitors at the hotel go around looking like that."

"Mike, will you just shut the fuck up?"

Yeah, shut the fuck up, Mike.

Sal zipped his pants and headed back inside, deliberately dragging his feet in the dirt. As he came up to the steps leading up to the trailer door, he got a good look at this Mike character. Sal didn't like his looks. Tall, built like a light heavyweight, the type who thinks he's good-looking. Straight dark hair falling over his forehead, deep-set eyes. Probably thinks he looks like Tom Cruise or something. Suspicious eyes. A real wiseass. Sal didn't like his looks at all. He looked like a fucking cop. Prick.

As Sal lumbered by, he deliberately bumped into the guy's shoulder, hard. He stared the asshole in the eye. "You my brother? You Joseph? You ain't Joseph. No . . . Where's my brother Joseph?"

The guy shook his head and stared right back at him. "In there, genius," and he jerked his thumb at the door. Real arrogant little prick. Typical bodyguard, all balls and no brains.

Sal climbed the steps and opened the metal door. It was like a piece of cardboard in his hand. He shut the door behind him and turned the bolt, glanced at Joseph and the Golden Boy, then went back to his chair, the metal folding chair. He didn't like the other ones in here. They all had arms. He usually didn't fit in chairs that had arms.

"Sal, why don't you take one of these chairs? They're more comfortable," the Golden Boy said.

Sal looked at the floor and shook his head. He never risked getting stuck in a chair with goddamn arms when someone was watching.

"Okay. Whatever makes you happy, Sal. So where were we?"

Sal reached into the pocket of his warm-up jacket and pulled out a black rubber ball. As he started to squeeze it he stared at Nashe, the Golden Boy, standing behind that drafting table.

Russell fucking Nashe. Mr. Cash. He better be. Jesus, please, he better be.

Sal pulled a pack of Dentyne out of his other pocket. He stopped squeezing the ball long enough to unwrap two pieces and stick them in his mouth. He looked at Nashe blankly as he rocked back and forth in his seat, chewing his gum and squeezing the rubber ball, giving the man a good show. Nashe was smiling at him, leaning over the drafting table in his two-thousand-dollar banker's suit, his knuckles on the blueprints, smiling with his eyebrows, like he was posing for the cover of *Time* magazine. Sal kept rocking back and forth. Russell fucking Nashe. Bright blue eyes— probably bright blue contacts. Wavy dark hair slicked back with that mousse crap they use now. A skinny guy but with a big head—too big for the rest of him. Chubby cheeks, like he always had something stuffed up his mouth. And those stupid buckteeth. Sal switched the ball to his other hand. Billionaire, huh? Nashe looks like a goddamn rabbit. He looks like Bugs Bunny. How can you trust a guy who looks like Bugs Bunny?

Nashe crossed his arms, rubbed his chin, shifted his smile over to Sal's older brother Joseph, who was sitting in one of the good chairs, the chairs with the arms. "Twenty-nine million . . . That's a lot of money. I can't just write you a check, just like that. What do I look like? Donald Trump?" Nashe flashed that wiseass smirk of his with the rabbit teeth sticking out. No, not this time, you fucking jerk. Don't wanna hear the song and dance anymore. Time's up. For both of us.

Sal looked at his brother, waiting for him to say something, but Joseph just sat there, stroking his silver-gray pencil-thin mustache, glaring up at Nashe. Another fucking jerk. Joseph thought he was tough. He thought he looked like Burt Reynolds too. Maybe Burt Reynolds with a pot belly and without the wig. Maybe. Joseph thought he was being real cool now, but his red face gave him away. He was pissed as shit, ready to explode. He wasn't saying anything now because he knew he'd start screaming like some kind of cuckoo bird if he opened his mouth. Burt Reynolds, huh? How about Elmer Fudd? These two were a fucking pair. They deserved each other.

Sal turned away and looked out the window, biting his bottom lip. He scanned the muddy construction site outside —the big hole they dug last November, the cement trucks revving their motors and spinning their drums, the construction guys yelling at each other, telling each other what to do, the big sign down by the boardwalk with the twelve-foot redhead in a Hawaiian-print sarong: "The BIGGEST name in Atlantic City is building the BIGGEST casino hotel in the world. NASHE PARADISE. Coming Soon." Sal lowered his head so he could see the giant silver letters on top of Bugs Bunny's other casino down the other end of the boardwalk. He wanted to see if Nashe was using the same typeface for the new casino. The letters were blinding in the sun, so it was hard to tell. C'mon, Joseph, say something, for chrissake.

"Twenty-nine million, four hundred thousand," Joseph finally said, struggling to hold his temper. *"Today."*

Nashe was grinning at him. "I made my original deal with Seaview Properties, Joseph. I think it's only proper that I continue with them."

Joseph kept stroking his mustache. "We *represent* Seaview Properties. Two weeks ago you could've dealt with them. Now you're late, so you deal with us." Joseph sucked on his teeth. Must've seen that one in an old gangster movie. Cagney maybe. What a jerk.

Nashe shook his head, still grinning. "You know, Joseph, you come here to the construction site to find me, no appointment, no warning, nothing. This isn't my office. I've got no papers with me, no files. You expect me to just give you a check right here? Is that what you think? Be real. I have to review the contract. I don't have the exact terms of the contract in my head."

Joseph straightened his tie. Now he was gonna be Rodney Dangerfield. "You don't remember the terms, huh? Well, I'll remind you. Down the other end of the boardwalk you happen to have a casino—you remember that one? Nashe Plaza? Well, under that big casino of yours, there's land. And that land under your casino was leased to you five years ago by Seaview Properties. Is it coming back to you now? The terms of that deal were that you'd put down five mil—which you did—pay two million a year for the first five years—which you also did—then in the fifth year, you'd make up the balance in a balloon payment, which you *haven't* done yet and which is now two weeks overdue. *That* was the deal. Okay, now? Anyway, you should know the terms, because you were the one who came up with this balloon-payment idea in the first place."

Sal chewed the cinnamon-flavored gum with his front teeth and squeezed the ball harder. Bugs Bunny knows all this, Joseph. He's just jerking you around, for chrissake. Stop playing around and just put it to him.

Nashe rolled up the blueprints on the table and crossed his arms with the roll in his hand, like some fucking king. "Of course, I remember *that,* Joseph, but there are details in the contract that have to be checked."

"I don't want to hear this crap, Nashe. Just get the money up."

Nashe tapped the back of his head with the blueprints and stared at the floor for a minute. Then he started pacing.

Sal dug his fingers into the rubber ball. He could feel his heart thumping. Now what, you son of a bitch? What's the excuse gonna be now?

Nashe puckered his lips and nodded before he spoke. "Joseph, let me say from the outset that you *will* get your money. That isn't even an issue here. The issue is commitment, and that's what I don't think you and your brother understand. We are all in the business of making money—that goes without saying. But you have to recognize that there are different *styles* of making money. Some people stick their money in the bank, and they're happy getting that nice little five-percent interest. It's safe, it's what they want. Other people are a little more adventurous with their investments. They're willing to accept a certain degree of risk for a better return. But when you're talking about making *big* money, you're talking about *major* projects, and for that you've got to really commit your money. And that means tying it up."

Joseph waved his hand at Nashe. "Hey, hey, I don't want to hear this shit. All I know is—"

"No, Joseph, just hear me out for a minute. Where I am standing right now will be the biggest casino in the world, *in the world*. Nothing else will even come close. Thirty-two hundred slots, one hundred seventy-five blackjack tables, fifty craps tables, fifty roulettes, twelve big sixes, fifteen baccarat tables. We're gonna have *two* showrooms. Big names playing all the time and *at the same time*. Just try to imagine this. We'll have, say, Liza in one room and Sammy in the other. They'll do walk-ons on each other's shows. People won't believe it. It'll look totally spontaneous. Can you imagine this? You're sitting there listening to Liza singing 'New York, New York,' say, and all of a sudden Sammy walks out onstage. *That's* entertainment, my friend. *That's* what brings people in. And *that's* what the Paradise will be known for. But you can't wait till the place is built to start lining up talent like that. No, no, no, no, no. To get big talent like that you've got to line them up long in advance.

And that's what we're doing right now. But that takes capital, Joseph."

Joseph straightened his tie again. "I don't give a shit about your two rooms. All I want is—"

"Hey, take a look out that window." Nashe pointed with the rolled-up blueprints. "See all those guys working out there? If I gave you your twenty-nine million today, how many of those guys would be there tomorrow? None. That's how many. And what about all the people who're waiting for jobs here? I'm talking about *thousands* of jobs, jobs that I promised the governor I'd give to Atlantic City residents first. Why? Because I'm the only casino owner in this whole town who gives a damn about this community. It's time the casinos stop taking and start giving a little. This city is a disgrace. This town is *built* on money. There shouldn't be slums here. There shouldn't be poor people here. These people should have jobs, and if I have to do it alone, I will make sure the people of Atlantic City get good jobs and are treated right so they take pride in this place."

Sal squeezed the ball in half. Gas pains were piercing his gut.

Joseph sat forward with his elbows on his knees. "I don't give a good goddamn about these jigaboos down here. I got my own charities to worry about."

Sal rocked and nodded. Yeah, that's right. Cil's place. Sal looked at Nashe, wondering what other bullshit excuses the rabbit was gonna pull out of his hat.

"Joseph, if the Paradise was the only project I had going right now, you wouldn't have to be here. You would've had your money by now. But I'm also in the middle of promoting this fight." Nashe pointed with the rolled-up blueprints to the poster taped to the wall. "Two weeks from this Saturday. The biggest fight in the history of professional boxing with the biggest cash purse in the history of professional boxing. Forget the Rumble in the Jungle. Forget the Thrilla in Manila. This is the ultimate, *the War Down the Shore.*"

Nashe was grinning again, pleased with himself. Joseph

was glaring at him, ready to jump out of his skin. Poor Joseph didn't know what the hell to do next. Sal squeezed the rubber ball and rocked. Joseph don't get no respect. That's 'cause he doesn't demand it. You gotta *demand* it, Joseph. C'mon! We gotta get that money!

"Look, Joseph," Nashe said, waving the blueprints around, "I know you don't want to hear any of this, but I want you to understand where I'm coming from. Originally I had no intention of getting involved with this fight to the extent that I have. What the hell did I know about promoting a fight? But the opportunity came my way and I grabbed it. Why? Because there was big money to be made with this fight. But once again, to make big money, you've got to *commit* big money."

Sal's gum was beginning to lose its flavor. He tuned out Nashe's bullshit, tired of hearing it, and stared at the two fighters on that poster on the wall, two heavyweights facing off, arms bulging, faces mean, skin oiled and shining. Sal didn't like the reigning champ, Dwayne "Pain" Walker. He was a street punk, the kind who'd rape your grandmother. Sal liked the challenger, Charles Epps. He was bigger and had a longer reach. Unfortunately he was also a lot slower and a lot older than Walker. Christ, Epps had fought Ali— that's how long he'd been around. Still, Sal liked Epps because he reminded Sal of himself when he was fighting. Same kind of body, same style. No footwork to speak of, but a killer right. When Sal fought he never fooled around working on the body. He went right for the head, looking for the knockout. Epps used to fight the same way, but his time had passed. They were just rolling him out now to face Walker because he used to be a big name and had held the title for about ten minutes in the late seventies. Epps wouldn't go more than four rounds, no way. Sure, Sal liked the guy, but he wouldn't put any money on him.

Joseph was raising his voice now. He sounded like Grandma. "I'm getting tired of the crap, Nashe. I want to know what the hell you're gonna do here." Joseph was begging now. Bad, very bad.

Nashe threw Joseph a patronizing smile as he moved a stool around the drafting table and sat down in front of Sal. He was through talking to the dummy—he wanted to deal directly with the ventriloquist now. "Sal, as I said, you're going to get your money. With interest, of course." Nashe toned down the snake-oil pitch, but he was still flashing the Bugs Bunny grin.

Joseph's eyebrows started twitching. "What the hell you talking to him for? Leave my brother alone. You don't talk to him. You talk to me."

Nashe nodded to Joseph but kept talking to Sal. He knew who the boss was. "Sal, I know you understand what I'm talking about. A good opportunity cannot be overlooked. So you have to steal from Peter to pay Paul. So what? You make it up to Peter later and you do right by him. As God is my witness, I genuinely wish I didn't have so much tied up with the Paradise and the fight right now, I really do. I *want* to pay you. Just ninety days. That's all it'll take. Ninety days at ten percent. Does that sound fair?"

Sal looked out the window at the cement trucks and started to shake his head, laughing to himself. Ninety days? That must be a joke, right? Mr. Mistretta gets out of prison in a couple of weeks. He doesn't want to know nothing about no ninety days. Mistretta wouldn't give you nine minutes, you fucking clown. He won't give *me* nine minutes. He wants that money waiting for him when he gets out. And if it's not there . . . Sal started rocking again. He didn't even want to think about it.

Nashe leaned closer. "Talk to me, Sal. Say something. Everything is negotiable. What don't you like? Tell me."

Sal almost spit out a bitter laugh. He didn't like much of anything lately. He stared at the rolling drums on the concrete trucks and squeezed the black rubber ball a few times. He'd been acting boss of the Mistretta family for almost four years now, and nothing had worked out the way he'd wanted it to. He had big plans when Mr. Mistretta left him in charge just before he went to prison. It wasn't like Sal wanted to take over or anything. That wasn't his intention.

What Sal wanted to do was bring the family up-to-date a little, get more into legitimate businesses the way the other families were doing. Why reinvest gambling money back into gambling and whore money back into whores? Drugs aren't even worth the risk anymore, not with the fucking Colombians controlling all the coke and the Chinks bringing in heroin. And crack—forget about that. You gotta be crazy to deal with those fucking nuts. Mistretta doesn't like to hear it, but the smart thing to do is go legit with your profits. And that's what Sal had wanted to do. He even had the businesses he wanted to buy all picked out and everything. Three concrete plants, one on Staten Island and two here in Jersey. They could've consolidated them and had a nice little monopoly for themselves in that area. Sal had it all planned out. He even promised Joseph he'd set him up as president of the company. You clean him up a little, shave off that stupid mustache, get him some nice conservative clothes, and he could almost be one of those Knights of Columbus types, very respectable. But things just didn't work out that way.

Sal shook his head, staring at one of the concrete trucks, the drum spinning round and round, red and yellow stripes spiraling. Mistretta, that clever bastard, left him in charge, yeah, but he squirreled away most of the family's money where Sal couldn't get at it. So any major purchases Sal wanted to make had to be made with money he made himself. In the beginning, Sal still thought he could pull it off—they were making good money with gambling and girls, and they were doing all right with the garbage trucks too—but then one thing after another happened. One guy needed money for this, another guy needed money for that, Mistretta's daughter wants a new house, his wife wants a condo in Florida, then his nephew wants to buy into an auto mall, then the bail money for everybody and his uncle, and the next thing you know, there's no money for what Sal wants. The three concrete plants are still up for grabs, but all he's got is about thirty mil to work with. Personally he could come up with another two himself, but what the hell's that? Nothing. Enough for one of the concrete plants maybe. But you've gotta have all three or it's no good. You won't have the control otherwise. Well, fuck it. Mistretta gets out at the end of the month and then it's his problem, thank God. Better to go back to running the crew again. Just be a captain, worry about your own guys. The concrete thing would've been nice, but it's too late now. Just get Mistretta his goddamn money and keep him happy. That's all that's important now.

Sal glanced up at Nashe who was waiting for an answer like a dog waiting for dinner. Fucking jerk. Yeah, he could smile. Joseph too. They weren't gonna be the ones to tell Mistretta that he didn't have the money yet. No, that wasn't gonna be their job. Even if he broke both of Nashe's legs right now, he'd be getting off easy by comparison. Mistretta did not like to be disappointed. Sal remembered what Mistretta did to Tommy Ricks, and a pain shot through his gut so bad he nearly doubled over.

Nashe suddenly put his hands up as if he were being robbed, except he was still grinning with those big stupid teeth of his. "Sal, I give up. Just tell me what you want. I can accommodate you. We can work something out. Just *talk* to me."

Joseph stood up, mustache twitching, eyebrows squiggling all over his forehead. "Hey, I already told you. You don't talk to my brother. He's a very sick man. He doesn't know what the hell you're talking about. *I'm* the one you talk to—"

Sal stopped rocking then, raising the hand with the rubber ball and waving his brother off. Enough! They had to have that money and they had to have it soon. Joseph wasn't gonna get it out of Nashe. It was time for Sal to speak for himself. No sense playing dumb with Nashe. Bugs Bunny knows the score.

"Listen to me, Russ," Sal started, then cleared his throat.

"Sal! Whattaya doin'?"

"Don't worry about it, Joseph." Sal pointed his finger at Nashe as he turned back to him. "Let me tell you something, Russ. When I want something, I pay for it. I just pay for it. No credit cards, no leveraging, no junk bonds, no fancy mortgage arrangements. I pay *cash*. That's all there is to it. Now, five years ago you wanted something from us, the land on the boardwalk, and so we leased it to you. *You* drew up the conditions, we didn't. Now, according to those conditions, it's time to pay. So naturally we expect you to live up to your promise and pay up. That's not unreasonable, is it?"

"No, of course not, Sal. But by the same token you're not appreciating my point of view here." Nashe was on the edge of the stool, hovering over him, still grinning that stupid rabbit grin.

Sal looked at the floor and shook his head as he switched the rubber ball to his left hand and made a fist with his right. He had to make Nashe "appreciate" *his* point of view.

"You see, Sal, I can make it worth your while if you—"

Sal's fist shot up like an erupting volcano, a solid uppercut to the middle of Nashe's chest that knocked the Golden Boy off his stool and back over the drafting table. He crashed to the floor on his shoulder, the blueprints crushed underneath him. Bugs wasn't grinning now. Sal was.

"Mr. Nashe. Mr. Nashe!"

Sal glared at the voice coming from the other side of the trailer door. It was that wiseass bodyguard, Mr. Mike.

"Are you okay, Mr. Nashe? Mr. Nashe?" The asshole was pounding on that flimsy aluminum door like he was gonna break it in.

Joseph looked jumpy. "Who the hell's that?"

know what the hell you're gonna do here." Joseph was begging now. Bad, very bad.

Nashe threw Joseph a patronizing smile as he moved a stool around the drafting table and sat down in front of Sal. He was through talking to the dummy—he wanted to deal directly with the ventriloquist now. "Sal, as I said, you're going to get your money. With interest, of course." Nashe toned down the snake-oil pitch, but he was still flashing the Bugs Bunny grin.

Joseph's eyebrows started twitching. "What the hell you talking to him for? Leave my brother alone. You don't talk to him. You talk to me."

Nashe nodded to Joseph but kept talking to Sal. He knew who the boss was. "Sal, I know you understand what I'm talking about. A good opportunity cannot be overlooked. So you have to steal from Peter to pay Paul. So what? You make it up to Peter later and you do right by him. As God is my witness, I genuinely wish I didn't have so much tied up with the Paradise and the fight right now, I really do. I *want* to pay you. Just ninety days. That's all it'll take. Ninety days at ten percent. Does that sound fair?"

Sal looked out the window at the cement trucks and started to shake his head, laughing to himself. Ninety days? That must be a joke, right? Mr. Mistretta gets out of prison in a couple of weeks. He doesn't want to know nothing about no ninety days. Mistretta wouldn't give you nine minutes, you fucking clown. He won't give *me* nine minutes. He wants that money waiting for him when he gets out. And if it's not there . . . Sal started rocking again. He didn't even want to think about it.

Nashe leaned closer. "Talk to me, Sal. Say something. Everything is negotiable. What don't you like? Tell me."

Sal almost spit out a bitter laugh. He didn't like much of anything lately. He stared at the rolling drums on the concrete trucks and squeezed the black rubber ball a few times. He'd been acting boss of the Mistretta family for almost four years now, and nothing had worked out the way he'd wanted it to. He had big plans when Mr. Mistretta left him in charge just before he went to prison. It wasn't like Sal wanted to take over or anything. That wasn't his intention.

What Sal wanted to do was bring the family up-to-date a little, get more into legitimate businesses the way the other families were doing. Why reinvest gambling money back into gambling and whore money back into whores? Drugs aren't even worth the risk anymore, not with the fucking Colombians controlling all the coke and the Chinks bringing in heroin. And crack—forget about that. You gotta be crazy to deal with those fucking nuts. Mistretta doesn't like to hear it, but the smart thing to do is go legit with your profits. And that's what Sal had wanted to do. He even had the businesses he wanted to buy all picked out and everything. Three concrete plants, one on Staten Island and two here in Jersey. They could've consolidated them and had a nice little monopoly for themselves in that area. Sal had it all planned out. He even promised Joseph he'd set him up as president of the company. You clean him up a little, shave off that stupid mustache, get him some nice conservative clothes, and he could almost be one of those Knights of Columbus types, very respectable. But things just didn't work out that way.

Sal shook his head, staring at one of the concrete trucks, the drum spinning round and round, red and yellow stripes spiraling. Mistretta, that clever bastard, left him in charge, yeah, but he squirreled away most of the family's money where Sal couldn't get at it. So any major purchases Sal wanted to make had to be made with money he made himself. In the beginning, Sal still thought he could pull it off— they were making good money with gambling and girls, and they were doing all right with the garbage trucks too— but then one thing after another happened. One guy needed money for this, another guy needed money for that, Mistretta's daughter wants a new house, his wife wants a condo in Florida, then his nephew wants to buy into an auto mall, then the bail money for everybody and his uncle, and the

"One of my bodyguards," Nashe rasped, holding on to his chest.

Sal watched Nashe crawl to his knees. The Golden Boy was rubbing his chest, sitting on his heels, staring up at the poster on the wall with fear in his eyes, like he was praying to it for mercy or something. Sal looked at the poster, the challenger and the champ eyeballing each other, nose to nose, muscles rippling, legs like tree trunks. When he looked at Nashe again, the Golden Boy was nodding at the poster. His Bugs Bunny teeth were sticking out, but he wasn't smiling. Good. Maybe he was ready to get serious now.

"You know, Sal, I may have an idea for you."

Mr. Mike was still pounding on the door, going crazy out there.

Sal nodded toward the door. "Take care of your man first."

Nashe nodded. "It's okay, Mike," he called out as he got off his knees and brushed himself off. He unlocked the door and opened it. "What's the problem, Mike?"

The asshole bodyguard stood in the doorway, glaring in at Sal and Joseph. Real tough guy. "I heard a big noise, Mr. Nashe."

"It was nothing, Mike. I knocked over a stool. That's all."

Mr. Mike looked very suspicious. He was staring at the crushed blueprints on the floor. "You sure you're okay, Mr. Nashe?" He was eyeballing Sal.

Nashe clapped him on the shoulder and came up with a confident bunny smile. "You're doing a good job, Mike. Believe me, everything's okay. I'll let you know when I need you. I promise. Okay?"

Sal stared right back at the guy, right in the eye, but the asshole didn't flinch. Sal didn't like this guy at all.

Mr. Mike looked around the trailer one more time, then finally left. Nashe closed the door and locked it.

"What's his problem?" Sal asked.

"Yeah, what the hell's his problem?" Joseph chimed in.

Nashe bent over to pick up the stool, squinting a little as he felt his chest with the other hand. "Mike? Mike's a good guy. Don't worry about him. He's new, that's all. Eager to please." Nashe set the stool down behind the drafting table and sat down. "One of your *paesans,* by the way. Tomasso's his name. Mike Tomasso."

Sal shrugged, unimpressed. He didn't need any more *paesans.* He needed the money. "So what's your idea?"

Nashe looked up at the fight poster again and flashed his nervous-rabbit grin at Sal. "I think you're gonna like this, Sal," Bugs said. "I think you're gonna *love* it."

Sal glanced at the two fighters on the poster, then tilted his head back and looked at Mr. Bunny. "Oh, yeah? Tell me what I'm gonna love."

Bugs showed more teeth. "It's gonna be a big fight. The biggest there ever was. Two weeks from this Saturday."

"So?"

"You a betting man, Sal?"

He tilted his head to the side, staring at the big rabbit with the chubby cheeks in the expensive suit, and started squeezing the black rubber ball again. "Keep talking."